THE DAY OF THE LORD

Only He will be Exalted

BORTOLAZZO
Publishing

A Last Days Trilogy

Only He will be Exalted

PAUL BORTOLAZZO
~ Author of *'Til Eternity*

The Day of the Lord
© 2011 Paul Bortolazzo
Published by Bortolazzo Publishing LLC
P.O. Box 241915
Montgomery, Alabama 36124
bortjenny@juno.com
www.paulbortolazzo.com

All scripture quotations are taken from The New King James Version of the Bible (NKJV), copyright © 1992 by Thomas Nelson, Inc. Used by permission.

Cover design by Elizabeth E. Little http://hyliian.deviantart.com
Interior design by Ellen C. Maze www.ellencmaze.com

PRINTED IN THE UNITED STATES OF AMERICA

"THEN I LOOKED, AND BEHOLD, A LAMB

standing on Mount Zion, and with Him one hundred and forty-four thousand, having His Father's name written on their foreheads."
Revelation 14:1

DEDICATION

This biblical novel is dedicated to the 144,000 men from the twelve tribes of Israel. After a great multitude of saints are gathered out of the Great Tribulation, the first fruits will be sealed for protection from *the Day of the Lord*, God's wrath against the wicked. When the fullness of the Gentiles ends, the Deliverer will return to earth to fulfill the mystery of God, the spiritual salvation of Israel.

TABLE OF CONTENTS

THE SEVENTH SEAL

"...He opened the seventh seal,
there was silence in heaven for about half an hour."
Revelation 8:1

Coming in the clouds the Son of Man descended in the glory of His Father with His holy angels. 1 The image of His face was still fresh in the minds of those who saw Him. 2 His hair was white like snow; His eyes like a flame of fire. A golden band was fastened around His chest. 3 Believers looking for His glorious appearing leapt with exhilaration as their Blessed Hope encircled the earth. 4 All who died in the faith were with Him. 5 When the trumpet of God sounded, a shout from the Lord pierced heaven and earth. In a moment, in the twinkling of an eye, the dead in Christ received their glorified bodies. 6 Immediately living believers were translated into His presence, never to taste the sting of death. 7 On the last day, all in Christ were gathered to meet the Lord in the air forever. 8

Last month, celebrated TV producer Wes Mackish signed Natalie Rene Roberts to a five year eighty million dollar contract. Her news program was the highest rated in America. This captivating forty-five year old had reached the pinnacle of broadcasting in record time. For a woman to rule over such a male dominated profession was a miracle. Even so, Ms. Roberts could feel the invisible boundaries surrounding her. One wrong move and her shining star could fall.

Her worried producer knew what had to be done.

"Nate, they aren't fooling around. We have been ordered not to even mention His name."

"I can't do that!"

"So you're going to disobey the New World Coalition directive?"

"C'mon, Wes, you gave me my first break. You've taught me what real broadcasting can do. You instilled in me a conviction to report the truth without personal bias."

"Truth!" he fumed. "So you think you know what just took place?"

"I know what I saw."

"There's no time to argue, Nate. The NWC directive says we can't mention Jesus Christ, second coming, the coming of the Lord, the day of the Lord, or the rapture."

"What are the other networks saying?"

"Who cares what they say! For God's sake, Natalie, you're the best anchor I've ever had. If you announce the lightening that just hit this earth as the second coming of Christ, you can kiss your dreams of broadcasting goodbye. Anyone who does will be arrested. Aren't you aware of the consequences?"

"Okay, Wes, let's do it. Just give me a minute to re-think how I'm going to report it."

"That's my girl. Listen up everybody; the commercial break is my call. I want her lighting a notch higher than normal. And don't worry about..."

She had always been so poised, so believable to her nationwide audience. Nothing had ever been able to shake her confidence. Sitting behind her massive glass desk, she closed her eyes as her makeup artist re-did her eye shadow.

"You ready, Nate?"

"Let's roll."

"Alright, everybody it's a go. And don't forget, Nate, no Bible references."

A pre-recorded tape announced, "We interrupt programming to give this Emergency Update."

"Good evening everyone, I'm Natalie Roberts. Early this afternoon we all saw a gradual blackout of the sun, which was followed by a red eclipse of the moon. Then our star system somehow lost its light. Several minutes ago, the world witnessed the most spectacular lightening shower ever seen..."

Just days before the Jerusalem Peace Accord was broken, 144,000 God-fearing men secretly slipped away to a place prepared by God. 9 This remnant was heading for the secluded Jordanian wilderness. Members from the tribe of Judah were the last to arrive. By the time the Abomination of Desolation and his armies invaded Jerusalem; these men from the twelve tribes of Israel were safely hidden away. 10

Standing before the 144,000 he raised his hands and asked for quiet. This rabbi sensed the urgency of the hour. He had just witnessed Yeshua coming in the clouds during the Feast of Trumpets. 11

Opening his Bible he read, "After these things I saw four angels standing at the four corners of the earth, holding the four winds of the earth, that the wind should not blow on the earth, on the sea, or on any tree. Then I saw another angel ascending from the east, having the seal of the living God. And he cried with a loud voice to the four angels to whom it was granted to harm the earth and the sea, saying, "Do not harm the earth, the sea, or the trees till we have sealed the servants of our God on their foreheads." And I heard the number of those who were sealed. One hundred and forty-four thousand of all the tribes of the children of Israel were sealed..." 12

Tears trickled down his wrinkled cheeks into his gray beard. Their supernatural sealing by God from the imminent wrath of God took only a moment in time.

"Men of Israel, Satan was not able to hurt us during the days of the Great Tribulation. Now God has sealed us for protection from His wrath during the Day of the Lord! The prophets foretold of a time when a Holy God would judge the rebellion of mankind. Joel warned, "'Blow the trumpet in Zion, and sound an alarm in My holy mountain. Let the inhabitants of the land tremble; for the day of the Lord is coming, for it is at hand.'" 13

These men now understood the day of the Lord would begin with fire. 14

Angels watched as a great multitude of overcomers gathered from every nation kneeled before the throne of God. Reaching forth the Lamb opened the seventh seal of the heavenly scroll. 15 There was no sound in heaven for a half an hour.

The atmosphere within the Chicago newsroom was teetering on hysteria. The irrational calls from the public sounded more like fantasy than fact. Any observations coming from the average Joe on the street couldn't be trusted. Very few had any real answers about the lightening storm that had just filled the earth's atmosphere. Most believed it was a brilliant meteor explosion. Major tabloids were pushing the spectacular light show as a UFO visitation. Some were convinced it was the actual second coming of Christ. In reality, it didn't matter what label was attached to it. Most just wanted to know when life would return to normal.

His glory was radiating from His throne as seven angels received a gleaming trumpet. 16 Another angel appeared holding a golden censer. He was given incense to offer on the golden altar with the prayers of the saints. 17 Instantly smoke from the incense ascended before God. Without any hesitation, the angel filled the censer with fire from the altar and threw it to earth. Immediately lightening storms and earthquakes erupted around the world. 18

FIRST TRUMPET: HAIL AND FIRE

"The first angel sounded. And hail and fire followed, mingled with blood, and they were thrown to the earth. And a third of the trees were burned up, and all green grass was burned up."
Revelation 8:7

Dropping to her knees, the terrified teenager screamed, "Somebody answer me!"

The echo of her defiant words bouncing off the damp walls of the deserted cave offered no help. This gnawing conviction had plagued Reenie Ann Tucker ever since she entered this Watchman camp.

"God, this isn't fair. I never worshiped the Beast or took his mark. I left my family and friends. I even risked my life for You. Why was I left behind?"

It was true; the slender sixteen-year-old had made several escapes from New World Coalition agents. She knew something was wrong the day her father tried to convince her to register. Kneeling in the dirt, the haunting memory seemed so overwhelming.

"What are you trying to say, Reenie?"

The brunette with sad green eyes was struggling. Everybody at her school had an ID. Her church friends never hesitated. So what was this crippling fear that wouldn't go away?

"Daddy, I know this may sound weird but I'm gonna pass on registering today."

"No way, you know we can't allow our sign up date to expire. We must register today. Have the fanatics at Lakeview been scaring you?"

"Naw, most just disappeared before registration became mandatory."

"No one believes their phony end time predictions. Homeland Security calls them resisters. Besides, our God is a God of love not fear. Come on, what's really bothering you?"

"I dunno. Ever since you told me we're going to register, I can't get Luke Appleby out of my mind. He believes NWC registration is the mark of the beast."

"But the church won't be here for the Beast!"

"That's not what Luke taught me. He believes the Abomination of Desolation must come before the Son of Man gathers His elect." 1

"Don't even go there."

"What about when Kayin and his armies invaded Jerusalem? He was the one who took over the nations by creating the NWC. Now everyone has to register for a chip on their right hand or forehead."

"Honey, we've been members of Bethany Baptist since you were a little girl. Pastor Ryals baptized our whole family. He teaches the rapture must come before the Man of Sin reveals himself. Now who are you going to believe, Luke or our pastor?"

"Daddy, Jesus warned no one knows the exact day or hour of the coming of the Son of Man. When He comes with His angel's it will be like the days of Noah and Lot, deliverance then wrath. The righteous will be taken to heaven; the wicked will be left to suffer His wrath. This is the rapture!" 2

"Why are you making this so hard? How can you just dismiss what we've always been taught?"

Reluctantly she asked, "And what's that?"

"Instead of worrying about end time events, we should be out winning souls. Now let's go; the lines are huge."

As her father searched for his car keys, the slender brunette sprinted upstairs to her bedroom. Sprawled across her bed her recent birthday party came to mind. Rosie, Shay, Alonzo, Kim, all her friends were there; except for one.

"Why did you leave us, Luke? Nobody cares about the resistance."

In her mind she heard, "For what profit is it to a man if he gains the whole world, and loses his own soul? Or what will a man give in exchange for his soul?" 3

Pounding the steering wheel, her father cursed, "What's taking her so long? Travis, will you please go get your sister?"

A strong wind from the farms on the west side was whipping through town. A cold shiver shot down the spine of the thirteen-year-old as he climbed the steep stairs. Opening her bedroom door, he could see her leopard skin drapes flapping in the wind. Inside her closet, Reenie was jamming clothes into her leather backpack.

"What's up with this, Ree?"

Double checking to see if she had everything, the intense teenager rushed to the window over her desk. After opening it, she stared at her bewildered little brother.

"Travis, it's just something I gotta do. I can't explain it."

"Try me?"

"I'm not registering before I get some answers."

"What kind of answers?"

"Will you come with me? Maybe we can make it together?"

"Naw, this is your thing."

They could hear his honking from the driveway.

"Will I ever see you again, Ree?"

Hugging him she whispered, "Something tells me we will."

"Don't worry about, Pa, I'll stall him."

Helping her out the window he watched as she crawled down the old oak tree. Growing up they had played in this tree many times. Travis remembered the night he fell from a branch and broke his arm. He felt so scared, so all alone. Then he heard Reenie running around the corner of the house. She was crying out to God for help.

His booming voice erupted from the bottom of the stairs.

After pausing at her bedroom door, Travis hollered, "She's gone."

Bats bouncing off the ceiling of the cave brought her back.

"Thinking about the past can't help me now," she muttered.

The day Reenie Ann Tucker arrived at the Watchman camp, only Luke Appleby had the discernment to see through her deceptive mask. The naive teenager had always harbored her dark secret with a charming smile. She felt like such an outcast watching everyone praising the Lord as the moon turned red. Earlier in the day, when the sun went black, she wanted to tell Luke the truth. There were other demons assisting on that cold rainy night. Reenie's decision to keep it a secret only helped her bitterness grow. Jezebel rejoiced over its deception. This demon vowed her soul would someday burn in the eternal lake of fire.

The two Witnesses looked out over the spectacular valley. Rows and rows of beautiful flowers lined its basin. One would have thought such a miraculous transformation of this barren land would have spiritually prepared the Jewish people to receive their Messiah. But instead of repenting of their rebellion, many looked at this miracle as a result of their own ingenuity. A covenant people supernaturally sustained by God for thousands of years had developed a deaf ear to His warnings. Soon their beautiful gardens would be engulfed in fire.

Crossing the Kidron Valley, the two Witnesses approached a panicky crowd lingering in the streets. The aftershocks from the earthquakes were dying down.

Raising his hands the taller Witness shouted; "'Alas for the day!

For the day of the LORD is at hand; It shall come as destruction from the Almighty.'" 4

From the angry crowd, an incensed Rabbi pointed at him.

"You there, the one speaking, do you know what you are prophesying? We are Hashem's chosen people; we will never suffer His wrath."

Another shouted, "Look at the filthy sackcloth they're wearing. 5 Who gives them the right to pass judgment on us?"

"'O Jerusalem, wash your heart from wickedness, that you may be saved. How long shall your evil thoughts lodge within you?'" 6

"Why listen to such fear mongering! Hashem is our protector."

Above their mounting accusations, the other Witness hollered, "Enter into the rock, and hide in the dust, from the terror of the Lord and the glory of His majesty. The lofty looks of man shall be humbled, the haughtiness of men shall be bowed down, and the Lord alone shall be exalted in that day." 7

"If this is true," pleaded a teenager, "then we're all doomed!"

"Children of Israel, you are living in the days foretold by the angel Gabriel. The Messiah is coming back a second time for the salvation of Israel. At the end of the seventieth week, the Deliverer will save a remnant believing in Him. 8 Beware, Satan's wrath against the elect has been cut short. The day of the Lord, the wrath of Almighty God, will soon destroy those who refuse to turn away from their evil."

Their angry threats meant nothing to these two men of God.

The taller Witness boldly declared, "Gather yourselves together, yes, gather together, O undesirable nation, before the decree is issued, Or the day passes like chaff, before the Lord's fierce anger comes upon you, before the day of the Lord's anger comes upon you. Seek the Lord, all you meek of the earth, who have upheld His justice. Seek righteousness, seek humility. It may be that you will be hidden, in the day of the Lord's anger." 9

The large scroll lay open. The thirty minutes of silence had prepared the heavenly host for the horror of the day of the Lord. 10 The Lion of Judah stood beside His Father. The saints were worshipping when the first angel sounded its trumpet. A shower of hail and fire followed; raining down on the trees and grass of the earth. 11 Mingled with blood, the wrath of God was being poured out on a Christ rejecting world. 12

Astounded by the fires, another angel warned, "'Beware, inhabitants of the earth, I was there when Moses faced the Pharaoh. Yea, I was there when God sent forth hail and fire upon the land of Egypt. 13 For those who still can repent, do it quickly, for the wrath of God will soon cut off man from the face of the land.'" 14

The cavern was jammed with empty sleeping bags. There were barely enough torches lit for Reenie to find her way out. Lifting off the ledge the spirit of Anger fluttered above her and hissed.

"You're wasting your time. No one cares what happens to you."

Then she spotted a lit candle beside Luke's sleeping bag. In the midst of his study notes was his worn Bible, a picture of his family, and a note.

"Can you tell me where Luke is?" taunted the foul spirit.

With her trembling left hand cradling the candle, she read, *"Reenie, I'll never forget the day you made it to our camp. You looked so alone; like someone who didn't want to face the future. After our first talk, the Holy Spirit exhorted me to intercede for you. The more I prayed, the more I sensed a dark cloud hovering over you. I know we talked about this before. You kept saying you were born again. Yeah, I know you've gone to church all your life, even gave up your family and friends to come here. But I have to ask you again, Reenie. When the sun, moon, and the stars lose their light will you be ready to meet the Son coming in the glory of His Father?"*

Lines of ink were running together from her tears.

Bending over, she shrieked, "Lord, I don't even know You!"

"Everyone you trusted has used you," screeched Anger. "No one loves you; everyone is gone."

Rolling up like a ball on Luke's sleeping bag, she cried out for mercy. Deep down, this angry teenager really wanted to cut loose and be real. But the fear of what her friends would think had always controlled her. Being labeled a Jesus freak was never an option. Over the years Reenie had many opportunities to get saved. Now there were no excuses left.

The brush fire sweeping across the camp started at the base of the hill. Suddenly the cool nightly breezes stopped. Yellow flames were entering the mouth of the cave. Leaping to her feet, she tried to get out, only to be met by a descending wall of smoke. Turning back, she frantically headed for the rear tunnel. Someone was blowing out the torches.

"You'll never make it without light," whispered Fear.

Crouching beneath the smoke, Reenie begged, "Lord, I need your help; I can't do this on my own."

As dark billows filled up the cavern, the Holy Spirit gently spoke in her mind, "'Listen now to my voice; I will give you counsel, and God will be with you...'" 15

Straining to hear, she could barely make out another voice.

"Is anyone down there?"

"Here I am, here I am!" she cried.

For a brief moment, her fears seemed to disappear. The naive teenager could hear heavy footsteps. His loud coughing didn't sound good. Leaning forward, she grabbed his outstretched hand pulling him free from the ever-increasing gray swirls.

"Are you alright?"

In between coughs he blurted out, "Yeah, how about you?"

"A little confused, what's happening out there?"

"Some idiot must've set fire to some brush. This is scary. Are you alone?"

"Yeah."

"We don't have much time. Is there a way out of here?"

"Follow me."

Pausing at Luke's sleeping bag she quickly gathered his study notes, his well-marked Bible, and all his money.

Retreating into the damp cave she miraculously found the opening to the rear tunnel.

"Thanks for the help. My name is Reenie Tucker."

"I'm Bret Santino. I heard about this camp from a friend. Guess I got here a little late. When the earthquake hit I slipped between two rocks. Next thing I know everybody was gone."

"I missed Him, too," she mumbled back. "Jesus gathered His elect. They were taken and we were left." 16

Her hands were shaking as she tried to regain her composure. Since early afternoon, Channel 6 had provided continuous coverage of the sun's eclipse. On the other side of the world, the moon was turning red. Then the stars gave up their light. The blackout coupled with enormous earthquakes was fueling a catastrophic panic.

"Good evening, this is News with Natalie Roberts."

It was anyone's guess what country was hit first. The popular anchor had no clue how to report such a terrifying event while maintaining an air of optimism.

"A few minutes ago nations from around the world were hit by immense firestorms. Whipped by powerful winds these fires are burning up trees and grass at record speed. Excuse me; I have just received a new update. The hail has stopped. Even though the fire damage is extensive, World Leader Joshua Kayin is convinced the worst is over. From his headquarters in Jerusalem he announced: "It appears we have just experienced the biggest cosmic explosion in history. After reviewing the scientific data from our research teams, I am certain the end of these fires is in sight. The hail coming from this lightening has ceased. Our Emergency Task Force Teams are prepared to extinguish every major fire on our planet.'"

As soon as Natalie finished Kayin's quote, Channel 6 was overwhelmed with callers. Skipping the commercial break, she gave a report on fires scorching through some of the largest forests in America.

"As of now, the most severe fire damage has been in the states of California, Oregon, and Washington. For an up close exclusive, let's go to Northern California."

"Hello everyone, I'm Trevor McCray reporting to you live from California's world famous Sequoia National Park. As you can see, these mammoth yellow flames are swallowing redwood trees that stand over twenty stories high. Thousands of firefighters have courageously created a firewall to take some steam out of this devastating forest fire. An army of volunteers have joined in trying to save some of these two thousand year old redwoods. Right now, there is no way of knowing how long it will take to get these flames under control. The NWC has implemented evacuation procedures for those in danger. If a fire is threatening your area, please check with your local authorities for a legitimate evaluation. I'm Trevor McCray reporting live from Sequoia National Park."

The flashing red light was from an overseas affiliate. Natalie immediately switched to her teleprompter.

"Let's now go for a live update from Israel."

Reporter Joel Friedman had just finished interviewing several petrified land owners.

"This morning disaster struck just north of Tel Aviv. Suddenly, a wall of fire engulfed our beautifully landscaped hillsides."

"Joel, how much damage are we looking at?"

"Natalie, I can see rows and rows of roses burning. Tragically, when our firefighters extinguish one blaze, another mysteriously pops up. Flowers are a valuable commodity for Israel. This has to be a dagger in the heart of our economy."

"Aren't flowers one of Israel's greatest miracles?"

"That's correct. An Old Testament prophet prophesied Israel would bloom in the last days. Isaiah predicted, "The wilderness and the wasteland shall be glad for them, and the desert shall rejoice and blossom as the rose." 17

"How is everyone responding?"

"The final death toll from the Jehoshaphat massacre isn't even in yet. 18 You can quote me; the surrounding Muslim nations won't stop until Israel is destroyed."

"Didn't the major blackout confuse their armies?"

"That's the spin our Prime Minister is putting out. He believes the God of Abraham, Isaac, and Jacob has intervened to save our people."

"Then why hasn't God protected Israel from these fires?"

"Obviously, neither God nor man has been able to stop the devastation of one of Israel's largest commercial businesses. We are anticipating an official announcement any time now. This is Joel Friedman reporting live from Tel Aviv."

The old fisherman from Gulf Shores, Alabama, had just delivered his best catch of the year. It was a five-hour drive from this popular ocean city to Birmingham. The sale was well worth the trip. He would usually pick up hitchhikers along the way to break the monotony. The young couple with him this morning looked anxious.

Pulling over, the bald fisherman shook his head, "Almost on empty."

The stench of fish was permanently etched into the cloth seats of his olive green truck. Bret Santino and Reenie Ann Tucker sat in the back with the windows wide open. The lonely driver had tried some southern hospitality but to no avail.

"Not the talking sort," he muttered to himself while filling up.

The old timer paid his bill by extending his hand for an ID scan.[19] After starting his engine he glanced over his shoulder.

"I'm glad you two ain't in a hurry."

"What's going on?" asked an uneasy Reenie.

"A huge checkpoint is up ahead. Reckon it's gonna be quite a spell before we get through this mess."

Waiting at crowded checkpoints was now the norm. For an elaborate ID system to work, constant surveillance was a necessary evil. For most in America, the benefits from security far outweighed the infringement upon one's personal rights.

It was a humid day as the fisherman wiped his forehead. Suddenly lines of cars were moving.

"We're in luck; they're checking every other car."

The old-timer kinda felt sorry for his anxious passengers. He didn't even know where they were headed. After another stop, he turned around and asked, "How would you two like a red snapper dinner?"

The Gulf Shores Truck Stop was only a quarter of a mile away. Even so, crossing a highway on foot near a checkpoint was a risky proposition. Mingling among the customers was their best bet. The air-conditioning was a welcome reprieve from the nasty aroma of the old timer's truck. Bret read a newspaper while Reenie hid in the woman's restroom.

After questioning the old fisherman at the checkpoint, the agent called for backup.

"I've found Santino... There's a girl with him... No, I don't know her... My guess is Bret is going home to see his folks... It will take me a couple of minutes to reach the truck stop... And remember no sirens."

THE JUDGMENT SEAT OF CHRIST

"For we must all appear before the judgment seat of Christ,
that each one may receive the things done in the body,
according to what he has done, whether good or bad.
Knowing, therefore, the terror of the Lord, we persuade..."
II Corinthians 5:10-11a

The base of the glorious Bema Seat stretched as far as the eye could see. In the background was the breathtaking brilliance of the New Jerusalem. The streets of the city were made with pure gold; like clear glass. 1 The four walls were shimmering with the glory of God. Each wall had three gates with the names of the twelve tribes of Israel written on them. 2 Each gate was made of one single pearl. The Holy City was laid out in a square having twelve foundations. The names of the twelve apostles were ascribed on each foundation. 3

The Christ gazed upon those standing before His judgment seat. 4 "Whoever desires to come after Me, let him deny himself, and take up his cross, and follow Me. For whoever desires to save his life will lose it, but whoever loses his life for My sake and the gospel's will save it. For what will it profit a man if he gains the whole world, and loses his...soul? Or what will a man give in exchange for his soul?" 5

A lonely voice cried out, "Lord, we want to know why we haven't received our glorified bodies?"

"Just because you call Me, Lord, doesn't mean you will enter the kingdom of heaven. The Holy City is only for those who did the will of My Father." 6

"What is the will of the Father?" asked a frightened mother.

"For whoever is ashamed of Me and My words in this adulterous and sinful generation, of him the Son of Man also will be ashamed when He comes in the glory of His Father with the holy angels." 7

A well known prophet shrieked, "Lord, I've prophesied in your name for many years. How can you be ashamed of me? This judgment is about rewards, not about my salvation. I don't deserve this!"

An arrogant evangelist bragged, "Lord, I've cast out demons in your name. My deliverance ministry has set thousands free from the bondage of the enemy."

Another claimed, "Lord, You know all the wonderful works I did in Your name. I never missed church, I tithed, and I supported whatever my pastor taught. I don't understand what's happening."

Such terror was indescribable. Their pleas only grew louder.

"You once prophesied in My name, cast out demons in My name, and did many wonders in My name? 8 '...Why do you call me, 'Lord, Lord,' and not do the things which I say?'" 9

Waves and waves of souls dropped to their knees hysterically beseeching the Lord for mercy. It was awhile before warrior angels encircled them and asked for quiet.

"Enter by the narrow gate; for wide is the gate and broad is the way that leads to destruction, and there are many who go in by it. Because narrow is the gate and difficult is the way which leads to life, and there are few who find it." 10

Nothing could undue their past. Those who were once saved, who denied the Lord while on earth, would soon experience the darkness of Hades where there is weeping and gnashing of teeth. 11

Raising His hand, the Son uttered these final words, "...Depart from Me, you who practiced lawlessness." 12

The Lakeview High School auditorium was swarming. Several classrooms were set up with TV's to handle the overflow. Most parents knew their children's lives would never be the same. Walking toward the podium, his nervous twitch was a dead give-away. He looked overwhelmed. After brainstorming with his staff, the principal knew a strong hand of leadership was desperately needed. But what answers could he give? Raising his hands, he invited everyone to take their seats.

"I welcome you all to this special assembly. I'm Principal Fyffe. We are here to discuss the fall schedule of classes for Lakeview High School. I can assure you, my staff is coordinating..."

A disgruntled father interrupted, "Mr. Fyffe, I know the School Board is pressuring you to close our school. You can't do it. My son has been offered a college scholarship and he needs his credits."

Hands shot up all over the auditorium. The avalanche of questions during this three hour assembly was predictable. The sheer fear on their faces was even making the security guards uneasy.

"Please, I can assure you our class schedule will eventually return to normal. Obviously, it's going to take some time. What my staff and I need is your patience."

The Prince of Darkness had personally summoned Baphomet. Satan's towering throne was made of pure stone. His domain was icy cold. Left of the throne was the book of the dead bound in human flesh. To the right, stood Kur; the herald of the underworld. Under the Devil's decree, there was no demon more powerful. Kur smiled when Baphomet hurried off with his new assignment.

This small church was once filled with a vibrant body of believers. One could hear joyful singing almost any night of the week. Today, a different service was planned; one that couldn't be seen nor heard by man. On this overcast afternoon in Bethany, Alabama, a horde of demons were waiting inside this abandoned church on Cherry. The constant complaining was a given, nevertheless, this meeting had an edge to it. No one had seen their Master since his defeat by Michael the archangel. 13 They lowered their voices as the powerful demon entered the sanctuary. Baphomet's black robe smelled of death. His face looked like a goat's head; his body like a strongman. His red eyes were glowing from beneath his hood. His pacing was a clear sign of his preoccupation. Every demon knew that much. Following him was the spirit of Fear.

"We know the One from Above takes great joy in accomplishing prophecies written in His book."

"You mean the Beast's power to overcome?" mocked Hate. "Look at how many have his mark!"

The demons howled with approval. There was no reaction from Baphomet. This foul spirit knew the boundaries of their attacks had been radically changed.

"The days of the Great Tribulation have been cut short." 14

"But look what we accomplished!" boasted Religion. "The falling away of so many has brought much pain to the One from Above." 15

"Has the day of the Lord really begun?" questioned Doubt.

"The first trumpet has sounded you fool!" wailed Baphomet.

Their stirring was predictable. Baphomet loved to threaten but he never entertained the subject of fire. Even though most of the world was deceived by the two beasts, this foul spirit refused to gloat. He knew if something wasn't done, his future would also lie beneath the lake of fire.

"No human will live through His wrath," seethed Death.

"I prefer such panic," lauded Suicide.

"These new converts don't understand His Word," boasted Deceit.

"Exposing their weaknesses will be easy; just more opportunities to deceive for eternity."

"What if we can't prevent what has been decreed?" posed Doubt.

Baphomet detested such ignorance.

"Soldiers of darkness, we know the consequences if the Deliverer is ever allowed to return. 16 We need to heed the words of our Master. The sounding of the seventh trumpet means nothing, if the mystery of God never comes to pass. 17 Confusion, come to me."

The cowering spirit slithered down the center aisle and touched the hem of Baphomet's robe.

"All hail, Satan. The destiny of these believers rests in our deceptions. Before my next visit, may these young ones be marked for eternity!"

Bret Santino knew this coastline like the back of his hand. The quaint café surrounded by palm trees looked safe enough, at least for a few hours. Most agents on Gulf Patrol concentrated on the real action: the trendy beachfront bars. From California to Florida, the story was the same. All anyone wanted was some normalcy back in their lives. For many, the sun and sand was the perfect place to reflect and regroup. The deep blue ocean had higher than normal waves. It was early afternoon, a hot eighty-one degrees with no clouds in sight. Fishing boats were returning to the harbor, as children built white sandcastles under the watchful eyes of their parents. Amidst rows of serious sunbathers, a group of high school kids were picking sides for volleyball. Most seated outside the cafe started laughing while some frat boys carried a baby seal down the one-way street.

Bret sarcastically shared, "Are we tripping or what?"

"Just another day at the beach," smirked Reenie.

Losing the agent who spotted them at the truck stop seemed like a miracle. Even so, slipping inside this attractive city was much more difficult than Bret ever imagined. Always having to be alert was emotionally draining; especially for his new friend. An hour had passed and Reenie had hardly touched her chicken salad.

"How much did this food cost you?"

"Call it a freebie; the owner and I are friends."

"This hide and seek is a bit much for me. I ain't going to make it."

Bret was having doubts too. His hands were shaking as he tried to light a cigarette. Her desperation was contagious; an invisible force he had resisted up 'til now.

"I suppose we're looking a bit ragged?"

Her abrupt giggle was a dead give-away for her age. He really liked her smile.

"I want to thank you for saving my life."

"There wasn't much time once the fire spread. I just happened to pick your cave."

"My lucky day."

"I'd say it was more like fate than luck. I can't explain it; it was like something guiding me."

"You mean the Lord?"

"No, I'm not religious if that's what you mean."

"Bret, what were you really doing? If you're not a believer, then why were you looking for a Christian resistance camp? Are you an agent; maybe an informer for the NWC?"

Avoiding any eye contact he flicked his cigarette into the gutter.

"Heard they pay well," he playfully teased.

Slipping a clip of bullets under his paper napkin got his attention.

"Do these go with the neat looking gun inside your jacket?"

"Just added protection, so what was it like hanging out with the holy rollers? Why were you left behind?"

Her tears seemed to come and go as they wished. His question had already plagued her mind many times. Reenie's deep-seated anger, a demonic stronghold from an early age, could manifest at any moment.

"Haven't a clue. That's God's problem."

The direction of the conversation was making him feel uncomfortable. Not knowing how to reply he just looked away.

"You from around here?" she curiously asked.

"I used to live with my parents on Dauphin Island. You can use the ferry to get there from here."

The redness of her cheeks stood out in the sun as she twirled a lock of her dirty brown hair.

"They taught us at camp never to return home. Agents can pick up a trail in no time."

"How long did you hide in this camp?"

"Almost a year, why do you ask?"

"I saw you gather some money from Luke's sleeping bag."

"He won't be needing it."

"You won't either. A lot of stuff went down this past year. The United States was the last nation to go cashless. Your money is worthless. The only way to make it without an ID is to barter. Of course, bartering has also been outlawed. The NWC taxes anything bought or sold."

"I'm not surprised. The overcomers were telling the truth. Most gave up everything they had just to call Jesus their Lord."

"You know, Reenie, you don't sound like someone who is ready to cash in your chips. What else did you learn at this Christian camp?"

His eyes shifted. They were hesitating; as if they were searching for someone.

"I've got two agents in my sight."

Sitting perfectly still, she asked, "Where?"

"Crossing the street, this café has an exit, a mile south is a surfboard shop called Tipper's. I'll meet you there in an hour."

"You know you're right."

"About what?"

"There's too much at stake to fold now."

Arriving at their deserted table, both agents cursed.

"I know it was Santino. He's become one of them."

"Was this the girl at the truck stop?"

"Yeah, she must be a resister too."

"You check the inside; I'll circle around back."

"Be careful," cautioned his partner, "Bret's armed."

The assembly was officially over. Atop a hill overlooking the Lakeview High parking lot, two teenagers anxiously watched those exiting. Turning away, a confused Jessie Hyatt clenched her fists.

"How could this have happened?"

Sitting on the edge of the hill, a shaken Jake Jamison was thinking.

"Jess, if we had just listened to Luke's warnings. Joshua Kayin is the Antichrist. Pope Michael is his false prophet. Even the Ryan's description of the mark of the beast was right on."

"Why did we wait so long? It didn't have to happen this way."

The memory of long lines registering was painful. Media moguls, Hollywood celebrities, even well known religious leaders, led the way.

The parking lot was almost empty.

"Jake, I really felt a peace last night when we prayed with Elmer. But now, God feels a million miles away. We aren't going to make it, are we?"

"Luke taught the day of the Lord would erupt after the Son of Man gathers His elect to heaven. Let's try going over what we know."

"Not again. Remember what Rachel told us? She said once the sixth seal is opened, the sun, moon, and stars, will lose their light."

"I meant..."

"Then Jesus will send forth His angels to gather His elect." [18]

"Jess, you don't have to..."

"Thirty minutes after the Lamb opens the seventh seal..." [19]

Picking himself up, Jake walked over and gently took her hand.

"Yeah, the day of the Lord came like a thief for those not watching. Like Noah, deliverance then wrath on the same day. [20] Luke said four of the seven trumpets will be fire. [21] Remember the first siren after Elmer left us? I've never seen so many losing it."

"Just robots programmed to survive," wept Jessie.

"Survive what? Zephaniah predicted mankind would be cut off the face of the earth. He prophesied God would consume everything during the day of the Lord." [22]

Dropping to her knees the teenager buried her face in her hands. Joining her, Jake bowed his head.

"Father, Jess and I know You sent Pastor Elmer Dyer to pray with us last night. We gave our hearts to You by believing in Jesus as our Lord and Savior. Luke used to say, You care about Your children. Father, we need to ask two questions if You don't mind. Will there be a lot of people spiritually saved after the coming of the Son of Man? 23 And is Your wrath going to destroy every person on this earth?"

After a few minutes Jessie playfully nudged to her best friend.

"Get anything?"

"I asked the Holy Spirit what He wants us to do."

"And?"

"I keep seeing Elmer's face."

"That's it, Jake! Pastor Dyer will be able to answer our questions! Do you remember the name of his church?"

WHOEVER DENIES ME

"But whoever denies Me before men,
him I will also deny before My Father who is in heaven."
Matthew 10.33

The Lentz's escaped just before agents raided their home. They had no choice but to hide. The downtown shops were busy as they made their way toward their haven of safety. An already tired Judah Lentz looked at his watch.

"Once I meet our contact we must be ready to move quickly."

His wife Hanna softly replied, "We're ready dear."

The Hilkiah's arrived in Jerusalem first. They were to enter only when the guards were short handed. A couple hours later the Lentz's miraculously made it through their checkpoint. The families in front and behind them were arrested.

Clutching her mother's hand, an eight-year-old Ruth, was silently praying. The Lentz's knew they had to stay focused in order not to draw any unwanted attention.

"That's enough praying. I can't wait for the Hilkiah's any longer. It's better if I go alone."

Judah dreaded leaving instructions of what to do if he didn't return. Turning toward his wife, he kissed her on the cheek.

"Hanna, no matter what happens; you'll always be the love of my life."

Tears welled up in her eyes for the only man she had ever loved.

Ruth begged, "No, Papa, don't leave us!"

"Everything will be fine, my little flower. I'll be right back."

They could only watch as he disappeared down the busy street.

Eleazar Hilkiah had always been a pillar of strength for his wife, Deborah, and his two sons, Jabez and Joash. Up ahead agents were randomly scanning shoppers. His wife had never seen such fear in his eyes. Eleazar knew time was running out. If they missed their contact everything was off. The securing of a hiding place through the Israeli underground would instantly become an ugly memory of what could have been. Motioning for his family to follow, they retreated down a narrow street.

He was watching from a bus stop a half black away. A stranger was sitting on a park bench reading a newspaper in front of a popular bar. Judah Lentz patiently waited for several minutes. There could be no mistakes. Strolling down the sidewalk he took a seat on the park bench and coughed three times. A minute later his contact folded his newspaper, tucked a brown envelope under his arm, and walked across the street. He nodded slightly before entering the law firm of Moshe, Yosef, and Waxman. Judah could hardly restrain his excitement. He knew his family had only a short time.

When worldwide registration was introduced, pockets of resistance spread quickly. That was expected. It wasn't long before the indoctrination by the media achieved its goal. Within eighteen months most became citizens of the New World Coalition. As Chief of the Bethany ID Force; it was Doyle Mercer's job to arrest anyone who refused. 1

"Chief, an official from FEMA wants to talk with you."

"About what?"

"Their camps holding resisters for execution are empty. This guy has no clue how to report this to Washington."

"That's his problem. We must stay focused on our objective."

"Since these fires we also are struggling with surveillance."

"They're out there; it's our job to find them."

"Chief, I just received a report from an operative that discovered a resister hideout outside Wetumpka, Alabama. It's deserted. He has no idea where they are."

"Now listen up. You can call this visitation in the sky, the return of Muhammad, a UFO reunion, or the second coming of Jesus, I don't care. I'm sick of your excuses. I'd better see some arrests real soon."

Doyle Mercer knew the consequences. NWC security was in real jeopardy if its ID system could successfully be subverted.

The law office of Moshe, Yosef, and Waxman, was typical. The sound of copiers was a constant as clerks examined their work. The receptionist lowered her reading glasses as he closed the front door.

"I'm Judah Lentz. This is my wife, Hanna, and my daughter, Ruth."

"Do you have an appointment?" she suspiciously asked.

"Yes, it's about your advertisement in the paper. My family loves playing tennis."

"Are you a good player, Judah?

"I'm afraid not; I have a weak backhand."

From a drawer she removed the brown envelope the contact left.

"This is everything you need. Take the stairs as far as you can and wait."

"Have you seen the Hilkiah's?"

"We can't talk here. Please go."

Reaching the third floor, the Lentz's stood in front of a bookcase filled with dusty law books. Seconds seemed like minutes. With her eyes closed, Ruth held her mother's waist. Slowly the bookcase moved away from the wall.

"Hurry," beckoned the old lady, "agents are coming."

Myra looked jittery as she fumbled with her niece's picture. None of the family knew what she was doing. Her chances were slim if she was turned away.

"C'mon," pressed the agent, "I don't have all day."

"Hello, uh, my name is Myra Santino."

"Okay, Myra, what's your story?"

"I haven't seen my niece in months. She has always been such a good girl."

"Please stick to prescribed procedure. May I have her original registration date?"

Looking down, she handed him a picture of Jessica Hyatt.

"Lady, what's your angle?"

"I thought if I gave you her description you could..."

With no emotion he tore up the missing persons report.

"Myra, you contact Jessica's parents and get her registration date. Then we can begin our search for your niece."

"But that could take..."

"What if she is a resister? I could arrest you right now for attempting to contact her. Take my advice and forget about her."

Her lonely walk out of the station was agonizing. The line of desperate parents was already spilling out onto the sidewalk. She could feel their despair. Some looked more hopeful than others. For many, they would never see their children again.

The hideaway above the law office could hide two small families. To ensure security every decision had to be approved. One careless mistake and each family member would be arrested then executed. For now, the Lentz's were safe. Their flat had enough food and water for two months. Waving a final goodbye, the wrinkled old lady who greeted them, disappeared into the darkness of the city.

"Mama, does this lady have a family? Will she be safe?"

Hanna's smile was one of admiration. Her little Ruth was always reaching out for those in need. Just before the Jerusalem Peace Accord was signed, the constant killing between Muslims and Jews was unbearable, especially for the children. 2 As more and more kids were being separated from their parents, there was rarely a dinner at the Lentz home without a guest. The streets were Ruth's playground. This sandy blonde, hazel eyed, five-foot ball of energy was determined to make a difference. Her rescues naturally gravitated toward the hurting. Their daughter was not afraid of the pain of others. Amidst such suffering; people were more important than her own safety.

"Come to Papa," beckoned her smiling father.

While gently hugging his only child, painful memories of Judah's childhood flashed in his mind. The screaming in the halls when a Palestinian bomber blew up his school; the tragic loss of his uncle's wife after a drive-by terrorist shooting; the echo of loud sirens under streams of white light as his family rushed to hide in an underground shelter. Enough, Judah thought to himself. He should be grateful to God for supernaturally protecting his family.

"Ruth, you are our pride and joy; do you believe this?"

"Yes, Papa."

"Remember what I said when we left our home?"

"You mean about obeying the rules even when it hurts?"

When Judah Lentz and Eleazar Hilkiah met with an operative from the Israeli underground, they knew what they had to do. In their eyes they had no choice. Soon they would take their families to a hideaway deep within the city of David, Jerusalem.

"Jabez and Joash aren't coming are they?"

"Hashem will be with them."

"Papa, what if God wants us to help them?"

"Ruth, we made a pledge never to leave this flat until our oppressors are expelled by the Messiah."

"Yes, Mama, but what about the Hilkiah's pledge?"

Her glance toward Judah was one of conviction. Hanna knew how loyal her husband was to their friends. She also knew he would never risk the safety of his family for something that was no longer achievable. Hanna Lentz had already decided to abide by whatever decision her husband would make. At least she thought she had.

BLESSED IS HE WHO READS

"Blessed is he who reads and those who hear the words of this prophecy, and keep those things which are written in it..."
Revelation 1:7

The Sunday morning chimes were ringing at Bethany Baptist. Since last Monday's firestorms, the rumors among this prominent fellowship were non-stop. Several influential families arrived early in order to get a good seat. Most were huddled in passionate conversation.

"So, Dwayne, what if Pastor doesn't show?" asked a board member.

"He'll be here. I'm confident John can explain what has happened."

"What if he resigns like some of the other pastors in town."

"What for?" scoffed the respected deacon. "Sure, it was terrifying at first. I can even see why some believe it was the coming of the Lord."

"The Bethany Herald is reporting the underground resistance has been decimated."

"Such yakking is meaningless."

"Firefighters in mountain areas are finding resister hideouts. They've discovered at least thirty-three camps in Northern Idaho. Dwayne, these camps are empty!"

"If you're saying the resisters were raptured, then you're crazier than the two Witnesses. C'mon, let' keep our speculations in the ballpark."

The pastor's study remained dark. It was a hard sell for those seeking answers. After singing three hymns, the assistant pastor approached the podium. His expression was apprehensive at best. He was one of a handful who talked with Pastor Ryals the night the heavens went black.

"Good morning saints. Let's welcome our new visitors. Our women's auxiliary has a gift for..."

"Where's our Pastor?" interrupted a restless choir member. "You told me he would be speaking this morning."

"Excuse me; I'm afraid I don't..."

"You're afraid, what about us?"

Dwayne Pressley knew he had to take over before the questions got out of hand. Heading toward the podium the confident deacon announced, "May I speak?"

The assistant pastor nodded before making a beeline to the bathroom. Standing before the most prominent congregation in town; a rush of adrenaline shot through his veins. Most pastors were dreading this morning's confrontation but not Dwayne.

"Most know I've talked with Pastor Ryals. He told me he was planning on attending this morning's service. In my opinion..."

Crossing the street, he couldn't remember ever walking to church on a Sunday morning. There were a lot of things he never took the time to do. When he opened the door to the beautiful foyer, the rays of the sun lit up a stain glass portrait of Jesus tending His sheep. A hush captured the audience as he sauntered down the center aisle. The deacon had not anticipated his late arrival. It didn't matter; Dwayne doubted his confused pastor could last more than five minutes.

From the podium John Ryals scanned the audience. It didn't matter how effective a shepherd he once was, or how good a speaker he was, or how much he was loved. The damage had been done.

"My sermon this morning is entitled, A Great Multitude No One Can Number. The text is Revelation 7:9-14."

In the first row, a teenager nudged his father, "What's up with this? We need answers, not another sermon."

"He knows what he's doing; give him a chance."

John had come without his wife. His wrinkled blue suit looked like it had been slept in. His smudged brown shoes with unmatched socks didn't help either. This polished congregation wasn't accustomed to this; especially on a Sunday morning.

"After these things I looked, and behold, a great multitude which no one could number, of all nations, tribes, peoples, and tongues, standing before the throne and before the Lamb, clothed with white robes, with palm branches in their hands.'" [1] Folding his arms he paused. "Did you know The Revelation of Jesus Christ has more about the coming of the Lord than any other book in the Bible? Jesus promised, 'Blessed is he who reads and those who hear the words of this prophecy, and keep those things which are written in it... If anyone takes away from the words of the book of this prophecy, God shall take away his part from the Book of Life, from the holy city, and from the things which are written in this book.' 2 The holy city in this verse is referring to the New Jerusalem. 3 The bride will live forever within this foursquare city. 4 Some of these believers died in the faith not having seen their Messiah. They were strangers on this earth. 'But they desire a better, that is, a heavenly country. Therefore God is not ashamed to be called their God, for He has prepared a city for them.'"5

His lips were moving but his words were barely audible.

"King David will be there. So will Abraham, Isaac, and Jacob. These men of God were looking for a heavenly city. John saw a vision of this city filled with the glory of God. The high wall of this city has twelve gates. Written on the gates are the names of the twelve tribes of Israel. 6 The names of the twelve apostles are written on the twelve foundations. 7 How can you explain..."

For most he was just rambling.

The impatient deacon interrupted, "Pastor, we appreciate your sketch of what heaven is going to be like. But right now, we have some shook up folks who really need..."

"Have a seat, Dwayne. This morning I am painfully aware of what we're facing. Last Monday night the wrath of God came upon all living in darkness; like a thief in the night. 8 Jesus exhorted believers not to be deceived amidst such widespread compromise. Genuine repentance and watching for the events Jesus highlighted helped many saints overcome."

A confused teenager challenged, "Where did Jesus say that?"

John Ryals couldn't remember ever being interrupted during a Sunday morning sermon; especially by a member of the youth group.

"Jesus warned, 'Remember therefore how you have received and heard; hold fast and repent. Therefore if you will not watch, I will come upon you as a thief, and you will not know what hour I will come upon you.'" 9

"Is that a fact," the boy sassed back. "It appears things are getting a bit hot."

An usher quickly whisked him out of the sanctuary. Tragically, buried beneath the jokes, the gossip, and the Sunday morning masks, was a growing spirit of terror.

"So what about our future?" asked his staff secretary.

"In Revelation 7:14, a multitude of believers from every nation were delivered out of the Great Tribulation to heaven. I never understood this critical passage until I saw it happen. 10 Last Monday night, at His coming, angels gathered His elect from earth. "But in those days, after that tribulation, the sun will be darkened, and the moon will not give its light; the stars of heaven will fall, and the powers in the heavens will be shaken. Then they will see the Son of Man coming in the clouds with great power and glory. And then He will send His angels, and gather together His elect from the four winds, from the farthest part of earth to the farthest part of heaven.' 11 In Revelation 7 and Matthew 24 His elect are gathered to heaven after the sun, moon, and stars lose their light." 12

"Pastor John, this sign precedes the Word of God coming at the battle of Armageddon, not the rapture of the church."

He knew what he had to say. Worthless questions, irrelevant opinions, even personal attacks, would not sidetrack him.

"In Revelation 5:9, John saw the Lamb of God who shed His blood to redeem man out of every tribe, tongue, people, and nation. In Revelation 7:9, this same phrase describes a multitude delivered to heaven out of the Great Tribulation. This proves..."

"Pastor, what do you think..?"

"It doesn't matter what I think! Jesus warned us to watch for the events preceding His gathering of believers to heaven. The events we've experienced the past five years were the six seals on the outside of the heavenly scroll in Revelation 6."

"What are you trying to say, Pastor?"

"According to Jesus, '...He who endures to the end shall be saved.' 13 If the days of the Great Tribulation were not shortened, no flesh would be saved. The Blessed Hope promised to cut short the persecution of the Beast by delivering His elect." 14

"When is the Lord going to do that?"

"Last Monday God blew His final trump. In a twinkling of an eye, angels gathered the dead in Christ followed by believers alive on earth."

"Have you utterly lost it?" threatened an angry board member. "If that was the rapture then we would be with him. You can face God's wrath but we aren't sticking around."

"Hey," joked a teenager, "for something that takes place in a twinkling of an eye, a whole mess of people sure do know a lot about it."

"The day of the Lord immediately followed the coming of the Son of Man. Like in the days of Noah and Lot, both events came as a thief for those living in darkness."

"But you taught us the rapture is different than His second coming?"

"His coming is more than a singular visitation; it's an event having a beginning and an ending. The coming of the Lord began with the gathering of His elect by angels. Thirty minutes later, fire was poured out on our Christ rejecting world."

"That's not scriptural!" challenged the worship leader. "Pastor, you taught us the church would be caught up before the seven year tribulation begins. God promised to keep us from this hour of trial. 15 God's wrath isn't against Christians but will test all unbelievers who dwell on the earth."

"Yes," moaned John, "the hour of trial was the Great Tribulation. In James 1:3, the word 'test', comes from the same Greek word 'tempt'. God cannot be tempted by evil and He cannot tempt anyone. So I ask you, if God cannot tempt anyone, how can the hour of testing be His wrath?"

"Then what is the Great Tribulation?"

"It was Satan's wrath against the saints." 16 Dejectedly he read, "'Then Jesus was led up by the Spirit into the wilderness to be tempted by the Devil.' 17 The word tempted comes from the same Greek root word as temptation. Satan is the source of temptation, not God!" 18

Questions were erupting from every direction. Wiping perspiration off his forehead he wondered if any could still be saved.

"Jesus said, 'Then they will deliver you up to tribulation and kill you, and you will be hated by all nations for My names sake.' 19 In the past year and a half, the persecution of overcomers reached an all time high."

"You mean the resisters?" hollered an irate choir member.

"They were hated by all nations on account of Jesus' name."

"So now you're calling these fanatics believers in Christ? Why you used to label them as instruments of the Devil!"

"Last week when the light from the sun, moon, and stars ..."

"For a false teacher, you've got some nerve showing your fat face."

"Those who understood the events coming before the day of the Lord were ready." 20

Another member mocked, "Imagine John preaching this heresy to the Bethany Ministers Association. No one believes the unscriptural nonsense he's feeding us this morning."

Acting out his part perfectly, Dwayne Pressley stood and softly shared, "Okay, okay, let's show some grace for our pastor. I'm a little surprised at how hot and bothered some of you are this morning. Of course, the best way to diffuse a deception is to expose it to the light. Tell us, John, who do you think Joshua Kayin really is?"

"He's the Beast of Revelation 13:2 and Daniel 7:25."

"And what about those of us who registered?"

"The NWC microchip is the mark of the beast." 21

"Are you sure of this?"

"Try reading Revelation 13."

"Pastor, allow me to read this passage of scripture. 'Let every soul be subject to the governing authorities. For there is no authority except from God, and the authorities that exist are appointed by God. Therefore whoever resists the authority resists the ordinance of God, and those who resist will bring judgment on themselves.' 22 How does this scripture apply to those who willingly break the laws of the NWC?"

"Using this to justify taking the mark won't fly, Dwayne."

"John you once taught the judgments during the day of the Lord will destroy every man, woman, and child, on earth. Do you deny this?"

His reply was not audible.

"Speak up," taunted Dwayne. "According to your warped theology we're all going to suffer His wrath. Is this something a loving God would approve of?"

"Will you please allow me to finish?"

Glancing back at the congregation, he whispered, "You'd better go."

The ushers had to restrain several members before John reached the side exit.

"You're so deceived!" yelled a prayer partner. "My God isn't an author of confusion."

Walking toward the street he could hear teenagers chanting, "Apostate, apostate, apostate." 23

Over thirty years ago, John Henry Ryals achieved his dream of becoming a minister. Never in his wildest imaginations did he ever think he would end his ministry in such disgrace. Ironically, those he had helped the most yelled the loudest.

Walking by Sluman's Garage he quoted this passage to himself: "The Son of Man indeed goes just as it is written of Him, but woe to that man by whom the Son of Man is betrayed. It would have been good for that man if he had not been born." 24

The wind felt good as she walked the sidewalk lining the beach. It brought back memories of board surfing with Travis, collecting seashells with her mother, even feeding the seagulls bread with her father. At the time it didn't seem special. Somehow she had taken it all for granted. Reenie Ann Tucker was beginning to feel cheated.

The shouting up ahead interrupted her daydreaming. The struggle between the teenager and the agent didn't last long. After cuffing his suspect, he scanned him for an ID.

His partner hollered, "I told you he was a resister!"

The arrest quickly drew a crowd. Most Americans rarely witnessed a resister being apprehended. Of course, when Congress approved televised executions, the thirst for revenge only grew stronger.

A veteran jeered, "Hey, punk, try living in Iran."

His blonde bangs covered his eyes as they cuffed him. Wearing a red sweat shirt and baggy blue jeans, he looked preoccupied.

"Barely my brother's age," sighed Reenie.

As the agent led the boy away, he yelled, "Don't register; it's the mark of the beast. Believe in Jesus as your Savior. He'll never forsake you!"

The other agent discreetly slapped a strip of tape over his mouth. These would be the last words this overcomer would ever speak. Reenie watched as they drove away. The delight from the crowd was heartbreaking. She couldn't understand their hostility.

"So, God, why didn't You protect the kid?" she naively asked.

In her mind she heard, 'He who overcomes shall inherit all things, and I will be His God and he shall be My son." 25

"Yeah, right, You didn't protect me either."

The frightening memory was never far away. The demon

possessing Reenie Ann Tucker made sure of that. The nightmares did the trick. Her heart was now callous due to the repeated attacks of terror. The flashback of her babysitter's face still produced thoughts of suicide. It happened in the house her family was still living in. Turns out her parents didn't even know the teenager who wound up at their doorstep that cold rainy night. They were in a hurry to make a surprise birthday party so they called a babysitter service. Rushing out the door barking instructions, they didn't bother to check the package under the teenager's arm. Just a fun game her mother thought.

After reading a book about bunnies to Travis, the babysitter put him to bed. Removing the wooden board from her package, she asked the tiny five-year old to join in.

"C'mon, Reenie put your hands on top of the board."

The little girl had never seen a Ouija board. The fun really started when the marker on the board moved by itself.

"Look, Reenie, she is asking you a question."

"Who is? I can't see her, Cassandra."

"She wants to be your friend."

After Cassandra's command, the wooden board lifted into the air by itself. Looking under the board, the wide eyed little girl expected her new friend to surprise her.

"If you want see your friend just ask her into your soul."

"What is a soul?"

"It's a place in your heart where your friend will meet you. My friend is called Baphomet."

Getting up off the floor, an excited Reenie took her babysitter's hand.

"Will my new friend love me?"

"Always."

"Will my friend ever leave me?"

"Never."

"Promise?"

"I promise in the name of the Prince of Darkness."

"Is that my friend?"

"No, the name of your new friend is Jezebel. She will never leave you nor forsake you."

In the distance, Reenie could still see the flashing blue lights. There was something about the boy that touched her heart. He wasn't scared. His main concern was for others not to be deceived. So why did God allow him to be arrested?

"Sounds familiar; where was the Lord when I needed Him?"
From within her soul, Jezebel hissed, "You'll never know."

Later that afternoon the disorientated pastor arrived at Lance and Lee Ryan's home. Sprawled on their living room sofa he began to reminisce. It was not the type of daydreaming seeking an answer. For now, self-pity was in control.

Over and over, he replayed the events of the past week in his mind. Pastor Greg Hudson had just wrapped up a lunchtime devotional with his staff when the eclipse of the sun began. After a quick glance everyone just went back to work. No really cared until News Anchor Natalie Roberts started posting pictures from overseas.

The other side of the world was simultaneously experiencing a red eclipse of the moon. Glancing up at the Ryan's severely cracked ceiling, Greg vividly recalled the first earthquake. The eclipse of the sun was an hour old when he decided to drive home and check on his family.

Ivy was the love of his life. A devoted mother of two, she was a faithful intercessor, especially for those in need. Ivy loved to testify how God answers prayer. Ethan was eighteen, Greg's best friend. Good looking, kind, responsible, his son was studying for the ministry. Misty was thirteen, a spitting image of her mother. Always the life of a party; among her classmates she was more of a leader than a follower.

As Greg drove by a used car lot, suddenly it was a struggle to keep his car going in a straight line. It was laughable, as rows and rows of parked cars began bouncing up and down. For a split second the pastor wondered if this was a sign from God. Somehow the events of this day had to be explained. But not now, his family was the only thing on his mind. It was a strange feeling to see the front door of his house wide open. There was no note, no phone message; no voices coming from the family room. Stepping outside he sat down on their wooden porch. Just another storm passing through, he thought. He watched as neighbors hastily boarded up their windows.

That day Greg Hudson never moved from the top step of their porch. Gradually the black sun dropped behind the Alabama hills, only to be replaced by a blood red moon. No one needed to tell this shepherd what had happened. Jesus had come like a thief. After the glory of His Father filled a black sky, angels caught up his family.

Greg couldn't explain his urge to visit the Ryan's. Their house had the same empty feeling as his. While agonizing in their living room he noticed a CD taped to their TV. Curiosity got the best of him. After slipping the CD in; he pushed play.

"I'm Lee Ryan. If you saw Him in the clouds, and your still here, then you've missed the Lord coming for His saints, Matthew 24:21-22, 29-31, I Thessalonians 4:15-17, II Thessalonians 2:1, and Revelation 7:9-14."

Heaving the remote off the wall, he shrieked, "I could've been with them!"

Trying to grasp such hopelessness, he slammed his hands on their coffee table. Just the thought of his wife and kids worshipping the Lord without him was too much to bear. Suddenly his instinct was to run. Jumping up, the dazed pastor rushed out the backdoor. A heavy smell of smoke was still in the air. With his blue dress shirt hanging out from his beige slacks, his tan loafers smeared with black soot, he lunged toward a park bench. His lungs were burning. He had no idea how far he had run; two maybe three miles. Gasping for air, he knew the danger. Agents could spot a disoriented resister a mile away.

"It doesn't matter," he cringed, "there are no second chances."

From the shoreline, Bret Santino could see clouds of smoke hovering over a deserted Dauphin Island. During the past year, his partnership in his father's fishing business was very profitable. The local rock band he started was getting super reviews. Owning his own red polyurethane powerboat made him feel like a celebrity. Many envied his reputation, especially the groupies from the Gulf Shores party scene.

"Why did everything have to change," he cursed. "Life would be slamming if my folks had just laid off the booze."

Bret had a lot of ifs. The physical and verbal abuse over the years by his parents had produced a deep seated rebellion within his spirit. His decision to move out and join the local ID Security Force was motivated by pure revenge; an avenue to really hurt someone. His first arrest was a real rush. Even so, the young agent could sense bitterness taking control of his life. After apprehending several underage resisters, informant Santino was granted a promotion. His next assignment was the infiltration of a resister camp hidden north of Birmingham, Alabama.

"Yeah, my folks should be proud of their son, the bounty hunter."

Deep down, all Anthony Bret Santino ever really wanted was love and respect from his father and mother. Kinda like the respect Reenie Tucker had for her friend, Luke Appleby. Even the tone of her voice changed when she spoke of his unselfishness; his concern for others. Secretly, the ex-agent was hoping to find what really changed Luke's life.

WHILE WE WERE STILL SINNERS

"...God demonstrates His own love toward us
in that while we were still sinners, Christ died for us."
Romans 5:8

Everyone could hear the shofars. All twelve tribes were assembling.

Raising his hands, an elated Rabbi Hillel announced, "My brothers, for such an hour as this our God has provided us with a refuge of protection. We will become the first fruits redeemed from among Israel when our Messiah returns to earth." 1

It was during the Feast of Trumpets the prophet Ezra read God's law to His people. It would become a defining moment in Israel's history.

"Last Monday we witnessed the new moon ushering in the Feast of Trumpets. 2 Remember the tiny crescent of light that night? As we worshiped on Zikhron Teruah, this sliver of light turned blood red."

Bowing, the 144,000 worshiped their Savior. At the trump of God, they witnessed the resurrection of the elect. Yeshua fulfilled the Feast of Trumpets for all who believed.

"After His coming we were sealed with our Father's name on our foreheads. 3 We now have experienced the saving knowledge of Yeshua, the one and only Christ."

Their spontaneous praise was glorious; none more than the tribe of Judah.

"My brothers, we must intercede until the end of Daniel's seventieth week. 4 When the times of the Gentiles are fulfilled, the Messiah will atone for Israel's transgressions on Yom Kippur. 5 Yeshua will make an end of their sins and grant reconciliation for their iniquities. Only the Most Holy can usher in everlasting righteousness."

Twenty years ago Louis Cooper decided to quit his job as a software salesman and accept a pastorate of a small Assembly of God congregation in Bethany, Alabama. After two decades, Reverend Cooper was now a well respected fixture among the religious leaders of this quaint farming town. From day one, the Cooper family was befriended by J.W. Brown, Pastor of Bethany Presbyterian. Despite their theological differences, Louis and J.W. forged a strong friendship. Pastor Brown became the spiritual mentor Louis had hoped for. Even so, it was the Assembly of God pastor who convinced J.W. of the imminent return of Christ. Tragically, in the past week, his friend was nowhere to be found.

"What are you thinking, J.W.?" Louis sadly reflected.

This was not the first time a well-known minister from Bethany suddenly vanished. Who could forget the dramatic disappearance of Pastor Mark Bishop of Bethany Assembly? Or the mysterious circumstances surrounding Pastor Allen Colson of Calvary Community? His congregation's only clue was a puzzling resignation. Louis Cooper could still remember the day he heard the news.

"Pastor, have you heard about the Colson's?" posed his secretary. "They secretly left their church. Do you think they are hiding out with the Bishops? Who knows," she chuckled, "maybe they joined the underground resistance movement."

"What a disgrace," Louis whispered to himself while rereading his Sunday evening sermon.

In anticipation of the overflow crowd, the regular morning service had to be rescheduled. Several carloads from around the county had already arrived.

"Good evening everyone," boomed the poised pastor.

The congregation represented every age group. By their faces one could discern a wide range of emotions: anger, confusion, fear, remorse, even denial. Most were coming for some sort of assurance about their future. The pressure of having to deal with so many unanswered questions had become a major irritation for most pastors.

"This evening our board has asked me to speak on, The Resurrection of the Saints. In John 5:28-29, we see the physical resurrection of all people on the last day. John wrote, 'Do not marvel at this; for the hour is coming in which all who are in the graves will hear His voice and come forth- those who have done good, to the resurrection of life, and those who have done evil, to the resurrection of condemnation.'" 6

A frightened Sunday school teacher anxiously asked, "Pastor Cooper, do you believe last Monday night was the resurrection of the elect?"

"It couldn't have been and I'll show you why. Jesus spoke of only one bodily resurrection of the elect to heaven. 'And this is the will of Him who sent Me, that everyone who sees the Son and believes in Him may have everlasting life; and I will raise him up at the last day.'" 7

An elated teen stood and asked to speak.

"So we couldn't have missed His coming because the last day is still future."

The different reactions didn't seem to bother the nodding pastor.

"I admit I used to believe in a secret coming of the Lord. After all we've experienced, I don't anymore. Our Lord promises a resurrection of mankind on the last day. The last day will come when everyone has heard the gospel. Jesus said, 'And this gospel of the kingdom will be preached in all the world as a witness to all nations, and then the end will come.' 8 We need to pray for spiritual discernment, saints. The resurrection on the last day is still future. Only the preaching of the gospel can usher in Christ's return. Now let me ask you, are there still people who need to hear the gospel?"

Instantly hands shot up.

"What about these firestorms, Pastor Cooper?" pleaded a deacon.

"Of course, we all see through a dark glass concerning the events of the last days. The suffering coming from these worldwide fires is tragically beyond description."

"The two Witnesses are prophesying the Day of the Lord has begun! These fires are from the sounding of the first trumpet. God's wrath is going to melt this earth!"

"Now listen up!" cautioned Louis. "The day of the Lord is the consummation of the kingdom of God when all believers are raised. Last Monday night we experienced the blackout of the sixth seal. Then Jesus opened the seventh seal. Thirty minutes later the first trumpet sounded and the vegetation fires erupted around the world. You've got to understand only the seven bowls are called the wrath of God."

"Where does it say that?"

"Revelation 15:1. Ask yourselves; didn't God protect us from the seven seal judgments? If we just have faith, He'll do the same during the seven trumpet judgments. Trust me, those found faithful will not face God's wrath."

"Does this mean Joshua Kayin is the Antichrist?" asked another panicky teenager. "Luke Appleby used to teach he was."

"Stop right there! The Holy Spirit warns in the latter times some will depart from their faith by giving heed to deceiving spirits and doctrines of demons. Does everyone realize how unstable the spiritual climate of Lakeview High is? Just look at how many professing Christians have left their families from this school."

"Pastor, what are you saying?"

"It's clear Satan is deceiving anyone believing Joshua Kayin is the Antichrist."

"What about Elmer Dyer? He believes our ID's are 666."

His disheartened friend could only pause and bow his head.

"Pastor Dyer is a wonderful man of God with a big heart. This is why he is so overwhelmed. He is confused, that's all. There is not one Christian leader teaching ID registration represents the number 666?"9

"But why is there so much uncertainty?"

"Now that's enough! I'm concerned with the lack of faith I'm hearing tonight. You must realize not all who call themselves Christian are saved. Don't believe these wild predictions about a coming Antichrist taking over the world. The books of Daniel, Matthew, and Revelation, provide us with an extensive overview of events coming before and after Christ's 2nd coming. Antichrist is never mentioned in these books."

"How can you stand there and deny what we saw?" shouted an usher.

"I know, I know," shrugged Louis, "even some of my neighbors are convinced they witnessed His coming. Even so, Monday night's shower of lightening couldn't have been the rapture. Clearly there is one resurrection and one final judgment. These are back-to-back events occurring on the last day. Trust me, the coming of our Lord for His church is still future."

"What about Pastor Ryals? Members of his church can't find him."

"Now let's not rush to any false conclusions. Obviously we're facing a major breakdown in communications. Yes, there are still people missing. How many we don't know. I'm confident the Ryals are safe. Let's stay positive and think good thoughts. Didn't Jesus promise, '...I am with you always, even to the end of the age.'" 10

It was easy to spot deserted homes; an overgrown yard, no lights on, no sign of movement. She knew agents were searching for resisters hiding in such houses. Waking up to an agent's revolver sticking in her face was not her idea of fun. It was a gamble she was willing to take. She couldn't relax enough to sleep anyway. Nestled between two wool blankets salvaged from the garage, Reenie Tucker would mostly daydream about Luke Appleby. Her questions about God were growing.

"Well, if I can't talk to Luke maybe he can talk to me."

Reluctantly she began reading his notes. It only took a minute.

"Who am I kidding; this is such a waste of time."

It was true. The power of God's word had always eluded the defiant teenager. Her major stumbling block was her refusal to come to the Father by believing in His Son. What she needed was a little help from above. The stranger easily scaled the fence. Peering through the small window of the garage door, he could see her reading. His knock startled the weary teenager. Before she could react, he made his move. 11

"How ya doing?"

"What do you want?"

"Just looking for a place to crash, do you mind?"

The days after missing her rendezvous with Bret had become a living nightmare. Just the idea of searching for another place to hide was too exhausting to consider.

"It doesn't matter, I'll be leaving soon."

Sitting on the floor, his back against the dryer, his elbows on his knees, he closed his eyes.

"So what are you reading?" he curiously asked.

"Some Bible study notes on the end times."

"You study the Bible a lot?"

"Not really. These notes belong to Luke Appleby. He was a friend of mine."

"Where is Luke now?"

"What's with the questions?"

"Whoa, lighten up. Just wondering, that's all."

Reenie knew she had overreacted. Not being able to trust anyone was a real drainer. It really didn't matter, she thought. If this guy was an agent, she knew she was just being pumped for information before being arrested.

"Luke was a Watchman for the Lord. We hid out in the same camp."

Her candid confession didn't seem to faze him.

"Why were you left? Aren't you a Christian?"

"I've gone to church all my life. I'm a good person; never hurt anybody."

"The Bible says a sinner is saved by grace through faith. No one can receive salvation because they're a good person. If people could get saved by doing good works then that would make Jesus' death on the cross meaningless."

"What's with the sermon; you a preacher?"

"No, I would consider myself more of a messenger."

In a mocking tone, she asked, "Who's your message for?"

"For those who have ears to hear."

Avoiding eye contract, she whispered, "I ain't going anywhere."

"The Son of God became flesh to die on the cross for your sins. 'But God demonstrates His own love toward us in that while we were still sinners, Christ died for us.'" 12

"My pastor taught on salvation all the time. We are saved by grace alone."

"You're close. Grace is God's part; responding in faith is your part."

"I believe Jesus Christ is the Son of God."

"Faith is more than believing something to be true. Continually acting upon God's Word is the result of saving faith."

The bewildered teenager was feeling an uncomfortable conviction.

"Are you saying I didn't act out my faith good enough?"

"I'm talking about saving faith which must take place for one to receive salvation. Before you can be born from above, you must ask Jesus to forgive you of your sins. Repentance is how you say yes to the giver of the gift."

"I repented of my sins when my pastor baptized my whole family. My parents thought we should since we were new members."

"Grace is a divine influence upon one's heart. Those who abide in grace bear the fruit of the Spirit. Grace is not passive you know; it's a dynamic force."

"What are you getting at?"

"I'm talking about a relationship. Grace changes one's life through faith."

"So what stops people from having real faith?"

"Peter said, 'Repent, and let every one of you be baptized in the name of Jesus Christ for the remission of sins; and you shall receive the gift of the Holy Spirit.' 13 Notice the phrase, 'for the remission of sins.' God's Word doesn't say 'believe' for the remission of sin but rather, it instructs us to repent for the remission of sin."

"Are you saying I'm going to hell because I didn't repent of my sins? My pastor says my sins, past, present, and future, have been wiped away."

"Reenie what about the stronghold of rebellion in your spirit you're hiding from everyone?"

"Nice try, you don't know anything about my past."

"Grace provides the way on His terms, not yours."

"Wait a second, how do you know my name?"

"You were five the night it happened. You know God doesn't forget."

"Then why didn't He help me? He just watched as my life was stolen away."

"'In this the children of God and the children of the Devil are manifest: Whoever does not practice righteousness is not of God, nor is he who does not love his brother.' 14 You need to forgive the one who deceived you, Reenie."

"Why should I? That witch should beg for my forgiveness. No telling how many others Cassandra has infected. Just leave me alone."

The stranger waved goodbye before walking out.

The slender brunette didn't want to talk about that night. Her spirit guide made sure of that. Even so, the spirit of Jezebel was on edge when the gospel angel was talking. 15

As the ferry neared the dock, Bret Santino was reading some bible notes he discretely lifted from Reenie's backpack. After her no show at Tipper's Surf Shop, he retraced his steps three times. The slender brunette was nowhere to be found.

"She's not my responsibility. We wouldn't have lasted a month."

He didn't know why he was going home. All his friends had the mark. The surveillance of his parents house was a given.

The night fog hugging the coastline was thick. A neon sign, 'Welcome to Dauphin Island,' was barely readable as the ferry reached the dock. Stepping between passengers, he saw a stranger waiting underneath the sign. He was talking on a red cell phone. Bret decided to make a run for it. Within seconds he reached the gravel parking lot. Hiding behind some trees the ex-agent knew the consequences.

"Sorry, folks, maybe another time," he whispered aloud.

After the ferry was out at sea, the stranger made the call.

"It's Santino... The girl isn't with him... Bret is heading for his parent's house. Send an experienced agent to pick him up. And remember, I want him alive."

"No, no, you can't make me!" she screamed.

It took a few seconds for her to recognize it was another nightmare. Reenie was used to them. Her parents sent her to several Christian counselors. Even talks with her pastor, John Ryals, didn't help. The key to breaking the bondage of Jezebel had always eluded her. The smell of oil in the garage brought her back to reality. Soon agents would be paying her a visit. The food she had didn't last as long as she thought. Most resisters waited too long. The weakness brought on by a lack of food would eventually render them helpless.

"Lord, did You really send that stranger to help me?"

Climbing through the broken kitchen window was easy enough. After a snack of instant oatmeal and crackers she began her search for some clean clothes. The upstairs bedroom was decorated in pastels. On top of a stack of teen magazines was her high school yearbook. Reenie couldn't resist. Abby Jean Bryant was eighteen, had short blonde hair, blue eyes, and an attractive smile. A collage of the teenager's family hung above her desk. After checking Abby's closet, she decided on a light blue sailor top and white cotton pants. A hot shower was too inviting to pass up. While drying her long brown hair, Reenie couldn't stop thinking about her family. Her daddy would be at work. Everyone knew he preferred his job over spending time with his children. Her mother never really demanded very much. Her passion was working in her prized flower garden. And then there was Travis. Growing up, she yearned for a closer relationship with her younger brother. It never happened. When her friends would ask about Travis, she could only answer, "Oh, we care about each other, it's just we are so different."

Masking her pain was a way of life. Excuses were her way of avoiding confrontations. Constantly shifting the blame was an effective way to numb her painful secret. Most of the time, Travis would cover for his sister's outbursts.

Suddenly Jezebel prompted Reenie to rip Abby's pictures off the wall. The frenzied attack lasted only twenty seconds. Laying face down on the soft white carpet the shame was overwhelming.

"Say it," hissed her spirit guide.

"Not this time."

"You know what will happen."

The possessed teenager cursed Jesus. Satisfied, the demon relented until another time.

"Look how happy Abby is. Her whole family was caught up. This isn't fair. Why didn't You save my family? I can't take this any longer."

Her despair was crippling. From the window she could hear the waves crashing to the shore. A storm was hitting the shoreline. Suddenly Bret's face surfaced in her mind. She wondered if he ever visited his parents on Dauphin Island. Reenie was already missing him. And what's with the gun he was packing? It didn't matter; he could take care of himself. Deep down, she really wanted to help him. He too was searching for God. After stuffing some of Abby's clothes in her leather backpack she walked down the stairs and out the backdoor. From the sidewalk, she could see heavy showers coming down over the ocean.

His search for the Hilkiah's was nearing two hours. Soon Judah would be forced to return to their hideaway empty handed.

The plain-clothed agents surprised the resisters from behind and threw them to the ground. Back tracking, Judah watched as a crowd rushed toward the arrest. Waiting at a red light, he spotted Jabez Hilkiah sucking on a piece of candy. Up ahead was another sting. Desperately he tried to get their attention without being noticed.

"Papa, where are we going?"

"Jabez, we are going to visit some friends."

Pointing across the street he replied, "You mean Ruth's daddy?"

Moments later, Eleazar Hilkiah gratefully hugged Judah Lentz.

"Have you met our contact? Are you inside?"

"Yes, it's a perfect hiding place. Stay close and follow me; there are stings all around us."

With Eleazar grabbing Jabez and Deborah holding Joash, Judah led the way. After an hour of turns they entered the law office. After three knocks, Hanna opened the bookcase. Once the locks were secured, Hanna hugged Deborah. While Eleazar thanked his good friend Judah, Ruth was already showing Jabez and Joash their bedroom. After praising Hashem for His protection, each family retired for a well-deserved rest.

THE BRIGHTNESS OF HIS COMING

"And then the lawless one will be revealed,
whom the Lord will consume with the breath of His mouth
and destroy with the brightness of His coming."
II Thessalonians 2:8

The old motel suite had a musty smell. Flies hovered over dirty dishes in the sink. Newspapers were spewed across the floor. Laying on his bed the bewildered pastor kept re-reading Matthew 24. Just over twenty-five years ago, the Holy Spirit led this committed bachelor to pioneer a United Methodist congregation. It was a labor of love he thoroughly enjoyed. God would have His way with His people; everything had its own time. Elmer Dyer had always believed this; that is until the coming of the Son of Man. For the past four Sundays his ministerial staff took turns preaching. They had no idea where he was. Something had to be done to stop the panic plaguing so many church members. The incessant phone calls were a living nightmare for his secretary. Oddly enough, due to several heavy rainstorms, the fires were now just an ugly memory.

The Sunday evening service began with another packed out sanctuary. After leading the congregation in two short hymns, the worship leader asked everyone to stand.

"May our Lord bless hearts as we recite the affirmation of our faith. I believe in God the Father Almighty, maker of heaven and earth; and in Jesus Christ His only Son our Lord: who was conceived by the Holy Spirit, born of the virgin Mary, suffered under Pontius Pilate, was crucified and buried; the third day He rose from the dead; He ascended into heaven, and sitteth at the right hand of God the Father Almighty; from thence He shall come to judge the quick and the dead. I believe in the Holy Spirit, the communion of saints, the forgiveness of sin, the resurrection of the body, and life everlasting. Amen."

After everyone was seated the youth pastor waited for their undivided attention.

"Tonight, our youth drama team has prepared a skit for us on overcoming fear. But first I have some announcements. Tomorrow night, our women will host a cake sale. For those in children's church, a prize will be given to anyone who can memorize the Book of Jude..."

He knew agents could be watching. It didn't matter; he couldn't wait any longer. His goal was to contact anyone who still could be saved. Entering the side door to the sanctuary, he never looked up.

"Well, uh, welcome back Pastor Dyer. It appears we will have a change in our program tonight. Let's all greet our Pastor."

During their warm applause, he knew this was a final goodbye. Some resisters had to be watching. His aim was to pray with them after the service.

"I remember the moment the Lord led me to establish this church. My goal was to shepherd a body of believers that would make a difference in our community. Of course, one can only accomplish this by the power of the Holy Spirit. There were times when I felt God was leading us; when it was actually my own self imposed agenda."

"Excuse me, Pastor; none of us have heard from you in a month."

"I'm afraid my days of pastoring are over."

"What are you talking about?"

Jesus said, "...when you see all these things, know that it is near-at the doors." 1 What things? The Son of Man was admonishing Christians to watch for six events warning us of His coming."

This board member had always been a close friend and an avid supporter. Everything was different now; his smile was not genuine.

"So tell us, Pastor Dyer, in your humble opinion how many Christians have been deceived since October 3rd?"

"The Beast deceived more than we ever imagined. John warned, "It was granted to him to make war with the saints and to overcome them. And authority was given him over every tribe, tongue, and nation." 2

Turning away, the board member sarcastically asked, "You believe Joshua Kayin is controlled by the Devil, now don't you? How can the takeover of Israel by the Middle East Federation somehow make our former President the Antichrist?"

"When Kayin defiled the Temple on Mount Moriah he became the Abomination of Desolation of Matthew 24:15."

"That's not true! The Antichrist must come from the revived Roman Empire, the European Union."

"The ten nations that invaded Jerusalem were from the old Roman Empire."

"Jesus couldn't have come last month. The Bible says the Lawless One will be consumed with the breath of His mouth and destroyed with the brightness of His coming. 3 This can only take place when Jesus casts the Beast and his false prophet into the lake of fire at the battle of Armageddon." 4

A candid Elmer just stared.

"II Thessalonians 2:8 is describing two separate events within Christ's second coming. The Word of God is going to consume the Beast and his armies at Armageddon. But before this takes place, Jesus will destroy the Man of Sin by the brightness of His coming. Destroy means to 'paralyze'. This restriction of power took place at the brightness of the coming of the Lord after the opening of the sixth seal."

"Pastor, you taught us the rapture comes before the first seal?"

"I was wrong. Tonight, I've come to share the truth concerning..."

The demons perched high across the huge wooden crossbeams had come in anticipation of this heated conflict.

"What fools!" scoffed the spirit of Confusion. "They all have the mark of the beast, yet they persist in such worthless interpretations."

"Not all," hissed Fear. "Look who just walked in."

Both overcomers slipped in unnoticed. Jessie Hyatt stood behind the sound booth, while Jake Jamison joined the youth group.

Confusion bristled at the followers it so ineptly lost.

"Easy now," warned Fear, "timing is critical."

Moving over for a better look, the foul spirit grinned, "I remember. Our Master is targeting these two. The plans the One from Above has for them will never transpire."

The traumatized pastor asked for quiet.

"I did teach believers would be caught up before the Abomination of Desolation invaded Jerusalem. I believed the body of Christ wouldn't be here for the Great Tribulation."

The murmuring from the youth group attracted several stares as two agents slipped inside the packed out sanctuary. Jake knew he was in trouble. Bowing his head, the new convert silently prayed for a miracle.

A devastated single mother in the first pew shouted, "Pastor, you told me and my girls to register. You said our ID's have nothing to do with the Bible. Have you changed on this too?"

Swooping toward the podium Confusion hissed, "He sure has."

Instantly his mind was flooded with demonic accusations. Looking down, the frail pastor accepted the fact he would never be allowed to share the truth. Those experiencing the most rage were itching for revenge. Others, who believed they had missed His coming, looked despondent. Sporting blood shot eyes, with heavy bags under each, Elmer didn't look any better. A member of the youth asked to speak.

"So what's the next event on God's prophetic calendar?"

Glancing up, Elmer recognized Jake. Then he saw Jessie nodding her head.

"My friends, one of the keys to understanding the timing of Christ's coming is to distinguish Satan's wrath from God's wrath. 5 During the first half of the seven years, the beginning of sorrows, Michael the archangel restrained the mystery of lawlessness. 6 In the middle of the week, Michael cast Satan and his angels out of heaven. 7 This is when this angelic restrainer was taken out of the way. Revelation 12:12 says Satan will exercise great wrath, knowing his time is short."

"Was this the beginning of the Great Tribulation?" Jake boldly asked.

"Yes, this is when Satan gave his power to the two beasts. It began when the first Beast and his ten nation army invaded Jerusalem. He then seized control of the nations and eliminated the World Faith Movement. 8 The second beast, the false prophet, then ordered the execution of anyone refusing to take the mark of the first beast."

"That's ridiculous!" seethed a retired missionary. "How can a government financial system somehow represent the mark of the beast?"

"The Great Tribulation was Satan's wrath against the saints. Look at the Christians the Beast killed for refusing to register." 9

"No one believes that. This is just your warped opinion."

Elmer took one last look at the people he so dearly loved.

"A month ago the Son of Man came in the glory of His Father. In the twinkling of an eye, angels gathered a multitude before His Father's throne. 10 The days of the Great Tribulation were cut short by the catching up of God's elect. The day of the Lord, the wrath of God against the wicked, has begun. Like Lot, fire struck on the same day believers were delivered." 11

"You're deliberately adding to the Book of Revelation! Jesus will return the same way He left. His second coming takes place at Armageddon when the Word of God splits the Mount of Olives. Last time I checked the Mount of Olives was doing just fine. You've been wrong before, Pastor, what makes you think you're right now?"

He took a deep breath. This would be his final plea.

"Those of us who registered have been deceived by the Beast, Joshua Kayin. His false prophet is Pope Michael. For anyone who hasn't I beg you to resist..."

Receiving his order several agents pushed through the double doors of the sanctuary and hustled down the center aisle.

Reaching the podium Commander Doyle Mercer shouted, "Elmer Dyer, you are under arrest for teaching unlawful propaganda against the NWC. Okay, take him away."

Doyle's evil smile wasn't much comfort. He knew most of the parishioners; just regular townsfolk trying to make a living. Most wouldn't harm a fly. Still he had his orders.

"Please settle down; this will only take a minute. Agent Abernathy will be scanning each of you as you leave. So let's do this right and line up in single file."

Slipping under a car, Jake avoided an agent checking the parking lot. Moments later, this same agent saw a girl running through the shadows of the church's soccer field.

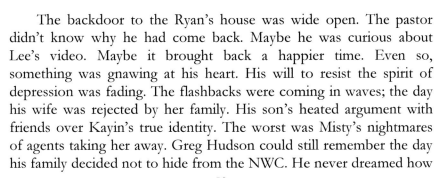

The backdoor to the Ryan's house was wide open. The pastor didn't know why he had come back. Maybe he was curious about Lee's video. Maybe it brought back a happier time. Even so, something was gnawing at his heart. His will to resist the spirit of depression was fading. The flashbacks were coming in waves; the day his wife was rejected by her family. His son's heated argument with friends over Kayin's true identity. The worst was Misty's nightmares of agents taking her away. Greg Hudson could still remember the day his family decided not to hide from the NWC. He never dreamed how difficult it would be to survive without having an ID. Being at the wrong place at the wrong time; that's all it would take. It didn't matter to Greg; he was willing to sacrifice anything for his wife and two children.

After retrieving the remote, he sat on the couch and pushed play.

"Hello, I'm Lee Ryan. If you saw Jesus in the clouds, and you're still here, then you have missed the coming of the Son of Man for His saints, Matthew 24:21-22, 29-31, I Thessalonians 4:15-17, II Thessalonians 2:1, and Revelation 7:9-14. Jesus has taken His elect to heaven and left those who denied Him, Matthew 24:40."

Slumping over, he pushed pause.

"But, God, what about my love for You? Look how many people I have helped? What about my calling as a pastor?" 12

Debate wasn't an option anymore. After graduating from Bible College, Greg entered the pastorate to please his parents. He felt better about himself when people's physical needs were being met. Through it all, his wrong motives were hidden from the very ones he loved the most. His good works rewarded by man were like filthy rags to God. With the video still on pause, tears of repentance drew him to his knees. Pastor Greg Hudson was in no hurry. For the first time in his life he was ready to truly repent of his sins before a holy God.

THE LORD IS MY GOD

Climbing up the tree next door was easy. He was hoping to get a decent look inside the Ryan's house. Since escaping, Jake couldn't get Lee's face out of his mind.

"Lord, agents are searching every abandoned home in this area. Why bring me here? Jessie must be waiting for me near Elmer's church."

The past few weeks were so challenging. At times His voice was clear; at other times Jake wondered if the Holy Spirit had left him.

"Lord, I'm feeling really useless right about now."

From a low hanging tree limb he softly dropped to the ground. The unlocked backdoor was a pleasant surprise. The exhausted teenager could easily hear the TV from the kitchen.

"Come on in!" hollered Greg.

It was as if this stranger had been waiting for him. Shaking his hand he felt a peace from God.

"Hi, I'm Jake Jamison."

"Nice to meet you, I'm Greg Hudson. The Ryan's were friends of my family."

"That's cool. I'm from Lakeview High. Lance used to share the gospel with us."

"He won a lot of souls, didn't he?"

"Lance and Lee were popular with the Christians."

"Some believe they joined the resistance. I've seen two NWC cars in the past hour. They love to scan this neighborhood. You're a Watchman, aren't you, Jake?"

"I'm an overcomer for the Lord."

"Me too, are you hungry? There's food in the kitchen."

"I got separated from a friend. I was kinda hoping Jessie would meet me here."

"Trouble with the NWC?"

"Jess and I want to do God's will. But we have so many questions. We were trying to meet with Pastor Elmer Dyer."

"Was he preaching at his church tonight?"

"He was trying to explain the difference between Satan's wrath and God's wrath. They weren't buying it. Then agents showed up and arrested him. Jessie and I were praying Elmer could give us some answers."

"Maybe I can. I used to pastor my own church."

"No way!" uttered the shocked teenager. "Would you really do that?"

Avoiding agents was becoming more difficult. Each morning, security offices would circulate detailed printouts of at large resisters. Eliminating leaders from the growing underground was now a top priority for the NWC. Only a handful knew about this covert operation. After a suspect was identified, a trained agent from Special Forces would be assigned. Once the package is eliminated, the agent simply disappears.

The third story balcony of the pricy beach condo was a perfect lookout. Entering the bedroom, Death Angel could hear a beeping from a specialized laptop. Within seconds, superiors would be sending pictures of newly assigned packages. Sitting on the side of the king-size bed, the sniper was cleaning a fifty caliber Bushmaster bolt action long range rifle, equipped with Mark 4 16x40 mm LR/T M1 scope. Across the bed were two 22 caliber white pearl pistols in a black leather shoulder holster. On the night stand was a 45 ACD Springfield XD Glock. The metal briefcase on the coffee table contained a wide array of explosives. Grenades, nitro, plastic clay; this assassin would use whatever was necessary for the elimination of a package. Of course, an assignment could never be personal. No agent was ever allowed to assassinate anyone they personally knew. Oddly enough, Death Angel only pursued underage resisters. Most would never see their killer until it was too late. Remarkably, this assassin had never been publicly identified.

Fastening a silencer to the semi-automatic Glock, the secret agent smiled. The NWC had just committed a serious error. This assassin had met this package before. Procedure required a reassignment. This wasn't an option for this killer.

After reading her PO, the agent whispered, "Her code name will be RAT. Reenie Ann Tucker is just one step away from Hades."

The Java House was a popular hangout where one could read a novel, study for exams, or just chat with friends. The locals even tried to keep it a secret from the tourists. It wouldn't matter tonight. Rather than quiet reflection, most were busy partying at the popular beach front bars.

Aimlessly wandering the streets, Reenie couldn't miss the aroma of the Columbian coffee. The soft lights, the mellow background music, the oversized leather chairs with large pillows; a short visit to the Java House couldn't hurt. Slipping between customers, the teenager flopped down on a small couch in the rear of the café. Seated next to the large picture window was a college student studying new age philosophy. In front of the roaring fireplace, two professors were debating the dangers of the global warming. To her right were two women holding hands and kissing while browsing in the spirituality section. This newly married couple was oblivious of the events that would soon destroy their world.

As the weeks ticked by, the routine of surviving was taking a toll on the frail teenager. From Luke's notes she picked a paper entitled: The Day of the Lord: A New Heavens and A New Earth.

Softly she read, "'But the day of the Lord will come as a thief in the night, in which the heavens will pass away with a great noise, and the elements will melt with fervent heat: both the earth and the works that are in it will be burned up.'" 1

Squinting, she read some verses scribbled in the side column.

"'And I will show wonders in the heavens and in the earth; blood and fire and pillars of smoke, the sun shall be turned into darkness, and the moon into blood, before the coming of the great and awesome day of the Lord.'" 2

The slamming of the front door by a customer jarred her for a moment. This time she refused to be distracted.

Continuing, she read, 'Behold, the day of the Lord comes, cruel, with both wrath and fierce anger, to lay the land desolate; and he will destroy its sinners from it. For the stars of heaven and their constellations will not give their light; the sun will be darkened in its going forth, and the moon will not cause its light to shine.' 3 Gee, this happened on October 3rd; the night the elect were delivered."

Then she read, "'immediately after the tribulation of those days the sun will be darkened, and the moon will not give its light; the stars will fall from heaven, and the powers of the heavens will be shaken.'"4

The fatigued teenager was trying to put it together.

"According to Joel and Isaiah, the day of the Lord is God's wrath in the last days. After the sun, moon, and stars, lose their light, the day of the Lord begins. In Matthew 24:29-31, the Son of Man comes with His angels and gathers His elect to heaven. His coming also takes place after the sun, moon, and stars, lose their light."

She was already sensing the stirring of her spirit guide.

"Could this mean the day of the Lord began on October 3rd?"

Reviewing a chart taped inside the cover of Luke's Bible, she paused.

"In Revelation 6, the sun goes black, the moon red, and the sky recedes like a scroll. In Revelation 7, a multitude of Christians from every nation arrive in heaven. In Revelation 8, Jesus opens the seventh seal. This means all seven seals had to be opened before God's wrath is poured out on the earth."

Reenie's desire to study was the result of someone's prayer. Her heart was softening toward facing the dark secret of her youth. Jezebel's threats were losing power.

After reading II Peter 3:10-13, the lonely teenager asked God, "The day of the Lord came like a thief just like you said. As far I can see, four out of seven trumpets are fire. Yet Peter says we are supposed to be watching for a new earth and a new heaven. I don't get this? If Your wrath melts everything, then when does the new earth come in?"

She was used to the silence, Jezebel made sure of that. Looking at Luke's notes, she noticed a passage from Isaiah underlined in red.

'For behold, I create new heavens and a new earth; and the former shall not be remembered or come to mind. But be glad and rejoice forever in what I create; for behold, I create Jerusalem as a rejoicing and her people a joy. The wolf and the lamb shall feed together...'" 5

Reenie remembered Luke telling her about Jesus someday ruling from Jerusalem. She had just never thought about the timing of it.

"Lord, this world is ready to crash and burn. I need to know when the day of the Lord ends? When are You going to restore this earth? 6 And who is going to live here?"

At first, she didn't notice the flickering of the lights. It was closing time. While gathering her notes, she overheard one of the professors.

"These fires have partially destroyed the protective layer of our ozone. If mankind expects to overcome global warming, we must rely on the best minds of our scientific community. I've always believed a catastrophe like this would force the super powers to clean up our polluted environment."

Stepping around them, Reenie wanted to say something.

Within her spirit she heard, "Not one word!"

"That's right, Jake, I met the Ryan's through my son. It was Ethan who invited Lance to preach to our youth. Two weeks later, I asked him to fill in for me on a Sunday night service. Some of the members of my church thought his teaching on the end times made a lot of sense."

"Were your wife and two children taken by the Lord?"

"They're before the throne right now."

A more relaxed Jake curiously asked, "Was Ethan my age?"

"Yeah, you remind me of him a lot."

"So what really happened to the Ryan's?"

"Haven't you heard? Lance was meeting with a student from Lakeview High. He supposedly had questions about the Lord. His name was Damien."

"I know Damien Haley. Luke and Hope used to witness to him. Jessie knows him too. That's why I'm here. Jess and I got split up. The Holy Spirit led me here to find Jessie. But the Lord sent you."

"It was a set up, Jake. Damien was an informant. That night, behind the Industrial Arts building, an agent shot and killed Lance's partner in the resistance. Hours later, the NWC executed Lance."

"So Damien got paid for trapping Lance?"

"Some people will do anything for money."

"You mean they were both martyred for the Lord?"

"Yes, every believer needs to count the cost my friend. Are you ready for your first lesson on Bible prophecy?"

"You bet I am."

"Do you have a Bible?"

"Not on me."

Reaching over, Greg picked up a worn black leather Bible.

"Here, Lance would consider it an honor for you to have his Bible."

Doyle Mercer was thinking about the growing resistance movement. Of course, picking resisters up one by one would require more manpower than was humanly possible. The Commander dreaded losing the infamous Jason Wylie. He vowed if he ever saw him again, the end result would be different.

"There she is, just like you said," whispered the rookie agent.

"I love this part," grinned Doyle.

"Do you think Jessie Hyatt is hooked up with Wylie's operation?"

"Naw, Jason disappeared with his family the very day he was outed."

"C'mon, Chief, let me arrest her. I'll interrogate her myself. She will be running at the mouth before our first coffee break."

Doyle wasn't amused. He didn't want any mistakes over this suspect.

"What if we cut her loose?"

"Too risky; she could stir up trouble for us at Lakeview High. We are talking one big headache; especially from her folks. C'mon, let me close this deal."

"What's the hurry? I want to play this hand out."

"But, Chief, the media will crucify us if she escapes."

"So, Greg, what should we study first?"

"Up for a video highlighting the fourteen judgments that are going to melt this earth?"

"Seriously?"

"Lee Ryan gave us the scriptures painting the picture."

"What an awesome answer to prayer."

Her eyes, her voice, her intensity was obvious. In the

introduction, Lee highlighted the events warning the saints of His coming. Between the sixth and seventh seals of the heavenly scroll, a multitude of believers from every nation were gathered to heaven by angels.

"A roadmap a child could understand," cringed the former pastor."

"Thirty minutes after the bodily resurrection of the saints, the Lord will begin to pour out His wrath. This judgment against the wicked is called the day of the Lord. It begins with the sounding of the first trumpet when one third of the earth's trees and grass are burned. It ends after the pouring out of the seventh bowl. Now this is critical. The coming of the Lord is more than a singular visitation; it's an event. It began with the resurrection of the dead in Christ and the translation of believers who are alive. It ends when the Lamb of God returns with His bride inside the New Jerusalem."

Greg hit pause after the young overcomer raised his hand to speak.

"You mean the coming of the Lord ain't over yet?"

"It appears Jesus still has some unfinished business."

"Now get this," cautioned Lee. "The very day the Abomination of Desolation defiled the Temple; God sent two Witnesses. These two prophets will prophecy the second half of the seventieth week (1260 days). They have already been sharing the coming of the Son of Man, the day of the Lord, the physical return of the Messiah, Armageddon, and the coming New Jerusalem. Once the seventieth week ends the Beast will kill the two Witnesses. On this same day, the Deliverer will return to earth."

"Time-out! I thought Jesus returns to earth during the battle of Armageddon when He splits the Mount of Olives."

"I once thought that too," Greg sheepishly replied.

"The scriptures tell us what the Lord does just before He splits the Mount of Olives. Check this out. Jesus will first gather the 144,000 from the Jordanian wilderness. The 144,000 will be the first fruits redeemed from His Jewish remnant. Two days later, they will arrive in Jerusalem and our Redeemer will fulfill the mystery of God. After the fullness of the Gentiles has come in, the mystery of God will be accomplished. [7] This mystery is when Jesus Christ forgives those from Israel who confess, '...The Lord is my God.'" [8]

"Wow, are you saying Jesus is going to save a remnant three days after the seventieth week ends?"[9]

"Seems God's promise to Abraham is forever," beamed Greg. 10

"The day after Israel is saved; Jesus will breathe life into the two Witnesses. These two prophets will rise from the dead and return to heaven. The next day the Lamb will lead His first fruits, the 144,000, to the Temple Mount. 11 At the sounding of the seventh trumpet; the Lord will take back authority from Satan and begin to spiritually reign." 12

"Hold up. When will Jesus do this?"

"It appears the Lord will take back authority from Satan the day after the two Witnesses are raised from the dead."

"Then what happens?"

"Let's find out."

"After Satan's authority is stripped away, the Lamb of God will lead His remnant down the Kidron Valley and up to the Mount of Olives. After splitting the Mount, His remnant will flee down a valley to Azal. 13 These believers will be protected from the seven bowl judgments."

Hitting the pause button, Greg sat back on the couch.

"There's your answer bro. The reason why Jesus splits the Mount of Olives is to hide His remnant from God's final wrath."

"You mean the seven bowls in Revelation 16?" 14

"That's right. The Lord will hide them after the sounding of the seventh trumpet. It makes sense. Why would the Word split the Mount of Olives during Armageddon to hide His remnant from His wrath? His wrath ends at the supper of the great God."

Shaking his head Jake asked, "So where in Israel does the battle of Armageddon begin?"

"North of Jerusalem at the base of a hill called Megiddo. Some think armies from the East will destroy Israel before facing the Word of God."

"You mean Satan is going to wipe out the Jewish people?"

"That's his ultimate goal."

"What about us?"

"Zephaniah prophesied mankind would be cut off from the face of the earth during the day of the Lord." 15

"I don't wanna die; do you?"

"Let's finish watching."

"Whatever."

Lee reappeared on the screen with a concluding remark.

"At the end of this video there is a list of verses concerning the thousand year reign of Christ. During His millennial reign, the Lamb will rule with His bride over those surviving the day of the Lord." 16

Jumping up, Jake yelped, "Did you hear that, Greg? Some people will survive the day of the Lord. They'll be living on the earth during the Millennium. 17 This means we still have a shot of making it alive. Jess will go ballistic when she hears this."

She was hesitating. Every window was covered. Hiding in the brush against the house, she could barely hear the muffled talking coming from the living room.

"Oh, Lord, what do you want me to do?"

The last few minutes seemed like hours to the frightened teenager.

"Father, I won't allow the fear of man to control me. In the name of Jesus, I rebuke these demons. Whatever happens, You take over Lord."

"Chief, the brush in their yard is pretty thick. We could lose her."

Doyle had made hundreds of arrests. This experienced agent had always acted decisively. He was never afraid to give an order. But on this damp night, he was wavering. Agents under his command knew his lust for revenge was affecting his judgment. Suddenly the outside lights shut off. An automatic timer had done its job.

"Get her!" cursed Doyle.

Through the blinds Greg could see the agents running toward the front door.

"Just stick to our plan, Jake. I'll see you behind Sluman's garage in one hour. If I don't make it, then meet me at my house at 2:00 am."

Sliding out the bathroom window, he could hear footsteps. Jumping over the neighbor's chain link fence the boy vanished into the darkness. Jake was two houses away before he turned around and saw the flashing blue lights.

IT WILL COME TO PASS

'And it shall come to pass that whoever calls on the name of the LORD shall be saved. For in Mount Zion and in Jerusalem there shall be deliverance, As the LORD has said, among the remnant whom the LORD calls.'
Joel 2:32

"The more noise the better!" hollered the elated Commander.

After handcuffing the frightened girl the agent put her in his squad car which was parked in the Ryan's driveway. With revolving blue lights illuminating the front of the house, Doyle Mercer read Jessie her rights. A half a block away Jake could barely make out her face.

"Well, little lady, your escape from Elmer's church was quite a feat. You think your God is going to give you another chance?"

Staring straight ahead she didn't bother to answer.

Another agent jogged out the front door.

"Just tell me you got Jamison?"

"Chief, he must have escaped out the bathroom window. He could be hiding in one of these houses. Do you want us to begin a search?"

"Not for this lousy punk."

"You'll never catch him."

"Whoa, the little lady finally speaks. Funny, I don't see your hero trying to save you."

After motioning for someone to tape her mouth, Doyle's deep-set eyes summoned his agents into a tight circle.

"What's wrong with you guys? Now we've lost this kid twice. Jake Jamison doesn't get another chance, do you hear me."

It was just after midnight and Reenie still hadn't found a place to sleep. In her mind she heard, 'But the Lord is faithful, who will establish you and guard you from the evil one.' 1

Manifesting, her spirit guide grabbed her throat and shook the teenager violently.

"I beg you, Jezebel, don't do this."

"You register tomorrow and I will leave you and indwell another."

"You mean I will be completely free?"

"I give you my word."

"How do I know you will keep it?"

Slowly encircling her, the demon picked up speed, flying faster and faster.

"Stop it! Stop it! You're making me dizzy."

Beads of perspiration slid down into her eyes as she crumbled into a flower bed next to the park bench. Within seconds red fire ants covered her left arm.

"Keep my word!" taunted Jezebel. "Maybe; maybe not, you don't have much choice now do you?"

The arrest of famous resisters was still hot news. Just last week, a popular movie star was executed for refusing to register. Even amidst a propaganda campaign promising a smooth transition into a one-world financial system, somehow the Christian resistance was being rekindled. A surging underground was clearly a major embarrassment to the NWC.

The agents parked their car behind the downtown Security Station.

"Hurry up; I can smell snooping reporters in the air."

With her eyes blindfolded, the agent shoved Jessie through the backdoor entrance.

"Easy on the merchandise," teased his partner.

Tightening his grip, his disdain was obvious.

"Everything's cool, I've just got a few questions for her."

"C'mon, bro, you know she can't talk here."

"Maybe she knows my boy. He was her age when he left us."

Slipping between them, the other agent couldn't look the other way.

"Let me check her in. The guys in the Green Room know what they're doing."

Reluctantly the bitter father released her. As the terrified teenager was led away he pounded the wall and pleaded, "Son, what could this cult offer you that would make you deny your own kin?"

The two families were done with lunch. Ruth volunteered to watch Jabez and Joash in her room. Cloaked in darkness their parents discussed their future.

"No one will survive His wrath," wept Hanna. "Amos prophesied, '"Woe to you who desire the day of the Lord...It will be darkness, and not light. It will be as though a man fled from a lion and a bear met him..."' 2

A resigned Judah shared, "The two Witnesses quoted this passage last month. The lion represents the slaughter of our people for the past eighteen months. Our people have escaped the lion only to meet the bear, the day of the Lord."

"But how can we know for sure?" pleaded a desperate Deborah.

"Joel prophesied, 'The sun shall be turned into darkness, and the moon into blood, before the coming of the great and awesome day of the Lord.' 3 The world saw this sign the night we were celebrating the Feast of Trumpets."

"A sign lasting almost eight hours," reflected a perplexed Eleazar. "This is so hard to believe."

Judah reached over and took his wife's hand.

"My love, Joel speaks of a remnant which will be protected during the Lord's righteous judgment of our people. 'And it shall come to pass that whoever calls on the name of the Lord shall be saved. For in Mount Zion and in Jerusalem there shall be deliverance, as the Lord has said, among the remnant whom the Lord calls.'" 4

"So how do we become part of this remnant?"

"This remnant of the Lord will find deliverance atop Mount Zion."

"What deliverance?" scoffed Eleazar. "These fires have practically destroyed the souls of our people, so many are trusting in Kayin's evil vision for the world."

"The two Witnesses are prophesying Yeshua gathered His elect that night. Those who believed were caught up to heaven."

"That's impossible!" challenged an angry Hanna. "There is no such thing as the resurrection of the living." 5

"These fires aren't manmade. The day of the Lord has begun. We've always trusted our Messiah will protect us."

For a brief moment they could hear their little ones playing.

With a candle flickering, Eleazar said, "Maybe next year, here, in Jerusalem."

Jessica Esther Hyatt was taking her eye scan when Doyle Mercer walked in reading her arrest report.

"Good job, guys, fresh coffee is in my office."

"Okay, Chief, Hyatt is in our system."

"Tell agent Abernathy to take her to the Green Room."

"Chief, regulations say we must first..."

"Our suspect has some guests. Abe can assist me in the integration."

No one liked special treatment for resisters. Their bitterness was obvious. Most agents wouldn't have wasted ten minutes on this case. In their minds, Jessie Hyatt's execution was a done deal.

The Green Room had a long table and several dark green plastic chairs. A water cooler and soft drink machine were side by side in the corner. On the wall was a large one-way glass mirror.

"Morning, this is agent Abernathy, I'm Chief Mercer."

"Thanks for seeing us. I'm Jon Hyatt and this is my wife, Shelby."

Motioning through the glass, Doyle asked, "This is your daughter?"

Bent over in her chair, her long hair hanging down, her hands were shaking.

"Jessie looks so different since she disappeared."

"And that was?"

"Over a year ago."

"Your daughter has been busy. She's met with members of the underground, has actively promoted hate propaganda, even tried to barter for food without an ID."

"That couldn't be our Jessie."

"Why not, Mr. Hyatt?"

"Why should she? Give me a motive?"

"So you wouldn't know a Mr. Jacob Jamison?"

"They were once friends," fumed Shelby.

"Practically inseparable if you ask me."

"May we see our daughter?"

"Mrs. Hyatt, that depends on what you're going to tell her."

"I don't understand?"

"Your daughter is under arrest for helping Jamison escape. I don't know where you're from but in Alabama this is called treason."

"Chief Mercer, my daughter would never willingly break the law. Maybe this cult is threatening her. Can't you give her another chance?"

Glancing at his watch, he yawned.

"Here's my offer. You convince her to register tonight and I'll drop all charges. Who wants to talk to her?"

"Let me, Jon. You know the bond we have. She'll listen to me."

In her mind the Holy Spirit spoke, "'but it will turn out for you as an occasion for testimony. Therefore settle it in your hearts not to meditate beforehand on what you will answer; for I will give you a mouth and wisdom which all your adversaries will not be able to contradict or resist.'" 6

"This is happening so fast, Lord. Please give me the strength to overcome."

The heavy door swung open. Both mother and daughter froze when their eyes met.

"Mama!"

Meeting half way, they embraced. Jon Hyatt was cheering from behind the one-way glass mirror. Their nightmare was over.

"We love you Jess. Your daddy and I thought we'd lost you."

"Jesus is with me, Mama. I've got so much to share."

"Yes, baby, I can imagine."

"Where's Daddy? I wanna share my testimony with him."

"He's waiting outside to see you."

"It happened the night Jesus came."

"What happened?" asked a confused Shelby.

"That night I became a Christian."

Her mother knew she was walking a fine line. Anymore talk about Jesus and the agents would certainly intervene.

"Guess what, Jess? All charges against you have been dropped.

Chief Mercer has graciously offered to register you himself."

Her words felt like a punch to the stomach. Bending over, Jessie couldn't breathe.

It was closing time as two college couples stumbled out of the bar. No one was sober enough to drive, so they decided to walk.

"Hey, check out the flower bed."

"Well if it isn't Snow White catching some zzz's," teased her boyfriend.

"That's not funny, this girl is in trouble."

"Watch it, she's got fire ants," slurred his buddy.

Suddenly a red dot edged up Reenie's left arm.

His patrol was almost over. For the third night in a row his partner was a no show. Spotting some suspicious movement, the sleepy police officer pulled over and hit his overhead lights.

"Okay, don't anyone budge. Who's the girl?"

Before they could answer the officer saw the red dot moving up her neck. Stepping out of his car, he drew his loaded revolver.

"We have no clue, sir. I think she needs to see a doctor."

"Help me move her to my car. I'll take her to the downtown Emergency Room."

The red dot disappeared the moment she was moved.

The spirit of Doubt signaled to Confusion, "How original, a new convert being comforted by her unsaved mother."

"C'mon Jessie," screamed Shelby, "Please say something! Hey, we need some help in here."

Jumping up, Jon shouted, "What type of operation are you running..."

"Sit down and shut up."

"I know my rights."

"You have no rights," snarled Doyle. "If it weren't for extenuating circumstances your daughter would have already been executed by now. She has valuable information we need. Now relax, she's in no danger. She's just putting on a show."

From the water cooler, Jessie mumbled, "I'm okay."

"C'mon, hon, let's go home."

"Mama, I'll never register. I'm looking for a heavenly city; the

New Jerusalem." 7

"That's wonderful. Jon and I go to church now too. Jess, don't you believe God understands our hearts? He is helping Joshua Kayin save our world. Having an ID doesn't mean you don't love God. For heaven sakes, it's the law."

"Your friends miss you," whispered Doubt. "God doesn't want his children to suffer." 8

"Please, Jess, do you understand the seriousness of your rebellion?"

"God wants you back with your family," spewed Confusion. "You don't have to die. God doesn't care about the rules of the NWC."

"I...I... I'm a bit confused right now."

"Confused about what, baby?"

"The Holy Spirit wants me to share the gospel with those who still can be saved."

"Yes and that's not possible if you allow the NWC to take your life."

Barging in Doyle shouted, "Okay, Jessica, are you willing to register?"

"I don't know."

"Tell me, if Jesus is so great, why are you so confused? Hey, we all go to church. Let's just pray and ask God to show us His will?"

"I already know His will for my life."

Doyle Mercers smile meant nothing as he pulled up a chair.

"I also have a teenage daughter. Sometimes she just needs her space. It's almost 2:00 am and the women's cells are full. Why don't you take Jessica home for a few days, call me when she's ready to discuss her future with the NWC."

"You're willing to do that?" asked a stunned Shelby.

"Absolutely, I know how easy it is for kids to be swayed by the wrong crowd."

As agent Abernathy fastened a security bracelet around her ankle; Jon Hyatt rushed into the Green Room and hugged his daughter.

"We're with you now Jess."

"Rule one; your daughter is to have no contact with anyone but immediate family. Two, she is never to be left unsupervised. And three, she must never leave your house."

"We understand, Chief Mercer."

10

AT THIS PRESENT TIME

'...At this present time there is a remnant according to the election of grace.'
Romans 11:5

Driving toward the hospital the police officer cursed.

"I apprehend an underage girl without reporting in. I didn't request back up. And I leave the scene without telling my dispatcher where I'm going. I must be losing it."

Deep down, he knew what he was doing. The red dot tipped him off. Pulling in he parked in an emergency parking space in front of the ER.

"Musta been a Special Forces sniper. A few more seconds and I would've had a bloody mess on my hands."

This veteran cop had seen enough killing. The deep-seated hatred for resisters was something he could never understand. They were no threat. He knew she would be arrested, no questions asked.

"She ain't any older than my Annie."

Sitting back he daydreamed of life before the NWC.

"Hey, Daddy, my church group is having a party. Everyone is bringing their best friend. It's so cool; we play a game asking our friend all sorts of questions."

"So who's your best friend, Annie?"

"Why you are, Daddy. You're my best bud."

He stiffened when he saw the approaching blue lights of an NWC cruiser. It had been two months since Annie's execution.

Opening her eyes a dazed Reenie looked up from the backseat and saw a cop arguing with an NWC agent.

Walking back he spotted her running through the dimly lit parking lot. Closing the backdoor to his squad car, the police officer smiled.

"Fly little one; like my Annie. Fly where no one can hurt you."

Lingering behind Sluman's garage was not the smartest move this early in the morning. It was twenty minutes past two and the young Watchman couldn't wait any longer. Moving in and out of shadows across town, Jake arrived at Greg Hudson's home. Popping open the backdoor, the entire house was dark. After making it down the hallway, he turned on a light in his study. Greg's large oak desk was overflowing with notes. Tacked to the wall was a seven-year calendar. His leather Bible lay open to II Peter 3:10.

"The firestorms came like a thief in the night," winced Jake. "The world was worshiping the image of a man; just like it says in the Bible." 1

An hour later, a key turned in the front door. Peaking into his study he could see the boy praying.

"Greg, you got away!"

"Praise God for lazy agents, Jake. They never checked the basement. I guess you saw Jessie's arrest in the Ryan's driveway?"

"Why did God allow this to happen?"

"He has His reasons."

Across the room the boy gazed at three full bookshelves.

"Wow, have you read all these books?"

"Not a chance. Most are from my days at Seminary. You know, a lot aren't even biblical."

"Have you heard the new lie from the NWC? Pope Michael is saying the firestorms are the two Witnesses' fault."

"Yeah, his phony signs and wonders deceived billions into worshipping the Beast. What heresy."

"What's a heresy?"

"A heresy is a denial of the doctrine of Christ.'

"Can you give me another example?"

"Sure. From day one Satan has sown the lie Jesus is not the only begotten Son of God. 2 In the past decade the enemy deceived many ministers into teaching a heresy many call the Manifest Sons of God.

These heretics taught Jesus became a sinner on the cross, died spiritually, and had to be born again."

"I don't get it, wasn't His physical death enough?"

"That's right, Jake. The only way to be saved is through His shed blood. 3 The sinless Lamb of God never died spiritually."

"So they taught born again believers were Sons of God equal to Jesus?"

"Tragically, anyone that embraced such heresy denied the Lord!"4

Scratching his head, the teenager's attention was drifting.

"So when are we going to rescue Jessie?"

"In the morning, I know four hours of sleep doesn't sound like much. You can have Ethan's room. It's at the top of the stairs. I'll wake you around seven."

"Greg, I have a question about when Jesus returns to earth. It sure would help me if we are ever spilt up again."

"Sure."

"On her video, Lee outlined a peace treaty between Israel and the Antichrist. She called it the seventieth week of Daniel. At the end of the seven years the Messiah is supposed to physically return. The Ryan's tried sharing this with Jessie and me. Can you help me understand it?"

"In 538 B.C., Daniel was confessing his sin and the sins of his people to God. The future for Israel looked bleak because of their disobedience. While the prophet was praying, the angel Gabriel arrived with a vision."

"What kind of vision?"

"This vision is about Christ's first and second coming. Because of their refusal to repent, God is going to allow Israel to suffer 490 years of Gentile domination. After sixty nine weeks (483 years) the Messiah was cut off. When the domination of the seventieth week ends Jesus will return and deliver a remnant who believes in Him."

"So when did this Gentile domination begin?"

"Persian King Artaxerxes issued a decree allowing the Jews to rebuild their city in 445 B.C." 5

"So when was the Messiah cut off?"

"Jesus was crucified in 32 A.D. Exactly 483 years from the time the decree was issued by King Artaxerxes to rebuild the holy city."

"So this was Jesus' first coming?"

"Yes, Jake. The leaders of Israel rejected Jesus as their Messiah. Sixty-nine weeks (69x7=483 years) of Gabriel's prophecy were fulfilled the day Jesus died on the cross. There is still a seven-year period that must be completed before the Messiah physically returns and saves a remnant from Israel. 6 In Luke 21:24, Jesus calls the seventieth week the times of the Gentiles. In Romans 11:25, Paul calls it the fullness of the Gentiles."

"So the seventieth week began when Kayin brokered the peace between the Jews and Muslims?"

"We are now living in the second half of the seventieth week."

"How can we know for sure?"

"Jesus quotes Daniel 9:27 in Matthew 24:15. Our Lord warned those living in Jerusalem to flee when they see the Abomination of Desolation standing in the Jerusalem Temple. 7 This evil ruler will break this covenant with Israel in the middle of the seven years."

"You mean a year and a half ago when Kayin's armies invaded Jerusalem?"

"Joshua Kayin is the abomination who caused the desolation of the Jewish Temple. Satan gave this world leader power over the nations just after the fourth seal was opened. 8 The coming of the Son of Man for His elect took place after the sixth seal was opened in Matthew 24:29-31."

"That's what the two Witnesses prophesied last week."

A mesmerized Jake pointed at the calendar hanging above Greg's desk.

"What's with the date circled in red?"

"A very special day in history God calls Yom Kippur; the Day of Atonement."

"What does it represent?"

"Paul wrote about a remnant of Jews being saved in the last days. 9 Right now, the Jewish people have spiritual blinders on until the seventieth week is finished. When the persecution by the Gentiles is over, all Israel will be saved. The Deliverer will return from heavenly Zion and forgive them of their sins." 10

"You mean our Lord is the Deliverer?"

"Yes, Jesus will save a remnant on the Day of Atonement."

"I wanna be here to see it, don't you? When does this take place?"

"Between the sixth and seventh trumpets, the same day the Beast kills the two Witnesses." 11

"Weren't the firestorms the first trumpet?"

"Yeah, the second trumpet can sound any time now."

"Wow, five more trumpets until Jesus returns. Do you think anybody will believe us?"

"That will be a great discussion over breakfast. If agents surprise us while we're asleep, Ethan's room has a balcony with an outside ladder. This time meet me behind the Go-Cart Center. Let's say two hours after we escape."

"Do you think they're gonna force Jess to take the mark?"

"The Holy Spirit is leading her, bro. In the morning, we'll find her."

"Good morning. I'm Dr. Charles Kyle from the Alabama Presbyterian Counsel of Churches."

Their lack of applause was understandable. This early morning meeting was suspect for such an important matter. Even so, the sanctuary was almost full.

As a teenager, Charles Everett Kyle felt the call of God on his life. In the past forty-three years he pastored four churches, served on several mission committees, while writing ten books on Reform Theology. Currently the Superintendent of over one hundred Presbyterian Churches in the state of Alabama. Thoroughly versed in his denomination's stance on eschatology, his mission was painfully clear.

"Thank you all for coming this morning. I'm here to announce the retirement of your pastor. Last week, the Reverend Brown submitted his resignation to our District Office. As your Superintendent, I will assist your pastoral search committee in finding a new pastor."

"Why did J.W. resign?" interrupted a member of the church board.

"Pastor Brown regrets he and his wife could not be here this morning. Under the circumstances, a retirement dinner can be arranged at a later date."

"What do you mean under the circumstances?"

"My brethren, I am compelled today to speak the truth from the scriptures. As Presbyterians, we are facing a biblical crisis we've never experienced before. In the past few years, false prophecy teachers have preyed upon many within our membership. They boldly teach Jesus is going to come back and gather His elect to heaven."

"That's what Pastor Brown taught us," insisted a deacon.

"He believes the Antichrist has deceived us!" added a teenager.

The experienced leader raised his arms.

"If you agree to listen to our doctrinal position concerning the second coming, then I will allow a time for questions."

Most hands dropped, some slower than others.

"Let me assure you, last month's eclipse wasn't the coming of the Lord. I know it was convincing, but it wasn't Jesus. No one but the Lord can usher in the eternal state of the saved and unsaved. This final bodily resurrection at the white throne judgment follows the coming of the Son of Man. Jesus said, "'Do not marvel at this, for the hour is coming in which all who are in the graves will hear His voice and come forth-those who have done good, to the resurrection of life, and those who have done evil, to the resurrection of condemnation.'"[12]

"What about us?"

"There is only one bodily resurrection. This resurrection must take place on the last day. 'And this is the will of Him who sent Me, that everyone who sees the Son and believes in Him may have everlasting life; and I will raise him up at the last day.'" [13]

Another member shared, "Pastor Brown taught us the judgment seat of Christ takes place in heaven after the rapture of the church. The resurrection of the unsaved at the white throne judgment takes place after the Millennium. How can they be the same event?"

"I'm afraid J.W. wasn't adhering to proper Presbyterian theology."

"Pastor told me our ID's are the mark of the beast."

"That's a bold faced lie!" challenged a gray haired grandmother. "I've sat in this here pew for over forty years and never heard such nonsense."

"Pastor Brown believes the Beast and the False Prophet will be cast into the lake of fire before the Millennium begins."

The Superintendent paused before asking for quiet.

"My friends; a lot of the events you're talking about are pure fiction. Show me where there is a literal thousand-year reign of Christ on earth."

A Sunday school teacher hollered back, "The Millennium, which means thousand in the Greek, is used six times in Revelation 20."

"This passage is referring to our Lord reigning in heaven with those who have died. It speaks of two resurrections. The first was spiritual and has already taken place. The resurrection of the body is a general resurrection taking place at the end of the age."

"It says the Devil will be bound for a thousand years."

"The Devil was bound at the cross. God did this so Satan wouldn't hinder the spread of the gospel."

"Doesn't the Devil give the Antichrist his power in Revelation 13:2?"

"There is no Antichrist in The Revelation of Jesus Christ."

"Ain't that a fact," howled an old timer. "I told them Satan had no power."

"As Presbyterians we don't believe in a future thousand year earthy kingdom. The prophecies concerning an eternal kingdom will be fulfilled on the last day. Thank you so much for your time."

Bidding goodbye, Dr. Charles Kyle didn't even try to relate to their needs. Their uncertainty was not his concern. His mission was to articulate Presbyterian theology. He and Pastor Brown were once good friends. He knew J.W. believed in a rapture of the church. Of course, before reprimanding a pastor for teaching doctrinal error, the Superintendent would have to take into consideration his seniority within the denomination, his popularity among his peers, and the financial status of his church. In J.W.'s case, the reprimand from the District Office never came.

It was mid morning when rays from the sun hit his eyes. After a three minute shower, Jake tried on some black jeans and a dark blue sweatshirt from Ethan's closet. Racing down the stairs he could smell the hot bacon. Greg was preparing their breakfast.

"You sleep well, Jake?"

"Naw, had three nightmares. Why didn't you wake me up? Jessie needs our help."

"Just after sun up this morning the Holy Spirit led me to drive by the Hyatt's house. I saw Jessie looking out the second story window."

"She's at home? But they wouldn't let her go unless she registered."

"That's what I thought. Excuse me for a second."

Turning his back on Jake, he grasped the handle of the skillet and poured the hot grease into the sink.

"So I had a friend make some calls. Nobody knows why but Chief Agent Mercer let Jessie go. Something about her being under house arrest. She didn't register."

Looking up Greg froze. Bolting from the kitchen the former pastor ran through the dining room. The front door was wide open. There was no sign of the young Watchmen.

A NEW COVENANT

'...The days are coming...when I will make a new covenant...'
Jeremiah 31:31

Her house was a mile away. His thoughts raging; Jake's run wasn't the smoothest.

"You're too late," whispered Lying. "Jessie is marked for eternity!"

"Lord, I can't handle this."

Pausing to catch his breath, he remembered. Luke Appleby was warning a group of students about the mark of the beast. He was losing their attention. Someone was cracking jokes.

"Jamison, this isn't funny. Anyone who doesn't register is going to be persecuted big time."

"Not in my lifetime," he teased back.

It was like yesterday. Then Jake received a word from the Holy Spirit.

It was after midnight when both families met in the living room.

"Within the next hour we are going to have a special visitor."

"Daddy is he going to live with us?"

"This is only a visit, Ruth."

"Why bring him here?" Hanna nervously asked.

"He risked a lot hiding us. We need to hear him out."

Sitting in silence, the three knocks on the bookcase seemed louder than they really were. The soldier was tall, good looking, with partly graying sideburns. The creases under his dark brown eyes were obvious. Since Kayin took control of Jerusalem, over a year and a half ago, this Israeli freedom fighter had hidden over five hundred Jewish families. Tragically, the stranger holding little Ruth in his lap had also become a killer. For many, the boundaries of right and wrong could easily be blurred by the heartache of war. A war not led by humans but by the ruler of this world, Satan. 1

After sharing a desert with their guest, the children left to play games. The soldier then methodically outlined the assassination of Joshua Kayin.

"My brother, is this really necessary?"

"Judah, this tyrant has to be stopped."

"What is your name?" asked Hanna.

"My soldiers call me, Matthias."

"Do you have a family?"

It was obvious he did not appreciate such questions.

"My family was killed by Jordanian terrorists."

"Hashem will deal with Kayin in His timing, not ours."

"What are you saying, Judah? Millions of our people have been killed."

"Matthias, do you believe the Messiah will rescue Israel?"

"I'm a Zionist. The land from the river Egypt to the river Euphrates is the land God promised our people through Abraham. 2 In 1917, world leaders approved a Jewish homeland. The land we presently possess is twenty-five times less than what was originally allocated. Since becoming a nation in 1948, our Muslim neighbors have tried to take away our land. We can't permit this, no matter what the cost."

"Hasn't God brought His people back to Zion? He will protect us."

"What about the Valley of Jehoshaphat massacre?"

"Didn't God supernaturally intervene?"

"Slow annihilation isn't what I call protection. Since the Jehoshaphat invasion, Kayin has lost his nerve. Now is the time to attack. This is why I've come. Our soldiers need more weapons. Can you help us, Judah?"

"May we share a prophecy given by Jeremiah? God has promised to make a New Covenant with the house of Israel." 3

"Only if we defend ourselves from Kayin's madness."

"Eleazar and I participate in the Feasts of the Lord. 4 These holy days depict the redemptive career of the Messiah. He will soon fulfill Yom Kippur and the Feast of Tabernacles. Only the Messiah can usher in the Kingdom Age."

"What fulfillment? You mean the defilement by the pagan deity of the crescent moon?"

"Matthias, soon the Shekinah glory will fill our Temple."

Turning to leave, he seethed, "If we don't defend ourselves there will be no Israel left to witness such a miracle."

It had been two days. The guilt was unbearable. Greg knew the risk as he drove by Jessie's house. After combing the neighborhood again, he visited Lakeview High, the Go Cart Center, George Wallace Park, and the Factory. No one had seen or heard of Jake Jamison.

The people lining the Mediterranean stretched for miles. TV networks were set up on ships just off shore. Cameramen were poised for the first glimpse of the prophets. Rumors spread by NWC were working. Worldwide hatred of the two Witnesses was growing.

The Bethany Ministers Association's monthly meeting was underway.

"Good morning. Before we begin..."

"Is there a reason why Chairman Ryals isn't with us this morning?"

"And what about Pastor Dyer?" interrupted another minister. "I've heard he's threatening our kids with end time propaganda."

"Has John Ryals really been fired by his board for teaching heresy? Isn't our creditability in jeopardy if we don't hold our members accountable?"

The entire BMA Committee stood. Then one of its members coldly announced, "Regrettably John Ryals submitted his resignation last week. I'm pleased to announce Pastor Louis Cooper of Lakeview Assembly of God is our new Chairman."

Without any hesitation, the preacher stepped up to the podium.

"Thank you so much. We all know our parishioners need us now more than ever. There is only one way to alleviate the fears plaguing our people. With the help of our Committee, I plan to deal with issues our former leadership never addressed."

"Pastor Cooper, what type of issues?"

"Concerning the end times we must speak as one voice. Chairman John Ryals taught a secret rapture of the saints at any moment. I did too. But the more I study the scriptures, the more convinced I am of a bodily resurrection coming at the last trumpet. 'Behold, I tell you a mystery: We shall not all sleep, but we shall all be changed-in a moment, in the twinkling of an eye, at the last trumpet. For the trumpet will sound, and the dead will be raised incorruptible, and we shall be changed.'" 5

Control and Confusion knew the ministers they had to persuade.

"Paul has the resurrection of believers coming at the last trumpet. I ask you, can we put the gathering of the elect in any other place and still remain faithful to the Word of God?"

"So we will be caught up at the sounding of the seventh trumpet?"

"My brother, Jesus has the elect gathered to heaven at the sound of a great trumpet. Paul spoke of a mystery, in the twinkling of an eye, at the last trump. John prophesied the mystery of God would be finished at the seventh trumpet. Obviously this mystery is the coming of the Son of Man for His elect."

"Praise the Lord, Pastor Cooper. I've taught this for over forty years. There is no rapture in the Bible. After the seven year tribulation is over, the last trump will be blown, and the elect will be resurrected."

"I've always taught the last trump will sound on the last day," bragged another. "Jesus promised to raise up all believers on the last day." 6

"I'm so confused," moaned a pastor from the front row. "If this is true, then why isn't the church ever mentioned again after a voice like a trumpet sounds in Revelation 4:1?"

"Please, brethren," interrupted Pastor Cooper. "What exactly does God mean by the last trumpet? The last trump means the end of a sequence. Yes, I'm aware several pastors in the BMA teach the events in the Book of Revelation are merely symbolic. They believe John's vision represents the struggle between good and evil. I'm not judging them. But since the recent firestorms, I now take a more literal interpretation."

"You can't mean we are suffering the first trumpet of Revelation 9?" asked a stunned priest.

"I'm afraid so, father. It appears we must endure six more

trumpets."

"What about other faiths who have never read the Bible?"

"Yes, father, we are all God's children. At the last trumpet, God will find those who truly are seeking after the truth."

"So you believe the seventh trump is the last trump?"

"That's right. The sounding of a trumpet in I Thessalonians 4:16, I Corinthians 15:52, Matthew 24:31, and Revelation 11:15, are the same event."

"The last trump is blown on the last day!" shouted a Baptist pastor. "The seventh trumpet takes place before the last day. Have you forgotten about the seven bowls?"

Another minister added, "The last day is the day of the Lord. The wrath of God isn't completed until all seven bowls are poured out. Armageddon follows the seventh bowl."

Raising his voice Louis Cooper confidently announced, "Gentlemen, the ultimate goal of our Association is to give people hope amidst such tragedy. Jesus has not forsaken us. He promises to be with us 'til the end of the age. May we assure our parishioners, the bodily resurrection of the elect will not take place until the last trump sounds."

Waiting at a red light, a tourist asked an Israeli soldier, "Any news on the two Witnesses?"

"I heard they are prophesying in the vicinity of Netanya. What a disgrace for our country."

"Some believe they are speaking the truth."

"Do you know I can arrest you for saying that?"

"Then why doesn't the NWC stop them? This only helps fuel the rumor they are being supernaturally protected."

"The crowds following these fakes have become unmanageable. Within forty-eight hours, the issuing of new visas will stop. Our army has been called in to restore order."

"So you don't believe in them?"

"The media is to blame. Such extensive exposure has guaranteed their creditability. Now their lies are spreading around the world. I say shoot them both."

"Wow, think of that. Whoever kills the two Witnesses would become famous overnight."

Stepping out on the ledge of a high hill facing the Mediterranean Sea, the smaller Witness raised his staff above his head.

"He's east of the rock formation," hollered a cameraman.

The massive crowd turned around and faced their accusers.

The taller Witness shared, "For those who have not worshipped the Beast, his image, or received his mark, hear me. 7 May you repent of your sins and confess with your mouth the Lord Jesus. 8 May you believe in your heart The Father raised His Son from the dead and you will be saved. Only by believing will you be able to discern between the righteous and the wicked; between those who serve God and those who don't! 9 Soon, another trumpet will sound. Many creatures in the sea will die. The oceans of this world will be as blood. The fire of God's wrath will destroy ships, yea; the Spirit of the Lord has confirmed it!" 10

THE TRUTH SHALL MAKE YOU FREE

'And you shall know the truth and the truth shall make you free.'
John 8:32

Shaking his hand the excited pastor eagerly shared, "Hi, Mayor Hayes, I just read about it in the Herald. Dr. Marcus Jacobs is one of the most sought after prophecy speakers in America. How did you ever persuade him to visit us?"

"All the pieces just fell into place, Reverend. The Robert E. Lee Conference Center was sold out in less than an hour. He'll be speaking this Saturday night on the future of mankind."

"My church will be praying for him."

"That's mighty kind of you. I'm glad we raised our ticket prices. Jacobs's has an assistant, a publicist, a bodyguard, a nurse, and two pilots. Even has his own jet. They're landing near the old Spivey farm Saturday afternoon."

"Mayor Hayes, he's so worth it. I've heard Dr. Jacobs has a way of calming people down."

"Hope he can expose these doomsday prophets! Have you heard their new prediction?"

"No, but I bet ya it won't be as bad as the firestorms."

"A third of the critters in our oceans are going to die. They're also predicting a third of our ships will be destroyed."

"Mayor, this is just the Devil inciting fear. Such grandstanding by them doesn't scare me."

"Reverend, you may have something there. Seems to me that good ole horse sense will tell ya that if these two voices aren't speaking for God, then who are they speaking for?"

The metal bars on her windows made escape impossible. Jessie's silence since breakfast seemed odd. A suspicious Shelby listened for a moment before knocking on her bedroom door.

"Hi Jess you up for a visit?"

Stepping between several prophecy charts on the floor, Shelby tried to hide her disgust. Across the room was a wastebasket filled with crumpled posters and broken CDs.

"Gee, honey, what's with the housecleaning?"

"Whew, won't be needing this garbage anymore." 1

Sitting down next to her daughter, Shelby picked up a torn poster.

"Isn't this your favorite band Blood Curse? What's going on?"

"I've trashed everything evil. I only listen to music glorifying Jesus."

"Some of these CDs were gifts. What will your friends say?"

"Mama, we need to talk."

"Okay but go slow, I've still got lots of questions."

"Bottom line, my life is devoted to God. The Father sent His Son to earth to die for the sins of mankind. When the Holy Spirit overshadowed the virgin Mary, the Son of God became flesh. 2 Jesus chose the cross as our sinless Passover Lamb. On the third day He rose from the dead and defeated death. He is my Lord and Savior. I'm His, no one else's."

"So you believe by registering you're somehow denying God?"

"The ID chip was a deception created by Satan."

"So the two Witnesses are for real?"

"They quote scripture to prove what they say."

"So does every preacher I know. Have you heard their latest prediction?"

"Must be the second trumpet, God's wrath is going to hit our oceans."

"Stop this charade, Jess, you're scaring me."

"Do you know anyone who lives near the beach?"

Caught off guard, Shelby mumbled back, "Sort of."

"We must warn them!"

From her Bible, Jessie removed a photo of a couple playing at the beach with their baby.

"Where did you get this?" asked a shaken Shelby.

"In yesterday's mail a letter was addressed to me. But there was no note, no name, no explanation, just this picture."

Her eyes never left her mother's.

"I guess you saw the postmark?"

"Dauphin Island is just off Gulf Shores. I believe God wants me to help this family."

Shelby had always dreaded this day. Yet telling her daughter the truth may be a way of bringing her back.

"Jess, you have never met the woman in this picture. She is my older sister."

"I don't understand. Why would you hide her from me?"

"This picture is seventeen years old. This is your Aunt Myra and her husband Anthony Santino. The baby is their son, Anthony Bret. I took this picture while we were vacationing together. We were celebrating Bret's first birthday."

"You mean Bret and I are first cousins?"

"That's right. The Santinos used to live outside Ogden, Utah. When the economy fell apart a few years ago, their grocery store went under. That's when Anthony decided to move to Dauphin Island and try the fishing industry."

"Do you ever visit them?"

"We helped them move in. Their house is right on the water."

"They're Christians aren't they?"

"Heavens no! Anthony and Myra are drunks. I'm talking knock down drag out fights. They swore so much Jon decided to never let you see them. We actually bumped into them a few weeks ago outside Bertha's. The firestorms damaged their home and they came to Bethany for supplies. Funny, Jon couldn't detect any liquor on their breath."

"I've got to warn them."

"You need to take care of yourself. You're under house arrest."

Restraining herself Shelby somehow shifted to hopeful desperation.

"Tell you what if you register we'll take you to see the Santinos."

"I will never register."

After locking Jessie's bedroom door behind her, the bewildered mother quietly wept. All she could hear was her daughter praying for the salvation of Anthony Bret Santino.

"Got a second, Chief... We've got trouble in high security again...

The prisoners are griping about Elmer... Yep, you're the only one who can make the call..."

"If he would just pay his fine, we could let him go."

"That would probably be our best move, Chief."

"You know the prophet?"

"From my wife's side."

"That's just it. Everybody in this whole stinking town knows him."

"He's no threat. Just a little confused, that's all."

"I'll be the judge of that. Cuff his legs and hands. I'll meet you in the Green Room in ten minutes."

In the past month, Pastor Elmer Dyer had been reported over twenty times for illegal witnessing. His scuffle down the corridor produced a hail of catcalls. Those walking behind the pastor offered no assistance. There were no favors for anyone violating the Religious Tolerance Act. An already annoyed Commander was waiting.

"Have a seat Elmer. As pastor of Eastside United Methodist you've created food programs for the poor, helped drug addicts get clean, even organized the building of homes for the homeless. So tell us, Prophet, what else have you done for our fine town?"

"Pastor Dyer mediated a truce between the Black Knights and the Diablos."

Another agent added, "He also saved the life of a rookie cop who was shot in the crossfire."

"My, my, such a fan club, tell me, why are so many interested in what happens to you?"

"You wouldn't understand."

"C'mon, Elmer, share with us sinners how such a respected pastor can so royally screw up his life?"

"Chief, it's only fair if we see..."

"That's enough! This man of the cloth has been manipulating children into joining the underground resistance. He threatens them. Says they're going to hell if they register. For those he deceives, he encourages them to leave their families."

"Chief, Pastor Dyer has helped..."

"Is anyone listening? Remember Jessie Hyatt and Jake Jamison? The Prophet here was the one who brainwashed them. They were trying to reach him the night we busted him."

Most could only shake their heads in agreement.

"So, Elmer, one moment you're an upstanding pastor and the

next you're a raving fanatic with an obsession for children. I was there the night you dropped the bomb on your congregation. Not very edifying, especially the part about our former President disguising himself as some evil Antichrist. Where do you get such nonsense?"

"The second trumpet is imminent."

"The Prophet speaks. So you believe in these doomsday Witnesses huh? Aren't they foretelling the destruction of our world by God's wrath?"

"They're in the Bible," mumbled agent Abernathy.

"Who is?" seethed Doyle. "Where in the Bible do two prophets predict the killing of millions of people in the last days? Have you lost your mind, Abe?"

Elmer whispered, "Zechariah prophesied two thirds of the Jewish people will perish during the day of the Lord. The one third believing in the Messiah will be...'" 3

"Is this the propaganda you're selling our kids? Reverend, why do you hate the Jews so much? Maybe you get your kicks in a God who burns innocent children. Do you know how many people will eventually die because of these fires?"

"After the sixth trumpet, one third of mankind will be killed." 4

"That's it, boys, we've got a real nutcase on our hands. I wouldn't be surprised if the Prophet has been comparing notes with Johnnie Ryals of Bethany Baptist."

"Anyone who hasn't registered can still be saved. Seek the Lord..."

"This is a waste of our time, Abe, DQ him."

"But, Chief, everybody loves Pastor Dyer. He doesn't deserve to be executed."

"We have legal grounds. Let Elmer be an example to other ministers who endanger the safety of our children. I want his execution in the Herald by this Saturday."

"Has Jess said anything?"

"Not a word. All she ever does is read her Bible, pray, and take notes. She left these notes on the kitchen table after eating lunch."

After spot-checking several pages, Jon Hyatt had to sit down.

"She is obsessed with something called the day of the Lord. This chart actually highlights the killing of billions of people."

"She believes these fires are going to hit Gulf Shores."

"What can we do?"

"Have you heard the news about Dr. Marcus Jacobs?"

"You mean the famous Bible teacher who's always on TV?"

"He's speaking this Saturday night at the Conference Center."

"Why would he come to our little town?"

"Maybe he could reach Jess with the truth."

"We'll be breaking the law if we help her leave our house."

"What choice do we have? We've totally underestimated the power of this religious cult. If we don't do something the NWC is going to pick her up and execute her."

"Alright, if Jess agrees, we'll go. You know this could blow up in our faces?"

"I also know our daughter. When she sees her old friends, without any influence from Jake Jamison, she'll come around. She just needs to hear the truth, that's all."

"That's funny, last night at dinner Jess told me, "The truth shall set you free." 5

THEN YOU WILL CALL UPON ME

'Then you will call upon Me and go and pray to Me, and I will listen to you.
And you will seek Me and find Me, when you search for Me with all your
heart.'
Jeremiah 29:12-13

Most Saturday nights in rural southeastern Alabama were so predictable. That would not be the case tonight. A special guest was coming with a message of encouragement. Since the announcement an eerie anticipation was steadily growing. In his honor, blinking white lights lined the trees on Main Street. With the Conference Center parking lot already full, most folks parked their cars behind the library. Their causal walk under the lights brought back fond memories when life was simpler. A lifestyle of innocence that had been eaten away, sadly, any attempts of recreating the past would never be able to change their future.

"Jon, can't you just drop us off in front of the Center?"

"Honey, getting in and out will take forever. It's only three blocks."

"Mama, are you worried about my security bracelet? I'm okay, it's no big deal."

"Jess, the gossip train in this town is disgusting. You know how people are."

Suddenly screams erupted from across the street. Within seconds a cluster of girlfriends surrounded the tall brunette for a group hug.

A hopeful Becca Clawson asked, "Mrs. Hyatt can Jessie sit with us tonight?"

Shelby glanced in Jon's direction before nodding.

"C'mon, Jess," whispered Becca, "we have some serious scoping to do."

He smiled as his daughter strolled down Main Street with some of her closest friends.

"Jon, what if any agents see her?"

"Our girl is in good hands. If there's trouble; I'll intervene."

The standing room only crowd applauded as he ambled down the center aisle. Encircled by his entourage, the seventy-two year old slowly made his way up the steps of the portable stage to his oversized lavender chair. Seated to his left, was a group of ministers affectionately called, The Amen Corner. Their goal was to pump up the crowd. He sat perfectly still with his eyes closed as everyone sang Amazing Grace. Most thought he was meditating. Others were convinced he was asking God for a word. Just last week, this theologian received a standing ovation at the Georgia Dome. His schedule was booked solid for the next three years. Some couldn't help wondering why this renowned lecturer would ever come to a little town like Bethany.

"Tonight," announced Mayor Hayes, "we have the honor of hearing a prophetic scholar who has no equal. The author of over thirty books on Bible Prophecy, he has written such bestsellers as, The Spiritual Parousia, The Apocalyptic Revolution, and The First Century Gathering. His thought provoking style is respected by scholars worldwide. His new book, 'A Sentinel at the Door', is on sale in our lobby."

Taking a glance in the speaker's direction the Mayor smiled.

"Now wasn't that a mouthful?"

Not receiving any response he cleared his throat and continued.

"This man of God needs no introduction for those who love the scriptures. Tonight, he has graciously consented to help us understand prophetic events that have the power to shape our future. Let's open our hearts to a voice of compassion; a voice coming from the very throne of heaven. I give you the honorable, Dr. Marcus Jacobs."

From his chair the fashionable scholar waved. His tired expression was gone. Nothing energized him more than the approval of man.

"Thank you for such a kind reception. For me the essence of our Creator is love. If I have learned anything from my studies, it is that I choose to love and not judge. My message tonight is entitled, 'A Look

Back in Time.' My text comes from the lips of an Old Testament prophet who was often misunderstood by the people he ministered to. Jeremiah prophesied, "'For I know the thoughts that I think toward you,' says the Lord, 'thoughts of peace and not of evil, to give you a future and a hope. Then you will call upon Me and go and pray to Me, and I will listen to you. And you will seek Me and find Me, when you search for Me with all your heart.'" 1

Sitting with her girlfriends, Jessie spotted one agent at the rear exit and another by the concession stand. There was still no sign of Jake.

"This passage testifies of the tenderness of the Author of Life. Tragically, the recent fires have pressured many to doubt His love. Of course such thoughts will never produce the peace we need. Tonight, I would like to expose the fears holding so many hostage. In order to overcome such strongholds we need to understand what God really says about His children."

Stepping away from the podium, the polished speaker positioned himself between the Amen Corner and the audience.

"Concerning His creation, does God desire to pour out His love or His wrath? If we seek God tonight will He turn a deaf ear? 2 Was Jeremiah emphasizing thoughts of peace or evil?"

The desperation of those in denial was obvious. The sheer emotion generated by his opening words was infectious.

"In my new bestseller, 'A Sentinel at the Door,' I examine the false assertions of those interpreting events from their local newspaper. For example, after our recent blackout, some teachers are declaring God is somehow pouring out His wrath on mankind."

From the first row someone shouted, "So where did these fires come from?"

"These deceivers teach God is sending fire upon our world to judge our sins. Obviously, they're using this intimidation to gain followers."

"Do you mean the two Witnesses?" asked Mayor Hayes.

A Catholic priest from the Amen Corner stood.

"These two imposters are visiting the cities of Israel wearing dirty potato sacks and quoting scripture. They're predicting God's wrath is only going to get worse."

The speaker froze. He didn't mind an occasional interruption. But as soon as the two Witnesses were mentioned, his patience quickly dissolved.

"Trust me, my friends; there is no credence to the fanatical predictions given by these false prophets. Jesus warned us to let the dead bury the dead."

"The two Witnesses prophesied the days of the Great Tribulation were cut short by the coming of the Son of Man. The fires around the world are from the day of the Lord."

"There are many prophetic passages outlining the coming of the Son of Man followed by the day of the Lord. The only way to understand these two events is to compare scripture with scripture. Only then we can understand the timing of His return."

"Dr. Jacobs, won't Jesus return at the end of the age?"

"Yes, our Lord is very precise about those who saw the events preceding His coming. 'Assuredly, I say to you, this generation will by no means pass away till all these things take place.' 3 Now I ask you, what generation of people was our Lord speaking of?"

He purposely paused as a hush came over the crowd.

"The believers living before the destruction of Jerusalem in 70 A.D. experienced the birth pangs of war, famine, and pestilence. They saw the rise and fall of the Antichrist. Many were martyred for their faith."

A skeptical pastor blurted out, "But how could these events take place in the first century?"

"This truth is repeated over and over again. Jesus warned believers living in the first century, 'Behold, I am coming quickly.' 4 John promised first century believers, 'The Revelation of Jesus Christ, which God gave Him to show His servants-things which must shortly take place.' 5 The apostle was also instructed not to seal the words of this prophecy."

"How come, Dr. Jacobs?"

"Because Jesus clearly stated, '...For the time was at hand.' 6 Tonight, we must reject the lie of those who glibly prophesy Jesus has recently gathered His elect and is now pouring out His wrath. This is scripturally impossible. The second coming and the events of the Apocalypse took place before the destruction of Jerusalem in 70 A.D."

"How can you prove that?"

"Jesus promised His disciples that some would see His coming. "'For the Son of Man will come in the glory of His Father with His angels, and then He will reward each according to his works. Assuredly, I say to you, there are some standing here who shall not taste death till they see the Son of Man coming in His kingdom.'" 7

"But how could the events of Revelation come before 70 A.D.? If this is true, then who was the Antichrist?"

The celebrated scholar boldly shared, "The majority of believers living in the first century believed Nero Caesar of Rome was the Antichrist."

"What about the falling away of believers during the Great Tribulation?" 8

"John also saw the falling away of Jews prior to the destruction of the Jewish Temple. 'He was in the world, and the world was made through Him, and the world did not know Him. He came to his own, and His own did not receive Him.'" 9

Trying to maintain a mask of composure amidst such spiritual warfare wasn't easy for Jessie. She could feel her friend's uneasiness. The stares she was receiving didn't help either. But even after a year, most still didn't understand why Jessie Hyatt and Jake Jamison ran away.

"Jessie, why is this dude spending so much time on our past? We need help now or this world ain't going to make it!"

"If you only knew, Becca."

Another minister asked, "The Beast was given authority to make war with the saints. When did this happen?"

"Nero fulfilled this by his persecution of Christians who refused to worship him as God. In 55 A.D., a statue of Nero was worshiped in Rome's Temple of Mars. In Ephesus, he was worshiped as the Savior, the Almighty God."

"But what about the seven bowls of Revelation? How could these judgments have taken place before 70 A.D.?"

These types of questions could go on for hours. His publicist was already signaling from the front row for the tiring teacher to cut them off. The distinguished historian paused then looked up.

"It's obvious several of John's prophecies have not come to pass. My friends, if the Lord had not cut short the persecution of Christians by the Jews in the first century, the elect never would have survived."

Witnessing a sea of uplifted hands, several pastors looked relieved.

Crouching behind the Amen Corner, the spirit of Religion bragged, "Our Master knew religious tolerance cloaked in false unity would eventually become fashionable."

Stepping forward; Jacob's announced, "According to Jesus' own words the saints were delivered in 70 A.D. This is beyond debate."

"Then what about now?" yelled a confused teenager.

"This is why I've come. How many of you tonight are optimistic about our future? Or are you pessimistic of our chances of surviving this so called wrath sent from above? Personally, I'm an optimist. The Word of God admonishes us to look forward to a glorious eternal kingdom. Some may ask why did Jesus return in 70 A.D? Did He not predict the wrath of God would visit those who persecuted His people? Was not the nation of Israel the greatest persecutor of the early Church? Ladies and Gentlemen, infant Christianity was at a crossroads. In order for the body of Christ to grow, God had to judge those who persecuted them. The people who the Messiah was sent to missed their time of visitation. At His coming, Jesus promised to deliver His elect. He also spoke of His wrath, which would immediately be poured out. The apostle Paul wrote of this time, '...The Jews are forbidding us to speak to the Gentiles that they may be saved, so as always to fill up the measure of their sins; but wrath has come upon them to the uttermost.' 10 Do you see the time reference of God's wrath coming upon Israel?"

The theologian could see more and more bobbing heads.

"We have the advantage of looking back. History cannot lie. Christians would never have reached the world with the gospel if the Jewish people had not been scattered around the world at the destruction of Jerusalem in 70 A.D."

With an enthusiastic Amen Corner leading the way, the overflow crowd erupted in loud ovation. Jessie was edging forward in her seat. If Jake was near, she was ready.

"Jesus delivered the elect from the wrath to come in the first century. The kingdom of God and the kingdom of evil will coexist until the final resurrection. The Christ will then create His eternal state."

"Preach it!" praised a regular from Poppy's Bar. "We finally get to hear something meaningful; not just another emotional dead dog story."

"As I leave you tonight, I know the day of the Lord is behind us. Malachi prophesied Elijah would come before the great day of the Lord. Jesus said John the Baptist was the Elijah who was to come. This means the day of the Lord took place in the generation following Jesus' death."

Agents were scanning the crowd looking for any signs of

resistance.

"We can all sense the forces in motion which can't be altered. Everyone must serve God in their own way. For those who exhibit real faith, let us sow seeds of hope. There is nothing to fear. God will never forsake His children. I leave you with a promise to remember me and the anointed time we've had tonight. 'For I have given to them the words which You have given Me; and they have received them, and have known surely that I came forth from You...'"11

The bus honked as it pulled into the Gulf Shores terminal. The agent on night duty was reading a newspaper as the riders exited the bus. No one asked why he never bothered to check their IDs. Jake Jamison was praising the Lord for His protection. Even so, weaving through partiers near the beach was not easy for the young Watchman. The denial was much greater than he ever dreamed. Taking a seat at the counter he could hear laughing coming from the back of the diner. Some teenagers were playing a new surf video. It took all the courage he had to barter for a bus ticket to Gulf Shores. He just couldn't stop thinking of Jessie. Watching agents handcuffing her was the worst. Demons kept accusing him of deserting her. Except for God, nothing was more important to Jake than the safety of his best friend. Pastor Greg Hudson had been a blessing in so many ways. Their friendship grew so effortlessly. That was over too. Jake was now on his own.

The sign on the wall read:

ID ONLY, ALL BARTERING WILL BE PROSECUTED!

Pushing away from the counter the glance over his shoulder proved futile. The kids were gone. It didn't matter; this wasn't a time for games. Reaching the beach, Jake realized how much easier it was going to be hiding in a city where no one knew you.

"I don't understand, Lord, why Gulf Shores? Greg was such an incredible answer to prayer. He taught me the events of the day of the Lord. Then I get a chance to help Jess and You give me a red light. And neither even knows I'm here."

The teenager knew God wanted to use him. The new prediction by the two Witnesses was on every news channel. Many families were checking out and going home. Those staying could care less. To them, a fire reaching the shores of America was a long shot; one in a million.

Standing outside with her girlfriends, Jessie was trying to grasp the seriousness of her situation. Several ministers were raving over Jacob's anointed message. The excitement of those clutching his autographed book was hard to take. Even her parents looked happy as they chit chatted with members of their new church.

"C'mon, Jess," tugged Becca, "the Factory is waiting. Your folks said it was okay. They'll pick you up in an hour."

The Pizza Factory was a favorite with the teenagers on the weekends. It wasn't unusual to see a throng of kids hanging out; especially tonight.

"Hey, Jess, where you been?" teased a former boyfriend.

"Took a vacation."

"I can guess with whom."

The snickering from his buddies felt like a slap in the face. This type of bantering was fruitless. Just another setup by the enemy, she thought. Even so, it was still difficult to remain quiet and not defend herself.

While one of the girls went in to order peach sundaes, Jessie and the rest of her friends sat at an outside table.

"So how did you like Dr. J? He was awesome, wasn't he?"

"Tell me, Becca, what did you like about his pitch?"

"Pitch, what's up with that?"

"He was selling; I was just wondering who was buying?"

Overhearing their conversation from the next table he leaned over.

"Hey, Hyatt, heard you enlisted with the underground?"

Her time of being away had changed everything. Jessie felt so out of place; so uncomfortable mingling with kids whose future was already sealed for eternity.

"Hate to break it to you but Jesus didn't gather His elect in the first century."

"You sure?" asked Becca. "The old man made a lot of sense."

"The coming of the Lord and His wrath are back to back events. The resurrection of believers on October 3rd was followed by a worldwide firestorm. Like Lot and Noah, deliverance then wrath on the same day. It's a no brainer!"

A daughter of a pastor sitting behind Jessie couldn't resist.

"Dr. Jacobs taught the apostasy during the Great Tribulation took place under Nero's rule. His name adds up to 666. This proves Nero was the Beast. How can you argue with that?"

"Satan gave the Beast authority over every nation. Nero's persecution never covered the whole world. And he didn't give out the mark of the beast to every nation."

"Don't you all get it?" mocked the young man. "Hyatt thinks our ID's are the mark of the beast!"

Without thinking she shot back, "Kayin is a liar!"

"Jesus promised some of His disciples they would not die until they see Him coming in the clouds with His angels. This means His coming had to take place in the first century. What do you say, Jessie?"

"I don't know."

"You hear that everybody, miss underground doesn't even know. Maybe we should invite the two Witnesses to fly in for a hot debate."

"They're for real. Jesus warned of false prophets coming as wolves in sheep's clothing."

"You mean the potato sacks they're wearing? The two Witnesses sure ain't scoring any fashion points with the hip hop crowd."

Crossing the street was a skinny teenager smoking a joint. His bloodshot eyes were focused on one person. Before he could reach her, Becca blocked his path.

"Whoa, Ollie, what's your hurry?"

"I need to talk to Hyatt."

"No can do, bro, maybe another time."

Flicking his joint into the gutter, the boy grinned.

"I'm cool; just want to ask her about a friend."

Jessie knew it could be trouble if she refused.

"What's up?"

"You don't remember me?"

"Should I?"

"How about Damien Haley?"

"I know Damien."

"Does Lance Ryan mean anything to you?"

"Okay, Ollie, what's with the quiz show?"

"Hyatt knew Damien Haley, who wound up dead with two slugs from an agent. She also had a connection with Lance Ryan who was executed by the NWC."

"Sounds like fate to me," mocked Becca.

"Last Sunday night I was standing behind Hyatt when agents

arrested my pastor. She made a beeline across our softball field. Somehow she got away."

"I know, Pastor Dyer, what of it?"

"Not anymore you don't. The NWC executed him this morning. And I suppose you don't know anything about that either?"

"Hey, Ollie," teased Becca, "thanks for your conspiracy theory; it's time to say goodbye."

"Seriously everybody if you're chilling with Hyatt you best be looking over your shoulder."

Turning away Becca whispered, "How about a walk?"

Side by side, the two friends leisurely strolled down Main Street.

"You know, Jess, what you and Jake did took a lot of courage."

"Becca, do you know anyone who hasn't registered?"

Turning the corner, the stranger spotted her.

"It's hard to know for sure. I did hear a rumor of two guys and a girl hiding out at the Dooley farm. They enrolled at our school last year."

"Thanks, Becca."

As he closed in, her bracelet began to vibrate.

An agent cruising Main Street received the GPS signal.

"A block from the Factory!" barked the dispatcher.

Hitting his siren, the agent accelerated toward his suspect.

Frantically Jessie tried to remove her bracelet.

Reaching her, he pointed over his shoulder at Poppy's Bar.

"I have a message for you from Jake. He said, 'God is still with us.'"

"Where is he?"

"Follow me."

The stranger took off running.

"Becca, tell the agents I'm heading for Lakeview High. Just say I'm meeting Jake."

"No problem."

Reaching the dark alley next to Poppy's bar, Jessie disappeared.

A Saturday night at the beach was not the best time to testify of God's coming wrath. When the containment of fires was announced, the partiers in the bars spilled out into the streets. Most celebrations would stretch into the early morning hours. Up ahead, Jake could hear some teenagers arguing.

"You don't know how bad it's going to get."

"As if you knew the future," his friend shouted back.

"The NWC is feeding us crap," cursed a girl in a black dress.

Sitting across the street, in front of Ruby's Donut Shop, was a girl munching on a stale doughnut. At first, she didn't recognize her former classmate. Both had mutual friends at Lakeview High but had never met. Before Reenie could cross the street the group doubled in size.

"Who are you anyway?" challenged one of the boys.

"Let him talk, who knows, he might be a real resister."

Pretending not to care Jake nonchalantly looked away.

"Okay, bro, so what's this about a second trumpet?"

"God's wrath began with vegetation fires. Soon our oceans will be hit with fire."

The girl in black joked, "Hey, anybody up for sailing tomorrow?"

Their cheap amusement allowed Reenie to mingle in unnoticed.

"Do you know anybody who hasn't registered?"

"I told you he was undercover."

"For those who believe in Jesus as their Savior..."

"He's just another born-againer who missed his ride in the sky."

Teenagers blocking the sidewalks were never acceptable to those on patrol. Accelerating forward the driver called for back-up.

"You've got company," warned a passerby.

"What about hide and seek?" laughed the girl in black."

"Huddle-up," motioned the leader of the group.

The agent's car slowed to a crawl.

"Ready, ready, now!"

Screaming teenagers running in different directions was a real rush. Partiers outside the bars cheered after making bets on who would get caught first. This was no game for Christians. Jake headed for the seashore. After a minute of running in pitch darkness he disappeared. He never heard Reenie's cries for help over the crashing waves. Falling down the exhausted teenager pounded the wet sand.

"Is this some sort of cruel joke? Lord, why won't You help me?"

SECOND TRUMPET: THE SEA BECAME BLOOD

'Then the second angel sounded:
And something like a great mountain burning with fire
was thrown into the sea, and a third of the sea became blood.'
Revelation 8:8

A vast multitude bowed in adoration before the Ancient of Days. To
His right, was the Lamb of God. When an angel sounded the second
trumpet immense sheets of fire swept across the oceans of earth. 1

After observing this initial destruction, another angel cried,
"Beware you who have spewed arrogant threats against the saints of
the Most High. 2 For the fire of His jealously will destroy those who
have sinned against the Lord." 3

"Wes, these pictures of Alaska are horrific."

"They're gory, so what? We have a duty to report the facts.
Besides, didn't we just get through these dam fires?"

"Pictures like these will only escalate the panic."

"Nate, our oceans are on fire. People on ships have nowhere to
go. We could lose millions if something isn't done. Tell me, have you
ever smelled burning flesh?"

"Wes, I'm afraid..."

"Your dam right people are frightened. But what choice do we
have? We can't shield them from the truth. No one can soft play this!
You're not pulling any punches tonight, okay?"

"I'm hearing you."

Pausing, he softly whispered, "Are you up for this, Nate?"

Most of her colleagues were in semi shock. As the top rated

News Anchor in America, she couldn't afford to appear disoriented. After collecting her thoughts, she looked into the teleprompter. 3... 2... 1..."

"Good evening, this is an Emergency News Update with Natalie Roberts. Without any warning, the Pacific Ocean, the Atlantic Ocean, and the Gulf of Mexico, have been hit by massive firestorms. Thousands of ships have caught fire. Rescue attempts by our Navy and Coast Guard are top priority. The NWC doesn't see any evidence these firestorms have any connection with the recent vegetation fires. Our feature tonight takes us to the coast of Alaska. Tragically, this popular shoreline has been soaked with the blood of thousands of dead seals, whales, and sea lions. There is no way to assess..."

The producer signaled for a live shot of vacationers fleeing a south coast beach.

"Our next shot takes us to the coast of Florida. The red blotches on this Key West shoreline represent..."

The frail reporter was struggling. Most had bought into the lie everything would be okay. Her crew was already slipping into a surreal state of hopelessness.

"I've just received a report by Navel Commander Rodney Quan. A large number of naval vessels who didn't have sufficient warning, have been destroyed. Right now it's impossible to estimate how many casualties there will be. Scientists have no comment on the cause of this fiery assault. Our oceans have turned red with the blood of..."

He was anxiously waiting when Jessie emerged from the dark alley. Grabbing a hammer from his trunk, the stranger asked her to stand still. It took three blows before her bracelet cracked in two. The sirens were getting louder.

"It's best if we go east."

"Trust me, my friend told them we are heading toward Lakeview High. Do you know how to get to the old Dooley spread?"

Accelerating down a side street, the old 1953 Woodie wagon headed west. It wasn't long before the sirens faded.

"I've seen this car at my school. A blonde surfer used to drive it."

"That was my son, Ethan. He loved the ocean."

"Where is he now?"

"Worshipping in heaven. Nice to meet you, Jessie, I'm Greg

Hudson. Jake told me a lot about you."

"How's he doing?"

"We were in the Ryan's house when they arrested you. The next day Jake headed for your home."

"That's exactly what Mercer wanted."

"I don't know where he is. Agents may have picked him up."

Folding her arms she sarcastically muttered "Sweet move, Jake."

"There's no sign of him in any of the ID stations. He could've found a hiding place."

"Maybe the Holy Spirit told him to leave town."

"Not without you. What's up with the Dooley farm?"

"My friend thinks some kids from my high school are hiding there."

"The burned farms are deserted. The destruction is hard to fathom."

"My friend Becca says the Dooley farmhouse survived."

"Can we trust her?"

"She's clueless. The agents won't waste any time on her."

The old farmhouse was surrounded by black cornfields. Entering the gravel driveway they saw a light flickering in the second floor window.

"Their headlights just went out," winced Emma.

"C'mon, Carlos let's just hide in the cornfields."

"Kurt, the Holy Spirit is saying sit tight."

"This is too funny. Yesterday you would've been the first out the door."

Scurrying up the stairs, the three teenagers chose the master bedroom. Emma decided to blow out the candle in the window. The light from the radio was reflecting off the passengers' eyes.

"What are they waiting for?" whispered Carlos.

"For those missing family members in Pensacola, your contact code is PEN4478. For Gulf Shores, it's GUL4480..."

"Greg, our oceans have been hit. It's the second trumpet."

Staring toward the burnt cornfields, the former pastor looked pale.

"Each judgment will increase in intensity; divinely fulfilling its purpose."

"My aunt and uncle live on Dauphin Island!"

He could feel her desperation, but what could he say.

"What's happening to me? Jake could be executed any time now!

My aunt's family is about to be fried! And three overcomers may be hiding in this house! My mind is so messed up."

"Jessie, God never intended for us to carry such burdens. We must pray for those in trouble and then trust God to protect them. 'For as many as are led by the Spirit of God, these are the sons of God.'" 4

"So how can I learn to be led by God?"

"You've heard from the Holy Spirit. What is He telling you now?"

"It's difficult to accept. My burden to find Jake has kinda faded."

"Sounds like God is taking care of him."

"You think so? I still have a burden for my aunt's family. But you know what? I have an even stronger conviction to help the resisters inside this farmhouse."

"Me too, in fact, the Spirit of God just gave me a word."

"What's He saying?"

"The overcomers in this house are watching us right now."

All shoreline patrols were on high alert. The sidewalks were jammed with spectators. Ambulances had top priority on the congested wharf. Doctors and nurses were frantically working on those being rescued from burning ships.

It had been several days since RAT went into hiding. In that time Death Angel terminated six more resisters. It was only a matter of time before hunger pangs would force the package to resurface. Seated at an outdoor cafe, the agent smiled. The tired teenager was wandering toward the beach. Reaching under the table the assassin released the safety of a white pearl revolver before taking a final sip of hazelnut coffee.

Ironically, the hysteria among the people actually helped Reenie relax. Wearing sunglasses and a dirty Atlanta Braves cap, the weary teenager sat outside a closed down burger joint. The removal of dead fish was underway. The decay made her nauseous. One ecological agency announced the worldwide clean up would take thirty years.

As another bus passed by, Jezebel whispered, "You could have been on that bus. What about your folks? Your brother Travis is asking for you. They need you."

Bowing her head, she muttered, "This is the end, Lord."

Death Angel moved along the rim of the roof. The commotion from the wharf provided a perfect backdrop. Two shots could easily be squeezed off without anyone noticing.

The driver of the old truck slammed on his brakes just missing a car backing out of a parking space. Startled, Reenie took off running. After a block, the black truck pulled up again. She didn't want to look.

"Bretttt!" she squealed.

"Get in, girl! Where have you been?"

"You don't want to know."

As the truck drove away the sniper laughed.

"Anthony Bret Santino teaming up with Reenie Ann Tucker; how convenient is this."

"I'd say a father and daughter," guessed Emma. "What now, Carlos?"

Carlos transferred to Lakeview High just weeks before the NWC implemented mandatory registration. The Delgado's were illegal immigrants, so getting an ID wasn't possible. For protection, Carlos joined the Ek-Chuahs when he was fourteen. His love for gang life was a subject his parents avoided. They had hoped their son would grow tired of it. He didn't. A year later, the tall muscular youth with wavy black hair was elected war counselor. Almost overnight, the power of life and death was placed in the hands of Carlos Ramon Delgado. Even so, the respected street fighter was not at home when the drive-by shooting occurred. His father lay dead beneath the bay window in their living room. The spray of bullets was meant for Carlos. All she ever wanted for her son was acceptance. In the fifth grade, Carlos was expelled for fighting two boys who stole his lunch money. In the eighth grade, he was suspended for fracturing the skull of the school bully. In three years of high school, he was arrested ten times. That muggy night a heartbroken mother and her troubled son left Atlanta for good. Maria Delgado was hoping Bethany could be a fresh start for her boy. She was praying for a divine visitation on his first day at Lakeview High.

"Go for it, Reenie," as Bret helped her slip through the opening.

The old warehouse looked deserted. After sliding in, the dirty window sprang shut.

"Wow, the owners of this palace sure left in a hurry."

"It isn't much. I've got a sleeping bag, a radio, a lamp, and a small coffee maker. Hope you like tuna in a can."

"Thank You Lord."

Most of the time, nights were lonely. It was different tonight. Both had a lot to share and neither was in a hurry.

"Reenie, I've been studying some of Luke's notes."

"That figures; I was missing some."

"His research really makes you think about the future."

"You mean heaven or hell?"

"His notes cover those departing from their faith in the last days. 5 Is that what happened to you?"

"Nope, this passage is about those who were once saved."

"I don't understand. You went to church, you were baptized, and you didn't take the mark of the beast. You were even in a believer's camp when I found you."

"Just playing the game, if you know what I mean. I got involved with something real evil when I was young. What a fool I've been. It was a setup from Satan."

"I feel the same way. My folks drinking and fighting was pure hell. When I entered junior high the beatings got worse. When we moved to Gulf Shores all I cared about was revenge. I used to daydream how I could hurt them."

"I'm tired of being angry, Bret. Satan can take his threats and shove it. I want to be free from this bondage. Whatever it takes; I'm not afraid anymore."

"But how do we do that?"

"Luke said we must first admit we are a sinner in need of a Savior. 'For all have sinned and fall short of the glory of God.' 6 Then we need to confess Jesus died for our sins and rose from the dead. '...Christ died for our sins according to the scriptures, and that he was buried, and that He rose again the third day according to the scriptures.'" 7

"I know I'm a sinner, Reenie. And I have no problem believing Jesus died for my sins and rose from the dead."

"Me too, now let's ask Jesus to be our Savior. God promises, 'That if you confess with your mouth the Lord Jesus and believe in your heart that God has raised Him from the dead, you will be saved.'" 8

Reaching over, Reenie took his hand and bowed her head to pray.

Through her lips the demon cursed, "You're a blasphemer. You have no right to become a child of God. He'll never accept your pitiful pleas for mercy."

Holding her in his arms, only the whites of her eyes were showing.

A bewildered Bret pleaded, "Reenie, are you there?"

"Reenie Ann isn't here anymore," hissed Jezebel. "She's dead."

The back door of the farmhouse was unlocked. Cautiously walking across the rustic wooden floor of the living room, they paused at the bottom of the stairs.

Greg called out, "Anyone here?"

A nervous Jessie replied from behind, "It's awful quiet."

"We're Christians! If we were agents we would have burned this house to the ground by now."

At the top of the stairs, a dark figure stood motionless. Clicking the safety to his Colt 38 he shouted back, "We're coming down."

A stunned Emma asked, "Carlos, what are you doing?"

"Trusting the Lord, C'mon, Kurt, let's see what the dude wants."

The Abbotts arrived in Bethany the same day as the Delgados. Emma and her younger brother, Kurt, never knew why they had to leave their home in Memphis on such short notice. Emma thought it was because her father lost his job. Kurt was worried his parents owed a lot of money. God knew. Their time of visitation was scheduled for their first day at Lakeview High.

"Hi, my name is Greg Hudson. This is Jessie Hyatt."

"He's Kurt Abbott; I'm Carlos Delgado. What's up?"

"We heard three believers were hiding in this farmhouse."

"That's nice to know," smirked Kurt. "My sister was right; it's time we fly this coup."

"Why do you care?" asked a suspicious Carlos.

"The Lord led us here."

"You a preacher?"

"Used to be."

"If you're a preacher then what's the next judgment?"

"Second trumpet, our oceans have just been hit with firestorms."

"For real?" choked Kurt.

"Got a radio?" asked Jessie. "It's getting real crazy out there."

"What do you think, Kurt?"

"You got any food, Pastor?"

"Sure do; do you want some?"

"They're okay, Carlos, let's eat."

Hearing their laughter from the top of the stairs Emma shouted, "Hey, what's so funny?"

After finishing off some lukewarm coffee left by a customer, the tired Watchman settled back for a rest in the oversized leather chair. Warning people of God's wrath wasn't a popular subject. The peaceful Java House was a welcomed breather.

While refilling Jake's cup the curious waitress asked, "What are you studying?"

"The pouring out of God's wrath, it's called the day of the Lord."

"My teenage sons have been bugging me for weeks. I'm on break for the next ten minutes. Do you think I could ask you some questions about our future?"

"I'm new to end time prophecy myself. But I guess so."

"So where are we now? Do the scriptures really predict these fires?"

"Try Revelation 8:7-9. The second trumpet just sounded. After the sixth trumpet sounds, the Messiah will physically return and spiritually save a remnant from Israel who believe in Him."

"Don't that beat all, far as I can see most Jews don't even believe in Jesus."

"God Almighty made an everlasting covenant with Abraham. Old Testament prophets predicted the Messiah would come through Isaac, the son of Abraham and Sarah. This was fulfilled when the Holy Spirit overshadowed Mary and Jesus was born."

"Didn't Jesus come from the tribe of Judah?"

"How do you know that?"

"I used to take my boys to church when they were young. But the so called Christians treated us worse than my unsaved friends. I didn't need the headache of playing church. It was Jesus coming in the clouds on October 3rd, wasn't it?"

"Yes, the elect were taken to heaven." 9

"Are you a Watchman?"

"Four more trumpets must sound before the Messiah returns. One third of the world will die after the sixth trumpet is blown."

Bowing her head she whimpered, "Our world is doomed."

"Have you and your boys registered?"

She didn't bother to reply.

"You must know someone who hasn't?"

"I remember two brothers who used to come in and ask for handouts. They never said much. I don't know where they are now."

Waving goodbye, Jake got up to leave.

"There's another one. Don't know her name. Your age, brown hair, green eyes, slender, had a nice smile. She looked kinda out of it. Was a regular before an agent on patrol got suspicious."

"Thanks."

"Can you tell me when the trumpet judgments end?"

"Just listen to the two Witnesses."

"You mean they're for real?"

Their candle light dinner on the second floor bedroom seemed so surreal. Everyone ate in a circle while Emma stood watch by the window.

"So what else have you heard, Jessie?"

"Carlos, the NWC is saying the Witnesses are behind the fires."

"Figures, the Beast is running out of time."

"Seems the NWC is using snipers; no arrest, no trial, just another dead resister."

Changing the subject, Greg asked, "So, Carlos, how did you all find the Lord?"

"And how did you find each other?" beamed Jessie.

For the next hour, the lonely threesome gave their testimonies. Carlos shared their first day at Lakeview High. The second bell was close and he was still lost.

"Hey, do you know where the Chemistry labs are?"

"You talking to me?" asked the surprised freshman.

"Yeah, I'm new here."

"Me too, m name is Kurt Abbott."

"I'm Carlos Delgado. What's with the room changes?"

"The programmer messed up. C'mon, I'm heading for the

Education Office to find out where my Algebra class is."

The former gang member watched as his new friend backtracked.

"Kurt, where're you heading? The Education Office is this way."

"That's senior lawn, bro. If seniors catch us on the lawn during school hours they can roll us in a garbage can. Trust me, it ain't fun."

"We're going to be late, c'mon, it's no big deal."

Several football players looking for a fight spotted the two boys playfully scampering across the manicured lawn.

"Hey, you two! What do you think you're doing?"

Carlos shouted back, "Just minding our own business."

"Underclassmen aren't allowed on our senior lawn."

Another mocked, "Maybe they think they're privileged?"

While one senior grabbed a garbage can, his buddies surrounded the new students. A crowd quickly joined in.

"Ahh, they don't look happy. Who goes first, the redhead or the Mexican?"

The knife in his boot was hidden. It would only take a moment for Carlos to use it.

"Get out of our way!"

Before anyone could react another student intervened.

"That's the second bell, you guys better go. As a senior I can take your place."

"You mean they rolled this guy in a garbage can? Why did he do it?"

With a straight face Kurt replied, "He had a crush on my sister."

Carlos chuckled at her funny expression.

"Don't listen to him, Jessie. Denny was a Christian. The Holy Spirit led him to do it. That same day he shared the gospel with us. He warned us not to worship the Beast, his image, or receive his mark. A week later he left school."

"Another overcomer," praised a grateful Greg.

"The Holy Spirit used Denny's witness to bring us to Christ. He was a real gift from God."

"Sounds like a divine visitation to me!" praised Jessie.

HE WILL APPEAR A SECOND TIME

'So Christ was offered once to bear the sins of many.
To those who eagerly wait for Him He will appear a second time, apart
from sin, for salvation.'
Hebrews 9:28

Her heart was barely beating; a few more moments and she would be gone.

From his knees, Bret pleaded, "Help her, Jesus. I repent of my anger. I believe You died and rose from the dead. Be my Savior and I will follow You the rest of my life."

Clutching her lifeless body, he hollered, "Wake up, Reenie, wake up!"

Bret Anthony Santino hadn't cried since he was fourteen. It was the night his drunken father whipped him with his own belt. The next day, the boy vowed he would never cry again. With tears running down his chin, he uttered a final prayer for help.

From the shadows Jezebel was cursing its unconscious victim. The manifestation of light couldn't be seen by humans. The warrior angel had come in response to Bret's prayer. Drawing its sword the angel crouched low. His intention: to fight for her soul.

"Reenie doesn't believe in God. You have no right to interfere."

Spinning around, it caught the demon with a mighty backhand thrust. The fallen angel had never been struck with such power.

"She will always be mine!" hissed Jezebel.

Lunging forward the warrior plunged its sword into the spirit's neck. This wound would emit pain throughout eternity. Then it commanded Jezebel to leave by the power of Jesus' name.

"Reenie, Reenie, are you okay?"

Her green eyes cracked opened.

"Alllll rightttt!" yelped Bret. "God has done it!"

She barely whispered, "Yes, Lord, Your way not mine, I forgive Cassandra for what she did to me. I repent of my bitterness. Please forgive me for blaming You. Jesus, I ask you to be my Savior."

Reaching over, he covered his new sister in the Lord with a blanket.

Before slipping into a peaceful sleep she whispered, "I feel so free, so different."

Tonight; there would be no nightmares.

Returning with a hot cup of coffee from the kitchen, Greg could hear them in the living room. Kurt was telling one of his famous jokes to Jessie. Carlos was going along with it, while Emma just smiled. She had heard her little brother tell this story a hundred times but she didn't care. It was fun just spending time with her new friend. It was easy to see the respect they had for one another. Each had a testimony of Jesus Christ; a special bond among overcomers. From the living room, a giddy Jessie waved her arms.

"C'mon, Greg, you're missing this."

The foursome was sitting on a rug in front of a fire in the huge stone fireplace. Kurt Abbott was five foot five and had thick red hair. He was wearing a grey Lebron James sweatshirt and baggy blue jeans. The young teenager waited until Greg took a seat on the brown leather couch.

"So the lady and her husband were walking by a pet store. Outside the shop's entrance was a large metal cage with a talking cockatoo inside. When they walked over to the bird it whispered to the lady, "You're ugly."

"Kurt, where did you get this story?"

"No kidding, Jessie, this really happened."

In between giggles, she asked, "You can't be serious?"

"The lady's husband told the owner of the pet shop. He was shocked. So he puts on a pair of rubber gloves, walks outside, and slaps the bird around. He then tells the couple it won't happen again."

"The poor bird," sighed Jessie.

"The next day this couple was taking their morning walk by the pet shop and they see the cockatoo waving his wing to come over. The lady walks up to the cage and asks, "Okay, Mr. big mouth bird, what now?" The cockatoo pokes his beak through the bars and says, 'You know…'"

The teenagers broke into muffled cries. Greg was trying to join in. He knew there was a possibility agents could have interrogated Jessie's friend. It didn't seem to matter at the moment. Everyone needed a break, even if it was just for a few hours. As Kurt's jokes evolved from the silly into the ridiculous, a smiling Carlos sensed Greg's uneasiness. A quick glance from his buddy was enough. Kurt knew the fun was over. Emma immediately produced a pen and paper.

"I always take notes," she proudly announced.

"So what do you guys know about God's wrath?"

An animated Kurt raised his hand and shared, "This past year we've been studying as much as we can. But with no one to teach us it's kinda hard to figure out where everything fits."

"We've been studying the verses you gave us," added Carlos. "Seeing the timeline of events has helped big time."

A determined Emma posed, "We have a ton of questions. I guess some are more important to know than others, huh, Greg?"

"Right now we need to understand the consequences of the trumpet and bowl judgments. Of course, our main goal is to remain faithful 'til the supper of the great God, Armageddon."

"That's a lock," grinned Kurt.

"Greg, we've heard Jesus is coming back before the sounding of the seventh trumpet. We also have been told He will appear after the seventh bowl during Armageddon. So which is it?"

"Both are correct, Carlos."

"How is that possible?"

"In 14:1-4, John sees the Lamb of God gathering His Jewish remnant to the top of the Temple Mount (Mount Zion). Hebrews 9:28 says, 'So Christ was offered once to bear the sins of many. To those who eagerly wait for Him He will appear a second time, apart from sin, for salvation.'" 1

"How does this fit in with the coming of the Son of Man?"

"Carlos, the Son of Man didn't return to earth when His angels gathered His elect to heaven. Hebrews 9:28 is referring to Jesus' physical appearance on earth for the salvation of His Jewish remnant. The prophet Zechariah foretold, 'I will bring the one-third through the fire, will refine them as silver is refined, And test them as gold is tested. They will call on My name, And I will answer them. I will say,

'This is My people'; And each one will say, 'The Lord is my God.'" 2

"I see the difference," smiled a curious Jessie. "Jesus promised to save those who endure until the end of the age. The word 'saved' in Matthew 24:13 means physical deliverance. The elect were already spiritually saved at the coming of the Son of Man. The Blessed Hope cut short the days of the Great Tribulation by delivering the saints from the persecution of the Beast. Hebrews 9:28 is talking about when Jesus appears on the earth for the spiritual salvation of those who believe in Him."

"Yep, the Jewish people have been blinded spiritually. When the fullness of the Gentiles is over, Jesus will physically return and forgive those who believe in Him." 3

"So when is Jesus going to do this?"

"The same day the Beast kills the two Witnesses. On that day Jesus will gather the 144,000 who have been hiding in the desert for three and a half years. 4 These sealed with their Father's name will be the first fruits of Israel's salvation." 5

"You mean we could be here to see Jesus?" asked a shocked Emma.

"Whoa, no rock concert can beat this,"

After receiving a stare from his sister, Kurt sheepishly nodded.

"Uh, sorry, I promise no more weirdness."

"Isaiah prophesied, 'The Redeemer will come to Zion (Jerusalem), and to those who turn from transgression in Jacob...'" 6

"Now let me get this straight, Greg," reflected Carlos. "Jesus first comes as a Deliverer from heavenly Zion. 7 Then Isaiah predicted the Redeemer will visit Jerusalem where our Lord will save those who have believed in Him."

"That's the ticket."

"So where in the Bible does Jesus return for Israel's salvation?"

"Revelation 10:1 says, 'I saw still another angel (Holy One) coming down from heaven, clothed in a cloud. And a rainbow was on his head, his face was like the sun, and his feet like pillars of fire. He had a little book open in his hand. And He set his right foot on the sea and his left foot on the land, and cried with a loud voice, as when a lion roars. When He cried out, seven thunders uttered their voices.'" 8

"I gather this messenger ain't no angel?" laughed Kurt.

"Wow!" yelped Jessie. "This is like the 'appearance of a man' in Daniel 10:5. This messenger has the likeness of the glory of the Lord."

"Guys, there are several instances in the Old Testament where

Jesus appeared to people before His Incarnation. The Angel of the Lord was a pre-incarnate appearance of the second person of the Godhead. Revelation 1:13-16 describes Jesus standing in heaven amidst the seven golden lamp stands. His countenance is like the sun." 9

"In Revelation 10:1 He also has a face like the sun."

"That's right, Jessie. There is no other person in the Bible described like this but Christ. In this passage, angel should be translated 'Holy One'."

"No angel has the power to fulfill the Mystery of God! This has to be Jesus coming to earth between the sounding of the sixth and seventh trumpets for the salvation of the Jewish remnant." 10

"Go girl!"

"Look at how many taught Jesus' physical return to earth comes at Armageddon," winced Kurt. "Talk about wacked out theologians."

"How awesome," piped Carlos. "If the seventieth week ends between the sixth and seventh trumpets, then the final seven bowl judgments have to come after the seventieth week is over."

A confused Emma asked, "Greg, I thought the seals, trumpets, and bowls all take place within the seventieth week of Daniel?"

"It's clear the Beast will kill the two Witnesses between the sixth and seventh trumpets, just after the seventieth week ends. When you compare scriptures, the seven bowls must be poured out within thirty days from their death." 11

"Hold up," asked a dazed Kurt. "It's time for a review. Like Cliff notes when you get the message of the book in five sentences."

As Emma wrote, Greg highlighted Jesus' six day itinerary after the seventieth week ends.

"This is super important, so everyone listen up. The day the Beast kills the two Witnesses, the Deliverer will descend from heaven to bring salvation to Israel. On the Day of Atonement, Jesus will gather 144,000 redeemed men from the twelve tribes of Israel. 12 These servants were sealed for protection from God's wrath during the Feast of Trumpets just after the coming of the Son of Man. 13 As we speak; they're being protected by God in the Jordanian wilderness."

"So when will Jesus lead these believers into Jerusalem?"

"Jessie, from the Jordanian wilderness it's a two-day journey. As the Messiah leads the 144,000, those who don't have the mark of the beast will join them and be saved."

A blown away Kurt jumped up and shared, "Can you imagine

Channel 6's Natalie Roberts reporting on this hallelujah march?"

"By the third day, Jesus will bring spiritual salvation to Israel by completing the mystery of God. 14 At His first coming, the Messiah came to His own people. 15 Because the Jewish people rejected their Messiah; the Gentiles were grafted into the tree of life. To make Israel jealous, the Gentiles have received the promise of Abraham. But even though the Gentiles are saved, they never become natural Israel. Despite Israel's unbelief in their Messiah, God the Father has unconditionally promised to save a remnant from natural Israel who will believe in His Son."

"So three days after the seventieth week ends, Jesus will come to Jerusalem and a remnant will believe in Him as their Messiah?"

"This is God's everlasting covenant with Israel."

"So if the mystery of God is completed by the third day," asked Carlos, "then that means the two Witnesses must be resurrected on the very next day?"

"You got it; bro. John saw the two Witnesses resurrected from the dead on the fourth day. They're going to receive the breath of life from Jesus. Then a loud voice will call them up to heaven. 16 The fifth day after the seventieth week, the Lamb of God and His 144,000 will ascend Mount Zion, the Temple Mount. 17 With the salvation of Israel completed, an angel in heaven will sound the seventh trumpet. Loud voices in heaven shall proclaim, "'The kingdoms of this world have become the kingdoms of our Lord and of His Christ, and He shall reign forever and ever.'" 18

A wide eyed Kurt announced, "Am I loving this! God is affixing to take back control of this earth from Satan."

"Do you think we'll be alive at the sounding of the seventh trumpet?"

"Don't know, Jessie. I do know the only way for us to survive God's wrath is to be obedient to the Holy Spirit."

"Hey, Greg, will the world see the Witnesses rise from the dead?"

"Yes, Kurt, it says they will see them ascend into heaven." 19

"Now that's something I'd pay to see."

The dragnet by agents was crippling. All reporters were turned away from the Temple Mount. Any sound bites needed NWC approval.

"Good evening, this is Natalie Roberts live from Jerusalem. Minutes ago, an attempted assassination of NWC Leader Joshua Kayin was exposed. An Israeli militia unit was arrested after successfully infiltrating his Jerusalem headquarters. Their leader, Aaron Glazer, somehow escaped. Within the next twenty-four hours..."

The peaceful silence of the farm was a stark contrast to the constant surveillance within the cities. Greg had just replaced Carlos from his watch. The sun would be up soon. Grabbing his pocket size calendar from his wallet he circled another day. He now understood why so many believers dreaded spending time alone with God. It was an eerie responsibility knowing the future. Time was precious; not something to be wasted.

Suddenly a picture of a maze full of doors surfaced in his mind. A terrified little girl was trapped inside. She was trying to find a way out.

"Lord," cringed Greg, "she's opening the wrong door."

As the big door sprung open a bottomless black hole appeared. From behind some believers rescued her. Miraculously another door filled with the glory of God opened. Before joining the Lord, she said, "Thank you so much, I never would have made it without your help."

Then Greg heard, "The believers in this maze represent you, Carlos, Emma, and Kurt. I have sheep you know not of. I can hear their cries. 'Whom shall I send, and who will go for us?'" 20

From the stairs, Jessie called out, "Greg, are you alright?"

The preoccupied pastor moved away from the window and sat on the couch.

"Uh, yeah, isn't your watch not for another hour?"

Sitting beside the fireplace the perplexed teenager just nodded. She didn't know where to start.

"So, Jessie, what did you think of Dr. Marcus Jacobs?"

"He's quite a salesman! My parents bought several of his books. He may be famous but his message is way off. Calls himself a preterist; whatever that means."

"Preterist means past. Jacobs believes the events in the Book of Revelation took place in the first century. This includes the seals, the trumpets, the bowls, the Great Tribulation, the coming of the Son of Man, Armageddon, even a new heaven and a new earth. Preterists teach Jesus resurrected His elect during the destruction of the Jewish

Temple in 70 A.D. They believe the warnings in Matthew 24 were for Christians being persecuted by the Jews in the first century."

"I guess when you're desperate enough you can swallow anything if it's presented right."

"Jacobs believes Satan was bound at the cross so the gospel wouldn't be hindered."

"How can that be true? Just look at what the Devil has done since Jesus was crucified. Wasn't Paul's thorn in the flesh sent by Satan? Besides, the Devil won't be cast into the bottomless pit until an angel does it on the first day of the Millennium." 21

"Some Preterists believe we are living in the Millennium right now."

"How blind can you be? Aren't we supposed to be looking for a new heaven and a new earth? 22 Isaiah prophesied the wolf and lamb would feed together. 23 Isn't this a picture of a restored earth during the millennium? Obviously, this event is still future."

"It sure is. I was watching from across the street when Jacobs and his entourage arrived at the hall. What did your friends think of him?"

"Deceiving those having the mark is easy. They loved the part about Nero being the Beast."

"Preterists believe his name adds up to the number of the Beast."

"Greg, show me how can you prove Nero wasn't the Beast?"

"At the great day of God Almighty, Armageddon, the Beast and his false prophet will become the first two humans cast alive in to the lake of fire. 24 Preterists believe Armageddon took place in 70 A.D. when the Word of God returned and delivered His elect from the wrath to come."

"Yep, that's what Jacob's was painting. Everyone was taking notes!"

"Jessie, Nero committed suicide in 68 A. D. If Jesus came in 70 A.D. how could Nero be cast alive into the lake of fire?

"Talk about blowing something right out of the water."

"He must have really zeroed in on the time references Jesus used?"

"Yeah, my friends kept asking me, why did Jesus say He was coming quickly in the first century? I didn't have an answer. Later when I prayed, the Holy Spirit showed me this is about how the Lord will come; not when He will come." 25

"That's right, Jessie, the prophet Joel predicted the day of the

Lord was near several centuries before Jesus was even born?" 26

"John says every eye will see Jesus at His coming. 27 That never happened in 70 A.D."

The pastor slouched back in the soft sofa. Hearing a new convert share with such spiritual insight was miraculous.

"You know, I was friends with several pastors who believed like Jacobs. They were absolutely convinced preterism was biblical."

"What ever happened to them?"

His eyes had a glazed over look. He could remember their names, their faces, even their families.

"They had no idea they were living inside the days of the Great Tribulation. Receiving a microchip on their right hand was their way of supporting the New World Coalition. To these pastors it was no big deal."

MY REWARD IS WITH ME

'... I am coming quickly, and My reward is with Me, to give to everyone
according to his work.'
Revelation 22:12

Five backpacks, each having a sleeping bag, food, and water, were stacked side by side in the foyer. Their breakfast of fried eggs, French toast, and stale cookies went fast.

"Jessie, it's a miracle my brother let you have his sleeping bag last night."

"Kurt is such a blessing. I praise God for ya'll. Emma, being overcomers for Jesus is such an honor."

A brisk prayer walk around the farmhouse was invigorating. Taking a seat on the living room couch, Greg asked everyone to gather round.

"Early this morning the Holy Spirit gave me a vision about the day of the Lord."

"I don't care what the NWC does; I ain't taking the mark!"

"Amen, Carlos. The problem is there are believers that will if they aren't rescued."

"I thought we were the ones who needed help?"

"Kurt, the Lord wants to use us as a team. If we accept the challenge; the Holy Spirit will lead us to those in danger."

"How does this all work, Greg?"

"It won't be easy. We need to count the cost. No lie, guys, once we extend the kingdom of God we can expect some visitors. The spiritual warfare will be intense."

Jumping up, an animated Kurt blurted out, "My first prayer after getting saved was for God to use me to defeat the devil in these last days. We need a nickname."

"Prepare yourselves;" grinned Carlos.
"I got it, how about the Rescue Squad?"

Seated on the platform the energetic youth pastor could feel the tension as the guest speakers greeted each other. As the youngest member of the Bethany Ministers Association, he had no clue why he was picked to emcee this morning's Bible forum. In recent weeks, the debate only grew hotter. Trying to predict end time events was far too divisive for most members. Nevertheless, the BMA Committee decided to clear the air. Each speaker had a microphone clipped to his lapel. The soundman was ready.

"Good morning. On behalf of the Bethany Ministers Association I welcome you to our monthly Bible Forum. We all know each speaker in today's discussion on eschatology. Let's begin with an opening statement from Presbyterian Superintendent Dr. Charles Kyle."

"Since October 3rd many skeptics have blatantly challenged the creditability of the apostle's writings. Such attacks have the power to undermine the divine authority of Scripture. Understanding the events preceding our Lord's return can only be proven by the Word of God. This morning I will give you scriptures defining the timing and consequences of the second coming of Christ."

The emcee politely led the membership in a warm applause.

"Our next speaker has taught amillennialism at LaSalle University for many years. From Our Lady Redeemer Catholic Church, let's welcome, father Andrew."

"Certainly," reflected the knowledgeable priest, "all nations, peoples, and tongues, have sought to understand truth behind the horrific tragedy of these firestorms. The indescribable shock of our oceans on fire has only multiplied our fears. My friends, there is an answer. In the fourth century, Augustine wrote a theological masterpiece entitled, The City of God. This work of grace highlights the mission of the Church since Calvary. No one can deny the Kingdom of God is advancing. This morning I will humbly share this message of hope."

Several amens rang out as the poised priest shook hands with the popular Presbyterian leader.

"Our next speaker needs no introduction. From Lakeview

Assembly of God, Reverend Louis Cooper will now share the post tribulation view of the second coming of Christ. God bless you, Pastor."

"Unlike my two distinguished colleagues, I believe in a future Millennium ruled by the King of Kings. At the last trump, the Word of God will descend during the battle of Armageddon. After the great day of God Almighty, the Lord will set up His earthly kingdom. No matter what Satan does, we must persevere until the end of the age. This is the message of the hour."

This ovation was by far the loudest. The Committee Chairman had hit a nerve. The boundary lines for the debate were forming.

Seizing the moment the young emcee asked, "Dr. Kyle, do you believe in the resurrection of believers from the wrath to come?"

"This took place during the destruction of Jerusalem in 70 A.D. After delivering His elect, Jesus poured out His wrath on the Jewish people."

"Father Andrew, do you believe this interpretation?"

"Yes I do. The apostle Paul promised his hearers they would be spiritually changed. Of course this resurrection of spiritual bodies couldn't be seen physically."

"So if it was spiritual, then how can you verify it ever happened?"

"Just check the context. Who was Paul writing to?"

The Presbyterian scholar raised his hand and smiled.

"The apostle was predicting the resurrection in his lifetime."

"Any comments Pastor Cooper?" posed the nervous emcee.

"We are living in a day of unprecedented suffering. Our earth has never experienced such catastrophic fires. We all know we are being hurdled toward a climax. When our Blessed Hope comes for His elect, every eye shall see Him. Keep looking up saints; His coming is still future. It will take place at the last trump on the last day."

The emcee had to wait before the cheers died down.

"Dr. Kyle, if His first coming was fulfilled literally in all points, why not His second coming?"

The stoic Superintendent nodded barely showing any emotion.

"There is only one resurrection unto eternal life. This event took place on the last day. The Lord places His coming on the last day of the Jewish age in 70 A.D."

Another minister asked, "Pastor Cooper, didn't Jesus say the coming of the Son of Man would take place after the heavens lose their light. Isn't this what happened on October 3rd?"

"Men of God, I must say piecing together the events of these last days can be challenging. But where are we if we just spiritualize events? The only way to understand future prophecy is it to take it literally. Revelation 19 depicts the Word of God coming back with His saints dressed in white. This can only be the last event of the last day!"

"Pastor, there are reports of people still missing ..."

"Let's be clear, there is only one second coming. 1 Obviously, there is no evidence of any resurrection of the elect taking place in 70 A.D. As shepherds we can't afford to stray from two thousand years of biblical orthodoxy. The coming of the Lord is still future."

A visiting Rabbi asked, "Is it true the Messiah is coming back to save a remnant from Israel?"

The resolute priest stood.

"My friend, God's chosen people rejected Jesus as their Messiah. The Jewish people, the natural branches, were broken off because of their unbelief. Because of this, the Gentiles, the wild branches, were grafted in. This means the promises of God through Abraham apply not to physical Israel but to spiritual Israel."

"Dr. Kyle, do you believe this?"

Easing back in his leather chair, the theologian purposely paused.

"Gentlemen, it's unfortunate we have such a limited time for this critical discussion. Ask yourselves, is the body of Christ the Israel of God? Of course but it doesn't help arguing about it. 2 Our focus should be the great commission. Anything else will only deter us from doing the will of our Father. Scripturally speaking, the beginning of sorrows, the Great Tribulation, the revealing of the Man of Sin, the coming of the Son of Man, and the day of the Lord, all took place in the first century."

Another asked, "Could Joshua Kayin be the Antichrist and Pope Michael his false prophet?"

"Absolutely not!" snapped the angry priest. "I've taught theology for many years. I don't see any evidence of some antichrist taking over the nations. Let me remind you, those who continue to judge God's anointed place themselves in a very dangerous place. 3 Our focus should be on what these two great men have achieved. They need our prayers not some unwarranted propaganda!"

"Pastor Cooper, what can you tell us about the millennial reign of Christ?"

"Jesus is going to rule from His throne in Jerusalem for a thousand years. At the end of this Millennium, Satan will be released from the bottomless pit to deceive the nations. God's enemies will once again surround the beloved city. This is the final war. Fire will come down from heaven and devour all who follow Satan. 4 Then the Devil will be cast into the lake of fire." 5

"Dr. Kyle, your preterist view flies in the face of our historic faith. What if you're wrong?"

"The authority of scripture is greater than any manmade creed. Jesus warned, '...I say to you, hereafter you will see the Son of Man sitting at the right hand of the Power, and coming on the clouds of heaven. 6 ... And behold, I am coming quickly, and My reward is with Me, to give to everyone according to his work. 7 ...When they persecute you in this city, flee to another. For assuredly, I say to you, you will not have gone through the cities of Israel before the Son of Man comes.' 8 Clearly our Lord is referring to believers in the first century."

"Now hasn't this been an insightful discussion!" reflected the emcee. "I've certainly been inspired by the faithfulness of God's Word. We will now hear a final conclusion from each speaker. Dr Kyle."

"For those who think we are experiencing God's wrath, Jesus warned, 'Take heed that no one deceives you...' 9 Let us not be manipulated into relegating the horrific judgments in The Revelation of Jesus Christ to our future. This apocalyptic writing was addressing the historical background of first century believers."

"Father Andrew."

"For years we have been inundated with voices claiming to be from God. Our time honored creeds have been challenged by protestant relativism. The purpose of Revelation is to show how good triumphs over evil. Our focus should be on the four pillars of the Church: the Eucharist, Baptism, the Holy Spirit, and Mother Mary. Let us draw comfort from the queen of heaven; our blessed mother of God! May her spirit lead the world into salvation."

"Pastor Cooper."

"You all know me. I have to confess, over the years, a lot of us avoided teaching on the last days. My, my, looking back it's easy to see how many pastors believed in a secret rapture. Of course, we now know how wrong this teaching is. The second coming is a singular event. Our Jesus is returning soon. During His descent, in a twinkling of an eye, He will catch up His elect. Continuing downward with His saints, the King of Kings will set up His millennial kingdom. We must all remain faithful as we approach the end of the age. The Word says it; I believe it, and that settles it!"

Their late night Bible studies were commonplace. This led to afternoon naps. The rain was coming down hard on this brisk November afternoon. Everyone was asleep on the second floor while Kurt Abbott kept watch from the big picture window in the living room. While eyeing the entrance to the farm the young convert was praying.

"Lord, I don't understand what You're saying to me?"

Instantly the Jerusalem Peace Accord came to mind.

"Yes, Lord, President Kayin confirmed a seven year peace agreement between Jews and Muslims. In the middle of it he violated it by invading Jerusalem with armies from ten nations."

Emma and Jessie were chatting as they strolled into the living room.

"Jessie, the Holy Spirit just showed me when the seventieth week ends."

"You mean when the Beast kills the two Witnesses?"

"You got it. We know when the Abomination of Desolation invaded Jerusalem in the middle of the seven years. It was the same day the two Witnesses arrived. We also know the two Witnesses will prophesy the second half of the seventieth week. So all we have to do is add 1260 days from the day they arrived and presto, we got the day the Beast kills them!"

"So when is the final day of the seventieth week?" asked Jessie.

"Two years from now, on September 19th."

They could hear Greg and Carlos walking down the creaky wooden stairs.

"Yo, Greg, I've got a gargantuan question for you."

"Fire away, Kurt."

"You taught us Jesus will gather the first fruits of His remnant the same day the two Witnesses are killed by the Beast. Do you have a date when this will take place?"

"Two years from now on September 19th during the Day of Atonement."

"Why didn't you tell us?"

"You know what; I think it's time we launch out."

"You mean the Rescue Q Squad is operational?"

"Which room are the children playing in?"

Deborah gestured over her shoulder, "In our room; they can't hear."

Crouching forward Judah shared, "I just received this from the underground. The mercenary who tried to assassinate Joshua Kayin was Aaron Glazer. We know him as Matthias."

"If the NWC arrests Matthias he could lead them to us?" gasped Hanna.

"What about now?" agonized Eleazar. "Our people are being systematically slaughtered!"

"When we entered this hideaway everything seemed black and white. At the time, it was easy to say we wouldn't get involved. If we help, the NWC could easily expose our hiding place."

"My relatives are fisherman. Some have been badly burned. They will never make it unless someone helps them."

Eleazar's wife pleaded, "Most have already sworn their allegiance to Kayin. What can we do?"

"That's the point," sighed Judah. "We know our Messiah is coming back to Mount Zion for His people. Many are on the verge of giving in. How can we look the other way and not help?"

The Rescue Q Squad's first strategy session lasted over two hours. The floor was filled with maps of Bethany. The red dots identified ID Stations; the yellow lines covered areas being patrolled. Abandoned houses in blue would be used as temporary hideouts to evade agents.

"Greg, what if someone who is registered asks for our help?"

"Kurt, God has already sent forth a strong delusion to those who refused to receive the love of the truth by taking the mark. Our objective is to rescue the saved and those who still can be saved."

"Wow, remember the teachers who taught there would be no second chances after the rapture?"

A puzzled Carlos asked, "Why would the Holy Spirit lead us to rescue people from the NWC if He isn't going to save them? There must be a ton that haven't worshipped the Beast or taken his mark."

"What do you think, Greg?" asked Emma. "How many can still be born again?"

"There is no way of knowing."

"Hey, where's Jessie? Her watch was up ten minutes ago."

"Let's take a break. Kurt, can you take lookout while I check on Jessie."

Stepping outside on the porch, Greg spotted the tall brunette in deep thought. He silently prayed as he sat down on an old wooden rocking chair beside Jessie's.

"How's it going in there?" she softly asked.

"Everyone's missing you."

"Greg, what was your vision like?"

"Sorta like a picture in my mind."

"I wasn't in your picture, was I?"

"I was praying you'd tell me."

After handing him the photo, she looked away.

"Is this your aunt's family?"

Rising from her rocking chair, the troubled teenager paced the weathered porch. Her hands clenched; she couldn't hold it in any longer.

"I can't get the Santino's outta my mind, their faces won't go away."

He patiently waited as she sat back down.

"What is God showing you, Jessie?"

"That's what I would like to know. I love Jake and God took him away. Then God sends you to help me and I become friends with Emma and the boys. C'mon, Greg, I need some counsel. Just tell me what to do with my future. Pray to God and whatever He tells you, I'll do it."

"Only the Spirit of Christ can reveal the Father's will."

"But He is so quiet. I can't hear anything."

"Maybe it's because He has already told you."

"I wasn't in your vision was I?"

"Nope."

"I don't want to leave. I'm afraid of being alone. What if I fail?"

"Jessie, God won't force you. Just keep praying and your path will become clear. We all are learning how to trust the Lord with our lives."

"But after each victory, the next trial seems even harder. What's up with that?"

"You ever help anyone who couldn't pay you back?"

"A couple of times, it felt right."

"A motive is the reason why we do things. But even a good work with a wrong motive is unacceptable to God."

Closing her eyes she searched for the right words.

"The Holy Spirit showed me I wasn't in your vision. Aunt Myra and Uncle Anthony are waiting for me on Dauphin Island. My future is connected with their lives. I can even see when the confusion hit me. Everything went screwy when I tried to fit His will into my own desires."

"Praise God! The Holy Spirit just gave me Matthew 16:24-26? Do you know it?"

Using a dirty sleeve to wipe away her tears, she replied, "In my sleep."

THEN THE DELIVERERS WILL COME

"But on Mount Zion there shall be deliverance... Then deliverers shall come to Mount Zion to judge the mountains of Esau, and the kingdom shall be the Lord's."
Obadiah 17, 21

"Hey, everybody, I'm back."

Kurt could hear her sobbing. Dropping the bag of bartered food on the kitchen counter, he sprinted up the stairs. Emma was sitting on the sofa with her face buried in her hands. Greg was pacing as he prayed. Carlos stood watch by the window.

"Emma, what's wrong?"

Carlos motioned with his eyes. The confused redhead walked over and sat down with his back against the wall, his elbows on his knees.

"Kurt, a few minutes ago Jessie decided to leave us."

"No way, Jess said God wanted us to be together."

"The Holy Spirit is leading her to find her aunt."

"Dauphin Island isn't far; maybe we can help her?"

"Sorry, bro, she's going solo."

Greg noticed Kurt's usual dopey smile was gone.

"We all love, Jessie. She's a special lady who left us to fulfill God's will for her life. The less we know about her plans the better. We need to follow her example. We can't allow Satan to use this to distract us from our calling."

"Why can't we take her in your Woodie?" cried Emma.

Greg waved for the boys to join them.

"First of all, if we're going to work together in the dangerous area of rescue, we must learn to trust each other. Even with our very lives. So what's it going to be?"

They all nodded.

"Jessie refused our help. She knows any driver must show ID. She would never endanger us in something God is leading her to do."

Getting up Emma walked over and looked out the window.

"I hate this world. Satan can have it. All of it!"

"Afraid not," smirked Carlos. "After the thousand year reign of Christ all the Devil is going to get is a face full of fire for eternity." [1]

"God bless you, honey. You be safe now."

With a soft ocean breeze gently touching her face, a thankful Jessie waved goodbye. After hitching a ride with the gray haired kindergarten teacher the young overcomer silently interceded as they passed through three checkpoints without being scanned once.

The ferry office at the beach was selling tickets for the last trip of the night. In the distance was a dark silhouette of Dauphin Island. Two agents walked by without any incident. She causally approached a man in his mid-forties. He had just purchased a ticket.

"Hey, mister, do you know how much a ferry ticket costs?"

"Why do you want to go to the island?"

"To see someone who needs my help."

"Do your parents know you're here?"

Turning away she made no effort to answer. She could only watch as the passengers got on. The loud horn was the final warning.

"Lord, how can I buy a ticket without an ID? Please help me."

At first, she didn't realize the driver of the ferry was waving at her.

"Little lady, are you getting on or not?"

Rushing down the wharf, she jogged across the wooden plank.

"One of the passengers couldn't go. He gave me his ticket."

As the ferry pulled away, Jessie spotted the stranger waving from the breakwater. [2] He never moved until the boat was out of sight.

After spreading their food out on the bedspread they prayed.

"I was just about to quit when I met an old friend outside Wal-Mart. After we talked, she went inside and bought us two bags of food."

"How awesome, Bret. What an answer to prayer. Guess what; while you were gone, the Holy Spirit gave me a revelation."

"You mean about our future?"

"Did you know the Book of Revelation pulls together the promises given to Israel in the Old Testament with those given to believers in the New Testament?"

He playfully cautioned, "Now just remember to go slow."

"Ever wonder why Luke studied the seventh trumpet so much?"

"Funny, I was going to ask you about this yesterday."

"It appears the prophet Obadiah predicted deliverers will come to Mount Zion in the latter days." 3

"Who are these deliverers?"

"Luke believes they are the 144,000 from Revelation 14:1-4. Jesus is going to first gather them from the Jordanian wilderness. The first fruits will then follow the Lamb."

"Where is the Lord going?"

"The 144,000 will follow Him through the hills of Judea. Once inside Jerusalem, they will follow the Lamb of God to the Temple Mount."

"You mean we could actually see the Lamb of God returning to Zion with His remnant just before the sounding of the seventh trumpet?"

They both looked uneasy. Bret spoke first.

"Reenie, there is something I've got to tell you."

"Yeah, I know, I haven't been truthful either."

Under the light of one candle, Bret confessed why he became an agent. It was a way to vent his anger. The night he exposed the Birmingham camp he was supposed to report in. At the last second something convinced him to wait.

"I guess that's it. Do you mind hanging out with an ex-agent?"

"It all depends how you feel about my secret."

To her surprise, sharing her demon possession wasn't hard at all. She wasn't ashamed anymore. The bondage of what people might think was gone. All Reenie Ann Tucker wanted now was to be faithful to the Lord. Freedom in Christ was always her dream. To think it was only a prayer away. Hours flew by as they swapped stories.

"You mean you slipped and missed His coming?" teased Reenie.

That's all it took as they rolled in laughter. The anger that controlled them had lost its power.

"Hey, what about you playing cavewoman?"

"Kinda picked a bad time to hide from God, didn't I?"

Bret couldn't remember laughing so hard. Not something induced by drugs; but a clean joyful time of realizing how far short one comes from God's perfection.

"So, bro, what is the Holy Spirit leading you to do now?"

"I keep getting a burden to see my parents."

"Do you think they registered?"

"Nah, my father is a former Navy Seal. He isn't going to let anyone brand him. I once helped him outfit a cave with supplies. My folks are probably hiding there."

The boats in the harbor were bobbing up and down on this cold December morning. Glancing out the dirty window of the loft, Reenie looked troubled.

"I'll be okay if you want to find your parents."

"What do you mean?"

"Are you hanging around here because you feel sorry for me?"

"Reenie, I wouldn't be a Christian if I hadn't found you in that smoky cave. God has supernaturally put us together as a team. Now is not the time to become a lone-ranger for Jesus, at least not for us."

Her smile radiated her newfound freedom in Jesus. Just the benefit of sleep, without any demonic intrusions, had helped the teenager regain most of her strength.

"So what's our next move?"

"How about leading my folks to the Lord? But before we make the trip to their cave, I need to pick up some personal stuff at their house."

"Do you think it's safe?"

"The Lord will be with us."

"What's the first thing you're going to say to your parents?"

Shrugging his shoulders, he said, "I want to tell them how much I love them and how much Jesus loves them."

After looking up their address at a closed down gas station, her ten-minute walk seemed like an hour. The Santino's house was the fourth on the right. Reaching their driveway she thought about Jake.

"Where could he be, Holy Spirit?"

Even though she prayed for her best friend every day, there was never a reply. It didn't seem to matter to God, she thought.

"Father, I also pray for Emma's protection. May the Holy Spirit shield her from the attacks of the enemy. I just know You're going to lead Greg and Carlos in their rescues. Praise You Jesus; I'm so excited they're in Your perfect will."

From their red brick porch, she rang the doorbell.

"And, Lord, please help Kurt count the cost. Let him understand the warfare the Q squad has entered into is no joke."

IF WE DENY HIM

'If we endure, we shall also reign with Him,
If we deny Him, He also will deny us.'
II Timothy 2:12

Before the doorbell rang a third time, Myra Santino slipped behind the bookcase. Anthony built this secret compartment the week after the catching up of the saints. Circling around the side of the house, the Navy Seal was unsure how to defend his wife. If pressured he could easily kill an agent with his bare hands. Crouching behind an old oak tree in the front yard, he didn't recognize the tall brunette. She looked nervous, as if she was afraid who would answer the door.

"Myra, are you there?"

"Who are you?"

Holding up the beach picture, the teenager spun around.

"Hi, Uncle Anthony, I'm Jessie Hyatt. Are you and Aunt Myra okay?"

"Jessie, have you come alone? Did anyone follow you? Maybe someone who knew you were coming to see us?"

"I don't think so."

Unlocking the front door, he whispered, "We praise God for bringing you to us. Take the hallway to the living room. Then knock on the bookcase two times."

The loud ticking of a grandfather clock in the foyer put her on edge. She prayed for courage before entering the living room. After knocking: the bookcase moved away from the wall.

"Aunt Myra, is that you?"

"Oh, Jessie," she sobbed. "The Holy Spirit told us you'd come."

The neglected church was nestled between several large pine trees. The side entrance to the sanctuary was unlocked. From atop the raised podium was a spectacular view of the red streaked ocean. Jake Jamison could barely make out the large tankers gathering the dead fish. To his left, was deserted Dauphin Island. To his right, owners were diligently repairing their boats inside the Gulf Shores Marina. The Watchman could barely control his disgust.

"Look at them. Life goes on as usual. Isn't anyone going to repent?"

The flashback in his mind was so real. Luke Appleby was sharing the gospel with some kids outside the high school cafeteria. Then a member of the basketball team interrupted.

"So, Luke, what's it like spreading such racist propaganda?"

The once popular leader was now a symbol of religious bigotry.

"Everyone is commanded to pick up His cross. Either you follow Jesus with everything you've got or forget about it."

"That's just your opinion, Mr. Bible answer man."

"I don't have all the answers but I know the One who does."

"Luke, I might buy into what you're preaching except the part about God loving everyone. If He does, why would He allow a worldwide famine? Get real, most Christians I know could care less how many Muslims starve to death."

"Don't forget about the Christians that died," mocked another student. "I guess Luke's form of Christianity isn't so superior after all."

A senior majoring in religion was passing out leaflets.

"Anyone wanting to be excused from sixth period can hear a speaker from the World Faith Movement in the auditorium. Ms. Grimm is amazing. She'll be speaking on how to respect each other's faith."

The bell sent the students scurrying.

"Luke, wait up," shouted Jake from the crowded hallway. "Caught the end of your message; you preaching again?"

"Praise God, a girl in my math class has questions about Jesus."

"What about your reputation? Sorry, bro, but your mini sermons aren't selling anymore."

"Each of us has to count the cost."

"So working yourself into heaven is the answer?"

"If good works could get you to heaven then the death of the sinless Lamb of God would be meaningless. The purpose of Jesus' first coming was to die for our sins. His second coming begins with the deliverance of believers from God's wrath."

"Most are saying your message is a turnoff."

"Jake, a couple years from now, a multitude of Christians from every nation will be supernaturally gathered to heaven. After their deliverance, God is going to pour out His wrath on a Christ rejecting world."

"Except for the Bible Club, no one believes this world will ever end."

"Let me ask you, has anyone ever promised you something but never followed through with it?"

"Sure, it can be a real bummer."

"Jesus promised to come back and receive those who follow Him to heaven. He said, 'In My Father's house are many mansions; if it were not so, I would have told you. I go to prepare a place for you. And if I go and prepare a place for you, I will come again and receive you to Myself; that where I am, there you may be also.'" 1

"Is this His second coming?"

"Yeah, the key word in this passage is 'receive'. The Greek word for receive is paralambano. It means to receive intimately unto one's self. Jesus is describing when the elect will be intimately gathered into His presence from earth."

"That's cool."

"Jesus keeps His promises. This world is plunging toward a final judgment by a Holy God. Not another flood but a consuming fire!" 2

"Isn't His coming supposed to be like the days of Noah, one taken, one left?"

"Yeah, the word 'taken' also comes from the Greek word, paralambano. Just before judging the wicked, Jesus is going to take believers intimately unto Himself." 3

"Luke, how do you know for sure? Maybe it's just symbolic?"

Glancing at the ocean, the watchman could see seagulls circling dead fish. Hundreds of volunteers were cleaning the shoreline.

"Lord, how many times did Luke warn me? I'm so tired of using the 'but' word. I love you but... I'll obey you but... I'll warn them but..."

Wrapped in official Navy blankets, Jessie slept on their oversized couch. Her trembling wasn't because she was cold. The Santino's knew she was running on empty. Last week, Myra witnessed the heartache of a teenager who gave herself up to the authorities. News reporters were curious why an ex-resister would change her mind and register.

"Just share it, honey. That's why she's here. Maybe Shelby told her."

"Look at her Anthony; I can't push her any further."

Reaching over he gave his wife a reassuring hug.

"You're right; the Spirit of God will tell you when."

A few hours later, the new converts shared hot tea in the dark living room. The weary teenager wasn't noticing how the Santino's were sidestepping her questions. Her jubilation was clouding her discernment.

"Jessie, please come with me, we need to talk."

Walking down the hallway they held hands.

"Is this Bret's room? Been praying for him, can't wait to see him."

"Jessie, it would better if you never see my son."

"Is it because he doesn't know about me?"

"What did Shelby tell you about us?"

"She said you were hard core drunks."

"Yeah, Bret was no doubt humiliated by our drinking sprees. The abuse he suffered from us fueled his anger. So much so, he left home this past summer. Like you and Jake, Anthony and I became Christians a few hours after the resurrection. Our conversion was pretty dramatic. Anthony was instantly healed of cirrhosis. My migraine headaches caused by my drinking disappeared. Bret doesn't even know we're saved, much less members of the Christian underground."

"What's going to happen to the underground?"

"A remnant will survive the day of the Lord."

"Aunt Myra, what is a remnant?"

"A group of believers our Lord is going to save."

"You mean God's wrath isn't going to kill everybody?" 4

"Believers surviving the day of the Lord will live on a restored earth during the thousand year reign of Christ. 5 Jesus will judge between the nations from the house of the God of Jacob in Jerusalem."

"That's the answer to the question Jake and I asked the Lord the day after we got saved."

"Jessie, I have something to share. I knew this truth the day you were born."

"Wow, you came to Tuscaloosa when I was born?"

"Honey, you weren't born in Alabama."

"I gave up asking my folks about my birth. Was like pulling teeth to get them to share anything. Of course, your sister loves talking about her rebellious days at the University of Alabama."

"Shelby never attended the University of Alabama."

"Oh please," giggled Jessie.

"After Anthony and I got saved, I felt convicted about keeping the truth from you. I was the one who sent you the beach picture. We prayed you would see it before Jon or Shelby."

"Well, God heard your prayer. Tell me straight up, Myra, if I wasn't born in Tuscaloosa eighteen years ago, then where was I born?"

"In a small hospital in Jerusalem."

"This isn't funny."

"Your grandparents, Samuel and Nell Kaufman, came to America as Jewish immigrants in the 1960's. Two years later they had me. A year later, they had Shelby."

"So what's all this supposed to mean?"

"My real name is Miriam; Shelby's real name is Sarah."

"You're not making any sense. What are you saying?"

"My mother and father loved you very..."

"I never knew my grandparents."

"Yes, they were killed in a plane crash when you were two."

"If my grandparents moved to America, and my mother grew up in Alabama, then how could I be born in Jerusalem?"

"Jon Hyatt loves you very much but he's not your father. Your father is Aaron Phinehas Glazer. Your real name is Johanna Esther Glazer."

"No, Myra, please tell me this isn't true."

"My parents forbid me to marry a Gentile. I wouldn't listen. Anthony and I were in love; so we eloped. This is why your grandfather convinced Sarah to have an arranged marriage. Within a year, your mother married Aaron Phinehas Glazer. You were born a year later."

The weary teenage stretched out on Bret's waterbed, lying perfectly still she covered her eyes and began to weep.

"Myra where is my father?"

"I don't know exactly; somewhere in Israel."

"Why did he leave me?"

After a long pause, she slowly replied, "Aaron Glazer is a military activist who loves his people. When you were a baby, PLO soldiers kidnapped him during a demonstration near the Wailing Wall. Aaron was convicted of treason by a Palestinian court. He had no way of protecting you. It was Aaron's suggestion Sarah take you to America. A year later she married Jon Hyatt, changed her name to Shelby, the rest is history."

"So if we make it to the Millennium which remnant will we be part of?"

"Jessie, there is no Jew or Gentile in the body of Christ."

"So I'm not a Gentile?"

"Your father and mother are Jewish. Someday God will reveal the whole picture of your life. For now, let's trust in His timing."

"Does Bret know about me?"

"No he doesn't. My son is an informant for the Gulf Shores ID Security Force. He makes his living tracking resisters. He is a very dangerous young man."

"Do you think my daddy is still alive?"

"Aaron was released from prison two years ago. Israeli officials freed several Jordanian terrorists in exchange for his freedom."

"When can I see him?"

"You want to meet your father?"

"If daddy hasn't worshiped Kayin or received his mark, he can still be saved."

"You have no ID! How will you get out of the country; much less through Israeli security?"

"Myra, will you help me find my father?"

"You'd risk your life for someone who abandoned you?"

With tears dripping down her red cheeks she asked for a hug.

"Uncle Anthony said you could've been arrested for trying to find me."

"God was leading me."

"The Holy Spirit is going to lead us to my daddy."

Walking arm and arm, Myra and Jessie knew God had brought them together. Entering the kitchen they could hear him packing food.

"So how is the greatest niece in the whole wide world?"

She took two quick steps before dropping into his big bear hug.

"I appreciate you two so much, Uncle Anthony. I forgive you for yielding to those who pressured you. It must have been a big squeeze."

"We've always loved you, Jessie," smiled Myra. "We praise the Lord for putting the pieces of our lives back together again."

"I've heard Christians should be different," reflected Anthony. "I don't want to be different; I just want to be real."

Coming together for a group hug in front of the window over the sink, a red dot appeared above their heads. Slowly it moved downward.

"We have some big plans to share with you, honey man."

The red dot paused on his shoulder. Moving up his neck, it rested on his left ear lobe. At that very moment, a wasp stung his left leg.

"Ahh," he screeched, jerking his head downwards.

Shattering the kitchen window several bullets pierced the refrigerator. Dragging his wife and Jessie to the floor, Anthony covered their mouths.

"Listen to me. If this sniper is working alone, he is repositioning himself right now for his next shot."

"We've got to get to our car. Our food, our clothes..."

"No, Myra, he wants us to panic and run into his line of fire. While you were talking, the Holy Spirit led me to pack everything in Bret's boat. Here are the keys; use the bathroom window. The trees should shield your way to the boat. Now go, we don't have much time."

"What about you?"

"Jessie, a sniper can squeeze off ten shots in less than two seconds. I'm going to create a diversion. When you hear a loud noise, hit the accelerator full throttle."

"Noooo," pleaded Myra. "This killer will never let you leave this island alive!"

"Baby, I promise to meet you at our cave. You and I spent a long time serving the Devil. The drunken fights, the scary blackouts, the sickening hangovers, we were two lost souls searching for something better. Our new life in Jesus has given us a purpose we always dreamed of but never thought was possible. Now, instead of reaching for a bottle, we've taken the hand of our Lord. And we're never going to let go."

Hiding in the brush the sniper reviewed her options. The package had three ways to escape: by car, by boat, or by foot. Crossing the dark street was easy. The house next door provided a clear shot to the car and the boat. It would only take a few seconds to terminate all three resisters.

Slipping out the bathroom window, they raced down the gravel path leading to the water. Death Angel watched as two women entered the boat. Their plan of escape made her decision easy. Out of the bushes a barrel of a Remington 500 appeared. The red light moved along the hull of the boat, finally resting on Jessie's back. Moving between her shoulder blades, it paused. Myra froze when she saw it. Before she could utter a word, a shot rang out. A bright orange flare grazed the sniper's shoulder, knocking her backwards into the garden.

Walking down the street Bret and Reenie instinctually jumped for cover. Orange rays were lighting up his parent's backyard.

"You wait here, Reenie."

Breaking into a sprint right behind Bret, she thought, "Not this time."

Loading another flare Anthony fired just above the sniper's head. He was already sensing a familiar presence that had tormented him since his first drunk. This time it was different; he wasn't afraid. The voice from the bushes sounded evil. Dropping the flare gun; he raised his hands.

Bret could hear the acceleration from the road. By the time he reached the front lawn, his powerboat was almost out of site. Motioning for Reenie to stay back he took a quick peek around the corner of their house. A stranger was pointing a gun at his father.

"You're such a fool, Anthony. You thought God would protect you. And what about your son the bounty killer? Who knows, maybe he'll terminate Myra before I do."

"Who are you?"

"Special Forces call me Death Angel. Your son helped one of my packages. Her name is Reenie Ann Tucker."

"Never heard of her."

"Your son's interference led me here. Who's the girl with your wife?"

"Jessie is Myra's niece. You leave her out of this."

"Hey, a real family affair."

"Where is my son?"

"Shut up and turn around."

Pointing a white pearl pistol at his back, she removed a silver detonator from her jacket. Delicately the assassin released the safety.

"You see Tony; I was wondering why your son still uses his middle name. The agents downtown think it's because you're a pathetic drunk."

Stalling for time, he pretended to think over his answer.

"That was me, alright."

"My specialty is explosives. I was going terminate you all at one time but you really surprised me. Figured a coward like you would have saved his own neck. I was hoping the girls would make their getaway first. You see, I want your last memory to be..."

Removing a Glock from his jacket, Bret had the stranger in his sights.

"I give you my life, Father. I believe in your Son, Jesus Christ, as my Lord and Savior. I ask forgiveness for the abuse I inflicted on Bret. May You save my son's soul. May you please protect my precious Myra, and may You help Jessie find her..."

In his mind Bret heard, "Taking a life is not the answer. Trust the Lord in all things."

Squeezing the trigger it clicked. Desperately he searched his jacket for a clip of bullets.

Anthony never saw the shots. Blood from his back splattered when he hit the ground. Standing over his dead body, the assassin removed the silencer from her gun.

"So much for God's protection ladies….. Bon voyage."

Turning toward the ocean Death Angel pushed the button to the detonator.

"Myra, how much longer?"

"You see the lights above the tall palm trees. That's Gulf Shores."

"Does anyone else know about this cave?"

"No Jessie, just Bret."

After rechecking the defective switch, the irate agent cursed. Throwing the device to the ground, it broke into pieces.

THE CHILDREN OF GOD

'He came to His own, and His own did not receive Him...
He gave the right to become children of God,
to those who believe in His name.'
John 1.11-12

They hid in the kitchen until the assassin disappeared into the darkness. It was awhile before he spoke.

"My Dad got saved... God changed his heart... He even gave his life."

"I'm so sorry, Bret."

"Well, this killer won't be back. Did you catch what she said?"

"Some of it, I know who she is. I saw her face."

"She's tracking you, Reenie."

"What for? Honestly, I haven't seen her since I was five years old."

"You mean Death Angel was the babysitter who hooked you up with Jezebel?"

"Cassandra is an assassin for the NWC. How insane is this!"

"But who was in the boat with my mom?"

"Your father said it was Myra's niece, Jessie."

"My mom has no niece. And I don't know any Jessie."

"Yeah and why would the NWC want me so bad?"

"Cops will be here soon. We need to hide."

"Aren't you going to report Cassandra to the police?"

"Nope, she's part of the Beast's system. There's a better way."

While Bret gathered more ammunition from his father's gun case in the basement, Reenie grabbed any food left in the kitchen. In the distance was the faint sound of sirens.

The popular landscaped park was a perfect meeting place. Judah Lentz and Eleazar Hilkiah chatted while waiting for their guest. Dressed in a blue business suit, sporting sunglasses, and carrying a leather briefcase, Matthias was in no hurry as he carefully strode down the narrow street. The Israeli freedom fighter knew what he was coming for.

"Good morning, gentlemen."

Their hopeful smiles he had witnessed before. Mostly it was from those who wanted to surrender. Amidst people eating lunch, children playing, and an occasional jogger passing by, they pretended to be at ease.

"So, Judah, why have you arranged this meeting?"

"Heard you're planning another bombing; we want to help."

Matthias gratefully replied, "I knew you'd come around."

"Before we answer how, may I share why we believe we have entered the day of the Lord?"

"You can't mean Joel's prophecy?"

"During the Feast of Trumpets the sun, moon, and stars, lost their light. Then we saw His glory and His angels. Thirty minutes later the fires started."

"You sound like the two Witnesses."

Glancing down the street Eleazar whispered back, "They're speaking the truth."

Partially covering his mouth, the mercenary heatedly asked, "What do you two hope to gain by condoning the burning of innocent children?"

"The world is suffering the wrath of God." 1

"Are you crazy? Thankfully, Kayin isn't making public appearances anymore. My sources say he's paralyzed with fear." 2

"Matthias, only the Lord will be exalted during the day of the Lord." 3

"Your clever interpretations mean nothing to me. How blind can you be? And now you believe God is somehow causing this misery?"

"Do you know why His wrath has come?"

"Get to your point, Judah, my time is valuable."

"Our people have hardened their hearts. We're experiencing God's wrath because of our rebellion. Zechariah prophesied only a third will survive." 4

"So you believe in a physical resurrection?"

"Daniel prophesied a resurrection coming after a time of great trouble." 5

"He was speaking of the dead not the living."

"We have loved ones who disappeared," pleaded Eleazar. 6 "They left notes."

"Tell me," seethed Matthias, "how can one identify the true Messiah?"

"He alone will atone for Israel's sins."

"What Israel? The methodical killing of our people is not from God. No prophet predicted such evil in the latter days."

"The Messiah will return to Zion to redeem His remnant." 7

"So when is God going to stop His wrath?"

"We don't know for sure," sighed Judah. "Only the Messiah can restore the kingdom of Israel." 8

"Is this why you brought me here? And how can the hope of some future utopia help our people; whose hearts can only feel pain?"

"Zechariah predicted the Lord will fight against the nations who attack Israel." 9

"You're wasting my time. The nations are close to hysteria. World leaders are buying into the idea these fires are the Witnesses' fault. They're going to use these false prophets as a reason to destroy our country. As we speak, twenty-two Arab nations are discussing our demise. Within a year, maybe two, most nations from around the world will buy into their Jihad against us. Is this what you're talking about? Because if it is, and we allow it to happen; then we have no hope of survival. Can't you see what your empty promises have done? Millions have been killed."

"What about the future of our people, Matthias? You're committed to guerrilla warfare. Your assassinations have been widely publicized by the world media. Do you believe this is the most effective way to defeat the sworn enemies of Israel?"

"Since surrender is impossible, what else can we do?"

"The prophets gave us the best option. Daniel wrote of a time when the Most Holy will atone for the sins of our people. 10 Jeremiah spoke of the latter days when God would write a new covenant with Israel. 11 Isaiah prophesied of a Redeemer coming to Mount Zion for the salvation of a remnant. 12 And Zechariah saw the Lord splitting the Mount of Olives in order to hide an end time remnant in Azal. 13 Then and only then, will the Lord..."

"Come for what? Didn't Zephaniah predict everything would be consumed by God's wrath during the day of the Lord?" 14

"Not all. The Messiah will deliver those who believe and forgive them of their sins. He will create a Garden of Eden on a new earth." 15

A hopeful Eleazar added, "Isaiah also speaks of a new heaven." 16

"Gentlemen, everything within me is screaming to leave. But you have helped our movement with more than just words. Because of this, I will ask you, what did you hope to accomplish today?"

"If the Messiah is coming soon, how could that change you're..?"

"Judah, how can you possibly prove such insane predictions?"

"No one can stop what has been decreed. If you intervene, you'll only be fighting against God!" 17

The pain on his face was clear as he leaned forward in his chair.

"When I was a young boy my best friend's mother was blown up by a PLO bomber in a downtown shop. Later my older sister was kidnapped, raped, and killed, by Muslim fanatics. On my twentieth birthday, I found my dead father lying in his own blood. A Jordanian officer, who vowed to destroy Israel from a young age, proudly took responsibility for his murder. Later PLO terrorists arrested me and put me in prison. They even tried to kill my wife and daughter."

"Matthias, we can't..."

"I'm not finished. The Arabs have portrayed our country as an evil aggressor against defenseless Palestinians. With the world turning against us, the American President convinced our Prime Minister to give our land away to our enemies in exchange for a so called peace. Three and a half years later Arab tanks crossed our borders and massacred an unsuspecting people. Eighteen months later, they attacked us again in the Valley of Jehoshaphat. How can you forget the dead bodies scattered all over our streets? And now you say I am fighting against God?"

"Matthias, we are speaking of hope not judgment."

"Enough! I don't need your counsel, your money, or your prayers. On the grave of my father I never want to see you nor the faces of your children again."

While loading supplies, a curious Jessie asked, "Myra, Bret's powerboat was so awesome. How could you barter it for this old truck?"

"We needed transportation. Without an ID it's the best I could do."

Their trip to the cave wasn't easy. Anthony had meticulously trained his wife in detecting NWC shadows. Frequent stops were necessary. Their very lives depended on it. After reaching the secluded Alabama hills, Jessie realized the importance of such a hideaway. It would take a miracle for anyone to find this cave. An enormous pit filled with logs was capable of heating the main floor. Several torches lined the walls. After hiding the truck they settled down for a dinner of fish and sweet peas.

"Myra, I've got some questions. Gee, I've never even been inside a synagogue."

"Your father will be very proud of you."

"Does my daddy believe in Jesus like us?"

"I'm afraid not."

"He doesn't believe Jesus is the Messiah?"

"No, Jessie, he never has."

"So what does he believe?"

"Aaron believes God Almighty made an everlasting covenant with Abraham for our people. Seven feasts were divinely appointed for Israel. 18 These festivals are called *mo'edim*—appointed times to meet with Hashem. They are sacred times of rehearsing by our people. All seven feasts will be fulfilled by the Messiah."

"Does daddy believe the Messiah will come again?"

"He did twenty years ago. I don't know what he believes now."

"What about the Gentiles who believe in Jesus?"

"Yes, Jessie, salvation has come to the Gentiles." 19

"Yeah, I remember studying about the Jewish people rejecting Jesus. To make them jealous, God grafted the Gentiles into the tree of life."

"The Holy Spirit showed me this truth the day after I believed in Jesus as my Savior. 'He came to His own, and His own did not receive Him. But as many as received Him, to them He gave the right to become children of God, to those who believe in His name.'" 20

"So what are the names of these feasts?"

"The first is Passover, then Unleavened Bread, First Fruits, Weeks, Trumpets, Day of Atonement, and Tabernacles. These seven holy days represent the redemptive career of the Messiah from Calvary all the way to the Millennium."

"Myra, could you share the meaning of each feast with me?"

"I'll try. The first holy day celebrates the deliverance of our people from the Pharaoh of Egypt in 1445 B.C. This day is called the Feast of Passover. 21 On this day; an angel passed over any house which had the blood of a sacrificed lamb applied to its doorpost. The blood was a sign of those who had real faith. 22 Two thousand years ago, the Son of God came to Calvary to die as our Passover Lamb. 23 And guess what? Yeshua was crucified during the Feast of Passover."

"The blood of a sacrificed lamb couldn't take away our sins. So the Father sent His Son to shed His blood as our sinless Passover Lamb."

"For those who looked forward to the cross and those who look back."

"The Son of God becoming flesh to die for our sins; how miraculous!" beamed Jessie.

"The second holy day, the Feast of Unleavened Bread symbolizes the time our people fled Egypt. 24 The night before eating the Passover Lamb our people were instructed to cleanse themselves of all sin. There was to be no leaven in the bread. You see, leaven represents sin. On the third day Yeshua rose from the dead. His body didn't suffer corruption."

"You mean His body didn't decay?"

"David wrote, '...Nor will you allow Your Holy One to see corruption.'" 25

"What a miracle."

"Paul exhorts us, 'Therefore purge the old leaven, that you may be a new lump, since you truly are unleavened. For indeed Christ, our Passover was sacrificed for us. Therefore let us keep the feast, not with old leaven, nor with the leaven of malice and wickedness, but with the unleavened bread of sincerity and truth.'" 26

"Wow, the Old and New Testament actually go hand-in-hand. Jesus was our sinless Passover Lamb sacrificed for our sins."

While Myra searched for the next passage in her Bible, Jessie retrieved a pen and paper. In the glow of the fire, the passionate teenager started taking notes.

"The third holy day is called the Feast of First Fruits. This Feast is recorded in Deuteronomy 26:1-10. It marks the beginning of the harvest season in Israel. Spiritually, it's the study of first things. As a child I remember my father, Samuel..."

"You mean my grandfather?" the tall brunette proudly announced.

"That's right," grinned Myra, "your grandfather loved this Feast. First Fruits took place on the third day of Passover. 'But now Christ is risen from the dead, and has become the first fruits of those who have fallen asleep. For since by man came death, by Man also came the resurrection of the dead.'" 27

"So Jesus is the first fruits of those resurrected from the dead?"

"Yes, Yeshua was the first to be resurrected and never die."

"Wow, Yeshua rose from the dead on the Feast of First Fruits."

"Listen to this. 'For as in Adam all die, even so in Christ all shall be made alive. But each one in his own order: Christ the first fruits, afterward those who are Christ's at His coming.' 28 Do you see the connection, Jess?"

"The Lamb of God was sacrificed on Passover. He rose from the dead on First Fruits. As First Fruits, He has the power to resurrect those who follow Him."

A grateful Myra reflected, "All those who believed in Christ at His coming were made alive."

"Keep going, Auntie."

"The fourth holy day is called Shavuot, the Feast of Weeks."

"So how did the Messiah reveal His power on this day?"

"Shavuot (Pentecost) means fiftieth. It was during the Feast of Pentecost, fifty days after Jesus' resurrection that Christians received the Promise of the Father." 29

"What type of promise?"

"This promise is the baptism of power to witness the gospel under the anointing of the Holy Spirit. The evening of our Lord's resurrection, the disciples were assembled for fear of the Jews. Suddenly Jesus stood in their midst and showed them His hands and His side. They were pleased to see their Lord. Then Jesus said, 'Peace to you. As the Father has sent Me, I also send you. And when He had said this, He breathed on them, and said to them, 'Receive the Holy Spirit.'" 30

"So the disciples received the Holy Spirit the night Jesus rose from the dead?"

"That's right. For forty days Jesus preached the kingdom of God. Then He commanded His disciples not to leave Jerusalem until they received the Promise of the Father. 31 Ten days later, during the Feast of Weeks (Pentecost), the disciples were filled with the Holy Spirit and spoke in tongues. When you got saved, Jessie, you received the indwelling of the Holy Spirit. After salvation, every believer can pray and receive the baptism of the Holy Spirit with the evidence of speaking in tongues. Anthony and I received the Promise of the Father a week after we were saved."

"Do you speak in tongues, Myra?"

"A language I was never taught. When I pray in tongues I talk to God through the unction of the Holy Spirit."

"Does praying in tongues help you hear from Him?"

"Very much, when I pray in the Spirit, I feel edified by God. 32 It's a divine gift from Jesus."

"Myra, sometimes I feel so weak."

"Weakness in yourself isn't bad, Jess. Your faith is in God. Yeshua is the baptizer. Tell me, do you desire more power for the glory of God?"

"With all of my heart."

"When you feel led try reading Acts 1:4-8, 2:1-4, 8:13-17, 10:44-48, and 19:1-6. Then pray and ask Jesus to baptize you in the Holy Spirit. It's that simple; it's the Promise of the Father."

"Praise God, how exciting!"

Myra smiled before taking another sip of coffee.

"The fifth holy day is Zikhron Teruah, the Feast of Trumpets."

"Do you speak Hebrew?"

"I haven't since I was a child. When I was praying the Holy Spirit showed me I will speak it again when we reach Jerusalem."

"What a confirmation. The Spirit is leading us to find my daddy."

"Jess, you have to be careful what you pray for. If we find your father it could be very painful."

"Do you think he has the mark of the beast?"

"No, your father would die a martyr before taking Kayin's mark."

"We are going to see him; I just know it."

Reaching over, they hugged.

"So what does the Feast of Trumpets represent?"

"The only observance of this Feast is in Ezra 3:1-6. The Jewish exiles returned from Babylon and rebuilt the Temple altar. On this day of celebration, Ezra rehearsed God's Law to the people. Nehemiah wrote of a revival that followed. During this holy day, priests sounded silver trumpets with short blasts over reinstituted sacrifices. Another priest sounds a shofar with long sustained blasts."

"What does the long blast of the shofar represent?"

"The blowing of the ram's horn announces the coronation of a new king. To the Jews, the Messiah will return at the sounding of a trumpet. In 70 A.D., the Romans destroyed our Temple and our sacrificial system was abandoned. Our people were scattered around the world. The Feast of Trumpets inspires our people to look for the coming of the Messiah."

"You mean this Feast represents a future day when the Messiah will deliver His people?"

"Yes. The first four Feasts were fulfilled by the Messiah at His first coming. The next three, the Feast of Trumpets, the Day of Atonement (Yom Kippur), and the Feast of Tabernacles will each be fulfilled during His second coming."

Leaning back, a thoughtful Myra patiently waited for her reply.

"So when is the Feast of Trumpets celebrated?"

"This holiday coincides with Rosh Hashanah, the first day of the Jewish New Year. Rosh Hashanah means 'Head of the Year.' By the second century, this holiday eclipsed the Feast of Trumpets in importance. In order to preserve this memorial the priests put them together."

"I don't get it, Myra, why would a memorial pointing to the coming of the Messiah be overshadowed?"

"The Feast of Trumpets occurs when the new moon is almost completely dark. Only a tiny crescent of light is visible. The priests call it, Israel's dark day."

"So what does this darkness represent?"

"The darkness represents God's wrath. The Old Testament prophets continually warned the Jewish people of this future judgment, the day of the Lord." 33

"But why would God pour out His wrath on His own people?"

"God will use the day of the Lord to bring many into the New Covenant."

"Didn't Paul write about the day of the Lord?"

"He did. 'For you yourselves know perfectly that the day of the Lord so comes as a thief in the night... For the Lord Himself will descend from heaven with a shout, with the voice of the archangel, and the trumpet of God. And the dead in Christ will rise first. Then we who are alive and remain shall be caught up together with them in the clouds to meet the Lord in the air...' 34 The day of the Lord erupted after God blew His last trump and believers were caught up."

"Yeah, the networks were showing pictures of a red moon the night Jesus came with His angels. You could barely see a tiny crescent of light. Tell me, Myra, were our people observing the Feast of

Trumpets on Rosh Hashanah the same night our Blessed Hope appeared?"

From the mouth of the cave he could see them sharing. This wasn't the type of assignment anyone could be trained for. There was no turning back now. Turning around he blinked his flashlight twice.

ACCORDING TO THE SPIRIT

'There is therefore now no condemnation
to those who are in Christ Jesus,
who do not walk according to the flesh,
but according to the Spirit.'
Romans 8:1

While sipping green tea inside the expensive beachfront bar, the assassin pondered her next assignment. She hadn't returned any calls since Anthony Santino's termination.

"I hate their stupid procedures," she cursed aloud. "I'm giving them what they want."

Actually it was quite amusing for Death Angel to be warned of an ex-rookie agent shadowing her. What really was intriguing was his involvement with her assigned package.

"Their partnership won't last long."

The flashing red light was Special Forces.

Turning off her laptop, Cassandra bragged, "Seems the rules have changed."

All other assignments were now on hold. She would wait for Bret Santino to come to her. After eliminating him, this possessed killer would deal with her RAT package, Reenie Ann Tucker.

Their escape from the house-to-house search on Dolphin Island was a miracle. It took everything Reenie had to convince Bret to hide at Abby's house. Hearing his whistle, she unlocked the backdoor.

"How did it go?"

"Cassandra's playing cat and mouse. She'll only surface when we do. It's the smart move."

"I've been thanking the Lord for our escape. Doesn't it feel great being on the right side! Have you been thinking about your daddy?"

"For sure, it would've been special to spend some time with him. I'll never forget his prayer."

"I've been meaning to ask you about Jessie."

"She was probably an overcomer my folks were trying to help."

"What was the message the underground gave you?"

"They aren't happy campers."

"I know why. Cassandra's going to terminate your mama just like your daddy. She won't stop until someone puts her out of her misery."

"Reenie, have you ever studied Romans? Paul wrote, 'There is therefore now no condemnation to those who are in Christ Jesus, who do not walk according to the flesh, but according to the Spirit.' 1 Either you're walking in the flesh or the walking in the Spirit. 2 The only way to deny the desires of our flesh is to obey the Holy Spirit."

"So you're saying we can't stop this butcher?"

"Speaking for myself, my killing days are over."

"Bret, I was only five years old when this witch deceived me."

"Yeah and she murdered my father, so what?"

"What about your mama?"

"With the head start she got, there is no chance Cassandra will ever find her."

"So when are we going to visit her? First, you tell me how great this cave is then you make me memorize the directions on how to find it. And now we just sit on our hands. Don't you even want to know if your mama is okay?"

"Mom and Jessie will be safe once they reach the cave. Death Angel wants us to lead her to them."

"Are you saying Cassandra is coming after us?"

"Let's just say strolling down the breakwater wouldn't be the best for our health!"

The sun reflected off the Jordan River as they approached. Lining the river bank, the jeering from the crowd would soon reach a fiery pitch.

Raising his staff high, the taller Witness announced, "Those who have ears to hear what the Lord says do not allow unbelief to capture your soul. Did not the Lord deliver the children of Israel from the Rea Sea? Did not the Lord lead Israel through the Wilderness of Shur for three days with no water?" 3

"We have plenty of water to drink," yelled an angry news reporter. "And that includes enough water to put out your evil fires. Tell us, do you accept the responsibility for the innocent people killed by these firestorms?"

"Death will soon visit the rivers and springs of this earth. 4 Your water will become bitter as it was in the days of Marah."

"Why do you approve of such evil? All you've ever done is curse us!"

The other Witness testified, "'Thus says the Lord of hosts: Execute true justice, show mercy and compassion everyone to his brother. Do not oppress the widow or the fatherless, the alien or the poor. Let none of you plan evil in his heart against his brother. But they refused to heed, shrugged their shoulders, and stopped their ears so that they could not hear. Yes, they made their hearts like flint, refusing to hear the law and the words, which the Lord of hosts had sent by His Spirit through the former prophets. Thus great wrath came from the Lord of hosts.'" 5

"Do you really believe you're speaking for God?" challenged an orthodox priest. "How dare you misquote the prophets? These men are blasphemers!"

Before leaving, the taller Witness concluded, "Obadiah foretold: 'For the day of the Lord upon all the nations is near; as you have done, it shall be done to you; your reprisal shall return upon your own head. For as you drink on My holy mountain, so shall all the nations drink continually...they shall drink, and swallow, and they shall be as though they had never been.'" 6

Sitting beside the fire, Myra and Jessie were sharing the wonder of God's Word.

"Okay, Auntie, so far you've covered the first five Feasts. What about the final two holy days, the Day of Atonement and the Feast of Tabernacles?"

"Hey Jess how about a coffee break?"

"Okay, you take sugar?"

"No thanks, I only drink the real deal."

After a sip, a hopeful Jessie asked, "How long will it be before Uncle Anthony arrives?"

Suddenly a red light inside the cave started flashing.

"Where's my shotgun? We may have a prowler on our hands."

"Are you kidding?"

"Yeah, our Italian hero has arrived. He tripped the alarm to keep us on our toes."

After reaching the top of the ledge overseeing the entrance, Myra's smile dissolved.

"This doesn't look good."

"Do you know him?" whispered Jessie.

"Nope."

"What now?"

"We can leave through the rear tunnel, take him hostage, or shoot him."

"What are you feeling?"

"I'm not prepared to shoot him."

The stranger stopped near the fire and raised his hands high.

"My name is Hughes Jennings. I'm unarmed."

"We hear you, Hughes, what do you want?"

"I'm with the Christian underground. We received a message from Bret. I'm just a bookkeeper. They sent me because we ran out of..."

"You don't know my son."

"Surveillance checked out his story."

"Anyone with you?"

"Donnell Emery is on lookout. He's about twenty meters north."

"Is my son okay?"

"While acting as informant he never worshipped Kayin or took his mark. He's become a believer."

A stunned Myra slumped down in the damp dirt. She knew this was a favorite trick used by agents. With Jessie's help, she raised herself up.

"Hughes, I've got a loaded shotgun pointed right at your heart."

"I can see both barrels."

"I've got three questions for you. You answer all three and you can leave this cave alive."

The tense bookkeeper nodded.

"One, how did you find us? Two, why didn't Bret come? And three, what's his message?"

Hughes took a few seconds to think over his answers.

"At first, the underground was suspicious too. Bret's a smart man; he knew how to find us. In fact, he could have busted our operation anytime he wanted."

"Why didn't he?" interrupted an impatient Jessie.

"We thought you might know."

"Go on."

"The answer to your first question is simple. Your son gave us the directions to this cave. Of course, getting here took us a lot longer than we expected."

Beads of sweat drenched the collar of his blue button down shirt. For Hughes, this would be the hardest thing he would ever do for the Lord.

"What about our second question?"

"Bret didn't come because he's tracking a Special Forces sniper. She's terminated over..."

"Is this sniper a woman?"

"Twenty eight years old, five feet ten, black hair, make no mistake; Death Angel is a real killer."

"Why would an amateur like my son risk his life tracking a Special Forces sniper?"

Nervously shifting his feet he hesitated.

"That's the answer to your third question."

"We're waiting."

"Bret was at your house the night you escaped in his boat."

"How would you know that?"

"He saw Death Angel execute his father, Anthony Santino."

In between sobs, she howled, "You're lying!"

"Myra, I know you must..."

"How can you possibly know how she feels?" seethed Jessie.

"I don't, I just know how I feel. I guess that's why they sent me. Last year Death Angel terminated my wife."

REVEALED UNTO BABES

'I thank you Father, Lord of heaven and earth,
that you have hidden these things from the wise and prudent
and revealed them to babes...'
Luke 10:21

Rays from the sun filtered through the sheer drapes as Reenie opened her eyes. Birds chirping outside the window reminded her of her bedroom at home. She thought about someday visiting her folks and her little brother Travis. So far this vacant house had been a real lifesaver. For now, God had given them a green light to stay put.

From the bottom of the stairs, she could smell fresh coffee. Bret had a cup in one hand and a Bible in the other. The kitchen table was covered with Luke Appleby's notes.

"Hey, early bird, what are you studying?"

"Just checking out Luke's research, it would have been a blessing to hear him share the events that make up the beginning of sorrows and the Great Tribulation."

"It was for those who had ears to hear."

"But the events Jesus gave John in Matthew 24 and Revelation 6 are so clear. How could so many deny what they saw with their own eyes?"

"For a lot of reasons."

"I'd like to hear some."

"I remember it like it was yesterday. Some kids were eating lunch behind the Industrial Arts building. Rachel Pressley challenged Luke to explain the horrific worldwide famines of the 3rd seal."

"Was Rachel a Christian?"

"Big time. She's no dummy either. Rachel knew how deeply Luke believed. It all started with a supposedly innocent question."

"So, Luke, can you tell us when these famines will end?"

"This past year the rider of the black horse fueled these famines. They will end after Jesus opens the fourth seal. Riders Death and Hades will come on a pale horse. This is when Satan will give the two beasts the power to kill a fourth of the world during the Great Tribulation."

Sniggering with her friends, Rachel asked, "What beasts are you talking about?"

"The first beast is President Kayin. The second beast is Pope Michael."

"You must be joking. How can our President be the Antichrist?"

"The Antichrist has several names in scripture. John calls him the Beast. Jesus calls him the Abomination of Desolation. Paul calls him the Man of Sin. Daniel calls him the Little Horn."

"What exactly do these names have to do with our President?

"Under the guise of promoting peace he convinced several nations to join America in a concerted attack against Islamic terrorism. The world watched as Arab nations from the Middle East fell one right after another. 1 Kayin's goal was to force these Muslim nations lay down their weapons. When he brokered the false peace between Israel and her enemies the 70th week of Daniel began. 2 Even now, most Christians refuse to see this progression."

"Listen up everybody," shouted Rachel. "We are supposed to be watching for our Blessed Hope, never the Antichrist. 3 Show me one verse, Luke, which says the Antichrist must come before the rapture?"

"In Matthew 24:15, Jesus warns believers to watch for the Abomination of Desolation standing in the Holy Place in Jerusalem. This is when this evil leader will defile the rebuilt Temple and convince the world to follow him. Anyone refusing to become a member of his evil system will be persecuted. The Son of Man doesn't gather His elect from earth to heaven 'til the sun, moon, and stars lose their light." 4

"That's so off the wall. There are no events left to be fulfilled. Jesus could come right now if He wants to."

"Guys, don't be deceived by teachers insisting the Lord's coming has drawn near, at any moment. 5 Open your eyes; these famines are part of the beginning of sorrows. The days of the Great Tribulation will begin once Kayin seizes control of the nations. This is why Paul exhorts to watch for the revealing of the man of sin and not be deceived." 6

"My pastor teaches we should be out winning souls not arguing over when Jesus will come back. I'm not worried, Luke. I'm ready for the rapture, aren't you?"

"Rachel, being saved means you're ready to go to heaven when you die. Being saved in these last days doesn't necessarily mean you're ready for His coming. The only way to be ready is to heed Jesus' warnings concerning the future persecution of Christians."

"You just don't get it, do you? What good are your slick interpretations anyway? God is going to protect us no matter what happens. Once a person is saved, they can never lose their salvation. Have you ever read Romans 8:35?"

"You mean, 'Who shall separate us from the love of Christ? Shall tribulation, or distress, or persecution, or famine, or nakedness, or peril or sword?'"

"So, are you still worried about losing your salvation?"

"I never worry about my relationship with the Lord. I'm saved by grace through faith. Actually, my heart aches for those blinded to the eternal consequences of Jesus' warnings. The love of Christians is growing cold. 7 Many will be betraying and hating one another during the days of the Great Tribulation." 8

"What eternal consequences? Christians can't be deceived. My pastor, John Ryals, knows more in his little pinkie than you. He teaches once a person receives eternal salvation they are always saved. What don't you understand about the word 'eternal'? Nothing can change that."

"Tell that to the saints who follow the Beast." 9

"You're teaching believers are saved by what they do. My pastor says that's a false gospel. Your good works mean nothing to God."

The lunch bell couldn't have come any sooner. Most were tired of the bickering between Christians. As Luke gathered his notes, she took off with her friends.

"Hey, Rachel thanks for sharing."

Stepping over for another cup of coffee, Reenie took a peek outside through the blinds.

"Did Rachel say anything back?"

"Nope, I don't think she ever talked with Luke again."

"What ever happened to her?"

"She registered with her family."

"And her pastor?"

Pastor Ryals was the first to register from our church."

"You mean..."

"That's right; Rachel and I went to the same church. It's so sad. Deep down, I know there were times she really wanted to believe Luke."

"Did you ever ask her why she didn't?"

"I don't think anybody did."

Their truck was almost ready to go. While helping load supplies, Jessie was trying to find the right words. Myra finally broke the silence.

"Last night while you slept I had a good talk with the Lord. You know I'm just learning how to hear from God."

"Me too," sighed Jessie.

"Being able to reflect back on what happened has really helped me. After retracing the events, it's obvious there was no way the three of us could've escaped."

"You mean Uncle Anthony gave his life?"

"He sacrificed himself so we could go free. My honey man became a martyr for the Lord."

Jessie had to ask. She prayed silently for the right words.

"Myra, if Death Angel is such a clever assassin then why hasn't she killed Bret?"

"It must be God. And what about my boy watching his father give his life; what a testimony!"

The teenager raised her hands in thanksgiving as Myra worshipped the Lord by praying in tongues.

"Jessie, are you up for doing God's will?"

"For sure; Bret needs our help."

"Remember our talk about trusting the Lord and not our emotions? God knows the danger he is in. Bret is capable of taking care of himself."

"But what is more urgent than saving his life?"

"The salvation of your father."

"You really want to go to Israel?"

"Anthony and I owe you that much. This morning I received a word of knowledge about Aaron. He hasn't taken the mark."

"But what about security? You said yourself getting through the Atlanta airport is impossible!"

"Anthony has a close friend who exports fish to Haifa, a harbor in northern Israel. It would take awhile, but maybe we could catch a ride."

Her troubled expression was so unexpected.

"What's wrong, Jess?"

"Does the Holy Spirit want us to go right away?"

"He has given us a green light. Aaron must be in trouble. How are your sea legs?"

"But we can't buy food or water without an ID?"

"Relatives and friends will help us."

"The Coast Guard has quarantined the harbor. No boats are allowed out. Who knows if your friend can even make it to the Middle East?"

"The Holy Spirit just gave me Matthew 16:24-27 for you."

Jessie squirmed in her seat and looked down.

"A Watchman once gave me this passage. He said it was God's will for my life."

"What's he doing now?"

"Oh that's easy; Pastor Greg is about his Father's business."

The two agents were watching from across the street.

"Chief, I saw Hudson's station wagon at this house last week."

"This ain't adding up. Most would just high tail it to another city."

"His wife and kids left him. He must be feeling guilty."

"These Christians are like cockroaches when a light is turned on. I'll take care of them, Abe, you report back to the station."

Kurt could hear them arguing downstairs.

"My friend and I are leaving. We're not into all your rules."

Carlos motioned for the boy to lower his voice.

"You both asked for help this morning. Kurt brought you here for safety. An hour later you sneaked out for food."

"We were hungry."

"You could have been followed. Jesus can help you..."

"Skip the sermon; we've heard enough from Kurt."

"You can go now. If you get caught, you never heard of us."

"Yes sir, Captain," mocked the twelve year as he walked out the front door with his friend.

From an upstairs window, Kurt yelled, "Mayday!"

Carlos shouted back, "How many agents?"

"One just left in a hurry. The other agent is jogging through the parking lot. Uh oh, they're not looking. Wake up boys. Busted!"

"Don't move," snickered Doyle.

After cuffing the young teenagers he locked them in the backseat of his squad car.

Reaching the bottom of the stairs Kurt could see Carlos waiting at the backdoor.

"C'mon, bro, let's warn Greg and your sister."

Greg knew his son's station wagon was a liability. Even so, the two sisters they had just rescued didn't look scared at all.

"How long have you two been hiding?" Emma curiously asked.

The younger boldly replied, "Our folks were arrested by agents about a year ago. We miss them now but we'll see them in heaven."

Driving down the deserted street, the former pastor sensed trouble.

"Emma, I'm getting a red flag. Can you take the girls to the house we checked out last week?"

"What about Carlos and Kurt?"

"If we don't show up in three hours, call in a code green."

"Are you sure, Greg? You really want a code green?"

"You'll just have to trust my judgment."

"I'm on it. C'mon, girls, we've got a long walk ahead of us."

As soon as they turned the corner, Greg turned the station wagon into an empty garage. After closing the garage door, he took off jogging.

From a drainage ditch they watched the agent kick in the front door.

"Let's go, Kurt, they can't be helped."

"We just can't leave them."

Picking up a rock, the redhead broke into a sprint. The alarm erupted after he smashed open the driver's window. Jumping out, the two boys ran in different directions. The young Watchman froze when he heard the shotgun blast.

"One more step and I'll blow your peanut butt off!"

The boys' escape meant nothing to Commander Doyle Mercer. All he wanted was the fool who broke the window of his favorite squad car.

"What's your name?"

"Kurt Abbott."

"Are you a resister?"

"Guilty."

"I should shoot you right now."

"Hold up! I've got a Colt 38 pointed at your back. Now put the shotgun on the ground or you and I are going to play a game of chicken. Now what's it going to be?"

Doyle knew he meant business by the tone of his voice. Laying his gun down, the agent raised his hands.

"Grab his keys, Kurt; we'll use his car."

"You're Carlos Delgado, aren't you?"

"Who wants to know?"

"You've got quite a history. Drugs, armed robbery, extortion, even attempted murder. I always knew you'd turn out like your old man."

"You don't know anything about my family."

"I knew your mama. I could've sent her back to Mexico. It was too much paperwork so we executed her. She told me you were born again. Tell me, what's it like being a Christian? Doesn't the sixth commandant say thou shall not kill? 10 Or does that matter to a killer like you?"

For a moment the ex gang member thought about squeezing the trigger.

"Is it really worth it?" pleaded a voice from behind.

"Looky here, if it isn't Reverend Gregory Hudson in the flesh. Heard about your family running out on you; it's a dam shame."

"What's it going to be, Carlos?"

"Greg, this dude killed my mother."

"It's no secret he's a cold-blooded murderer. He takes his orders from the father of lies. Who do we take our orders from?"

"Our heavenly Father."

"Sure enough," taunted the commander, "my pastor says we should forgive one another."

After handcuffing his hands behind his back, Greg escorted him over to his squad car.

"Open the trunk, Kurt."

"What do you think you're doing?" threatened Doyle.

Taping his mouth shut Greg shoved him in the trunk and locked it.

"C'mon, it's time we disappear."

After a block, Carlos asked, "What now, Greg?"

"Guys, we just locked the head hog of the Bethany Security Force inside his own squad car. This area will soon be swarming with agents."

"What's your plan?"

"We need to split up. Kurt, when was the last time you saw a movie?"

"Outstanding. Does this date include hot buttered popcorn?"

"Emma is waiting for us at the Westside house. Carlos and I will meet you there in two hours."

For most it seemed like blue lights were coming from every direction. A major dragnet was underway.

Bartering for a movie ticket was easy for the redhead.

"Kurt's in. C'mon, Carlos, we don't have much time."

Running down an alley they scanned the side of an office building.

"What about the roof?"

"No way, they're still using a helicopter. Wait; see that open window on the third floor?"

"How do you know it's safe?"

Grabbing the metal ladder Greg pulled it down.

"You could say this is climbing by faith."

Reaching the open window, they climbed inside the medical supply room.

Sitting against the wall, Carlos grabbed two bags of chips and two sodas from his backpack.

"Sorry about what happened, Greg. When he threatened Kurt, my gangster days kinda kicked in."

"Naw, in your gangster days you would have shot the sucker."

Their laughter lasted a couple of seconds.

"So why did you cut Kurt loose? We aren't going to make it, are we?"

He didn't bother to reply to such a streetwise kid like Carlos.

"Greg, you hear about the protest at the Wailing Wall? The two Witnesses are saying Jesus is physically coming back to Jerusalem. Yesterday, thousands of Hasidic Jews were calling them liars."

"Not man, not Satan, nor his demons, will stop the Messiah from coming back and saving His remnant."

The immediate silence was not unusual for the two Watchmen.

"You know Doyle Mercer was right. The old Carlos Delgado was no good. Now that I have the Holy Spirit, God is changing me."

Greg loved the transformation he was seeing.

"Carlos, I have a verse for you from the Holy Spirit."

"For me?"

"Jesus once said, 'I thank you, Father, Lord of heaven and earth, that you have hidden these things from the wise and prudent and revealed them to babes. Even so, Father, for so it seemed good in Your sight.'" 11

THIRD TRUMPET: A STAR FROM HEAVEN

'Then the third angel sounded: And a great star fell from heaven, burning
like a torch, and it fell on a third of the rivers and on the springs of the
water.'
Revelation 8:10

Hiding among kids playing video games, Kurt watched as two agents
scanned everyone exiting the theater. A teenager standing beside him
could sense his uneasiness. This boy once heard the gospel at a
summer Bible camp. Some of his friends responded to the altar call
that day. The fear of what his parents would say kept him glued to his
seat.

"Hey, Red, you in some kinda trouble?"

"Not exactly, I just need to be going."

The teenager glanced at the agents and then looked back.

"There's a window in the men's bathroom on the second floor.
Use the ladder to the alley. When you hear the alarm, make your
move."

"You mean the fire alarm?"

"I'll take care of it. It should take you about twenty seconds."

"It will cost you big time if you get caught."

Rubbing his right wrist he muttered back, "So what if it does?"

The two sisters were safely on their way to a camp in Georgia. In
the past hour Emma was able to reroute six more believers. Standing
watch in the living room she fervently prayed.

The fire alarm worked like a charm. Even so, avoiding unmarked
cars could really make a resister sweat. Kurt wondered if he had made

it in time. Rushing through the kitchen Emma was praising the Lord. She could see her little brother opening the backdoor.

"Are Greg and Carlos with you?"

"They never showed. I had to call a code green. Everybody's being evacuated."

"You got any food?"

"I sent most of it with the girls."

"Okay, you watch for Greg and Carlos. I'm going downtown. I won't be long."

Raising the trumpet, the third angel sounded. A star burning like a torch fell from heaven. Soon one third of the rivers and lakes on the earth will turn bitter. 1

The fog covering the harbor was unusual for late December. For those exporting fish the red tape was endless. Since the firestorms most had gone out of business. A skipper for many years, Curtis Levy had no intention of giving up. His ship was loaded with iced flounder and red snapper. This shipment was bound for Haifa, Israel.

"Skip, what about the new restrictions on contaminated fish? If we get caught hauling infected cargo the government will put us out of business."

"We're leaving, notify the crew."

"What about our two passengers?"

"They should have been here an hour ago. The trip would've been too rough for them anyhow."

Coasting off the road Myra groaned, "Not a flat tire. We are almost there."

Jumping out of the old truck, Jessie stuck out her thumb for a ride.

Minutes later, his crew gathered round.

"Remember no sounds while leaving the harbor."

"Hey, Skip, we've got company."

Tipping his hat back, Levy smiled.

"It's Anthony's wife, help them aboard."

With a bag of food underneath his jacket Kurt opened the backdoor.

"Any sign of Greg or Carlos?"

From the kitchen table his sister sighed, "Not yet, any news?"

"Our contact filled me in. Code green was a disaster. Like catching fish in a barrel, agents were waiting when resisters fled the city."

"What could I do; Greg told me to do it?"

The claws on the roof sounded like sharp fingernails scratching a blackboard. They had come in response to her fear.

"You hear that?" she gasped.

"You stay here, Em, I'll check it out."

Stepping into the dark living room, he felt a coldness coming from the hallway. Heavy breathing followed. Once he smelled its foul odor, Kurt knew it wasn't human.

Blasting into the room, the hideous spirit bounced off the wall landing behind his victim. The demon hissed before circling around for a glimpse of Kurt's face.

"So where are your friends now? Why you little coward, you don't even know."

"My Lord will protect them."

"He didn't protect Jessie from registering. You turned her away."

"You shut your lying mouth."

Two other demons blocked the kitchen door as the spirit of Condemnation slithered closer.

"This isn't hard. You just leave your sister to us and you can go."

Kurt had never faced a demon before. He could hear Emma crying for help.

"What's it going to be, coward? You're an embarrassment to your God, your friends, why you care less about your own flesh and blood."

"I'm not leaving; you are."

"I sense your fear. You have no power over us."

"By the authority of Jesus Christ, I rebuke you!"

Lunging forward the demon was rendered helpless.

Running in a giddy Emma shouted, "Praise the Lord, they're gone!"

"What was that all about?" reflected her exhausted brother.

"We've got to get out of town, how about Dauphin Island?"

"Sorry, sis, if Jessie did find her aunt they could be anywhere."

"When I pray I see a girl that looks like Jessie, she needs our help."

"We just can't leave Greg and Carlos!"

"If the Holy Spirit is telling us to get out of Bethany, then He will also tell them." 2

"You know, I love the beach in December. The problem is the smell will probably kill us."

A grateful Emma hugged her little brother. She knew his joking was his way of coping with the pressure. Somehow the Holy Spirit would make a way.

WE WILL NOT LISTEN

'...I set watchmen over you, saying, "Listen to the sound of the trumpet.
But they said, "We will not listen."
Jeremiah 6:17

Everyone at Poppy's bar was watching News Anchor Natalie Roberts
on the big screen TV.

"Within the past hour, a meteor has exploded within our earth's
atmosphere. Burning fragments have contaminated many of our fresh
water systems. I must advise our viewers the pictures you are about to
see may not be suitable for children."

The holiday carnival at Lake Tahoe looked more like a B-rated
horror movie. Volunteers were frantically retrieving hundreds of
unconscious bodies from the infected lake.

"Under NWC orders, all rivers and lakes will be tagged with a red
flag. No one will be allowed to swim or drink from any river or lake
until it receives a green flag. It appears millions have been infected
worldwide."

Most at Poppy's could barely hold their drinks. Those overcome
with despair were cursing the two Witnesses. Natalie showed no
expression as she read from her teleprompter.

"Congress has declared a National Emergency. Every citizen
must conserve as much clean water as possible. As a protective
measure, water piped to private and public toilets will be turned off.
This is a temporary solution...excuse me, this is just in. The
Department of Environmental Hazards has successfully tested an
antidote that eliminates this poison many are calling Wormwood. 1
Every state will be responsible for its application. Please stay tuned for
an in-depth analysis by our scientists..."

With blue lights flashing, the NWC squad closed in.

Running toward Sluman's Garage, the out of breath pastor hollered, "Carlos, it's a code green! Get going, Emma and Kurt need your help!"

The teenager veered left; disappearing behind the Pizza Factory.

Speeding toward Sluman's, the agent called for backup.

After a long u-turn, a dark blue Continental screeched to a halt.

"Get in, Greg... C'mon, if you don't they'll execute you before the 10 o'clock news."

Lunging in, the Watchman hugged the floor. Hitting the accelerator, it wasn't long before the lights of the city were replaced by stars.

"Don't you just hate these NWC sirens? They give me a real headache. Would you like some water?"

Popping his head up, Greg took a double take.

"Thanks, John. That would be a blessing."

"The third trumpet is no joke. Water rationing is scary. Those waiting in line downtown are terrified. We need to get off this road. Agents started patrolling this area last week."

Turning into a cow pasture, John Ryals coasted his car behind a large billboard. From his trunk, he retrieved two bottles of water.

"Greg, the NWC is broadcasting executions left and right. I sure wasn't expecting you."

"They're trying to intimidate the children. Many are trying to get out of the city."

"The deception is awful. Now I can see why you left your church."

"How is Bethany Baptist doing?"

"My pastoring days are over. The board didn't appreciate my new interpretation of the last days."

"Are you still involved with the BMA?"

"Louis Cooper is the new Chairman. Heard God has given him a new vision. Some of the new members include Unitarians, Mormons, Jehovah Witnesses, even some sure fire New Agers."

"Wow, a real ecumenical circus."

So, Greg, how did you miss the coming of the Lord?"

"I wasn't saved. It was my wife and kids who convinced me not to register."

"Did you see Him coming in the clouds?"

"From my front porch."

"My wife and I were sitting by our pool."

"How is she taking it?"

"She's staying with her relatives in Nashville."

"Pretty overwhelming huh?"

"You mean evil. Oh, at first I was confused; even re-studied my notes. I always believed what my grandfather taught me on the coming of the Lord. Never dreamed his teaching would ever steer me away from the truth. I was convinced those who taught a Christian could deny their faith were fear mongers. The truth was always there; I just refused to see it. Jesus warned, 'He who overcomes shall be clothed in white garments, and I will not blot out his name from the book of Life; but I will confess his name before My Father and before His angels.' 2

"John, I..."

"The Word of God will soon appear in the heavens for the supper of the great God. The rider of the white horse is going to kill the armies following the Beast!" 3

Not knowing what to say, Greg sat back.

"So you're rescuing underage resisters?"

"The Holy Spirit is opening doors."

"How can I help you?"

"Honestly, John, most believers won't have anything to do with you when they see you have the mark."

"I'm asking you; not them."

"We need to pick up the Q Squad as soon as possible."

Whiskey was dripping off the corner of his desk as he read the casualty report.

"God, our crops are burned, our water is infected, why such vengeance?"

A shot glass shattering off his office door brought his aide running.

"Matthias, are you alright?"

"All these years I have sacrificed for my country. I've lost my family. Most of my friends want nothing to do with me. Millions have been killed, and for what?"

"For the safety of our people who are left."

"Do you believe in God?"

"Never have."

"Why not?"

"Believing in a supreme being controlling billions of people is a stretch for me."

"Judah Lentz believes Yeshua is going to return on the Day of Atonement. Five days later the Lamb of God is going to visit the Temple Mount during the Feast of Tabernacles." 4

"Seriously, Commander, how can such vain conjecture help anyone?"

"How long have we waited for the Messiah to crush our enemies? Maybe it's time for everyone to take their own stand for what they believe."

"What about the defenseless? Who will fight for them?"

Dismissing his aide, the distraught leader laid down on his couch. The flashback seemed so real.

The young boy screamed, "Mama, please answer me!"

"She's not coming home. Leah was in the wrong place at the wrong time."

"I don't understand, Mama. Why didn't God protect my sister?"

"Aaron, I pray someday you'll be in a position to recognize God's love. And when you do, remember the price Leah paid. May her death never be in vain."

Clenching his fists he screamed, "Where is Your love; God; I can only feel hate!"

His next memory was a dark courtroom. Every seat was taken. Verses from the Koran were written on the walls. The judge was announcing the sentence of a convicted terrorist. Sitting in the back of the courtroom, was his wife disguised in Muslim clothing. She was holding their one-year-old baby.

"Aaron Phinehas Glazer, you're guilty of treason. You deserve the death penalty but your country has freed three of our soldiers. Therefore, your sentence will be life in prison. May Allah be praised."

As guards led him out of the courtroom Aaron took one last look. His wife was waving goodbye with their baby girl's little hand.

"I miss my family so much. Oh, God, please protect them wherever they are."

His final flashback was of his father. Zionist Leader, Isaac Glazer, was dead. The red lights from the ambulance quickly drew a crowd.

The medics watched as Aaron placed his father's lifeless body on a stretcher. No one noticed the blood on the hands and feet of his son.

"What does this blood mean?" begged Matthias. "Lord, are you saying I will kill more terrorists than my father? Is this about my future?"

Reenie could hear Bret coming down the stairs.

From the sofa in the living room she asked, "What's up?"

"We're low on water; I need to barter some before curfew."

"Anything else?"

"The underground thinks my mother caught a ship to the Middle East. We need to get out of Gulf Shores too."

"I'll begin packing."

"We can't leave until the underground pinpoints Cassandra's location."

"You can't protect me forever. Let's ask the Holy Spirit. He'll tell us what to do."

"I'm losing it, Reenie. My thought life feels like a war zone."

She had never seen him so confused, almost panicky.

"This is spiritual warfare. Luke writes about it. He warns believers how Satan attacks with confusion. The Devil wants us to act outside of God's will." 5

"Before this confusion hit me I was studying God's wrath. This whole thing is too creepy. Daniel predicted, 'Then the king shall do according to his own will: he shall exalt and magnify himself above every God, shall speak blasphemies against the God of Gods, and shall prosper till the wrath has been accomplished...'" 6

"Wow, what a perfect profile of Kayin."

"So what does it mean, 'till the wrath has been accomplished'?"

"Satan's wrath against the saints was cut short by the coming of the Son of Man. We are now in the day of the Lord, God's wrath against the wicked. This day began after the first trumpet sounded and the fires started. The wrath of God will be completed after the seventh bowl is poured out. 7 Then the Word of God will cast the Beast and his false prophet into the lake of fire at the supper of the great God, Armageddon."

"What about the two hundred million released to kill a third of mankind in Revelation 9?"

"Pastor Ryals taught these are soldiers coming to attack Israel."

"I doubt it."

"Why do you say that?"

"This army attacks mankind just after the sixth trumpet sounds. Armageddon doesn't erupt till after the seventh bowl is poured out."

"Then who could they be?"

"The four angels bound at the Euphrates River are given control over this army of two hundred million. Only fallen angels are bound. This army has to be demons."

"You really think so?"

"Do you remember the invasion of Iraq in 2003? It took six months to move 140,000 American troops to Iraq. To move two hundred million troops to Israel would take several years."

"So the army released during the sixth trumpet isn't human?"

"Reenie, even if you combine the armies from every nation you couldn't even get close to twenty million; much less two hundred million. What a bloodbath. These demons are going to kill two billion by fire."

It was just after midnight. The only light on was in the living room. He slowly moved down the dark hallway leading to the stairs.

"Emma, Kurt."

"Freeze!"

The agent's flashlight covered the upper half of his body.

"I've got a gun. Don't make me hurt you. Now lay face down with your hands behind your neck."

Later that night, handcuffed to a chair in the Green Room, Carlos closed his eyes and bowed his head in reverence.

"Holy Spirit, no matter what they try, I know You will give me the right words." [8]

Raising his hands in worship, he heard in his mind, 'For to you it has been granted on behalf of Christ, not only to believe in Him, but also to suffer for His sake.' [9]

The drunken agents started laughing after slamming the metal door against the wall.

"Well now, if it isn't the gangster from Atlanta. This was the punk who threatened to shoot me. Instead he locked me in the trunk of my squad car. Do you deny this, Delgado?"

Kicking the chair out from beneath his suspect, Mercer cursed.

"How about a little respect! I'm asking you a question."

These agents were ready for some real hazing as they lifted him back into his chair.

"I'm a Watchman who will never register."

"Yeah, yeah, you religious fanatics are all alike. Hey, maybe Carlos can give us a word from God?"

"'...I set watchmen over you, saying, "Listen to the sound of the trumpet. But they said, "We will not listen... Behold, I will certainly bring calamity on this people..."' 10

"I told you our boy can quote scripture."

"He sounds like a prophet to me," hooted another agent.

"This spic ain't representing my Father in heaven."

"Your father is the devil."

"What was that?"

"'You are of your father the devil, and the desires of your father you want to do. He was a murderer from the beginning, and does not stand for the truth, because there is no truth in him... He is a liar and the father of it.'" 11

"You think you're special in the eyes of God, don't you Carlos?"

"All who overcome the Beast and his evil world system will never be blotted out of the Book of Life." 12

"How exactly are these overcomers going to do this?"

"By the blood of the Lamb and the word of our testimony." 13

"You mean the part about breaking the law and endangering people's lives? This is your testimony to the good people of Bethany?"

"My testimony is the doctrine of Christ. 14 Only those who believe in Jesus as their Lord and Savior will enter the kingdom of heaven. This world is burning up. The New Jerusalem is forever."

His evil gaze, his sudden outbursts, his inability to sit still, most under his command knew something wicked was eating away at their boss.

"I've heard Greg Hudson was your teacher. Is this why you sound like a broken record?"

"I pity you."

"DQ him in the next live TV execution."

"But, Chief, the paperwork will take at least..."

"That's an order! This holy roller is wasting our time. He'll never change. Make sure his execution goes down just like his mother."

"How long has this been going on?"

Shuffling behind, Kayin's aide looked frightened.

"Two hours, your grace."

"Why wasn't I immediately notified?"

"Lord Kayin asked not to be disturbed."

"Come with me and be discrete."

Slumped in a chair beside his picturesque window, the captivating visions he was receiving had his undivided attention. Pope Michael and the aide took seats behind his huge desk.

"Master, I see Mizraism, the Pharaoh of Egypt. He was your leader of the first beast kingdom. His armies are hunting the Hebrews like animals. Nooooo!"

In his mind he saw the drowning of the Pharaoh's armies in the Red Sea. His deep breathing was not a good sign; the Man of Sin was turning pale. 15

"Yes, Master, it's Assyria, your second beast kingdom. Shalmaneser courageously captured the ten tribes of Israel."

The picture of Assyria's destruction was so vivid. Dropping to his knees he begged for this torment to go away.

"Yes, I see the King of Babylon. Nebuchadnezzar is dressed in gold. Jerusalem is being overrun, the Temple is destroyed; the Jews are being led captive to Babylon. This was your third beast empire, the capture of the two remaining tribes of Israel."

His praise was interrupted by another vision. Babylon lay in ruins. Dressed in rags, a tormented Nebuchadnezzar was begging for mercy.

"Neverrrrr!" shrieked the Son of Perdition.

"Have you seen my fourth beast kingdom?" whispered Satan. "The Medes and Persians were greater than the Babylonians."

Kayin's face was mesmerized by the silver kingdom.

"Ahasuerus ordered the death of every Jew in his kingdom."

A queen appeared. Groveling at her feet was a frightened Haman.

"Is this the beautiful Queen Esther?"

A dead Haman hanging from the gallows took away his breath. Soon, the fifth beast kingdom surfaced in his mind. Alexander the Great of Greece was invading Israel with his armies. Then he saw Antiochus Epiphanies seizing control of Jerusalem. 16

Falling to the floor, Kayin roared with delight.

"I love Antiochus. We both deceived the Jews through flattery. We desecrated their Temple. We stopped their sacrifices. We declared ourselves to be God."

At first, he didn't recognize the white haired priest. Mattathias was leading the revolt against Epiphanies' evil kingdom. A future event followed. Thousands were walking toward the Temple Mount on the first day of Christ's thousand year reign over the nations. 17

"It can't be! Not the Shekinah glory returning to the Temple?" 18

Jumping up, the Lawless One began to pace.

"Yes, Master, you were there when Rome ruled the world. Your hand was upon Nero, the leader of the sixth beast kingdom. No not the fires!"

The burning of Rome was a memory Kayin wanted no part of. Satan countered with a picture of Jews fleeing Jerusalem in 70 A.D. Soon there would be no more Israel.

The false prophet whispered to the aide, "'...The seven heads are seven mountains on which the woman sits. There are also seven kings. Five have fallen (Egypt, Assyria, Babylon, Persia, Greece) one is (Rome), and the other has not yet come. And when he comes, he must continue a short time.'" 19

Closing his eyes the Beast saw immense crowds chanting, "Seig Heil, Seig Heil, Seig Heil."

The high stepping soldiers marching through the streets wore emblems resembling black spiders. One by one nations were falling under the demonic influence of Adolph Hitler. Over six million Jews were killed during the seventh beast empire.

"Master, your kingdom in the last days consists of seven heads and ten horns. I, Joshua Kayin, will soon usher in a thousand-year reign of your earth. I'm the eighth head; I'm greater than the seven!"20

Circling back, John could sense Greg's reluctance.

"Is this a set up?"

"All the lights are off. It must be a NWC bust."

The Lincoln made a quick left, then an immediate right.

"Greg, you should have never played with Doyle Mercer. He's vindictive; a real killer. I can't believe you lasted this long."

"My kids are counting on me."

"Not as a martyr. The Q Squad must be underground by now. I own a lake cottage about thirty miles north. The water is infected so no one will bother us. We need to hide out until the heat is off."

"I just pray they got out before the agents arrived."

"Any idea where they might go?"

"None of us know the other's hiding place."

In a strange way the ride around the polluted lake was peaceful. A cold wind was blowing across the abandoned yards. John led Greg down a crushed rock pathway to the porch.

"Make yourself at home. The grocery is a block away. It will be a miracle if it's still open."

Resting in his study, Greg could see pictures honoring his ministry. The most prominent was a meeting with former American President Joshua Kayin. Representing the World Faith Movement was a Muslim cleric, a Jewish rabbi, and a Catholic priest. They were all thanking John Ryals for his leadership.

"Somehow, somewhere, something went wrong!" moaned Greg.

Through the window he could see red flags placed along the shoreline. The smell of decay was nauseating. He could hear heavy breathing coming up the back steps. After tossing Greg a bottle of tea, John heated up two burritos in the microwave.

"Did you hear anything?"

"The NWC killed a member of your Q Squad. The store clerk saw the execution of Carlos Delgado on channel 19. He said the young man was praising the Lord."

Tears slid down his face. Greg could only reminisce.

"Carlos had such a love for God's Word. The Holy Spirit was teaching him truths it would take years to learn. He so much wanted to be here to see Jesus at the sounding of the seventh trumpet."

"Heard Pastor Louis Cooper is preaching the seventh trumpet in Revelation 11 is the last trumpet of I Corinthians 15:52, I Thessalonians 4:16, and Matthew 24:31."

"Afraid not! During the Feast of Trumpets, when the sun, moon, and stars, lost their light, God blew His final trumpet. The Great Tribulation was cut short when the overcomers were delivered to heaven."

"The seven trumpets will be blown by angels not God. Jesus will be on earth for the seventh trumpet alright. Not for the resurrection of the elect but for the salvation of Israel." [21]

The beleaguered pastor slumped down in his chair.

"I can't describe the pain I'm feeling."

"I understand."

"No, Greg, I hope to God you never do!" [22]

THE WAY OF ESCAPE

'No temptation has overtaken you except such as is common to man, but God is faithful, who will not allow you to be tempted beyond what you are able, but with the temptation will also make the way of escape, that you may be able to bear it.'
I Corinthians 10:13

Seagulls circled the blood-etched harbor. The unloading would begin as soon as his crew was scanned. Hiding in the ship's galley both overcomers were praying.

"Hey, Levy!" shouted an NWC agent. "Never dreamed you'd make it, looks like you're carrying an extra special catch."

The skipper yelled back, "There's no doubt about that."

As agents scanned crew members near the hull of the ship, Myra and Jessie made their move. Reaching dry ground they disappeared into a fish market. The skipper never said goodbye. He was convinced they would be arrested by the third checkpoint. Curtis Levy never understood why resisters risked their lives to share their faith. But he did know one truth. If he ever asked for help, Anthony Santino would have given him the shirt off his back.

Gazing upward, he nervously prayed, "I ain't good at this, God, but could You help Myra find what she is looking for."

———

"There they are," whispered John.

"How do you know?"

"Look at them. They're scared to death."

The Lincoln eased toward the mother and two daughters.

"Are you looking for a black and white tabby cat?"

"It depends," the mother anxiously replied.

"He's an original," a smiling Greg whispered.

"That's the password," blurted one of girls.

The trunk sprung open. The three believers jammed two large plastic bags inside and then slid into the wide backseat of the Lincoln.

"God bless you. We have been waiting for hours. Our contact never showed."

"These your girls?"

"My pride and joy."

"Hey, mister, why is God so mad at the world?"

Her mother glanced at Greg, then John.

"I've been trying to teach them. Explaining God's wrath isn't easy."

"Join the club. I pastored for over thirty years and never taught the difference between Satan's wrath during the Great Tribulation and God's wrath during the day of the Lord, didn't think any of us would be here for either one."

"My favorite prophecy teacher believed that. He taught these fires were nuclear explosions."

Both pastors could sense her confusion. The spiritualizing of scripture had deceived so many.

A blunt John shared, "The day of the Lord is a period of time when only the Lord will be exalted. 1 God wants man to know these judgments are from Him."

"There's not much time left, is there?"

"Those who survive the day of the Lord, that don't worship the Beast, his image, or receive his mark, will live on earth during the Millennium." 2

"How do you know that?"

"After the thousand year reign of Christ ends, Satan will deceive the nations like the sand of the sea. 3 If no one survives the day of the Lord to live on earth during the Millennium, then who does Satan deceive when the thousand years is up?"

"This is incredible. I've never heard this before."

The closed gas station was their drop off spot. The lights from the truck blinked twice before pulling up alongside the Continental.

"You looking for something?" asked the trucker.

"I'm looking for the largest city in America."

"That would be Jacksonville, Florida."

A relieved Greg turned toward the weary family and winked.

"This is your ride."

"We thank God for your faithfulness. We will always pray for you. And we loved the Bible study."

Both pastors watched as another family headed for safety. One felt joy; the other horror.

As the two Witnesses entered Bethlehem, the Palestinian crowd had to be restrained by soldiers.

The smaller Witness announced, "'Behold the day of the Lord comes, cruel, with both wrath and fierce anger, to lay the land desolate; and He will destroy its sinners from it... The Lord says, 'Therefore I will shake the heavens, and the earth will move out of her place, in the wrath of the Lord of hosts and in the day of His fierce anger.'" 4

"Is this another prediction?" taunted a suspicious reporter.

"At the sounding of the fourth trumpet, the Lord will strike the sun, the moon, and the stars. 5 Beware, the wrath of a Holy God has come upon you and who shall survive?"

For the right price, most taxi drivers would smuggle anyone into Jerusalem. Speaking in rusty Hebrew Myra tried to pass herself off as a Jewish settler. After several attempts the situation looked hopeless. Then a young driver heard about two Americans. After a chat with the clean-cut Israeli, Myra met with Jessie inside the harbor bar. Surrounded by partying sailors they looked out of place.

"Jess, I just got us a ride."

"How did you do that?"

"I had to use Aaron's name."

"You didn't!"

"The driver's name is Bela. He owns his own taxi. He's willing to smuggle us for free."

"Yeah, and how much will he get when he turns us in?"

"He says we'll have to hide in the trunk of his cab during our ride."

"For how long?"

"It depends on the lines; maybe two hours."

The noise in the bar seemed louder.

"Myra, do you remember my interrogation by agents? I didn't tell you but I had a claustrophobic reaction. I couldn't breathe. My greatest fear is being closed in."

"I don't understand; we were on the ship for over a month?"

"It sounds crazy; maybe I was okay because I could move around. Believe me; I can't last ten minutes in the trunk of a taxi."

Grasping Jessie's trembling hand she whispered, "When the Lord led us to come here we knew we couldn't do this in our own strength."

"Please, I'm not strong enough."

"We can't fly into Jerusalem and walking through checkpoints is suicide. The Lord opened this door. We can't afford to do it our way."

"I need to pray some more. Maybe God will show us a better way."

"He already has. 'Therefore let him who thinks he stands take heed lest he fall. No temptation has overtaken you except such as is common to man; but God is faithful, who will not allow you to be tempted beyond what you are able, but with the temptation will also make the way of escape, that you may be able to bear it.'" 6

"What if I flip out? No way. I'm not getting us killed."

"This is just another step in faith in reaching your father."

"When daddy got out of prison why didn't he come see me?"

"That's what we're going to find out, honey."

Bela was removing the back seats when they arrived. Myra crawled in feet first. After a long pause he looked up. Jessie wasn't moving.

"Miss, what's it worth to you to defeat your greatest fear?"

"I don't know; I've never thought about it."

"Little one of Judah, I promise to get you safely inside our city."

She prayed before sliding through the small opening.

"Remember, no talking. Be ready to run if we have a problem. If you have any trouble, knock on the back seat."

"We can't thank you enough Bela."

"Is this really Aaron Glazer's daughter?"

"Yes, this is Johanna Glazer."

"Your father is a patriot. He has risked his life many times for our people."

Hopping behind the wheel, he turned on to the main road.

The spirit of Fear wasted no time. Flicking on her flashlight,

Myra could see a glassy panic in her eyes.

"Lord, may Your power drive out all fear. I rebuke this evil spirit in Jesus' name. Grant Jessie the power to be a witness for You. Baptize her in Your Holy Spirit."

It wasn't long before the teenager was praying in tongues. The fear had been replaced by the presence of God.

"What a beautiful gift. I can feel His power so much more."

A grinning Myra whispered back, "Girl, instead of working by hand, it's more like power tools."

FOURTH TRUMPET: THE SUN WAS STRUCK

'Then the fourth angel sounded: And a third of the sun was struck, a third
of the moon, and a third of the stars,
so that a third of them were darkened.
A third of the day did not shine, and likewise the night.'
Revelation 8:12

Mankind watched in horror as the infection spread. Many died from
drinking contaminated water; others by cooking with it. ₁ The hysteria
from the two Witnesses next prediction was the worst the world had
ever experienced.

The ride took ninety minutes. Bela turned up his radio as he
edged within two cars of the border. In the past year this young man
had smuggled Russian Jews, government officials, Rabbis, even Israeli
mercenaries. But never was his cargo as dangerous as it was today. He
knew the risk. To assist the unregistered daughter of Israeli freedom
fighter Aaron Glazer was a capital offense. If caught, he would be
executed within forty-eight hours.

"Papers please," requested the agent without looking.

Bela casually handed him his monthly pass.

"Are you carrying anything?"

"I'm picking up a fare in Old Jerusalem."

"Have a good day."

While putting his papers away another agent spoke up.

"Well, what a surprise. How's your family doing Bela?"

"You know this guy?" asked the other agent.

"He opposed the roadmap to peace. Let's give him a through
exam."

Myra and Jessie could only hear the music from the radio.

"We'll never make our quota if we do."

"Bela, are you hiding anything from us?"

"I've got a fare waiting on me on David Street in Old Jerusalem."

"You best remember my face. Now get going."

It took a few minutes to reach a secret garage underneath a storage building. Waiting until it was clear, Bela drove down a ramp into the basement. The light coming through the tiny holes in the side of the cab faded. A ten-year-old opened the trunk door and helped them out.

"How do you feel?" the boy excitedly asked.

After taking a deep breath all Jessie could do was smile.

"Everything is okay," announced Bela, "you're safe."

Myra wasted little time. Their conversation in Hebrew was intense. The tall brunette knew her aunt was sharing the gospel. It only took a minute before a sad looking Myra gave him a final hug. As Bela drove away, the boy waved goodbye from the rear window of the cab.

"Are you ready to travel, Jess?"

"I will be after a good stretch. Was Bela interested in Yeshua?"

"Not anymore. When the Great Tribulation erupted, he and his family refused to register. A few months later agents arrested his wife near Zion Gate. Martyrdom wasn't an option. That day his whole family received the mark of the beast."

The fourth trumpet could be heard throughout the vast reaches of heaven. Soon the power of God would strike the sun, the moon, and the stars. One third of a day would not shine. 2 One third of the stars would lose their light. For thirty days a sign from a Holy God was written in the sky for the world to see.

The trip across the busy city was tedious, especially for Jessie. Avoiding agents on patrol was top priority. Myra desperately wanted to get settled in before nightfall. It had been almost two decades since her last visit. For those who have never been to Israel, there was no way to describe it. To actually visit the land where Immanuel ministered was life changing. To see the very place the Lamb of God died for the sins of mankind was a sacred experience. At least to some it was.

While walking, a curious Jessie asked, "Does Bela know my daddy?"

"He's heard about your father but has never met him. Aaron was the leader of the nationalists who tried to assassinate Joshua Kayin."

"That will never happen. Daniel 8:25 says he will never be..."

"Quiet, Jess."

Ducking inside a candle shop they hid behind a counter. The agent rushing bye was discretely holding a mini scanner by his side.

"That was close. So where is my daddy hiding?"

"Bela thinks somewhere in the Judean hills."

"What's our plan?"

"Bela will spread the word. Once Aaron finds out, he will find us. For now let's find the flat my friends told me about."

"Then what?"

"We can only pray and wait."

Suddenly a third of the sun turned black.

"It's the fourth trumpet!" squealed Jessie.

"Everyone is heading indoors. It's only going to get worse. Let's make a run for it. Please stay close to me. Our flat isn't far."

───────────

While resting in her deluxe suite, Cassandra sensed Baphomet's displeasure. Something was wrong. Counting down to ten, she summoned the demon. Manifesting near the bathroom, the foul spirit wasted no time.

"Our Master is weary of your excuses."

"Why blame me; Jezebel lost the girl."

"Soon I will have to punish you, Cassandra."

"They're underground; they could be anywhere. I suppose Jezebel isn't too thrilled, is she?"

"I wouldn't be making such foolish comments."

"Let's not forget, I was the one who gave this girl to Jezebel on a silver platter. Now when is she going to possess her again?"

"One never knows how Jezebel will act. You just be ready to terminate your subject when she reaches a backslidden state."

"I always finish what I start. Reenie Ann Tucker will never see it coming until it's too late."

26

THE ANGEL OF THE BOTTOMLESS PIT

'And they had as king over them the angel of the bottomless pit...'
Revelation 9:11

One could barely make out their silhouettes within the smoky bottomless pit. Abaddon had promised to someday return and free them. Every demon was waiting to hear the sound of a key turning. Once released, this unseen army would torment the inhabitants of the earth for five months. 1 Only those having the seal of God on their foreheads would be protected.

The team of John Ryals and Greg Hudson had quite a reputation among the Christian underground. Their rescues were miraculous to say the least. No one ever dreamed a pastor having the mark of the beast could be used in such a valuable way.

"Nice move, you lost them."

"Greg let's lose this blue hog. Agents can spot us two blocks away."

"Okay, we'll retire this baby after tonight's pickup."

"Do you want me to circle back?"

"One more time," sighed Greg.

The blue Continental slowly turned onto Hillsborough. The tired teenager hadn't moved. He was wearing black jeans, an old army jacket, and a dirty Atlanta Braves hat.

"Most would have bailed by now," whispered John. "He isn't afraid."

Easing past the park bench, they cut the engine and waited.

"Hey, kid, when does the Lord physically return to earth during

His second coming?"

"Revelation 10:1-7."

"Get in."

After three quick turns, they coasted into an abandoned garage. Greg got out and closed the garage door. Getting back into the Continental he could already feel the tension.

"You look mighty familiar mister. Aren't you a pastor?"

Looking straight ahead, John Ryals didn't answer.

"I wanna thank you both for helping me."

Greg nodded and replied, "Your ride will be here in an hour. Can you share your testimony with us?"

"Used to be a member of a Nazi gang called the Neighbors, it took awhile before I figured out Kayin cut a deal with the devil. For sure, that fascist's mark ain't part of my future. I've never been to church. I got saved last year."

"How did Jesus reveal Himself to you?"

"Met a friend hiding in an empty house over on Cherry, he told me how the Holy Spirit indwells those who repent and follow Jesus. 2 God is good; I was ready to surrender my life."

"Tired of running?" sighed John.

"It's been rough. I still don't get why so many checked out when the persecution hit?"

"You mean when it started to cost something to be a Christian? Satan can answer that one for you."

"I thought God was greater than the attacks from the enemy?"

"A greenhorn," John muttered under his breath. "Boy, you ever wonder how Satan deceived Eve?"

"My friend is talking about spiritual warfare. Satan did deceive many through threats of persecution. The lack of spiritual discernment during the Great Tribulation was heartbreaking."

"But how could so many Christians be so blind?"

They had heard this question many times. For John Ryals, it was like pouring acid on an open wound.

"Satan did it by sowing lies," Mark slowly confessed.

"But why would Christians listen to Satan? And why didn't anyone expose these lies?"

"Many who did were martyred. God is still using Watchmen to expose Satan's deception."

"Yeah, I remember a Watchman from Santa Barbara, California. The NWC wasted him in a run-down church. Don't recall his name."

Jerking around, he shouted, "His name was Reverend Steven Alan Corbin!"

"Easy, John, he didn't know Steven. C'mon, the kid is just sharing."

Turning back around John gripped the steering wheel and stared straight ahead.

"Yes, Steven Corbin was a Watchman. Tragically, at the time of his death, many pastors were teaching doctrines of demons." 3

"Still do," John added with no expression.

Resting his elbows on the back of Greg's seat, the inquisitive teenager asked, "What do you mean?"

John Ryals wiped away the perspiration from his wrinkled forehead. He had heard it before, but this time it was worse, much worse. After an awkward silence, the former Baptist minister looked at Greg.

"Go ahead; tell the boy how I deceived the members of my church."

"John, maybe we should focus..."

"For the entire time I've helped you in rescue, have I ever asked you for anything?"

"No, you haven't."

"You mean this dude has the mark of the beast?" gasped the teenager.

Jumping out of the car he lit up a cigar. Greg joined him by the side door of the garage.

"What's wrong, John?"

His lips were barely moving.

"I'm losing it."

"I don't know what to say."

"It was just a matter of time. What about the camp in Georgia you started?" You need to be getting out of Bethany."

"Been praying about it."

"I'm happy for you, Greg. Don't screw it up. Nothing is worth taking the mark."

"I'll never forget you, John."

Tossing him his car keys, he muttered back, "Sure you will."

It was painful to watch as the ex-pastor shuffled down the sidewalk cluttered with trash. As soon as he was gone, Greg walked back and slid into the driver's seat of the Continental.

"Where's your friend going?"

"You were right about John Ryals. He was one of the most respected pastors in our state. His congregation was the largest in Bethany."

"You mean they all took the mark of the beast?"

"Son, for almost two thousand years most ministers never understood the events warning believers Christ's coming is near; especially the falling away during the Great Tribulation." 4

"How is that possible?"

"Two reasons. The only way to understand the coming of the Lord is by Jesus' own words. This includes the prophets and His apostles."

"What about the Holy Spirit?"

"That's the second reason. Instead of seeking after the Holy Spirit many trusted in famous teachers. 5 The traditions of men were far more powerful than we ever imagined."

A crowd from Hebron watched in horror as the two Witnesses approached.

"They are visiting every city in Israel," warned a TV reporter. "Before their through, we'll all be destroyed."

It had been two days since the month long blackout ended. The two Witnesses were still prophesying salvation for those who hadn't worshipped the Beast, his image, or received his mark.

"Children of Israel," the taller Witness boldly announced, "the angel Gabriel spoke to Daniel concerning the salvation of our people. When the seventy weeks of Gentile oppression is complete, Israel's transgressions will be finished. The Messiah will return to earth on the Day of Atonement and forgive all believing in Him." 6

The truck stop had a dozen rigs parked on the back lot.

Pulling his sister inside the women's bathroom, he locked the door.

"The driver of the green rig will take us to Gulf Shores if we wash his truck."

"Can we trust him?"

The frail redhead collapsed underneath the sink.

"It would've happened if I hadn't played hero," he sobbed. "If I had only listened to Carlos."

"What are you saying?"

"Carlos and Greg are with the Lord. A trucker gave me the details."

Dropping to her knees Emma desperately tried to compose herself. It was always a possibility but she never really believed it could happen.

"Just tell me, Kurt."

"He saw Carlos' execution on channel 19. Greg was arrested a few days ago while trying to help a teenage boy escape. His execution was broadcast on FM 107."

FIFTH TRUMPET: TORMENTING LOCUSTS

'Then the fifth angel sounded: And I saw a star fallen from heaven to the earth. To him was given the key to the bottomless pit.'
Revelation 9:1

An army of angels stood back as the fifth trumpet sounded. They had their orders. This time there would be no interference. Abaddon loved feeling the texture of the key. The opening produced hideous shrieks, as demons emptied out of the bottomless pit. 1 Their king had anticipated their intoxicating reaction to freedom. He would grant them time to prepare themselves for their evil assault. Abaddon knew this would be the first of the final three woes (fifth, sixth, and seventh trumpets). 2 The stench from the smoke was still lingering in the air when the command to assemble was given. The power would come from their tails. His emissaries would torment for five months. 3

Wes Mackish, the popular producer of Channel 6, had somehow held his staff together through the month long blackout. But the invisible stings were the worst of all. Almost overnight an enemy was tormenting men, women, and children all over the world.

"Where's Nate?"

"She's still checking the sound bites. Wes, the pain from these stings is sickening. Natalie had a hard time reviewing the pictures."

"Doesn't matter, I scratched them, we're going live."

"Yesterday the NWC gave us strict orders not to."

"We're reporters. Our viewers deserve a straight call. Has Nate been stung?"

"Not yet."

The panic was escalating. Her cell phone was dead. Natalie had no idea how her parents were doing. Being famous wasn't worth much during emergencies like this.

"The truth still matters! We have a job to do. Ready, Nate?"

She looked grimly into camera one and nodded at her producer.

"This is Special Report with Natalie Roberts. Just minutes ago, a rare phenomenon struck nations around the world. Millions have been stung. There are no deaths at this time. Symptoms include high fever, cramps, and nausea. The NWC has issued an Emergency Medical Alert. Medicine will be distributed at the same stations used for the Wormwood infection. Let's check in with several on site reporters.

"This is Shelia Fisher reporting from the Miami Art Festival. As you can see, hundreds of visitors have been stung. Several doctors are treating those infected. As a veteran reporter, I've never seen anything like this!"

"We're thinking of you, Sheila, next up, Culver City, California."

"I'm Cade Ames reporting from the Los Angles Interstate 405. The exodus from downtown has been a nightmare. This twelve lane highway is at a total standstill. By law, gas stations and grocery stores must stay open till six o'clock tonight."

In a monotone voice, a reluctant Natalie asked, "Cade, how are the people reacting?"

"I'd say overwhelming fear to out of control anger. Most believe the two Witnesses are the cause. Those I interviewed want them executed."

"We're losing you, Cade. Our final report tonight is from Gulf Shores, Alabama."

"I'm Quentin Willis. Minutes ago, the Alabama High School Cheerleading Championships was brought to a stunning halt. The evacuation was pandemonium. Many were trampled on while trying to exit the gym."

"Quentin, how many girls have been stung?"

"I saw bunches collapsed on the floor screaming for help. The panic is horrific."

"This isn't easy for us either. You're in our prayers."

She could hear footsteps. A hasty retreat followed. Jessie then burst into tears behind the barricaded door. It had been five days since Myra left for food. The petrified teenager was on the edge of complete exhaustion. Her empty backpack lay in the corner of the room. The scenarios of what could have happened were suffocating her.

"Lord, if I leave how will I ever find Myra?"

She had no other choice, the Holy Spirit had spoken. Walking slowly down a street in Old Jerusalem the slender brunette was shocked to see so many pale numb faces. Like their Arab neighbors many were covered from head to toe. Transactions in the shops were abrupt; no one wanted to be caught out in the open. The only laughter was coming from those who had lost their mind. A gang of teenagers waved after spotting the disorientated American asking for directions.

"We can help you." shouted one of the boys. "What's your name?"

Pretending not to hear, Jessie turned away. After two blocks of running, she disappeared into an open market. Circling around, they trapped her on a street of apartments closed off by concrete barricades.

"What's wrong with you? We just want a little fun."

His blood curdling scream scattered his buddies. The puncture appeared just below his right eye. Within seconds, pleas for help began pouring out of the apartments. The hysteria spread as more people were being stung. Jessie never saw where the little girl came from.

"Are you lost? What is your name?"

"Jessie Hyatt. I'm searching for my aunt."

"I'm Ruth Lentz. Being out alone is too dangerous. Follow me!"

Taking Jessie's hand they hurried by several stores filled with frantic shoppers. After a couple turns, she knew her little friend was purposely avoiding agents. Then they stopped and waited.

"My family lives across the street. We cannot enter until the blinds are drawn half way down. Jessie, do you live in America?"

"Yes, Ruth, I live in Bethany, Alabama."

"Is Bethany near Disney World?"

"It sure is. Would you like to visit the United States?"

"Very much, my Papa says all kinds of people live there in peace."

"I'm fine, Mama... No, I didn't have permission from Papa... I know it was dangerous but we needed water... I just couldn't leave her... No, we weren't followed."

Their hug lasted a minute. The thought of losing Ruth was Hanna's greatest fear.

"Mama, this is Jessie Hyatt. She is from America."

"Nice to meet you Jessie, I'm Hanna. Would you like some hot tea?"

"That would be great."

"Mama, where are the boys? Have the Hilkiah's left us?"

"Your father will explain. He will be home soon."

After an hour the tapping on the bookcase was a welcome relief.

With a resigned expression he softly reflected, "I can see we have a new house guest."

"I'm Jessie Hyatt."

"I'm Judah, Ruth's father. So, my dear, I assume you are unregistered?"

"Yes, I'm a Christian."

"And where is your family?"

"I got separated from my aunt. I don't know where she is."

"I understand your position, Jessie. This presents us with a difficult problem. Somehow we are going to have to learn to trust one another. We too are unregistered. We believe in Hashem, the God of Abraham, Isaac, and Jacob."

"Papa, where are the Hilkiah's?"

"Eleazar took Deborah and the boys to a secret apartment outside Ashdod."

"But why would they leave us now?"

"Eleazar's family is very weak; they have no food. The Hilkiah's left to help them. The streets are a madhouse with these horrific stings."

"God gave us a miracle. Jessie and I were never stung."

"What now, Judah? What if agents are searching for Jessie?"

"Hanna, what can we do but trust Hashem."

"You mean it, Papa?" asked a shocked Ruth. "Can Jessie really live with us?"

THE DAUGHTER OF ZION

'Indeed the Lord has proclaimed to the end of the world: 'Say to the daughter of Zion, 'Surely your salvation is coming, Behold, His reward is with Him.'
Isaiah 62:11

One sting could take weeks to heal. At first most would just hide in their homes. After almost five months the embarrassment didn't matter anymore. Even being stung in public had lost its novelty. The harassment for those being protected was growing.

Seated at an outside table in front of Ruby's Donut Shop, a faint Emma Abbott wasn't doing so well. In the distance was Dauphin Island.

"C'mon, sis, we can do it."

"Everyone says the island is deserted."

"We have to at least try. Look how long it took us to get this far."

The older looking man looked gentle enough as he sat down. They discretely watched as he sipped his coffee and read his newspaper.

"You kids hungry?"

"Sure are!" grinned Kurt. "We'd love some fried eggs, sausage, pancakes and..."

A stern Emma interrupted, "No thanks mister we have a ferry to catch."

"Has the ferry reopened? After the murder most left the island."

"What murder, mister?"

"Can't recall his name, he was a fisherman who lived on the Dauphin Island. Shot two times in the back. There were no witnesses."

"What do you think happened?"

"The NWC isn't saying. My guess is the poor fellow was a resister."

"Anyone else involved?"

"Nope, they tried to locate his wife but she took off. You never mentioned who you were looking for?"

Emma wasn't expecting the nudging by the Holy Spirit.

"Our friends live on Dauphin Island, Anthony and Myra Santino."

"How do you know this couple? Are they your kin folk?"

"Just friends of a friend."

"I'm sorry but the fisherman murdered was Anthony Santino."

"Nooooo!" shrieked Emma, "I don't believe you!"

Turning away, Kurt steered his sister toward the beach.

"We gotta go!" pleaded her bewildered brother.

Across the street, a beach trolley was giving free rides around the city. After jumping on the steps of the trolley Emma glanced back. The stranger was gone. 1

She could hear her little friend crying in her bedroom.

"Jessie, would you like to share some soup with us?"

The worried teenager sat down on the couch.

"Hanna, why is Ruth crying?"

"Our neighborhood was bombed by terrorists yesterday. We heard about it through the underground. Several of Ruth's friends were killed."

"I'm so sorry."

"Jessie, it's been five months since you arrived at our home; the day the stings began. Isn't it strange none of us have ever been stung?"

"I've asked God to protect us. I pray every day no evil will touch us."

A thankful Hanna softly replied, "You're so kind."

A sober Judah muttered, "Without a promise to end this hideous judgment, we would be without hope."

"You mean the promise of the Messiah to come back and restore the kingdom of Israel?"

"Why yes, Jessie. At the end of days our Messiah will rule a physical kingdom that will bless all the people of the earth." 2

"One like the Lamb of God!" praised the slender teenager.

The Lentz's knew their houseguest was more than just an American. There was no doubt this young lady, whom they had come to love and respect, was a daughter of Israel. Her keen interest in Judaism and its relationship to Christianity was obvious.

"Judah, why do Muslims hate the Jewish people so much? And what about these terrorists threatening the world before Kayin took control? I don't get Islam. Where did this religion come from?"

"In the seventh century a merchant named Muhammad created Islam. His tribe, who lived in the desert, worshipped over three hundred pagan deities. From these deities, Muhammad picked Allah to be the only true God. Allah's wife was Allet. These pagan deities represent the worship of the sun and the moon."

"How did he do that?"

"He mixed the traditions of tribal deities with stories from the Bible. Muhammad had false visions. Combining his visions and these stories together, he created the Koran. Muslims believe Muhammad was the greatest prophet ever."

"So how does the Koran differ from the Old Testament?"

"The Messiah will come through Isaac, the son of Abraham and Sarah."

"Yes, salvation is of the Jews."

"Muhammad prophesied the Messiah would come through Ishmael, the son of Hagar, the handmaiden of Abraham."

"That can't be. How can Muhammad be a true prophet if he teaches something so false?"

A solemn Judah glanced at Hanna.

"At first, Muhammad was friendly toward the Jews. When they rejected his teachings they became an enemy of Islam. You see, Arabs are descendants of Ishmael; not Isaac. This is why Muslims hate Israel."

"My aunt taught me about Babylon. Nimrod and Semiramis were the king and queen of Babylon. They were also worshiped as the sun and moon gods. Does this have anything to do with Islam?"

"Absolutely, the Babylonians worshiped Semiramis as the queen of heaven. She believed her son Tammaz would be the future Messiah. Did you know there were Jews living during the time of Jeremiah that were rebuked for burning incense to Semiramis? They were pouring out drink offerings to the queen of heaven for material blessings." [3]

"What happened to them?"

"God refused to listen to any of them." 4

"What an evil counterfeit! Remember when the Temple was rebuilt. The wall separating it from the Al-Aqsa Mosque was so massive. Muslims want control of the Temple Mount, don't they?"

"Peace is the last thing they desire. Muslims won't rest until the flag of the crescent moon and star flies above Mount Zion."

"Jessie, how long have you been a Christian?"

"Hanna, I got saved just after the worldwide blackout."

"Do you believe a resurrection took place that day?"

The tall brunette had prayed for this opportunity ever since she arrived.

"Feel free to share, Jessie. We have other Christian friends we love very much."

"His glory was the sign of His coming. Jesus sent forth His angels to gather His elect to heaven."

"What about the people left behind?"

"The mystery of God will be completed soon. 5 The Lord is going to redeem a remnant from Israel."

Shaking his head, Judah shared, "Yes, the prophet Isaiah foretold, 'Indeed the Lord has proclaimed to the end of the world: "Say to the daughter of Zion (Israel), 'Surely your salvation is coming; Behold, His reward is with Him, and His work before Him...And they shall call them The Holy People, The Redeemed of the Lord...'" 6

"Is this passage about the Messiah?"

"Yes, our Redeemer is coming to Zion for the salvation of His people. Jessie, as a Christian, do you believe Jesus is the Messiah?"

"I do."

"Does Yeshua speak of His return to Jerusalem in the latter days?"

"Yes, Hanna, but it sounds harsh." Opening her Bible, she read, "'Looking out over the Holy City, He proclaimed, "'O Jerusalem, Jerusalem, the one who kills the prophets and stones those who are sent to her. How often I wanted to gather your children together, as a hen gathers her brood under her wings, but you were not willing. See. Your house is left to you desolate; and assuredly, I say to you, you shall not see Me until the time comes when you say, 'Blessed is He who comes in the name of the Lord.'" 7

"What does this mean?"

"The Messiah will not come back to earth until Israel proclaims,

'Blessed is He who comes in the name of the Lord."

"You mean, 'Barukh haba b'shem Adonai.'"

"Wow, Judah, that sounds so cool in Hebrew?

"When do you think this will happen?"

"Once the times of the Gentiles ends; Yeshua will physically appear on the Day of Atonement."

Judah and Hanna could fill the conviction. Their houseguest was explaining the mystery of God, the salvation of a remnant from Israel.8

He could hear her weeping as he walked to the rear of the trolley.

"Hi, can I help?"

Stepping between the stranger and his sister, Kurt stood his ground.

"We can handle this."

"What is your name?" asked a curious Emma.

"I'm Jake, what's yours?"

"Is your last name Jamison?"

"Who's asking?"

"I'm Emma Abbott, this is my brother Kurt. We are from Bethany. Seems like we have a mutual friend; we're looking for Jessie Hyatt."

"You mean Jessie is here in Gulf Shores?"

"She left us to find her aunt on Dauphin Island. We don't know where she is."

"It's a long story," gushed Kurt. "When Pastor Greg and Jessie drove to the farmhouse..."

"Greg found Jessie?"

"He sure did."

"Did Jessie register?"

Grabbing the redhead by his shoulders Jake pleaded.

"Just answer me; did Jessie take the mark of the beast?"

"Nope! Greg rescued her from agents the same night they found us."

All three kids plopped down on the backseat.

"How long have you been here?"

"Since the second trumpet, Emma, I've prayed with several for salvation. Helped a bunch of overcomers, it's a tough area. Most have registered. Is Greg coming here too?"

Glaring at her brother, Emma replied, "We don't know where he is."

Turning the corner, the bell rang. The trolley was returning to the beach.

"If we've been spotted, agents will be waiting for us at the end of this route. At the next red light, let's boogie. The Holy Spirit led me to a great hiding place. I've got food, water; it's a real blessing."

"How far is it?"

"A couple miles."

SIXTH TRUMPET: RELEASED TO KILL

'So the four angels, who had been prepared for the hour and day and
month and year, were released to kill a third of mankind.
Now the number of the army of the horsemen was two hundred million; I
heard the number of them.'
Revelation 9:15-16

While Emma prepared dinner in the church's kitchen, the two boys
watched from a tiny window in the balcony.

"Whoa this town looks like it's been hit by an F5. You can't miss
the ones with the blank faces."

"The stings sealed that. No one is home anymore."

Stepping away from the window, Jake laid down on his sleeping
bag.

"So how was Jess doing when you first met her?"

"She's a special lady. Emma and Jessie were tight."

"I praise God for her. Did she work with you in rescue?"

"The Lord had other plans. He led her to come here and find her
aunt. She loved talking about you; praying for you. Carlos prayed for
you too. He was a member of the Q. He was like my big brother."

"What do you mean was?"

Choking up, the redhead mumbled back, "The NWC executed
him."

"What about Greg?"

"It's hard to know exactly what happened to him."

"You're not a very good liar, bro."

"He's also with the Lord."

Fighting back the tears, the young Watchman excused himself.

Making her way up the stairs was a grateful Emma. While Kurt lit
a candle, she served their sandwiches in plastic bowls she found in the

church's pantry.

"Where's Jake? Did you tell him..."

"I ain't going to lie. He was already putting the pieces together."

Sitting on the blanket they each prayed for their new friend. Then they heard his deep voice.

"You guys ready to eat?"

After a prayer of thanks, Emma spoke first.

"We miss Greg. He taught us so much about the day of the Lord."

"He was a gift from God. At least for a few hours, he was my pastor."

"As a Watchman, Greg led by example. He didn't make us obey. Now thousands of children are carrying out his legacy. May his death never be in vain, the underground misses him."

From candlelight one could see the dark circles under her eyes.

"So, Emma, what was it like hanging out with Jessie?"

"I guess you could say her love was unconditional. She was never threatened by my weaknesses or my pain. She wouldn't let the sins of my past affect our friendship. That meant a lot."

The sandwiches went fast.

"Jake, you got any ideas where Jessie could be hiding?"

"No clue, Kurt. Didn't you say she has an aunt living on Dolphin Island? Funny, I don't remember Jess ever mentioning her."

"We have her aunt's number. Does this church have a phone?"

"Bro, the NWC has hacked every church in this town. If we use the phone, we could be receiving a visit. Besides I doubt if Jess is hiding on the island. It's deserted. Police found a dead resister in his backyard. He was Italian. Patino, Terino, something like that?"

Emma gave her brother a reassuring glance before sharing.

"Jake, we just found out who was murdered."

"Let me guess. Is that why you were crying on the trolley?"

"Afraid so."

"If we're going to work together in search and rescue we have to be honest. Trying to protect me doesn't help. Sooner or later you're going to have to tell me everything."

"You mean you want to join the Q Squad?"

"For the glory of God, Kurt."

"I know Greg and Carlos would approve. Bro, it's a done deal."

"So, Emma, who was the dude murdered on the island?"

"It was Anthony Santino, Jessie's uncle."

Standing to his feet a worried Jake started pacing.

"Am I missing something here?" confessed a perplexed Kurt.

"You tell him, Jake."

"Kurt, what would be the quickest way to pick up Jessie's trail?"

"I'd begin by visiting the Santino's."

"So what happened if Jess was visiting her aunt when her uncle was murdered?"

"You tell me."

"If they were witnesses, the assassin could be tracking them."

"Then what are we waiting for?"

"Bro, I deserted Greg because I thought Jessie had taken the mark of the beast. Just ran out the front door of his house. Didn't even bother to tell him where I was going. I never saw him again. I have no idea the pain I caused him that morning."

"We know," Emma gently replied. "Greg shared with us how it all went down. God used it to form the Q Squad. All things work together for good, huh, Jake."

"Hold up!" blurted her little brother. "That's in the past, guys, what about now? What if Jessie needs our help? I'm not willing to wait, are you Jake?"

The fight within his carnal nature was raging. God was speaking.

"Yesterday while praying in the Spirit I saw a cave filled with supplies. Then a fishing ship."

"Is this about Jessie?"

"The Holy Spirit is saying she left Gulf Shores. Even so, I still sense she's in trouble. Jess needs discernment. We need to intercede for her."

Their praying lasted two hours. Jake volunteered to keep watch from the sanctuary while Kurt and Emma slept in the balcony. It wasn't long before Jessie's arrest came to mind. Flashing blue lights were covering the front of the Ryan's house. Agents were searching their backyard. Then he saw her terrified face. She was handcuffed beside a NWC squad car.

"Lord, Jess and Greg risked their lives for me that night. I wouldn't be free without their sacrifice. Demons continue to accuse me of abandoning them. I now know that's a lie. You brought me to Gulf Shores for a reason. Tonight, I'm in Your perfect will. I thank You for sending Emma and Kurt. May You raise up other Watchmen like Greg and Carlos who gave their lives so others can be saved."

The ordeal of the past five months was beyond description. Most believed they would never survive. More and more were begging to die. Then came the jubilant news; the reign of terror by the two Witnesses was over. Worldwide celebrations were already underway.

On the shore of the great river Euphrates stood an army of two hundred million demons. 1

"Is it time?" inquired the spirit of Fear.

Death hissed back, "After the sixth trumpet sounds, the second woe will commence." 2

"Where are the four angels bound to kill one third of mankind?"3

"I see Belial in the north, Beelzebub in the south, Leviathan in the west, and Cerberus in the east. They can't do anything until the angel of the sixth trumpet releases them. Once the voice from the four horns of the golden altar gives the order, the three plagues will begin." 4

The small city bordering the Euphrates was a perfect setting. As mankind summoned the courage to persevere, the two Witnesses met with a crowd huddled by the river.

"Listen!" cried the taller Witness. "Those who can still choose to believe in Jesus Christ; today is your day of salvation. For the wicked who deny the Lord, the wrath of God has come upon you. 5 Prepare for the sounding of the sixth trumpet. 6 When the four angels bound at the great river Euphrates are released, one third of mankind will die!" 7

Judah and Hanna smiled as the two girls took turns cutting each other's hair. Jessie's love for God was a much-needed blessing to their household; especially for Ruth.

"Come everyone," called Hanna. "Cookies and hot tea are waiting for you in the living room."

Judah sat quietly in his brown leather chair studying.

"Jessie, your notes on the Messiah are very insightful; especially the passages predicting a Deliverer coming to Jerusalem."

"It was my aunt who taught me about a Deliverer coming from heaven and turning away ungodliness from Jacob. Try Romans 11:25-27; its underlined in yellow."

"This has Israel being saved after the fullness of the Gentiles ends."

"Judah, the persecution of Israel by the Gentiles will end between the sounding of the sixth and seventh trumpets. Remember when we studied the mystery of God? This mystery is when the Messiah visits Israel and saves those who believe in Him."

"We'd love to hear it again," smiled Hanna.

Reaching for her Bible, Jessie read, "'But in the days of the sounding of the seventh angel, when he is about to sound, the mystery of God would be finished, as he declared to His servants the prophets.'" 8

"So where are we now?"

"The two Witnesses are saying the sounding of the sixth trumpet is near. This will be the worst of the trumpet judgments."

"Worse than the stings?" asked a stunned Ruth.

"The scriptures say one third of the world will die by fire."

"How long will this judgment last?"

Before Jessie could answer, Judah asked, "Can you show us in the New Testament when a Deliverer comes?"

"In Revelation 10:1-7, an angel or Holy One descends in a cloud with a rainbow on His head. His face is like the sun; his feet like fire. 9 He comes from heaven to earth between the sounding of the sixth and seventh trumpets."

"That's an interesting description. The angel in Ezekiel 1:24-28 also has the appearance of a man. His likeness was of the glory of the Lord."

A keyed up Jessie replied, "The messenger in Revelation 10:1 is holding a small book in His hand. In Revelation 5:9 it says only the Lamb of God can open the seals of the large scroll. Some think only Yeshua can open the small book."

"So what's inside the small book?"

"Sweetness and bitterness. The sweetness stands for the salvation of Israel, the mystery of God. Jews who haven't worshipped the Beast will see Yeshua face to face and believe in Him as their Lord. Praise God, Yeshua is going to take back the authority Satan received in the garden."

"And the bitterness?"

"Hanna, the bitterness is God's final wrath being poured out on this earth."

An animated Judah reflected, "Hosea foretold of the Lord roaring like a lion as His sons come to Him. 10 The messenger in Revelation 10:3 also roars like a lion."

"Yeshua is coming for the salvation of His people. Hosea foretold the Lord will revive us after two days, and on the third day He will raise us up." 11

"Jessie, have you ever compared the Old Covenant with the New Covenant? In the Book of Exodus, God instructed Moses to have the people consecrate themselves for two days. On the third day God gave the people the Old Covenant." 12

"You mean the New Covenant parallels the Old Covenant when it comes to the salvation of Israel?"

"Jessie, if Yeshua comes for His first fruits on the day after the seventieth week, do you think it's possible He could come for the salvation of our people two days later?"

"Nothing is impossible for the Alpha and Omega!"

Looking at his wife, then his daughter, Judah smiled.

"Jessie, I know Hashem has sent you to us. We have asked you many questions about your faith. God has given you the ability to share the gospel with us with such sincerity. Such kindness can only come from above. We want to thank you with all of our hearts."

The command could be heard throughout heaven. A voice from the four horns of the golden altar cried out to the angel who blew the sixth trumpet.

"Release the four angels bound at the great river Euphrates." 13

Another angel warned, "'For their power is in their mouth and in their tails, for their tails are like serpents, having heads, and with them they do harm.' 14 Beware inhabitants of the earth, the fire coming from their mouths will kill...'" 15

The monthly Bible Forum was about to begin. The free breakfast buffet was wiped clean. Most didn't even bring their Bibles anymore. With Pastor Louis Cooper spearheading a new tolerance provision, the makeup of the Bethany Ministers Association was changing. Stepping up the new Chairman turned on the microphone.

"Let's begin this morning by having our new members introduce themselves. Yes, to my left."

"My name is Adam Clark. I am an elder from the Church of Jesus Christ of Ladder Day Saints located on Rivercrest."

"God bless you, Adam," affirmed Louis.

"I'm Rebecca Grim. I minister at the Unitarian Fellowship on Hillsbough."

The experienced preacher could hear the murmuring. Nevertheless, Louis Cooper was determined to follow through with the ultimate goal of his Committee.

"Welcome, Rebecca. For those of you who have never met Ms. Grimm, God originally brought her to Bethany as a spokeswoman for the World Faith Movement. Our Committee is thrilled to have her as our first female member."

Immediately several hands shot up.

"Yes, I see another familiar face near the back."

"I'm father Andrew from Our Lady Redeemer Catholic Church."

"Why, of course. Father Andrew was also a representative for the WFM. As a former speaker at our Bible Forum, it's an honor to have..."

The Chairman froze. At first, he didn't recognize the crumpled suit and his disheveled hair. Scuffling toward the dove shaped podium, this preacher was in no hurry. He wasn't even trying to hide his anger.

"Tell us, Louis, whatever did happen to the World Faith Movement? Funny how easy things can come and go these days?"

"I'm sorry, John, but you're in no shape to..."

"You're so right; I'm in no shape to do much of anything. I certainly did my share of deceiving. I just never thought the BMA would ever buy into the ecumenical fairy tale."

"Pastor Ryals, we all believe..."

"That's what I'd like to know?" challenged the former Chairman. "As members, you certainly must believe in the sin nature of man, the virgin birth, the resurrection of God's only Son, and His second coming. And let's not forget eternal damnation."

"The BMA is about fostering love, not arguing doctrine."

"Louis, what is the best way to foster love. Is that what your tolerance provision is all about; an agenda accepting all faiths? Or maybe your Committee could explain the recognition of ministers denying the divinity of Jesus? Please share with us, elder Clark, what do Mormons believe about the baby Jesus?"

The elder calmly replied, "Jesus had a human father and mother. His birth was no different than my own son. He is the first begotten of Elohim, His glorified father in the flesh. The Christ wasn't divine while he was on earth. He became God after His resurrection."

"Does anyone get a witness? Elder Clark, if this is true then why did the apostle John write, 'Therefore the Jews sought all the more to kill Him, because He not only broke the Sabbath, but also said that God was His Father, making Himself equal with God.'" [16]

"Please stop this, John!" seethed the irate Chairman.

"How about it, Ms. Grimm, do you believe Jesus was the Lamb of God who took away the sins of the world by the shedding of His blood on the cross?" [17]

"Of course not! Unitarians don't believe His blood has any special powers."

"Imagine that? So everyone gets a free pass from the lake of fire?" [18]

"Everyone is going to heaven, they just don't know it. Eternal damnation is an evil weapon used by the intolerant to control. There is nothing but light after death."

"Ms. Grimm, under the inspiration of the Holy Spirit Peter taught, 'Nor is there salvation in any other, for there is no other name under heaven given among men by which we must be saved.' [19] Now I ask you, saved from what?"

"You're wrong if you're implying salvation is only for Christians. We are all children of God. God loves everyone, not just those who believe in Christ."

"What do you say, Louis, isn't it true the agenda you're selling is a lie from the pit of hell?"

"Look who's judging now. I heard your board fired you for teaching heresy. You coming here to vent your bitterness is no surprise to me."

"What else have you heard Louis?"

"Please, Pastor Cooper," challenged a retired evangelist. "Pastor Ryals has helped so many of us. He certainly deserves to be heard."

At first, he had no intention of yielding to such a strong leader. Yet facing such a clear majority he had no other choice. Nodding, the Assembly of God minister took a seat with his Committee. The former pastor of the most prominent congregation in Bethany was coming with a warning. His agony was easy to see. Picking up the microphone he just stared.

"Walking here all I could think about was the coming of the Lord. Jesus said no one knows the day or hour of the coming of the Son of Man. At His coming the saved were taken up; the unsaved left for God's wrath. Just like Noah and Lot. Funny, even now most of you are still in denial. How many saw Jesus coming in the glory of His Father on October 3rd?"

Before he could utter another word, several pastors bid goodbye.

"My exhortation this morning concerns the wrath of God."

"Pastor Ryals, why would a loving God pour out His wrath on a people He created?"

As soon as the Mormon elder spoke, John's mind was bombarded with confusion.

Another minister coolly reflected, "You're asking what God requires of us. This type of teaching isn't popular in today's society. Everyone must be allowed to supply their own convictions. The path for spiritual truth is far greater than the goal of ever acquiring it."

"None of us would be here if we didn't love God!" laughed father Andrew. "You don't know what God will do. He can do anything He wants."

"The elect were delivered out of the Great Tribulation by their Blessed Hope. On the same day, God set our earth on fire. Deliverance then wrath; on the same day." [20]

"John, the good people of Bethany deserve more than a hell fire and brimstone tirade. Such spiritual arrogance doesn't help anyone."

"What do you suggest, Andy, maybe an escape hatch like purgatory? Actually, my arrogance has deceived more than I care to think about. Tragically, Jesus warned believers to watch and not be deceived." [21]

"The elect can never be deceived!" scoffed a Presbyterian pastor. "Jesus said, 'For false Christs and false prophets will rise and show great signs and wonders to deceive, if possible, even the elect.' [22] This verse clearly teaches it's not possible for the elect to be deceived."

"Matthew 24:24 isn't saying believers can't be deceived. This passage is about how deceptive the signs from the false prophets are. During the Great Tribulation a great multitude of Christians were deceived."

"Deceived by whom?"

"I'm only going to give it to you one time, so listen up."

Remarkably, the murmuring dwindled to a mere whisper.

"For those who haven't registered or worshipped Kayin, you still can be saved. I implore you..."

"Thank you," interrupted an energized Pastor Cooper, "your time is up! In order not to end on such a depressing note allow me to read a wonderful promise from Jesus. 'He who overcomes shall be clothed in white garments, and I will not blot his name from the Book of Life; but I will confess his name before My Father and before His angels.'[23]

"This promise is for believers who got the victory over the Beast in Revelation 7:14 and 15:2. The saints overcome by the Beast, Revelation 13:7, their names blotted out for eternity!"

The Presbyterian pastor stood and challenged, "This is comical! My God doesn't own an eraser. Apostasy is only for professing believers who depart from the faith."

"Please enlighten me, Reverend," countered John. "Exactly what is a professing believer? Are they part of the Church?"

"Professing believers are those who were never saved."

"Church in the Greek is *ekklesia*. [24] It means 'called out ones'. The body of Christ is the ekklesia. Ekklesia never refers to unbelievers. Tell me, how can a professing believer sever a relationship he never had? How can an unsaved person deny a faith he never believed in? Only a true believer can fall away and become an apostate." [25]

"I suggest you examine yourself to see if you're really saved?"

"God gave a sober warning to any believer who adds or takes away from the words of The Revelation of Jesus Christ. Now I ask you, who is written in the Book of Life?"

"Only believers are."

"Yes, Louis, and any believer who adds or takes away from this prophecy will have their part in the Book of Life and the holy city, the New Jerusalem, taken away." [26]

An irate Episcopalian priest asked to speak.

"The Bible teaches Christians, Muslims, and Jews, are all from the seed of Abraham. Your condemnation of other faiths only divides. After all, no matter how we may disagree on biblical doctrine, we are all part of the family of God."

"You have anything more to say John?"

"It's over Mr. Chairman. I'll see you at the great white throne. That's where Jesus judges the works of those not written in the Book of Life before casting them into the lake of fire. 27 Oh excuse me, how can I be so careless. I forgot, most of you don't believe in such mythology."

Not waiting for a response the distraught pastor walked out the rear entrance.

WITH GOD ALL THINGS ARE POSSIBLE

'...With men it is impossible, but not with God;
for with God all things are possible.'
Mark 10:27

The plague of the sixth trumpet lasted a year. 1 In the first four months over a billion people died. Worst hit were third world countries. For many, there was nowhere to hide from the immense flames. In India, most sought protection by petitioning their many gods. To somehow stop this curse, the people of Cuba held prayer vigils. As children carried the statue of the blessed virgin through the burning streets, parishioners would bow and confess their sins to the queen of heaven. Some were seen crawling on broken glass trying to atone for their sins.

Amidst resignations, mental breakdowns, and deaths, Channel 6's production team was practically decimated. The skeleton crew was barely able to produce live specials anymore A lethargic pessimism had replaced the energy of the popular news show. From the soundman to the cameraman, hardly anyone was reacting. The well-known News Anchor was taking medication to settle her nerves. She was just a shell of what she used to be. In the past year Natalie Rene Roberts lost her parents, her two sisters, and most of her friends. Her job, once the joy of her life, was now a daily drudgery of pain. No nation was immune, not even the United States, the greatest super power the world had ever known.

From across the street two agents watched as he left.

"Our informer was right. Their flat is hidden above the law office."

"Do you want me to follow Lentz?"

"Let him go, he'll be back. If Judah does meet with Glazer, it won't be long before Aaron shows up for his daughter. It's worth the wait."

Hanna and the girls finished their prayer time with a song.

"Mama, shouldn't Papa be back by now?"

"He'll be home soon."

Jessie smiled while quietly reflecting, "He is out helping others; his heart has changed."

"Tell us about the suffering of your people?"

"What do you mean, Hanna?"

"Jess," smiled an innocent Ruth, "we believe you're a daughter of Zion. Right, Mama?"

"When you first slipped through our bookcase, I knew there was something special about you. Judah noticed it too; especially when you shared the gospel with us."

"Hanna I want you to know..."

"When God brought you to us; we were struggling. Gradually, many of our questions had answers; answers from the lips of a Christian. Ruth's prayers were changing too. She prayed with more of a purpose. Many of her fears disappeared. My child was changing from someone who knew about God, to someone being led by God."

"Mama, I have something I need to share with you."

"I know sweet one; I've also become a believer in Yeshua."

"Mama, did you know the first Christians were Jewish?"

"You're Jewish, aren't you, Jessie?"

"Yes, Hanna, I am."

"So where are your parents now?"

"My mother's maiden name is Sarah Kaufman. After she got married she changed her name to Shelby Hyatt. She lives in Bethany, a small city in Alabama."

"So why did you come to Jerusalem?"

"To find my daddy, my Aunt Myra helped me get here. She is the older sister of my mother, Shelby."

"Where is your father?"

"I can't say at this time. Someday I will be able to share everything with you."

"What's most important is the Lord sent you. Your love for Yeshua is real."

His familiar knock produced an immediate hush.

"Papa!" beamed a wide-eyed Ruth.

With Jessie's help, Hanna unlocked the secret bookcase.

"Papa, we have lots to share with you, don't we Mama?"

"Let me guess; you both believe in Yeshua as your Savior? Hanna, it took me a while too. I couldn't deny the change in Ruth. Our God is a miracle worker. I prayed and received the Holy Spirit yesterday."

"So we're walking miracles, aren't we, Papa?"

Hugging his only child, Judah asked, "What do you think Jessie?"

"Yes, Ruth, salvation through Yeshua is truly a miracle."

The seizure began when she woke up. At first, Reenie didn't know what to think. Just calling out for Jesus was a struggle. From her bed, she let out a blood-curdling scream. Sprinting up the stairs, Bret began to rebuke the devil in Jesus' name. Opening the bedroom door, he found her shaking uncontrollably on the floor.

"Reenie, Reenie! Where are you hurting?"

Desperately she tried to move her lips.

"Has this ever happened to you before?"

She shook her head no.

For thirty minutes the new convert prayed for her healing. Her blood pressure was dropping. Soon, she would be collapsing into a coma.

Clenching his fists he pleaded, "Lord, I have prayed all I can. If this is from Satan then why won't You help us? What am I supposed to do?"

The silence was overwhelming. Hearing from the Holy Spirit was new territory for Bret. Grabbing his jacket he bent over and gently kissed her forehead.

"I'm going for help, Reenie. May the Lord protect you while I'm gone."

In his mind he heard, "Take her to the hospital."

"Your Word says believers shall lay hands on the sick and they shall recover." 2

"Take her to the hospital."

"That's suicide! They'll notify the NWC. Ask me anything other than that."

"Take her to the hospital."

Stripping a blanket off the bed he wrapped her lifeless body. The ten-block journey to the ER was excruciating. Not one car stopped to help. His arms were on fire when he arrived. Her lips were blue as he staggered in. The receptionist made the call.

"C'mon, girls, we've got a comatose on our hands."

As the nurses placed her on a gurney, Bret collapsed in the hallway. Reenie Ann Tucker had lost consciousness. This was the end. She had fought with all of her heart. Her family never understood her decision to become a resister. Her friends turned against her, and even now, a demon-possessed sniper was trying to kill her. Bret wasn't even trying to figure out why. The person God used to help him find salvation couldn't even speak. She couldn't defend herself. He never felt so helpless.

"Doctor, she has no ID... He could be her brother... I will ask."

From the hallway the receptionist called out. There was no reply.

The teenager in room 1-C was not responding.

"That's all we can do. We'll lose her if her vitals keep dropping."

A frustrated nurse shouted, "Doctor, if she just registered we would have her medical history. What's the big deal; it only takes a minute."

While massaging his eyes he shared, "I'll have to report her."

"Why can't we wait until she gets better?"

"You know the rules; I could lose my license. Besides, by calling the NWC we are actually helping her get back with her family."

It wasn't long before two agents were knocking on his office door.

"Doc, this patient may be Reenie Ann Tucker. She knows the whereabouts of Anthony Bret Santino. He is six foot, has black hair, brown eyes, and weighs a hundred and seventy-five pounds. Both are wanted for murder."

"The man who brought her in fits your description."

"How is Tucker doing?"

"Not good. Her chances of living are fifty-fifty."

The angel at the foot of her bed was dressed in pure bright linen with a golden band fastened around its chest. 3

"Bret, is that you?" she faintly whimpered.

"Hello, Reenie."

Squinting, she tried to focus.

"Who are you?"

"By now, you must know Satan is vying for your soul."

"You don't say?"

"I have come to share a glorious truth concerning your future."

"What future? No one understands what I've suffered."

Slithering down the hallway Fear was joined by Lying and Death.

"She's got company."

"Why wait?" pressed Lying. "Let's have some fun."

"Enough!" scolded Fear. "Master is sending his own messenger."

After explaining her mission, the angel waited for an answer.

"What you're asking me to do is impossible."

"'With God all things are possible.'" 4

"Why do I have to sacrifice everything dear to me?" 5

The demons hissed as the glass door opened. Dressed in tight leather pants and a black jacket, she slipped by the receptionist unnoticed.

A nurse was taking her pulse when she opened her eyes.

"Honey, you've just come out of a coma. What's your name?"

"Reenie."

"Can I get you anything?"

"My throat is really sore; maybe a cold soda?"

"I can't leave until your doctor arrives. Oh, it'll only take a second."

"Can't your questioning wait?"

"Sorry, Doc, not if this is Reenie Ann Tucker."

"She isn't talking with anyone. Come see for yourself."

Sauntering with a deliberate stride and stoic face, she could already sense interference. Joining a grieving family entering the emergency room, Death Angel veered off and started her search.

"How exciting, the girl in 1-C just came out of a coma."

"You better get your tail back there," rebuked the head nurse.

Moving through the double doors the doctor yelled, "Nurse, why aren't you with your patient?"

The agents hastily ordered everyone to stand aside.

Easing the door open, Cassandra smiled. Her victim was asleep. After locking the door, the assassin attached a silencer to her Glock. Opening the window she carefully placed one foot out into the garden.

"Tucker, I never believed what my Master said about your future.

It ain't happening. You care too much about yourself to serve God."

The three shots hardly made a sound.

After the nurse unlocked Reenie's door, the agents rushed in.

The first agent checked the footprints in the garden.

Ripping the sheets off her bed, his partner cursed, "Six stinking pillows."

WHEREVER THE CARCASS IS

'For wherever the carcass is,
there the eagles will be gathered together.'
Matthew 24.28

Meeting in an abandoned bomb shelter his officers were on edge. Their Commander was late. This was so unlike him. Twenty minutes away their respected leader was concluding business.

"Barging into his office his assistant blurted out, "Matthias, we think we have the driver who smuggled your daughter into Jerusalem!"

"Is he registered?"

"Affirmative."

"He only wants to blackmail me with lies about my daughter? Forget it. My daughter is dead."

"He could have some valuable information. You should see him."

"I'm already late. Two minutes, that's all."

Two soldiers ushered him in.

"My name is Aaron Glazer."

"I know. I'm Bela. Did you order these soldiers to kidnap me?"

"It was for your own protection."

"Why do I need your protection?"

"I just want some information, that's all. Bela, have you ever smuggled two American women into Jerusalem."

"I have told no one about these women."

"Then how did we find you? The NWC will execute you if they found out."

"Why threaten me?"

"Do you really think I'm your enemy, Bela?"

With his hands shaking, the taxi driver changed his mind.

"Two women approached me at Haifa during the Wormwood infection. They entered the harbor aboard an American ship. They were searching for Aaron Glazer. I drove them into Jerusalem that day."

"Who are they?"

"I know they are unregistered. The older woman never identified herself. She said the teenager traveling with her was your daughter."

"Guards get this liar out of my sight!"

"I'm telling you the truth. The girl's name was Johanna Esther Glazer."

"For years my enemies have used this lie. Who sent you?"

"The older woman gave me an idiom to use if I ever met you."

"Let's hear it."

'For wherever the carcass is, there the eagles will be gathered together.'" 1

Turning away he whispered, "Honey, what have you done!"

The remnant cheered for Rabbi Hillel.

"My brothers, we have all seen what our Lord has done by drawing us safely to this divine haven. For almost forty-two months, those who don't have the seal of God have experienced the most horrendous plaques ever suffered. They openly worship the image of Kayin. They are committed to the demonic idols of greed and lust. Even so, we must continue to pray for the Jewish remnant that will be saved when the fullness of the Gentiles is completed."

There was no way to describe their anticipation.

"Servants of God, on Yom Kippur, Kayin will have the two Witnesses killed. This same day, our Redeemer will gather us from this haven in the wilderness."

Their praises unto the Lord were electrifying.

"Micah foretold of the last days, 'I will surely assemble all of you, O Jacob, I will surely gather the remnant of Israel; I will put them together like sheep of the fold...The one who breaks open will come up before them; They will break out, pass through the gate, and go out by it; their king will pass before them, with the Lord at their head.'" 2

Yeshua is Lord echoed through the night air.

"We have prayed for the day when our Lord will lead us. For almost two years, we have interceded for the Holy Spirit to save the souls of our people. Now the time has come for us to prepare for our trip to Jerusalem. As we walk, believers hiding in the Judean hills shall join our procession. Hosea foretold, 'I will return again to My place till they acknowledge their offense. Then they will seek My face; in their affliction they will earnestly seek Me.' 3 Three days after the seventieth week ends, Yeshua will lead His remnant into the Holy City. He will fulfill the mystery of God by bringing salvation to the children of Israel." 4

The twelve tribes bowed and worshipped Yeshua.

"The day after the salvation of Israel, Yeshua will raise the two Witnesses from the dead. 5 Miraculously; these men of God will ascend into heaven in the sight of their enemies. Yes, my brothers, mankind will soon see this miracle."

"Rabbi, isn't the Feast of Tabernacles the next day?"

"Yes, my son, the Feast of Tabernacles will begin five days after Yom Kippur. During this Feast Yeshua will lead us to Mount Moriah. Then the seventh trumpet will sound and our Lord will reclaim the authority of this world back from Satan."

The roar of approval was deafening.

"The next day, the Lamb of God will lead us across the Kidron Valley, up to the Mount of Olives. Zechariah prophesied His feet will stand upon the Mount of Olives. Then Yeshua will split this mountain forming a large valley. 6 A remnant will flee through this valley to Azal. 7 The Lord is going to protect us from the seven bowl judgments. Let us prepare spiritually, physically, and emotionally, to meet our Messiah. For surely He will perform what His Word has spoken."

Ruth and Jessie were washing dishes while Judah and Hanna met in their room.

"There isn't much time. I've just received a coded message from the underground. We might have to find another place to hide."

"You mean leave right now?"

"No, I first have to meet with our contact this morning."

"Are the Hilkiah's in trouble?"

"I don't know. Just pack our essentials. You and the girls need be ready to leave when I return."

Ruth was asleep as the shops in the city were opening up for business. He knew this might be the last time he would ever see his wife and daughter again.

"I love you Hanna. If I don't return in two hours, you must leave. The Holy Spirit will tell you where to hide."

After securing the locks, she leaned up against the bookcase and sobbed.

The line stretched around the block. Some had come for bread, others for clean water. His contact was waiting near the back. Judah greeted him with a nervous smile.

"May the Lord bless you for helping us."

"Judah, the NWC arrested Eleazar Hilkiah last week. They threatened to kill his sister's family if he didn't reveal your hiding place. He caved in. The only reason they haven't arrested you is because of the Glazer girl."

"What are you talking about?"

"Aaron Glazer's daughter, Johanna, gents have been waiting for Matthias to contact her. Better yet, they're hoping she'll visit him. Your only chance of escape is to use her as a decoy. I suggest you split up and get outside the city right away."

His walk home seemed so surreal. Had they really sheltered the daughter of the highest-ranking officer in the Israeli underground? And why hadn't Jessie confided in them? And how could his closest friend betray them?

"We can't leave without Papa?"

"Ruth, we have no other choice. Jessie, are you ready?"

Forming a circle, they joined hands. Petitioning the Holy Spirit one last time before departing, they heard a familiar knock. After securing the locks, they anxiously surrounded him.

"Well, everybody, I believe it's time we move to another flat."

"How come, Papa?"

Sitting down in his favorite chair, Hanna and Ruth joined him on each side.

"Jessie, I still remember the day you arrived. The Lord sent a daughter of Israel to share the gospel with us. We would like to thank you for your obedience. Not many would have had the faith to travel from America to Jerusalem."

"Glory to God, Judah, I had no other choice."

"We always have choices. Is there anything else you want to share?"

"What do you mean?"

"Our dear friend Eleazar Hilkiah has been blackmailed by the NWC. He told them our hiding place. Agents are watching us right now."

"Why haven't they arrested us like the Hilkiah's?"

"Our contact said it was because of you."

It was a while before she could look at them.

"I came to Jerusalem to find my father. He left my mother when I was a baby. He's a leader in the Israeli underground. My Aunt Myra told me to never reveal my true identity. It was for your protection; as well as mine. My name is Johanna Esther Glazer. My father is Aaron Glazer."

Under her breath, Hanna gasped, "Matthias!"

"Agents are waiting to trap your father. We don't have much time. We must split up."

"Judah, I'm so sorry."

"The Holy Spirit has shown me your destiny. Soon you'll be a shining light for those in darkness. Johanna, will you take Ruth with you?"

"Why would you want me to do that?"

"Our daughter wants to be used for the salvation of our people."

"Is this true Ruth?"

Through her tears she uttered, "God wants me to be a Watchman."

As Hanna hugged Johanna; Judah whispered a final message to his daughter.

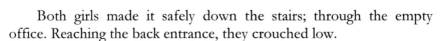

Both girls made it safely down the stairs; through the empty office. Reaching the back entrance, they crouched low.

"Do you see anyone, Johanna?"

"Trust me; they're watching even if we can't see them. When they move, we will make our escape."

Ruth winked and whispered back, "Yeshua will protect us."

The memory was clear as they walked down the stairs. The Lentz's hid in this flat to save their lives. Now, they were leaving to sacrifice their lives. Stepping outside, they covered their eyes from the bright morning sun. Within seconds they were surrounded.

"You're under arrest Lentz. Where are you hiding Johanna Glazer?"

Judah held Hanna as she quietly interceded.

"Move in!" barked the agent.

They could hear the explosion of the bookcase from the third floor.

"Sir, they must have escaped out the back door of the law office."

"They're heading for the marketplace. Get going. I want Glazer in custody within the hour."

"What about their daughter?"

"Judah, it's your decision. You cooperate with us and your daughter won't be harmed."

A few seconds passed before he shook his head no.

"If that's the way you want it. Eliminate her!"

YOUNG MEN SHALL SEE VISIONS

'And it shall come to pass in the last days, says God,
That I will pour out of My Spirit on all flesh;
Your sons and your daughters shall prophesy,
Your young men shall see visions,
Your old men shall dream dreams.'
Acts 2:17

Their prayer in the end zone of the football field was over.

A concerned Emma asked, "What now, Jake?"

"I just got a burden for someone who looks like Jessie."

"Here in Gulf Shores?"

"A Java house waitress told me about her. She must be in trouble."

"JJ, I once prayed for this same girl. Maybe we could…"

Kurt interrupted, "Hold up, the traffic at the beach is almost zero. Agents on patrol could spot us easily. There are only a few more days until the seventieth week ends. Jake, is this rescue worth it?"

"She isn't going to make it by herself."

"That's a good enough conformation for me."

"C'mon, bro, let's take a quick look downtown."

"Glory to God," shouted the naive redhead, "the Q ain't over yet."

She just stared as Jake gave Kurt a high five.

"What's wrong, Em?"

"Why don't you ask my brother?"

"Well, huh, it seems like my sister has been left behind before. Wasn't the best situation being alone and all; if you know what I mean."

"What girl in her right mind would trust two grimy thugs like you? You're going to need me."

Three hours later, waiting at a red light, Emma sadly reflected, "Well guys, after walking this shoreline twice, trust me, she ain't on the beach."

"My stomach is talking, JJ. How about Ruby's; she'll helps us."

"Go for it. We'll wait for you behind the palm trees at the Marina. If you're not back in thirty minutes we'll meet you at the church."

Dressed in baggy blue jeans and a faded Atlanta Falcons jersey, the teenager loved cruising down the sidewalk for donuts and coffee. He welcomed the opportunity to be normal, if only for a few minutes. The bells on the doorknob of Ruby's Donut Shop sounded great.

Her hands covered with white power she looked up and smiled.

"Where you been, Kurt?"

"God is faithful. Your sidewalk is looking grisly, Ruby."

Throwing him two garbage bags she pointed toward the exit.

"The back looks junky too. People just don't care anymore."

It didn't take long to fill up both bags. Two boxes of donuts were waiting for him on the counter.

"No way, Ruby."

"Share it with your friends. Besides, you're looking a bit skinny. Hey, you see the girl at the back table? She's alone; doesn't have a family."

The NWC was efficient at creating set ups. Walking back he knew the risk.

"Hi, I'm Kurt. What's that you're reading?"

"God's Word."

"Sharper than any two edged sword."

"Are you a Christian, Kurt?"

"A child of the King."

"Are you registered?"

Looking over his shoulder he thought about his answer.

"That's where the rubber meets the road."

"This is so confusing," she painfully confessed.

"Depends who you're listening to. Being a lone ranger during the day of the Lord is a tough road. When was the last time you prayed with another believer?"

"I had a close friend I prayed with. He's gone now. His parents got saved right after the saints were gathered. After Bret's father was killed..."

"You mean the overcomer murdered on Dauphin Island?"

"Anthony Santino was Bret's father."

"How do you know this?"

"Bret and I saw the shooting."

Rising from his seat, the wide-eyed redhead whispered, "I didn't catch your name?"

"Reenie Ann Tucker."

"Reenie, why aren't you in hiding?"

"Why aren't you?"

"A friend of mine named Jake Jamison received a vision this morning of an overcomer who needs help. 1 She has green eyes and dark brown hair. My sister and I have been helping him search the beachfront for her for the past three hours."

Burying her face in her arms, all she could do was cry.

"You're a walking miracle."

"Are you from here, Kurt?"

"Emma and I are from Bethany. We came here searching for Jessie Hyatt."

"Is this the same Jessie who escaped with Bret's mama?"

"Agents are coming!" shouted Ruby.

After the intersection cleared, they burst through the front door.

"Can I help you?"

"Shut up, Ruby!" hollered the agent in charge.

After a quick search both agents met at the backdoor.

"She was talking with a boy. They must have used the alley. Ruby do you know the names..."

"Afraid not."

"We know you're feeding them. We ought to run you in."

Stalling for time, the widow asked, "Tell me, what can you do to an old woman like me?"

His assistant saluted as he entered the bunker.

"Commander, we apprehended the woman who smuggled your daughter into Haifa. Her passport says she is Myra Santino. She is married to an American named Anthony Santino. Her maiden name is Miriam Kaufman. Her sister, Sarah Kaufman, is married to Jon Hyatt. Both changed their names; Miriam became Myra and Sarah became Shelby. We don't know why."

Sitting in a chair facing his desk, she knew her only way to find

Jessie was through her father. The creaking of the office door interrupted her praying.

"Hello, Aaron, it's been a long time."

"Yes, much too long."

"I guess you know why we have come."

"You should have never tried, Miriam."

"It was Johanna's idea. She wants to meet her father."

"Jon and Shelby Hyatt raised our Johanna. Don't you remember; it was your decision?"

"You don't need to remind me. After you were imprisoned, terrorists made two attempts on my life. They even tried to kidnap Johanna. I did what I had to do."

"I have no right to judge you. You did what you thought was best for our baby."

"Aaron; she's not a baby anymore."

"Where did you hide when you arrived?"

"An apartment on the Westside, last year I was making a trip for some water and agents blocked off the area for five days. When I got back, Johanna was gone."

"How did she convince you to come?"

"She's a lot like you; she is willing to sacrifice for the ones she loves."

"I can't believe the Hyatt's approved of this wild scheme?"

"Johanna had no choice; both Jon and Shelby took the mark of the beast."

"What about your husband, doesn't he care about your safety?"

"Listen here, Aaron, you have no right to lecture me like one of your soldiers. My Anthony gave his life so Johanna and I could escape from a NWC sniper."

His remorse was something she had never seen before.

"Miriam, I'm not the person you once married. My zeal isn't motivated by love anymore. 2 My heart is cold. Hate took control of my spirit a long time ago."

"I can relate. The bitterness from losing you and Johanna was devastating. Actually, Anthony joined me in my drinking. No matter what I tried, it became a bondage I was never able to beat, until now. After eighteen years of binge drinking, my insides eaten up, I've found freedom."

"What type of freedom?"

"Yeshua is my great God and Savior!" 3

"I've heard this testimony from those who need a crutch."

"Yeshua can take away your cold heart and give you a heart of love for eternity."

"You denied your faith; not me. Don't you realize how many are depending on me? Shall I reward their trust by becoming a Christian?"

"Your daughter has come to share the gospel. The Holy Spirit even gave her a scripture for you. 'So Christ was offered once to bear the sins of many. To those who eagerly wait for Him He will appear a second time, apart from sin, for salvation.'" 4

"Who is the Christ in this passage?"

"The first time, Yeshua came as the Passover Lamb to bear the sins of mankind. He's coming back a second time for the salvation of our people. Soon He will return to the Mount of Olives."

"Why there?"

"He's going to split the Mount and hide a remnant in Azal." 5

It wasn't hard for her to see through his tough mask. Through the years Matthias had fooled many people. But his stubborn will was fading. Somewhere in Jerusalem a young lady was interceding for the salvation of his soul.

"When is Yeshua going to return?"

"The day Joshua Kayin has the two Witnesses killed."

"When will he do this?"

"This week end. This same day Yeshua will gather His first fruits from the wilderness."

"You can't mean this?"

"God has protected the 144,000 Jews for 1260 days. They are ready to meet their Deliverer on the Day of Atonement."

"I've received surveillance reports of a large number of believers hiding out in the Jordanian desert. They have no weapons, there're harmless. All they do is pray."

"The Lamb of God is going to lead them to the Temple Mount during the Feast of Tabernacles."

"Miriam, if Kayin kills the two Witnesses, then what makes you think he won't kill this remnant as well? If they attempt to follow Yeshua into Jerusalem, they'll never make it alive."

"What's taking so long? Are Jake and your sister in trouble?"

"Naw, they're just being extra careful. Kayin is going to whack the two Witnesses this weekend."

Kurt could hear his whistle coming from the backdoor of the church.

"C'mon, they're here."

The foursome met at the bottom of the stairs.

"We thought we lost you bro, you alright?"

"Everything's cool. Jake and Emma meet Reenie Ann Tucker, the girl in your vision."

Later on, while eating in the church balcony, Reenie was amazed at how comfortable she felt sharing with fellow Watchmen. Experiencing such peace from the Holy Spirit was so special.

"Reenie, the past two years of your life could be used in a manual on spiritual warfare."

"You think so, Kurt?"

A concerned Jake asked, "So, Reenie, when was the last time you saw this sniper?"

"At the Gulf Shores ER."

"Do you think this Death Angel is still tracking you?"

"Probably, I'll leave if you want me too."

"No need for that. God has brought us together to help one another. If He can protect us from Satan, God can certainly protect us from this loser. We're almost there! Next week, we'll be watching on TV the Lord marching into Jerusalem with the 144,000." 6

"You don't know how much it means to me to hear these words. All the demonic attacks I've suffered would be worth it, just to see Jesus take back authority from Satan."

"That's a lock, Reenie!" winked Kurt.

"So how do we prepare for God's final wrath?"

"We better be ready to rock and roll."

"I don't know what Kurt is saying?"

"Most of the time we don't either," teased Emma. "He is saying we need to find a place of protection before the first bowl is poured out."

"What are our chances of making it through alive?"

"Does God love us? We plan on making it together. Would you like to join us?"

"Do I! I even know a place that can protect us from the bowl judgments. It's a cave Bret's father outfitted for protection from the NWC."

"The Q welcomes you, Reenie. Anyone else know about this

cave?"

"I don't think so. Bret helped his father stock it with supplies. He made me memorize the directions. Who knows, Bret might even be waiting for us."

"Hey, JJ, in your vision wasn't Jessie hiding in a cave?"

"Praise the Lord, Em, she sure was."

After two narrow escapes, Johanna and Ruth arrived at the Wailing Wall. Ever since the Holy Temple was defiled, public prayer was strictly prohibited. This was just another reminder of the true intentions of the Man of Sin. Ironically, Muslims continued to worship within the Al-Aqsa Mosque atop Mount Moriah. It was the Jewish people who were being targeted for elimination.

"Johanna, do you have a plan to find your father?"

"We need to locate your parents first."

"My papa has met your father."

"Ruth, are you serious? Why didn't Judah tell me?"

"He said to tell you once we were safe. It was your father who arranged for our hiding place. In return, papa gave money to outfit his soldiers. I can point him out if I see him."

"We'll find my daddy when Yeshua comes to Jerusalem next week."

"While praying I saw your parents worshiping near the Temple. You were between them."

Jessie looked away.

"What's wrong; don't you believe me?"

"That can't be, Ruth. My folks have the mark of the beast."

"I know what I saw. In my vision, your parents were holding their hands high, praising the Lord. Johanna, when is Yeshua coming to visit the Temple Mount?"

"Next week during the Feast of Tabernacles; this sounds crazy but if my daddy could just see Yeshua; I just know he would believe in Him. The problem is the crowds will be huge. That's it; we need to get to the Temple Mount. Let's ask the Holy Spirit to lead your parents, my father, and my aunt Myra, to the Feast of Tabernacles."

STEADFAST TO THE END

'For we have become partakers of Christ if we hold the beginning of our confidence steadfast to the end.'
Hebrews 3:14

Death Angel loved to prepare in the darkness of the early morning. From the roof of a downtown bank, the sniper meticulously assembled her Barrett XM500. This rifle could hit a package a mile away. All she needed was a moment in time. Peering through her scope she smiled.

"C'mon, man of God, it's time to show your sweet face."

Among the forty boats docked in the harbor, the Morning Star provided a perfect hiding place. The small window offered a bird's eye view of the sidewalk lining the beach. Two handguns and a dozen clips of bullets lay on his bunk. An hour passed. His contact was a no show. He wasn't surprised. Bret Santino was a marked man. Many within the resistance wanted nothing to do with the ex-agent or his girlfriend. Some believed her escape from the ER was a NWC decoy.

A panicky Bret prayed, "Cassandra has to be stopped. Lord, if You open the door, I'll take her out."

Donnell Emery's high pitched whistle was an answer to prayer. His contact was light on his feet as he stepped down into the lower cabin.

"Praise God, Bret, you're still with us!"

"Thanks for coming, Donnell, it took courage."

"That's what brothers in the Lord are for."

"You got any good news for me?"

"A Watchman named Jake Jamison is looking after Reenie. They are hiding in a church a couple miles from here. She's safe for now."

"Nobody is safe from Death Angel."

"I had to pray about coming. Angel is capable of squeezing off a shot a block away. You can't leave until resistance pinpoints her location."

"Can you get a message to Reenie?"

"I can try. There are no guarantees. Next week, during the Feast of Tabernacles, an angel will sound the seventh trumpet."

"Donnell, she won't last that long."

"A Watchman drove me here. He can take you both out of the city."

"Let's go."

"Are you sure? Have you asked the Lord?"

"This waiting game is eating me up. I gotta get outta here."

Exiting the boat the two overcomers strode up the breakwater. A strong wind was whipping off the rough waves as the sun edged above the horizon. Reaching the Marina entrance Donnell looked anxious.

"He left. Once spotted by the NWC, our drivers are instructed never to return. We gotta go back."

"If you know Reenie is alive, so does Cassandra. Let's find her."

"Walking out in the open is way too dangerous, Bret."

"I'm willing to risk it."

"Why is this little lady so special?"

"She led me to the Lord."

"Oh yeah, it can't get any better than that."

"Commander, we have news about your daughter. She has been hiding with one of our underground families for over a year. It's a delicate situation. NWC agents are tracking her right now. They're hoping she'll contact you."

"Who was protecting my daughter?"

"Judah Lentz. He and his wife have been arrested. He may be an informer."

"Judah would never cooperate. What about his daughter?"

"She escaped with Johanna."

"My ex-wife and daughter have become Christians. Who knows, maybe Johanna converted Judah's family. If this is true, then let their precious Jesus protect them."

Deep down he knew he was wrong. His survival instinct was now in control. Over the years his lust for revenge was far more important than his convictions, his friends, even his own flesh and blood. Aaron Phinehas Glazer couldn't afford to allow anything to deter him from his mission; not even the truth from his only daughter.

As everyone slept, Jake watched the sun reflect off the waves. He could hear the beeping of their two-way radio. Entering the kitchen he heard a wrap-up of the local news.

"Tragically our area has suffered another suicide. This young man died early this morning. A former agent with the NWC, Anthony Bret Santino was found dead on beach front property near..."

Pounding the kitchen counter, Jake cried, "No, not Bret, not now!"

"This wasn't God's will," spewed Doubt. "You all could have been in the Santino's cave by now. If you had obeyed the Lord Bret would still be alive. Reenie is going to hate you."

After washing their face and hands in the church baptistery, both girls were playfully chatting as they entered the kitchen.

An excited Reenie asked, "Any news on the two Witnesses?"

Sitting on the floor, his back against the counter, he turned off the radio.

"Not yet," he sadly replied.

"Guess what, JJ? I just received a word from the Holy Spirit."

"Let's hear it."

"Somehow the Holy Spirit is going to protect the Q squad. Bret wasn't mentioned but I know we'll see him again."

"I've got some bad news. Em, where's Kurt?"

"He's on watch. I'll tell him later."

"I just heard it on the radio."

"Is this about your mom?"

"Bret was found dead this morning. They're calling it a suicide."

Bending over, Reenie screamed, "They're lying!"

"You think it was Cassandra?"

"Looks like it, Em."

"What kind of butcher is she?"

"Reenie, God sometimes..."

"So why didn't He stop her? Doesn't God even care?"

"Bret is with the Lord."

"Tell me, Jake, did he get two shots in the back like his father?"
Not receiving a reply she ran out the backdoor.
"He meant so much to her, Em. This is so Satan."
"She can only get the victory by talking it out with the Lord." 1
"We gotta leave now. The Santino's cave is our best move."

A dunk in the cold baptismal was good enough. After toweling off, the redhead pulled on a pair of baggy blue jeans. While combing his wet hair Kurt could hear her cry for help.
"What's wrong, sis?"
"When I was getting food from the basement; Reenie came back got her stuff and left. She's trying to protect us. She thinks Cassandra will eliminate any believer connected with her."
"Wasn't Jake on watch?"
"He's gone too."
"No way! JJ wouldn't bail on us when we're this close!"
"This is such a setup. Satan is trying to pin Bret's death on Jake. Do you think he's going after Reenie?"
"Sis, if they return to Bethany, Death Angel won't be far behind."

He was sitting on the front porch quietly smoking a joint.
Turning the corner, she remembered the day she left. Sprawled on her bed she felt a supernatural conviction drawing her. Somehow she gained the courage to take a stand.
The teenager walking toward his house looked like an old friend. Her casual stride, her slender arms, even her clothes looked familiar.
At first she thought the sad looking man sitting on the porch was a friend of her father's. Picking up the pace she dropped her backpack on the sidewalk.
"Travis! Travis!"
Jumping off the third step of the porch, he hit the ground running. After she grabbed his neck, he twirled her around and around. Her piercing squeal sounded great.
"Wow, aren't you the ladies man?"
"You should talk. I didn't recognize you until I saw your famous gait."

"How are the folks?"

"Bertha's is still open. Let's go for a burger and some fries. C'mon, like old times?"

"Talk to me, Travis."

"How about the Factory, maybe we can visit some of your friends."

"You all alone?"

"Yeah."

"For how long?"

"Last year, Pa got stung three times in one day. It was too much for him. He committed suicide behind Sluman's."

"What about Mom?"

"She left to live with her brother on his farm in Iowa. She died a couple months ago from drinking infected water."

"Why didn't you go with her?"

"Didn't want to leave my friends."

"I don't believe you."

He awkwardly looked away like he was stalling for time.

"If I left, I knew I would never see you again. I always hoped you'd come home."

Pulling her close for a hug, he could feel her sobs.

"Thanks a lot for the ride."

The truck driver waved back; he didn't mind picking up resisters.

Jake Jamison felt strange walking through his old neighborhood. A few yards looked cared for, mostly by those who refused to give into despair. He could smell the stench from the garbage overflowing from the garage. A crumbled American flag lay on their dirty porch. The dark living room somehow looked lonely. The phone in the hallway was dead. Even the blinds in the kitchen were drawn. Cigarette smoke was seeping from underneath the double doors leading to the dining room. Seated at her favorite mahogany table, she poured herself another whisky. After taking another drag from her cigarette, she just stared, her blank expression never changing.

"Well, well, well, it's the prodigal son returning home. How about a whiskey? Or does your religion allow for such a great sin?"

"I've never seen you drink before, Mom."

"You missed a lot since you deserted us. I've thought about this moment for three years. You know why? I was the one who persuaded your father to let you go; something about following your own path."

"Where's Dad?"

"The Army sent him to the Florida Everglades to fight fires. It wasn't long before he was infected with Wormwood. He cried out for help but I guess your Jesus was just too busy. He's dead or don't you even care?"

"I care Mom; I care a lot."

"Then why did you leave us? So many families pulled together during this nightmare. Can you imagine the pain you caused us? Jessie must've been mighty convincing."

"It was my decision to leave."

Casting the empty whiskey bottle aside, she mumbled back, "So what did this cult offer you?"

"This isn't a good time to discuss the resistance."

"Why not," she cackled, "maybe you'd rather talk about how clean good ole Bethany used to be?"

His mother felt like a stranger. He had never heard her talk with such bitterness. Suddenly her eyelids lowered; her lips forming an evil smile.

"Seriously, how does it feel to see someone die because you disobeyed God?"

"I don't understand?"

"Ask Reenie, you stinking hypocrite."

"I command you lying spirit to leave her."

"I don't have to," it hissed. "She invited me in."

"By the power of Jesus, I command you to leave her. If you don't, I will ask the Lord to send you to the bottomless pit before your time."

Her body convulsed backwards. For several seconds she lay still in her chair. Sitting beside her; he held her hand.

"I'm so sorry," she whimpered. "Is the end near, Jake?"

"The Bible calls it the great day of God Almighty. But before Armageddon can happen, seven bowl judgments must be poured out. The bowls are God's final wrath."

"How loving; God finally grants us closure from these evil plagues."

"C'mon, Mom, I tried to tell you Joshua Kayin was evil. His invasion of Jerusalem with armies from ten nations was warning enough." 2

"If God loves the Jews so much, then why didn't He protect them? Over four million have been slaughtered. 3 Such killing makes no sense."

"The Word will soon cast the Beast and his False Prophet into the lake of fire." 4

"So now you believe in a literal fire for sinners. And I suppose Muslims, Hindus, and Buddhists, are all going to fry!"

"Jesus promised, 'That whoever believes in Him should not perish but have eternal life.' 5 Anyone who doesn't believe in Jesus as their Savior cannot inherit the kingdom of heaven. Everlasting fire was created for the devil and his angels. 6 It was enlarged to include humans who reject the forgiveness of their sins by a loving God."

She gently touched his face with her nicotine stained fingertips.

"Were you ever stung?"

"God protected me."

"Yeah, the resisters executed didn't have any blemishes either. Even the major networks were talking about it."

"I love you, Mom. I've always loved you. My decision to become a Christian doesn't mean I ever rejected you or Dad."

"Heard your loving God predicted families would split up?"

"Yeah, Jesus warned believers, 'Do not think that I came to bring peace on earth. I did not come to bring peace but a sword. For I have come to set a man against his father, a daughter against her mother... a man's enemies will be those of his own household.'" 7

"Tell me, why would Jesus predict something so evil?"

"You wouldn't understand."

The young Watchman now understood why he returned home. Reaching over he gave her a final hug.

"I gotta go."

"What are you going to do?"

"Something that will glorify God. Bye, Mom."

She didn't bother to reply. Stumbling into her dark kitchen there was only one thing on her mind: another bottle of whiskey.

As they walked downtown, Travis was itching with questions.

"So after you left us where did you hide out?"

"At a Christian camp outside Birmingham, did you all register?"

"Yeah, Pa would never lose his job. Ma didn't care either."

"What about you, Travis, did it mean anything to you?"

"C'mon, Ree, who was I supposed to believe? At the time my life was Little League and patching things up with my girlfriend. Even Pastor Ryals said registering had nothing to do with the Bible."

"How is he?"

"His wife left him after our church kicked him out. Sometimes I see him feeding the pigeons at the park. Talk about depressing."

"Travis, the night I left all I could think about was my friends who refused to register. I had to find out why. I finally got saved last year."

"What do you mean saved? You and I have gone to church since we were little. We've always believed in Jesus, haven't we?"

WHERE OUR LORD WAS CRUCIFIED

'And their dead bodies
will lie in the street of the great city...
where also our Lord was crucified.'
Revelation 11:8

As he walked downtown Jake couldn't resist reflecting back on his
days growing up: learning how to swim at his neighbor's pool,
winning a mother/son sack race at seven, scoring a touchdown in his
first football game at twelve. In the fifth grade, his mother stayed up
til two in the morning helping him finish his first book report. Or the
time he walked home with his father after losing in the City Wresting
Championships.

Reaching Main Street, he spotted an agent scanning teenagers
outside the Pizza Factory. A judicious backtrack brought him into one
of the oldest neighborhoods in Bethany. Most of the homes had wrap
around porches with big picture windows. Up ahead was Greg
Hudson's house. Every window was boarded up. Yellow tape circled
the front porch. Even the backdoor was gone. The kitchen, the living
room, the bedrooms, everything was trashed. Pushing the door to his
study open, Jake gasped. Greg's bible was still on his desk. End time
notes were everywhere. His seventieth week of Daniel chart was on
the wall.

"Lord, I ask forgiveness for leaving Emma and Kurt. After
hearing about Bret, I allowed Satan to yank me into a cloud of
unbelief. I took my eyes off You to fulfill my own needs. Then instead
of helping Reenie, I gave in to self-pity. And where is she now?
Please, God, may You put her in a place where this sniper can't get to
her."

He could hardly look at the picture of Greg, Ivy, Ethan, and

Misty.

Then the bewildered teenager cried out, "Why did it have to happen this way?"

The deep voice was coming from the dark hallway.

"Because you chose to be a Watchman for the glory of God."

"Gregggggg, you're alive!"

"Welcome home, my brother."

"The NWC has you dead."

"You can't always believe bogus radio broadcasts, now can you? I see Emma and Kurt found you. Any news from Jessie?"

"She left Gulf Shores on a ship headed overseas."

"Wow, I always thought she'd make a great missionary."

Their laughter felt good.

"The spiritual warfare is raging, Greg."

"We're almost there, bro. Remember studying Yom Kippur? The Day of Atonement begins tomorrow night in Jerusalem. Think of it, each year the shofar summons Jews to ask for forgiveness. But there is no forgiveness except through the precious blood of the Lamb. Habakkuk prophesied the Lord would come for the salvation of His people." 1

"Wow, Jews proclaiming blessed is He who comes in the name of the Lord."

"For the whole world to see," beamed Greg.

"What about the hailstones of the seventh bowl? 2 Rome, the headquarters of the Babylonian harlot, is affixing to be demolished." 3

"I know a camp in the mountains above Atlanta that can protect us."

"Sounds awesome! Got room for one more? I've got a friend named Reenie Tucker who is from Bethany. How far is this camp?"

"Depends on the traffic; a couple of hours for sure."

"How many campers are you expecting?"

"Three thousand and counting, we have RVs rescuing overcomers round the clock."

"Can we first pick up Emma and Kurt in Gulf Shores?"

"There's not enough time. We need to pick up Reenie and get going."

Their drive to the Tuckers house took less than five minutes. From the street, her home looked deserted. It took Jake less than a minute to complete his search.

"I found Reenie's backpack in the living room. She's gone."

While sharing with her brother Reenie felt a check from the Holy Spirit. She stiffened as a NWC car pulled up in front of Bertha's.

"Hey, Travis, you okay?" asked the curious agent.

"Sure, Abe, everything's cool."

"Who's your new friend?"

"You mean you've never met my older sister?"

"Can't say I have."

"Reenie, this is Agent Abernathy. Abe and Pa were good friends."

"Where are you living now, Reenie?"

"Gulf Shores."

"Kinda strange Travis never mentioned you before?"

"It's been awhile since we've seen each other."

Removing his hat the agent wiped his forehead with his sleeve.

"And when was that?"

Travis nonchalantly muttered back, "I'd say three years."

"Wasn't that the time mandatory registering kicked in?"

"Nice talking with you, Abe, we're going for some burgers."

"Reenie, I don't remember seeing you at your father's funeral. Funny, you living so close and not being able to attend? Tell me, have you ever received a blemish?"

"Nope."

"Now how is that?"

"Lucky, I guess."

"When was the last time you were scanned?"

"Don't remember."

"Hey, ease off, Abe! This is my sister."

"Sorry, Travis, you need to stay out of this."

"ID, no ID, no one gives a rip anymore."

"I do, it's my job. So what's it going to be, Reenie?"

"I've never registered."

"She doesn't mean it, Abe!"

She gently shared, "Sorry, Travis, I just don't care anymore."

Grabbing his handcuffs the agent smugly announced, "I don't know who you are little lady but I'm going to find out. Now stretch out your hands, you're under arrest."

As the truck pulled up to the Factory he spotted some classmates from Lakeview High.

"Hey, it's Jake. Never thought we'd see you again. Have you seen Jessie?"

"Not lately, Becca. I'm looking for Reenie Ann Tucker."

"Now there's a strange one. An agent just busted her at Bertha's."

The most solemn night of the year for the Jewish people was near. With their arms chained, both were ushered into his chambers. Slumped in his oversized chair Kayin looked listless. Seated to his left, was a livid Rabbi Shimon Melchior, a leader of the Jewish Orthodox Party.

Gazing at their prisoners, Pope Michael looked hopeful.

"Do you know what time it is?"

Both Witnesses stood motionless.

"Come now, soon your people will be praying the enchanting melody of Kol Nidre. Doesn't your Day of Atonement begin with this prayer?"

Rabbi Melchior was struggling to control his disgust.

"Please tell us the meaning of the Day of Atonement?" 4

"I object to such detestable dialogue."

"Shimon, you must pray for patience. Lord Kayin, may I ask some questions which can help us in our decision?"

The lethargic Beast simply nodded.

Stepping near the Witnesses, his prophet whispered, "Isn't this a day when your people will fast and repent over the sins they have committed in the previous year?"

"I implore you, what can be achieved by such mockery?"

"Why, forgiveness, my dear Shimon. Don't you think these two men of God need to be forgiven of their sins? Since arriving in the Kidron Valley forty-two months ago, these prophets have been busy. Look how many cities in Israel they have visited."

Kayin nervously shifted in his chair. Their silence was annoying.

"What about their Messianic prophecies? A Redeemer leading a remnant to Mount Zion is my favorite. 5 Don't these believers have their Father's name written on their foreheads?"6

Both beasts broke out in sarcastic laughter. 7

"On the Day of Atonement doesn't your High Priest enter the Holy of Holies and sprinkle blood on the Ark of the Covenant? 8 Oh, excuse me; I seem to remember your people losing the Mercy Seat when the Babylonians destroyed your Temple. I've heard prophesy experts teach the Ark of the Covenant is buried under the Dome of the Rock. Imagine that? Rabbi Melchior, shouldn't these prophets be able to tell us the exact location of the Ark of the Covenant?"

His eyes on the second beast, the taller Witness stepped forward.

"Soon, the Deliverer will come and forgive them of their sins according to the covenant He made with them. Their spiritual eyes will be opened as they will put their trust in the King of Kings and Lord of Lords. When the seventh trumpet sounds the Ark of the Covenant will be seen." 9

"Silence such blasphemy!" screamed the Rabbi.

"My, my," mocked Kayin, "another prediction?"

"For the past forty-two months these prophets have kept a challenging schedule," chided the priest. "Isn't that so? No wait, how about a quick review."

Reaching over Pope Michael picked up a thick folder from a small table. Thumbing through the pages, he focused on several passages underlined in red.

"Two years ago on Rosh Hashanah, they predicted the world's trees and grass would burn. They called this assault the first trumpet of the day of the Lord. Later, they predicted the eruption of fires upon our largest oceans. Then these righteous servants infected the Euphrates River with the Wormwood curse. Within a month, our earth's water supply was poisoned. Finally, they somehow knew when the sun, moon, and stars, would lose one third of their light."

"Must we be subjected to such biased projections?" demanded Melchior. "Such a mixture of truth and error proves nothing."

"It gets better. They actually predicted how long the fifth trumpet would last. 10 For five months, billions of people suffered countless attacks. Never in history have so many been tortured. But that wasn't enough, was it?"

The tension was rising. Each leader was near his breaking point.

"Their prediction of the sixth trumpet resulted in the death of over two billion people. Even so, we have reports the killing has stopped. This evil assault is over!"

His beady eyes resting upon the Witnesses, Kayin howled, "There will be no more predictions!"

The other Witness raised his hand to speak.

"The fullness of the Gentiles is over! Yeshua is coming to save a remnant from Israel on Yom Kippur!" 11

"Trust me," threatened the Beast, "this is something you two will never see!"

"Good evening, I'm Natalie Roberts reporting from the Wailing Wall in Jerusalem. The two Witnesses are dead. By order of the NWC, these tormentors will not be buried. At this moment their bodies are laying in a street in front of the Temple Mount. 12 Thankfully, the goal of these false prophets has failed. Within days, thousands of dignitaries from around the world will join us in this celebration."

Roped off by security, the overflow crowd erupted with cheers. Such jubilation was what this veteran reporter wanted to capture during the public viewing of the bodies. Surrounded by guards, Natalie began her interviews.

Over the elated crowd, she hollered, "What's your name?"

"May Allah be praised!"

Before he could give his name, the young Palestinian was hoisted upon his friend's shoulders. Turning to her right, Natalie spotted a small bent over man.

"This is Special Report. May I have your name?"

"I'm Magen David. I'm ninety-one. I've lived in Israel all my life."

"Have you ever seen such festivity?"

He couldn't contain his tears of joy. While the reporter steadied his left arm, he remembered.

"I was here in 1948 when we became a nation. In 1967, I prayed for our soldiers when they regained our beloved Jerusalem. Three and a half years ago, I watched Kayin's armies invade Jerusalem. Two years later, I survived the Jehoshaphat offensive. Yet nothing compares to this."

Moving down the line of partiers Natalie was searching for someone younger; someone who had trumpeted over every adversity. The popular reporter picked a boy who had burns on his arms and legs.

"What is your name?"

"My name is Titus Robison. I'm ten years old."

"And what do you think of the two Witnesses' execution?"

"The fires are no more. The dying has stopped. I am so happy the Witnesses are dead."

"There you have it, from a ninety-one-year old Magen David to a ten-year-old Titus Robison, the feeling is the same. Even though no one can be brought back to life; there is still a triumphant relief these imposters are dead. To celebrate this glorious victory over evil, many are exchanging gifts. 13 For anyone who believed God was protecting these prophets of doom we now take you live to their funeral."

The roar from the crowd was electrifying. This was a defining moment in history.

"Thank you for such inspiring interviews, Natalie," praised Israeli newscaster Joel Friedman. "Of course, such perseverance is evidence we can defeat whatever evil is forced upon us. Never before have we seen so many people killed, and for what purpose? All because of religious fanatics who have no tolerance, no conscience, no thought for anyone or anything but their own religious edicts. I can think of no greater good for our world than to permanently silence these spurious prophets."

"What's the holdup? She's taking her sweet time."

"Chief, she almost lost it a couple of minutes ago."

"Take off the kid gloves. No wait, I'll take over."

She couldn't remember when all the shouting began.

"Listen up, Tucker!" threatened Doyle. "We know you have information about other resisters. Your brother told us you were once in a camp outside Birmingham, Alabama."

Shielding her bloodshot eyes from the glare of the overhead lights she shook her head no.

"Your heroes are dead! The NWC just hung the two Witnesses in Jerusalem."

"It's over," she whispered back.

Agent Abernathy curiously asked, "What is over?"

"C'mon, kid, what's over?" demanded an annoyed Doyle.

"When the seventieth week of Gentile domination ends, the Beast will kill the two Witnesses. Then the Messiah will come and gather His first fruits. By the third day, He will enter Jerusalem and forgive the sins of those who believe in Him. The next day, the two Witnesses will rise from the dead."

Their spontaneous hilarity filled the room.

"Little lady you're a bit mixed up. The two Witnesses ain't going anywhere."

"The Bible predicts it."

"What if it doesn't happen?" interrupted Abe.

"Sometimes it's hard to see how everything fits."

"Girl, do you realize the consequences of your religious play-acting?" ranted Doyle. "How well did you know Bret Santino?"

"We were close friends."

"Did you say close? Close enough that he took his life. Isn't it true you were the one who converted agent Santino into your cult? You convinced him to go AWOL!"

"Bret believed in Jesus as his Savior."

"Are you nuts? He was so depressed he killed himself. Don't deny it; you got the ball rolling."

"Reenie, Travis is in our lobby. Just register and you can go home?"

Looking down she squirmed in her seat.

"All your friends have registered with the NWC," sighed Abe. "Jake Jamison, Jessie Hyatt, Emma and Kurt Abbott, it's no big deal."

"You're such liars."

"I thank God your friends have come to their senses."

After a long pause, the agents were gone.

Spinning around she heard a familiar hissing.

"Jezebel, you have no power over me anymore."

"My Master has some unfinished business with you. Your cooperation will determine your future."

"Go away."

"All you have to do is register."

"Never."

Lunging forward the demon clutched her throat.

Gritting her teeth, the teenager confessed, "Jesus is Lord."

"It won't work, you were once mine."

"By the authority of Jesus Christ I command you to leave!"

Slowly its grip loosened.

"I command you to return to the bottomless pit."

The demon vanished.

With her face touching the cold cement floor, an exhausted Reenie closed her eyes.

They were parked a half block from the Tucker's house.

"Hard to tell, Jake, it could be a setup."

"Naw, Travis would never sell out his sister."

His walk home was devastating. His bitterness was looking for an excuse to explode. He thought the agents that knew his Pa would help in her release. After seeing their faces, Travis knew that wasn't happening. The disillusioned teenager was sitting on the porch when they arrived.

"I don't care who you are; just get off my property."

"Travis, we are friends of your sister."

"Registered or unregistered?"

"Unregistered."

"Oh joy, more religious fanatics. She isn't here. What do you want?"

"We want to rescue her."

"You're a little late."

"Can we talk inside?"

"Why not, I ain't got any pressing engagements."

Seated at the kitchen table, Travis grudgingly asked, "You guys hungry?"

"Do you have any clean water?"

"I sure do; just lifted two bottles from the ID station."

"How did you pull that off?"

"With all the partying going on, it was easy."

"You mean agents were drinking on duty?"

"I don't blame them; the NWC just wasted the two Witnesses. Kayin had them hung."

"My name is Jake Jamison, this is Greg Hudson."

"I know; Reenie mentioned you."

"Did you see her?"

"They sent me to talk her into registering. After five minutes I guess they didn't like where our conversation was heading. An agent practically yanked my arm off getting me out of her cell."

"What did she say?"

"She's alright. When they were dragging me out I made a funny face. My sister isn't the same person I grew up with. She has a peace, a calmness I've never seen before, real spooky. I mean this girl was always afraid. Her nightmares were a real drag. I remember Ree sleepwalking when she was nine. She picked up her dresser and put it in her closet. It weighed over two hundred and fifty pounds. Go figure."

"There's a reason, Travis. Satan got a stronghold within her spirit at an early age."

"I know all about Jezebel."

"Her control of your sister is over. Reenie has been set free."

"More church lingo. Don't you know how bogus you sound?"

"We are talking about a new person in Christ."

"Your faith means nothing to me."

"Travis, we don't have much time. Armageddon is four weeks away."

"Yeah, I heard agents talking about another world war in the Middle East. What's all this crap over Israel? I wish God would just put this stinking country out of its misery."

"Make no mistake; God won't melt this world until His will is fulfilled." 14

"You know, Ree really blew Abe away when she told him she was unregistered, calm, cool, and collected, right to his face."

"You ever wonder why she did it?" asked Jake.

"She ain't scared anymore. It was Jezebel who made her live a lie. Dodging, running, putting the blame on me, that was my big sister. Ree couldn't help herself; it's easy to see now."

"What did your folks think?"

"The old man couldn't relate. He'd just call her a coward. She couldn't please Ma either. Didn't matter what she did, my sister could never measure up."

"Do you think your sister is a coward?"

"Not anymore, preacher!"

"By not telling the truth it prevented her from being loved herself."

"Ain't that the truth!"

"It seems a lot of people gave up on your sister."

"You figure God has?"

"No and we haven't either. C'mon, Travis, it's time we all take a ride downtown."

FIRST DAY: AS A LION ROARS

'He had a little book in his hand. And he set his right foot on the sea and his left foot on the land, and cried with a loud voice, as when a lion roars...'
Revelation 10.2-3

The Lion of the Tribe of Judah stood. A glorious rainbow covered His head. His face was shining like the sun; His feet burning like fire. 1 The prophets who proclaimed His mission were interceding. As the Holy One of Israel descended in a cloud the saints erupted in glorious praise. 2

Before the Throne an angel eagerly announced, "'And it shall come to pass in that day that the remnant of Israel...will never again depend on him who defeated them, but will depend on the Lord, the Holy One of Israel, in truth. The remnant will return, the remnant of Jacob, to the Mighty God. For though your people, O Israel, be as the sand of the sea, a remnant of them will return...'" 3

The Son of God raised His hand to heaven after His right foot touched the Mediterranean Sea and His left foot touched land. 4 There would be no more delay. Turning east, He saw blood-spattered bodies lining the road. 5

Reaching the lonely Jordanian wilderness the Lord spoke, "'I overthrew some of you, as God overthrew Sodom and Gomorrah, and you were like a firebrand plucked from the burning; yet you have not returned to Me,' says the Lord. Therefore thus will I do to you, O Israel; because I will do this to you, prepare to meet your God, O Israel.'" 6

In the solitude of the desert air the remnant was partaking in a sunset service. He could hear their cries of repentance. In the background shofars were resonating. The 144,000 watched in silence as the Lamb of God approached on the dirty sand.

His first fruits encircling Him, Yeshua shared, "'I will rejoice in the Lord, My soul shall be joyful in my God; For He has clothed me with the garments of salvation, He has covered me with the robe of righteousness, as a bridegroom decks himself with ornaments, and as a bride adorns herself with her jewels. For as the earth brings forth its bud, as the garden causes the things that are sown in it to spring forth, so the Lord God will cause righteousness and praise to spring forth before all the nations.'" 7

Looking toward Jerusalem the Lord smiled.

"'For Zion's sake I will not hold My peace, and for Jerusalem's sake I will not rest, until her righteousness goes forth as brightness, and her salvation as a lamp that burns. The Gentiles shall see your righteousness, and all kings your glory. You shall be called by a new name, which the mouth of the Lord will name. You shall also be a crown of glory in the hand of your God. You shall no longer be termed Forsaken, nor shall your land any more be termed Desolate; but you shall be called Hephzibah (My delight is in her), and your land Beulah; for the Lord delights in you...'" 8

Nearing the Security Station he spotted a signal from a group of shoppers.

"What's up, Greg, do you know this guy?"

"He's a Watchman from our camp. I need to talk with him."

Their ten minute chat seemed like an hour. An uneasy Greg jumped in and started the engine.

"The Vineyard is in danger. Satan is sowing discord. I can't wait; I gotta go."

"Hey, preacher, you promised to help my sister."

"Sorry, Travis, obeying the Holy Spirit is not always popular."

"You are so full of it. You knew saving her was a long shot. This was just your first chance to bail!"

"These campers are my top priority."

"Gulf Shores is so close. What about picking up Emma and Kurt?"

"Jake, you know God's timing is everything. You're welcome to come with me."

"I believe the Holy Spirit is leading me to stay."

Greg paused and whispered a prayer of thanks to God.

"The bottom line is obedience, isn't it?"

"Yeah, I know. Jesus is going to save believing Israel by Tuesday. The Witnesses will rise on Wednesday. Satan will lose his authority to rule on Thursday. The Mount of Olives will be split on Friday."

"What's all this yakking, Jake?"

"It's Bible prophecy, Travis, the world is moving toward a climax."

"What does this have to do with my sister, preacher?"

"Reenie knew the risk when she visited you. We must all live with the consequences of our decisions. Besides, her rescue doesn't depend on you or me."

The fuming teenager bristled.

"Easy, Travis," cautioned Jake, "it's tough to explain how God works sometimes."

Stopping the van in front of Tucker's home, Greg's eyes never left the road as the boys got out.

"I'll be praying for you, Greg."

"Keep trusting, bro, Jesus will soon enter Jerusalem."

God had prepared a place in the wilderness for His first fruits. 9 Moving northwest from Edom, the procession led by the Breaker were marching toward Jerusalem. 10 Those having their Father's name written on their foreheads were coming to worship the Lord before the eyes of the world.

SECOND DAY: THEY WILL LOOK ON ME

'And I will pour out on the house of David and the inhabitants of Jerusalem the spirit of grace and supplication; then they will look on Me whom they pierced...'
Zechariah 12:10

Arriving at the Dead Sea, the procession headed north. A throng of onlookers celebrating the death of the Witnesses had no idea who constituted the massive crowd.

Suddenly a jubilant believer boldly shared, "'Who is this who comes from Edom, with dyed garments from Bozrah, this One who is glorious in His apparel, traveling in the greatness of His strength? I speak in righteousness, mighty to save. Why is your apparel red, and your garments like one who treads in the winepress?'" 1

As cries of repentance rang out those having the mark cursed.

Stepping in front of the remnant, an old-timer raised his hands high and cried out, "Yeshua, You are the Messiah. Have mercy on me, O God, for I am a sinner." 2

Grief stricken, he collapsed in the dirt. Two believers from the remnant gently helped him up. Looking into Yeshua's eyes, the old man somehow knew his sins had been forgiven.

The jeers by followers of the Beast were intimidating. Yet, the procession was growing as they crossed over the Jordan River.

Running ahead, a teenage boy announced, "The Messiah is here; come and see."

Those in hiding couldn't wait any longer. It was a like a dam bursting; as thousands of believers poured out of the Judean hills. 3

His magnificent office seemed smaller with the shades drawn and the lights dimmed. While watching the funeral on his hundred-inch TV he sipped on a brandy. Throughout the world millions had been martyred. 4 He hoped to accomplish so much more. Their vision for the future, their destiny as leaders, was unraveling. Pope Michael had to confront him. He had no choice.

"So what does my prophet think of this glorious celebration? Many still believe in my vision for the world; they even worship me."

"It appears our grandiose announcements are premature."

"Michael, we gave them what they wanted; a dose of good ole fashion revenge. This counts for something, my pessimistic friend."

"I was at your side the day you seized control of the nations. 5 Even after the Valley of Jehoshaphat debacle, I never wavered. 6 The signs and wonders our Master gave you have freely flowed through me. Yet today, you jest and refuse to hear me."

"What are you discerning?"

"Have you noticed the world leaders that are absent? The list of our enemies is growing."

"Attack the NWC? Only these insane Jewish guerillas would dare do that. Every stinking Jew will soon be stamped for eternity."

The false prophet knew what Kayin's thinly veiled smile meant. In the background, they could hear the spontaneous cheers from the massive crowd flooding the city.

"Our Arab friends are still with us. Nation's not represented will not receive any oil for one year."

"There is another issue. A mob is marching toward the eastern border of Israel."

"When will they ever learn, how many this time?"

"At this time over three hundred thousand. This mob is growing."

"Are they coming to protest the execution of the Witnesses? Or maybe they are just trying to gain some belated sympathy for America?"

"This group represents a different challenge."

"I suppose they're claiming to have an arsenal of bio chemicals?"

"They have no weapons," the priest dryly replied.

"Within the hour I want to destroy everyone even remotely..."

"The Witnesses prophesied the Deliverer would come the same day they were killed. Our hedge of protection is gone. The Christ is coming to Jerusalem."

"Are you suggesting we flee in our moment of victory?"

"Large numbers of unregistered Jews are joining Him from the Judean hills. The talk on the streets has them entering the city by Tuesday." 7

"What are these fanatics hoping to accomplish?"

"They believe He can redeem their transgressions."

"Hah, the streets of Palestine are filled with dead messiahs."

"We cannot afford to be distracted. The Federation is waiting for us in Rome."

The afternoon crowd blanketing Jerusalem was drunk with revenge. Covering the Witnesses' funeral was a heavy responsibility for the rookie producer. His staff meeting wasn't going well.

"Resisters are coming out of the woodwork. Right now it's over four hundred thousand."

"This idiotic story could blow up in our faces," winced newscaster Joel Friedman.

"If they reach the city," reasoned Natalie, "it will get a lot of play."

"Is their leader really coming on foot?" laughed Joel. "What a tough way to gain a following. It's their funeral; just regular people shedding their blood for another fanatic. What's this joker's name?"

"Some say He's the fulfillment of Isaiah 59," winced the producer.

"Enlighten me, bro; my theology is a bit rusty."

"They believe He is Jesus."

The trendy reporter ripped his headset off and cursed God.

"Not another religious fairy tale. In the past two years two evil men predicted six judgments that killed over two billion people. The NWC decides to execute them and guess what, the dying stops. That is news, real news. I need a drink."

"Wait, Joel," pleaded Natalie, "don't go."

Answering his cell phone the rookie producer was stressing.

"Is that Wes from Chicago?"

"Nate, he wants to know if you're up for this?"

Her biggest weakness was never being able to say no. Most insiders knew Natalie Rene Roberts was a big time people pleaser. He patiently waited for her reply.

"What type of pictures do you have of this remnant?"

"Some real beauties, I've heard He may raise the two Witnesses from the dead."

"How sick is that. Don't expect me to pick up the pieces after this publicity stunt crashes. Wes must know how many lives are at stake?"

"He doesn't think Kayin will allow this mob to enter the city."

"Kayin's gone!" interrupted a soundman listening in. "Just heard it from a NWC official. He left on his private jet to Rome. Pope Michael is with him."

"C'mon, Natalie, we can't sit on the sidelines! Don't tie our hands; not this time."

"Let's shoot it from the Wailing Wall. And double check security; Kayin didn't take off for nothing. I'll need a few minutes to script it."

Everyone cheered after lights lit up the Eastern Gate.

"Live from Jerusalem, this is Natalie Roberts. With the funeral celebration of the Witnesses in its second day, it's official, the horrific plague overwhelming our world is over. Record levels of rainfall have put out the fires. Now we can look to the future with a new hope."

The cameraman scanned their joyous applause.

"Of course, there are some who still oppose the execution of the Witnesses. As I speak, a massive crowd is marching toward Jerusalem. Their leader is a mystery. Some believe He is the Messiah."

She paused as a teacher joined her under the lights.

"Rabbi, what do you make of this event?"

"The stranger leading this mob is no Messiah. When the Messiah comes, Israel will recognize Him; not just a few who believe they are special in the eyes of God."

"Tragically," announced the Anchorwoman, "another false messiah has convinced a half million people to march on Jerusalem during this funeral celebration."

"Natalie, this is Dell Cotton from our New York affiliate. Do you have anything else for us?"

"Some say this mob is against the failing ID system. Others believe they want to die as martyrs."

"Is it possible these resisters are hoping to gain sympathy for the Jewish people?"

"That's one scenario. Some leaders are convinced they intend to participate in the Feast of Tabernacles. This holy day begins Thursday night. Of the seven feast days of Judaism, Sukkot is the most joyous."

"A remarkable story, Natalie, lots of possibilities."

"There's one more. Some believe their leader is going to raise the two Witnesses from the dead. 8 They believe He will perform this miracle by Wednesday."

After a long pause, Dell asked; "Now why would anyone want to do such an evil thing?"

Running through the camp, she arrived at his office totally out of breath. Pushing past the outside sentry, she kicked open his door only to be met by two rifles.

"Stop! Miriam, these soldiers have orders. They could've shot you."

"Aaron, I must speak with you."

"Do you know how many of our people have been killed since the Witnesses' execution?"

"He is here. He is leading His remnant from the Jordanian desert. They'll enter Jerusalem by tomorrow."

"Who is, Miriam, speak up woman?"

"Jesus in the flesh, His Word says, 'To those who eagerly wait for Him He will appear a second time.'" 9

"Miriam, there is a vast difference between you and me. You live in a fantasy world filled with empty promises. Apparently you prefer this type of playacting. I understand such escapism. Many of our people hiding in the hills of Judea believe in such religious propaganda."

"They aren't hiding anymore. Thousands are joining Him. Tomorrow is the third day. The mystery of God will be accomplished. He is coming; we must meet Him."

"The NWC will never allow this remnant to reach Jerusalem. Kayin is evil. He can't be reasoned with or bargained with. He is heartless, merciless. He will destroy anyone who resists his authority."

"This is Israel's day of salvation. Hosea predicted the Lord would raise us up on the third day." 10

"You are so naïve."

"No one will stop Yeshua this time. At His first coming, on the Feast of Passover, He willingly gave His life as our sacrificial Lamb. His second coming has Him returning on the Day of Atonement for the salvation of Israel." 11

Slumping down against the wall in his office, he looked tormented.

"I want to believe but I just can't change."

"Aaron, have you forgotten what you have fought for since your father's assassination? What about your goal to expose Kayin's plan to wipe out Israel? God has used you to protect a multitude for this very moment. Paul wrote, 'And so all Israel will be saved, as it is written: The Deliverer will come out of Zion, and He will turn away ungodliness from Jacob; For this is My covenant with them, when I take away their sins.' 12 The Messiah is coming for those who believe in Him. We can't miss His visitation. You must grant your soldiers a chance to join the redeemed."

"If we show our faces we are dead men."

"Don't you understand? Ever since our people rejected Yeshua as their Messiah, Israel has lived in spiritual darkness, unable to perceive spiritual truth, until now. Those trusting in Yeshua as their Savior are being grafted back into the olive tree. There is no other way to receive eternal life." 13

"What about Johanna? If I agree to go will she join us?"

"Aaron Phinehas, you must remember the day you prayed for our baby girl? You asked God to use her as a light for those who are lost. Lord willing, she'll be there."

THIRD DAY: HE WILL RAISE US UP

*'After two days He will revive us, on the third day
He will raise us up...'*
Hosea 6:2

The next day, no one interfered as Yeshua walked through Jerusalem.

Over the crowd someone shouted, "This is the Messiah; the Anointed of God."

"How can this man be the son of Mary?" scoffed a Muslim teenager.

Both were speechless as He approached. Bending over Johanna lifted her upon her shoulders.

"The Son of God!" cried Ruth. "He has come just like He said He would."

Lowering her down, Johanna whispered, "We must leave for the Temple."

Ruth's attention was transfixed. Slipping through the legs of the crowd in front of her, she tried to get a better look. Suddenly a crushing surge followed Jesus down the road.

"Johanna, Johanna, I just saw your father!"

Stepping back from the massive stampede, she never heard her little friend. Within seconds, Ruth Lentz disappeared into a sea of bodies.

"The brunette leaning against the wall?"

"Are you sure?" the soldier suspiciously asked.

"That's Johanna Glazer. Can I go now?"

"We need you to lead her to our van."

"That wasn't part of our agreement."

"Bela, you do this and we will let your family live."

Crossing the street the beleaguered taxi driver could see her praying.

"Your aunt is dead!" threatened the spirit of Death."

"Your daddy never loved you," whispered Guilt. "You even lost Ruth. God is punishing you."

"Father, in the name of Your Son, I reject these lies. May You protect Myra wherever she is. May You save my daddy. And may You please help Ruth find her parents."

"Johanna, Johanna, do you remember me?"

"Bela, is it really you?"

"I've found your father. He's not far. Please follow me."

They cautiously walked several blocks before reaching a mysterious black van with one-way windows. The engine was running when the side door slid open.

"Are you Johanna Glazer?" asked the driver.

"Never heard of her, my name is Jessie Hyatt."

"If you want to see your father alive, get in."

The traumatized teenager grasped Bela's arm.

"Don't be afraid, Johanna, they will help you."

Once inside, the door automatically locked.

"Hey, what about Bela?"

"Shut your mouth and listen. You're our prisoner. If you cooperate we will let you live."

While one soldier tied her hands, another blindfolded her. The ride seemed longer than twenty minutes. The metal door closing from behind was jarring as she was escorted into his dimly lit office. Behind the heavy set officer was a mural of the prophet Muhammad. On his desk was a photograph of Anthony and Myra Santino.

"My name is Mullah Abdul Sheikh. You are Johanna Esther Glazer. I'm a sworn enemy of your father. Aaron Glazer has taken thousands of innocent lives."

"He has killed and you have killed."

"Silence! You have no idea the heinous crimes your father has committed against my people. When you were a baby, your father was convicted of treason. Your mother escaped to America with you. When she remarried and had another child; we realized you meant nothing to her. Your disappearance has always been a mystery to us."

"You're confused; I'm an only child."

The demonic oppression was stifling. Her mind was spinning.

"I wonder why the infamous Matthias suddenly wants to see you and your mother after all these years. His guilt is consuming him."

"My mother lives in America. I have come to share the gospel with my father. Yeshua will save those who believe in Him."

"You actually believe this imposter in Jerusalem is Jesus?"

"I've come to pray with my daddy. Salvation can only come through believing in the death, burial, and resurrection of the Son of God." 1

"Not only is your belief a lie, you don't even know who your real mother is. Take her away. She doesn't know where Matthias is."

The filthy cell had no heat. One guard watched as another chained her to a rusty steel bar attached to the wall. In the corner of the room sat a slumped over prisoner. She was dressed in prison clothes; a scarf was covering her face.

"Wake up!" yelled the guard. "You've got a visitor."

Raising her head, she couldn't believe her eyes.

"Glory to God! Jessie, are you alright?"

"Myra, how long have you been here?"

"I was arrested yesterday."

"I've seen Him, Myra. I've seen Yeshua."

"It can only be the mystery of God; the salvation of Israel!"

Their backs against the cold concrete wall they praised the Lord.

"I guess you know why they've captured us?"

"They want to trap Daddy. Did you ever find him?"

"Yes, the Lord opened the door. I got to share the gospel with him yesterday. So what did these terrorists say to you?"

"You can't trust anything they say. They're mixing lies with the truth. It's really pretty simple. The Holy Spirit wants me to remain calm and not be deceived by the devil."

"Jessie, there is something very important I have to share with you."

"What is it, Myra?"

"I'm not your aunt."

"You mean Shelby isn't your sister?"

"She's my younger sister. She never married Aaron Glazer, I did."

"I don't understand."

"Honey, I'm your real mother."

"How can that be?"

"I had you in Jerusalem twenty years ago."

"You and Shelby both told me you were my aunt."

"I want you to know why I kept this from you. When you visited us you were emotionally on the edge. Anthony and I decided to wait for a better time to tell you. Then he was killed."

"This is so crazy."

"These terrorists aren't telling you the whole story."

"You mean the part when you gave me to your sister. What a great feeling to hear my parents wanted nothing to do with me. If I hadn't visited you this would have never surfaced; just your dirty little secret."

"I know they tried to hurt you."

"How would you know? Were you there when they mocked my so-called Christian mother? Tell me why didn't you want me maybe you preferred a boy?"

"I was trying to protect you."

"So after having me, you drop me on your sister's doorstep. Then to hide your pain you rush off and marry Anthony Santino and have Bret."

"Jessie, I..."

"Can you at least call me by my real name?"

"I never wanted to give you up, Johanna. I've always loved you. Aaron will tell you the danger you and I were facing."

"Did you say danger? Any moment now we could die. In the meantime, I find out my mother has been lying to me my whole life. Because of this, I'll never know about the salvation of my real father, who could care less. Jake, my best friend, is probably dead. Lord, I have no idea why You let all this happen to me."

"Abdul, a patrol just picked up Matthias near the Knesset. He didn't resist."

"Why would he; he wants to see his family."

"No soldiers are with him."

"I don't believe it. He knows we'll execute him. We must be ready to defend ourselves once he enters our compound. Alert security outside our perimeter."

Their animosity was understandable as a blindfolded Aaron Glazer hopped out of the black van. Every soldier watching had lost a family member due to the direct orders of this man. The officer sat behind his desk as the prisoner was chained to a chair.

"Take off his blindfold!"

Both leaders stared at each other. The blood of many people was on their hands.

"Matthias, why have you come alone?"

"To offer my life in exchange for my daughter."

"You're not that courageous. So how many of your soldiers will die trying to rescue you?"

"May I talk privately with Johanna?"

"If it means anything to you, we also have your ex-wife."

"Let them go; they know nothing about my affairs."

"How can you say that; they're Jewish aren't they? Your evil seed has infected the entire world. Praise be to Allah, before long Israel will be no more. I just received a report of armies moving toward her borders."

"You know my men are holding several of your soldiers hostage?"

"You're such a liar. Why should I trust the man that ordered the execution of my nephew? Don't you remember him, he was just sixteen."

"You know the consequences of war."

"You're right; I have no apologies either."

"I do."

"Imagine that, coming from such a cold-blooded killer."

"It's over, Abdul. Our war has lost its meaning."

"So you believe in this imposter in Jerusalem?"

"I have seen Him."

"So after killing thousands of Muslims you now want to become a Christian?"

"Thinking about it, my wife read me a passage about God becoming flesh. 2 The Son of God humbled himself as a man to die as a sacrifice on the cross." 3

The officer lit up a used cigarette.

"Now why would God want to become a mere man? Jesus was a prophet not the Son of God. Allah doesn't have a son."

"Peter called Jesus the Son of the living God." 4

"So what, all believers are called the sons of God."

"Jesus responded to Peter's claim by saying, "Blessed are you, Simon Bar-Jonah, for flesh and blood has not revealed this to you, but My Father who is in heaven." 5

"Such blasphemy is punishable by death."

"What if Jesus really is in Jerusalem?"

"Just another false Messiah that's all."

"Then why hasn't anyone stopped Him? The NWC is paralyzed, the religious leadership is terrified, and now even Allah, the pagan god of the Arabs, is powerless."

"On judgment day you will regret such lies. I pity this pretender and His deluded followers."

"Have you ever seen a person raised from the dead?"

"Never, have you?"

"What if Yeshua raises the two Witnesses? Would you believe then?"

"What nonsense. Look at the pain these false messengers have caused. You don't actually believe this will happen?"

"My wife says by tomorrow."

"I'm well aware of her convictions. Your daughter was humiliated when she heard the truth about her mother the hypocrite."

"Miriam isn't a hypocrite. She had her reasons."

"I wonder how much of the whip she can stomach before she cries for mercy."

"What can you gain from such cruelty?"

"To see your face as we torture her will bring joy to my heart."

For hours they lifted up many prayers. But there was one that captured their hearts.

"Father, Johanna and I were drawn by the Holy Spirit to Jerusalem for the salvation of her daddy. Forgive us for the times we allowed unbelief to control our thoughts. You supernaturally opened doors for us. My visit with Aaron was a miracle."

"Mama, are visions for real? Recently, I was given the interpretation of a vision from a dear friend. Ruth saw you, daddy, and me, worshipping on the Temple Mount during the Feast of Tabernacles."

"Where is Ruth now?"

"I lost her in a crowd following Yeshua. It was her parents who protected me for a year."

"Father, we commit Ruth's family into Your loving arms. Wherever Aaron is, please save his soul for eternity. The Feast of Tabernacles is near. In Your Son's name, we ask that You make a way for Aaron to attend this Feast."

A determined Johanna shouted, "And may You confound his enemies!"

The cell door flew open. The officer waited until the guards chained him to the wall.

"Matthias, you have ten minutes to decide whether you will live. When I return, I will ask you some questions. If you refuse to answer, your daughter will be executed. If you refuse again, your wife will die. After their executions, you will be eliminated."

The slamming of the steel door had a hallow sound.

For several moments, no one spoke.

"Johanna, this is your father. Aaron, this is your daughter."

It seemed so natural when their eyes met.

"I love you, Daddy."

"Johanna, when I first heard you'd come, I was overcome with regret. Your whole life I was never able to protect you. Now the opportunity arises and somehow I fail again. It's like your mother and I are facing the very fears we had twenty years ago."

"Daddy, I've also had fears I tried to run from. What you did doesn't mean you didn't love me. When Mama gave me to Shelby it was her only way of protecting me."

Tears slid down his cheeks as he whispered, "Johanna, I don't know what to say."

"When Mama first told me the truth, I was angry and confused. Then I prayed. Satan wanted me to hurt you by lashing out. Instead, God has challenged me to reject the Devil's lie of revenge. It doesn't matter anymore, Daddy, I forgive you." 6

"Johanna, you have every right not to believe me."

"I gave up my rights when I became a disciple of Yeshua. I memorized this passage the day I became a Christian. 'Therefore as the elect of God, holy and beloved, put on tender mercies, kindness, humility, meekness, longsuffering; bearing with one another, and forgiving one another, if anyone has a complaint against another; even as Christ forgave you, so you also must do.'" 7

"You mean Christian's must forgive those who hurt them?"

"How can I harbor unforgiveness when Yeshua died so I could be forgiven?"

"You don't understand. My hate for those who killed my sister will never go away."

"God's love can erase your pain, Aaron, even the horror of your sister's death."

"And how would you know that, Miriam?"

"I also loved my Anthony. I will never know the name of his killer. It doesn't matter. I choose to walk in forgiveness, not by my own strength but by God's grace."

"Daddy, have you seen the Messiah?"

"A massive crowd is following Him, many from Egypt and Jordan." 8

"The ransomed of the Lord are using the Highway of Holiness! 9 They're being supernaturally protected. Hosea prophesied the Lord would come on the third day and forgive a remnant." 10

"I've done too much evil to be forgiven."

"God brought us together for you to be saved. Let's pray right now."

Slamming the door open, he ordered, "Stand them up."

"Abdul, I have one last request."

"You speak when you are spoken to. Recently you received three dirty bombs. I want the names of the operatives who sold them to you."

From the dark corridor a guard saluted.

"Abdul, it's a set up. Hundreds of soldiers have surrounded our compound."

Whipping around, to his surprise, Aaron Glazer looked meek, almost humble.

"Abdul just release Johanna and Miriam."

"Daddy, Yeshua can save..."

"You must trust me, Johanna."

After they were driven out of the compound, Aaron was taken to Abdul's office.

"Matthias, I was there the night it happened. Your father's killer is a friend of mine. He has a scar under his right ear. He will be pleased to hear I have apprehended the son of Isaac Glazer. His brother was killed by Israeli terrorists."

"Will killing me bring back his brother, my father, or your nephew?"

"Allah will soon bless those who obey his teachings."

"My wife believes the Son of Man is going to receive a kingdom from the Ancient of Days. This kingdom will never pass away." 11

"Do you believe Allah is the God of all mankind?"

"The Ancient of Days is the Father of Abraham, Isaac, and

Jacob. The allah of Islam is not God."

"You're so ignorant. In Arabic, Allah means God."

"The Allah Muslims serve isn't a father. Jesus once prayed, "And now, O Father, glorify Me together with Yourself, with the glory which I had with You before the world was." 12 The Father and Son were together before this world was created."

"Neither the Bible nor the Koran teach such a lie."

Outside his office door the guard stood at attention.

"Abdul, his soldiers have left."

"Well done. In which direction did they withdraw?"

"We don't know, Abdul. One moment they were there; then they were gone."

FOURTH DAY: THE BREATH OF LIFE

'Now after three and a half days
the breath of life from God entered them,
and they stood on their feet,
and great fear fell on those who saw them.'
Revelation 11:11

Slouched in a chair just inside the front door, a frustrated Jake was trying to sort out the events of the past week. Travis looked troubled as he crossed the street.

"Ree is still alive. Man, your preacher is a real loser."

"Greg is obeying the Lord."

"My sister is caving in and the reverend takes off; what a surprise."

"I'm not going anywhere."

"That's just it, Jake, this ain't a two man job."

Poking his head around the porch, the redhead playfully teased, "Don't you just love a challenge?"

"Kurtttt!"

"Besides craving a Bertha burger, we thought about helping you out."

"Is Greg really alive?" squealed a giddy Emma.

"In the flesh, Em, the NWC broadcast of his execution was bogus."

"So you're a Watchmen too?" asked a skeptical Travis.

"For the glory of God, so where's our Miracle Girl?"

"They're holding her in the Downtown Security Office."

"But, Jake, that doesn't figure?"

"We're wondering why they haven't executed Ree."

"Ease up, Travis, it ain't over yet. The Holy Spirit will lead us."

"What are you saying, Jake?"

"How awesome is this," winked Kurt, "the Q is making a comeback."

"I'm Natalie Roberts reporting live from the two Witnesses' funeral. This is the fourth day of this celebration and the enthusiasm from this glorious crowd hasn't diminished; it's actually getting stronger."

Standing beside her was a well known Catholic bishop.

"Father, these resisters are calling their leader, Yeshua." 1

"This is absolutely ridiculous. Matthew 24:23-26 clearly warns us not to look for Jesus on earth."

The veteran reporter moved on to the next speaker.

"Let's meet Aziz Yusuf Qasin, a cleric from the Al-Aqsa Mosque atop the Temple Mount. What is your opinion of this procession?"

"It's heartbreaking to see so many zealots parading after another phony messiah. Such Zionist propaganda will only escalate the tensions between Jew and Muslim."

"So why didn't the NWC stop this remnant from entering the city?"

"Kayin has lost his courage. Many are demanding he resign. Several world leaders are now convinced a war in the Middle East is inevitable."

Crouched behind a van in the Security parking lot, the Q Squad was silently praying. Agents on the late night shift were checking in.

"I don't get it, Abe. The two Witnesses are dead. What does the leader of these resisters expect to gain by coming to Jerusalem?"

"I could care less what He does or says; the dying has stopped."

"What about the rumor of another war in Israel?"

"Kayin has been losing it ever since the Jehoshaphat invasion. What leader can sit by idly and watch two billion people die? If he had just allowed Iran to nuke Israel we wouldn't be in this mess."

"Is everybody set?" whispered Jake.

"Tell me why these jerks will not let me see my sister again?"

"We are asking for a miracle, Travis."

"Kurt, I watched Ree pray her guts out all the way to the station. She never got an answer. Either God isn't listening or He doesn't give a rip."

"Sometimes the Lord wants us to take a step of faith."

"One more time; I ain't into your blind faith."

"Travis, God cares a lot more about your sister than you. Now are you into this or should we just forget about it?"

Sheepishly he shrugged his shoulders. He was ready.

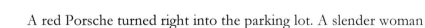

"Excuse me," blurted Natalie Roberts. "It appears Yeshua is offering up a prayer."

After raising His hands toward heaven, all eyes turned toward the one dressed in a robe sprinkled with blood. Suddenly those surrounding the two caskets gasped in fear. One Witness sat up; then the other. The onsite cameramen were trying to hold steady.

Lifting their hands toward heaven, the two Witnesses ascended in a cloud. 2 Without any warning, a huge earthquake rocked the old city. 3 Frenzied onlookers scattered for cover as thousands were killed. The brave News Anchor never moved.

"Rabbi, Rabbi, have we just witnessed the two Witnesses coming back to life?"

"That's impossible! Only God has such power."

"Will Yeshua participate in tomorrow night's Feast of Tabernacles?"

"I hope not. He has nothing to gain by disrupting our most joyous holy day."

"What exactly is this Feast about?"

"The Feast of Ingathering represents a time when the Messiah will gather believers before sending His final judgment." 4

A red Porsche turned right into the parking lot. A slender woman dressed in black got out and walked toward the Security Office.

"She fits the description," sighed Jake.

An uneasy Travis whispered, "Who is she?"

"Calls herself Death Angel, she's the assassin tracking your sister."

"Now listen up! I know my future and I'm making dam sure my sister isn't joining me."

Jumping up, he jogged out of the parking lot and entered the front entrance of the Security Office.

"What do you think, Jake?"

"If I were him, Em, I'd do the same thing."

The commotion erupted like a bomb. The dispatcher's lines were jammed with 911 calls. The agents pouring out of the station into their squad cars looked terrified.

"Can't you just feel an earthquake?" yelped Kurt. "Think about it, guys. Jesus must have just raised the two Witnesses from the dead!" 5

FIFTH DAY: THE LAMB ON MOUNT ZION

'Then I looked, and behold, a Lamb standing on Mount Zion, and with Him one hundred and forty four thousand, having His Father's name written on their foreheads.'
Revelation 14:1

Doyle Mercer hated emergencies. Waiting outside the station, his assistant wasn't surprised when his boss barely missed him before laying rubber down on the curb.

"Chief, you hear about the Witnesses?"

"I know everybody saw them disappear. What's our status?"

"Three more agents quit and went home."

"What a bunch of cowards."

Walking through the station his assistant started quoting fresh updates to his boss. Doyle wasn't listening. Her dark silhouette could be seen through the uneven glass of his office.

"Chief, you've got a visitor."

"Not until I review the emergency list."

"It's Death Angel."

His double take was more from intrigue than alarm.

"No interruptions for five minutes."

Sporting a new haircut, the Special Forces agent looked rested. As Doyle sat behind his desk, she crossed her long legs and lit a mini cigar.

"It's been a while, Mercer, how's your wife and daughter?"

"We're getting by, Cassandra. You okay? What's it like being AWOL for so long?"

"I've been specializing."

"Still using those pearl white pistols?"

"Wouldn't have it any other way, nothing tears up a body like a

22 caliber bullet."

"You screwed up at the hospital, Angel. Shooting up an ER isn't what Special Forces is about. You must think you're in the Wild West?"

"Doyle, how many packages have I delivered under your orders?"

"More than any agent I've ever had."

"So what are you whining about?"

"You're talking ancient history. You zoned out on us. Just how long have you been tracking this Tucker girl? Some are saying this teenage punk has your number. And what about the Santino hit? You were never authorized to terminate him, much less his son? I'm still getting heat for your free lancing!"

"I've come for RAT. She was originally assigned to me."

"You had enough chances. My boys know what to do."

"Your antics won't sway her. Bottom line, you cut her loose, you'll never see her sorry face again."

"This better be a clean hit; no loose ends. I want no more screw ups."

Reaching for his phone, he made the call.

"Chief, her brother is back."

"Just get them both out of my station."

Peeking through his office blinds, Death Angel smiled as Reenie and Travis Tucker strolled down Main Street hand in hand.

"Relax, Chief, how many times have I saved your butt?"

His hands clasped behind his head; he leaned back in his chair.

"So what did this itty bitty girl ever do to you?"

The annoyed assassin ran her fingernails through her long black hair.

"Doyle, I must say your tunnel vision has always been your biggest liability. This assignment isn't about the past; it's about her future. I call it preventive maintenance."

The next night their trail could be seen for miles. Thousands were holding candles. Imbedded within His remnant, the Lamb of God began His walk toward Mount Zion. 1 His followers were singing and waving palm branches.

"'Save now, I pray, O Lord... Blessed is He who comes in the name of the Lord. We have blessed you from the house of the Lord.

God is the Lord, and He has given us light...You are my God, and I will praise You; You are my God, I will exalt You.'" 2

"Only God can forgive sin!" begged a young woman. "Are you really the Messiah?"

Looking into her eyes, He replied, "'I am the light of the world. He who follows Me shall not walk in darkness but have the light of Life.'" 3

In the foreground was the majestic Temple. Baskets of fruit surrounding its base represented a harvest of souls preceding the final judgment of God. 4

A Messianic believer read from his Bible, "'And it shall come to pass that everyone who is left of all the nations which came against Jerusalem shall go up from year to year to worship the King, the Lord of hosts, and to keep the Feast of Tabernacles.'" 5

From the family room, a wound up Reenie announced, "C'mon everybody, Channel 6 is broadcasting the Feast of Tabernacles."

Travis and Kurt crashed on the leather couch. Jake and Emma sat in front of the old brick fireplace while Reenie sat in her father's recliner.

"Thanks guys. The Holy Spirit told me you would help me."

"It was your bro who made the play," reflected a candid Kurt.

"I thank God for you, Travis."

Looking at the TV he pretended not to hear his sister.

"No way, it's Nate Roberts," gawked Kurt. "She's a bulldog who doesn't know how to let go."

"Good evening, this is News with Natalie. Tonight, we are bringing you live coverage of the Feast of Tabernacles atop Mount Moriah. This Feast is also called Sukkot, which means 'tabernacle'. This celebration represents God's provision during the forty-year sojourn when the children of Israel dwelled in booths. Every year, five days after Yom Kippur, the Feast of Ingathering portrays..."

The frantic shouting from the bottom of the Mount was frightening. Cameramen near the Temple were already filming the massive gridlock.

"It appears Yeshua and His followers are attempting to participate in this Feast. Please allow me to give you a short rundown of the bizarre events of this past week. Five days ago the NWC executed the two Witnesses. This one act precipitated the largest celebration in history. Two days later, in an attempt to disrupt, a mob entered Jerusalem. Then on Wednesday, the leader of these resisters joined the Witnesses' funeral. Excuse me, can you hear the singing? They're singing the traditional song sung by those who celebrate this holiday, Psalm 118."

"Our Lord reigns!" praised Kurt. "Get ready, slew foot, the seventh trumpet is affixing to sound."

"The mystery of God is finished!" shouted an ecstatic Jake. "Jesus has redeemed the remnant from Israel believing in Him." 6

"Don't forget those who got the victory over the Beast," grinned Emma. "They are on the sea of glass in heaven preparing to sing the song of Moses and the song of the Lamb." 7

Everyone was worshipping the Lord but Travis. Suddenly the Miracle Girl sensed an evil presence from behind. A chill shot up her spine as she slowly turned around. Standing in the kitchen, the assassin cocked the triggers of her white pearl revolvers.

"Hate to break up your hallelujah party. How tacky, Reenie, the same drab furniture after all these years."

"What do you want, Cassandra?"

"Didn't Jezebel tell you? She's coming for a visit."

"Jezebel is a liar! She has no control over me."

"I knew you wouldn't register with Doyle's stooges. I've been sent to complete this job."

"You're dreaming. I'm a new creation in Christ."

"I'm afraid you're not seeing the whole picture."

Interrupting, Kurt shared, "The picture is..."

"Shut up!" seethed Baphomet, Cassandra's spirit guide. "Go ahead, Tucker, tell them all about you're so called future."

"Would love to; any time now the Lamb of God is going to take back control of this world from Satan. Everything you have believed in, everything you've stood for will be destroyed."

"You're such a mindless idiot."

"Your little game is over, Angel. The wicked charade you've lived since your last visit to my house is a lie. You have willingly been Satan's pawn, and for what?"

"Reenie's right," added Emma. "All Satan wanted was your soul."

"I've actually seen my Master's stone throne. There is nothing like it!"

"If Satan is so strong," challenged Jake, "why doesn't he stop this remnant from worshipping Jesus? The devil never had the power to stop what God has ordained." 8

Her hands were trembling. A war was raging from the demons indwelling her. Travis had never seen a demon-possessed person manifest. With her face contorting, her groans sounded like an old man.

"I have my orders; each of you must register or die."

Lunging forward he shoved her backwards into the kitchen. One gun went off.

"Travis!" shrieked Reenie.

Lying on her back she wasn't moving. Blood was spewing from the sides of her mouth.

"Cassandra what's going on?"

"Baphomet is gone. The demons under its control have left to indwell another."

"Why did you introduce me to Jezebel? I was only five years old."

"I had no choice; Satan was threatening to kill me."

"Why did the devil choose me?"

"He knows about your mission. He will never allow it."

"Cassandra, listen to me. I forgive you for what you did to me. Do you understand?"

"I hear you. Be careful this ain't over. Satan will send others."

Her pale face and chapped lips looked cold as it dropped to its side.

Getting up, Travis was speechless. Cheers were coming from the TV. The 144,000 were worshipping the Lamb of God atop Mount Zion.

"I can't believe she's dead," cried Reenie.

"Jake, we gotta get out of here," urged an anxious Kurt. "We can't be out in the open when the bowl judgments hit."

"Reenie, can you lead us to the Santino's cave?"

"Sure. But we still need a car and a full tank of gas."

"Give me two hours, Jake. I'll get one."

"Okay, let's split up. Kurt and Emma, you meet Reenie and me at the exit of George Wallace Park in two hours. Travis will meet us there with the car."

Burying her face in her little brother's chest, she began to sob.

Gently holding her, he whispered, "It's over, sis, Cassandra won't be bothering you anymore."

To see His blood stained robe brought renewed hope to those who had not yet worshipped the Beast, his image, or received his mark.

Her hands resting on her mother's shoulders, Johanna was jumping up and down.

"Save souls, Lord, lift up a standard against the enemy." 9

"It's the remnant of Jacob returning to Almighty God. Zechariah prophesied believers from the nations would worship the Lord during the Feast of Tabernacles." 10

Bowing her head, Johanna prayed, "Father, in Jesus name, may You protect Jake."

"This young man must be very special."

"I miss him so much, Mama. Maybe you can visit Jake during the Millennium?"

"I'd love that."

"I don't see Yeshua anymore. Can we move closer?"

"I don't see how."

"But what about Ruth's vision?"

"Sweet one, I know her vision was very specific. I also know we cannot make God's will happen through our own strength. If her vision is of God, it must come to pass in His timing not ours."

SEVENTH TRUMPET: HE SHALL REIGN

'Then the seventh angel sounded. And there were loud voices in heaven,
saying, "The kingdoms of this world have become the kingdoms of our
Lord and of His Christ,
and He shall reign forever..."'
Revelation 11:15

An angel from above announced, "But in the days of the sounding of the seventh trumpet, when he is about to sound, the mystery of God would be finished, as He declared to His servants the prophets.'" 1

The prophets stood in the magnificent light streaming from His glorious Throne. Spontaneous applause was rippling through the heavenlies. Amidst such adoration, the seventh trumpet sounded.

Loud voices were proclaiming, "...The kingdoms of this world have become the kingdoms of our Lord and of His Christ, and He shall reign forever and ever.'" 2

The twenty-four elders fell on their faces and worshiped God.

"...We give you thanks, O Lord God Almighty, The One who is and who was and who is to come, because You have taken Your great power and reigned. The nations were angry, and Your wrath has come, and the time of the dead, that they should be judged, and that You should reward Your servants the prophets and the saints, and those who fear Your name... should destroy those who destroy the earth.'" 3

The bride to be, the twenty-four elders, the four living creatures, and the angelic host, watched in awe as the Temple opened in heaven. Seraphim stood on each corner as a cloud of fire engulfed the Ark of His Covenant. 4

It only took a few seconds for a huge cloud to cast a dark shadow over the Temple Mount. Then a ring of fire settled upon His shoulders. Gripped by the fear of God; many fell prostrate to the ground and cried out in deep repentance to the One their forefathers had pierced. 5

"Look at His face, Johanna, Yeshua's eyes are on fire! This is like the glory resting on Him in the midst of the golden lamp stands." 6

The rush down the mount was terrifying.

"Watch it, Mama; the followers of the Beast are panicking."

No one knew where it came from. The swirling white light was captivating at first sight. Mankind had never seen this fallen angel in its original form. In shining brilliance, an enchanting Lucifer bowed. Vainly it tried to free itself. Grimacing in pain, it unsuccessfully tried to curse God before the world. For those who never believed in a literal devil, his physical manifestation was shocking. From the time of Adam, when the serpent first gained authority over man, Satan feared this moment. His obsession was always to be like God; to deceive as many as possible. Groveling at the feet of Jesus it was losing its light. Within seconds, it shriveled into the hideous creature it had become through pride. An infectious hilarity swept over the crowd. Covering its ears, the devil's humiliation was obvious.

"Silence!" it screeched.

Bowing to the Son of God, the foul spirit acknowledged in an agonizing voice, "I, Lucifer, declare, 'the kingdoms of this world have become the kingdoms of our Lord and of His Christ, and He shall reign forever and ever!'" 7

With his authority surrendered, the demon vanished. Another angel instantly appeared.

"'We give thanks, O Lord God Almighty, The One who is and who was and who is to come, because You have taken Your great power and reigned!'" 8

In the past two years, Louis Cooper hadn't missed a meeting. The room had a lonely feeling on this overcast afternoon. Staring into space, he was all alone. Even though the constant bickering among the membership brought about its demise, the evil pride controlling the Chairman of the Bethany Ministers Association wouldn't let him give up. He knew the two ministers approaching the podium.

"Mind if we join you, Louis?"

"Whatever."

"How are you feeling?"

"Lousy, Andrew, how about you?"

"Do you remember Dr. Charles Everett Kyle?"

"So, Doc, what brings you to Bethany? Maybe join the BMA?"

"Not interested. I'm here for J.W.'s funeral. Wasn't he your mentor?"

"Everybody knows that."

"Then why did you miss his funeral?"

"Why do you care?"

"Mrs. Brown was asking for you," whispered the priest.

"How did J.W. die?"

"He took his life after the Witnesses were executed. What was he thinking?"

"I guess it depends how you look at it," Louis reflected without any emotion.

"What's that supposed to mean?" pressed an angry Charles.

"I'm talking about the events of His coming. Standing in the batter's box; each of us was confident we could make contact. It didn't matter what pitch the Devil threw; we thought we were ready."

"Satan has nothing to do with it."

"Save it, Doc, your belief Satan was bound at the cross doesn't hold water."

"So you actually believe this metaphysical scene on the Temple Mount was somehow a confrontation between Jesus and Satan?"

"Not a confrontation. Satan just surrendered his power over this world to God."

"You have no idea what you're talking about."

"The Messiah has returned to Jerusalem for the salvation of Israel. It's history, Doc. What I never understood is how this visit fits into His second coming."

"God will do something no one expects," smirked the priest.

"He already has. Jesus highlighted the events warning believers His coming was near. Everyone had a clear view of the playing field. We all had our chance to hit. Then God allowed Satan to throw a changeup; a pitch most Christians never expected."

"You can't mean the religious harlot's lie? I've personally met Pope Michael. He is a humble man with a love for all faiths. For God's sake, Louis, just look what the Holy See has done for our world."

"Close Andy. Certainly the false signs from the second beast were deceptive. I'm not talking about that."

"Isn't it obvious," laughed Charles. "He believes Joshua Kayin is the Antichrist. He also thinks our ID's are the infamous mark of the beast."

"That's a lie!" scoffed Andrew. "Lord Kayin is a very religious man."

"Didn't Jesus say, "...Take heed that no one deceives you. For many will come in My name, saying, 'I am the Christ,' and will deceive many." 9

"Louis, I don't recall Kayin ever claiming to be the Messiah?"

"Try reading what it says."

"Not another Protestant revelation?"

"Most born again Christians would never have listened to the cults, New Agers, even the false prophets on TV. Only pastors saying Jesus is the Christ could deceive so many. We were sincerely wrong."

"That's not what Jesus is saying in this passage!"

"The changeup by Satan was the proper understanding of the second coming. The seventh trumpet has sounded, Andy. The Lamb of God has gathered the remnant who believes in Him."

"Did you hear a trumpet, Andrew?" chided Charles.

"In the past two years were either of you ever stung?"

"What does that matter?"

"Those stung will suffer a sore after the first bowl is poured out."

"So when will Jesus return to heaven?" taunted the theologian.

"After splitting the Mount of Olives and hiding His remnant in Azal." 10

"Why doesn't He just stay and watch?" chuckled the priest.

"He's returning to marry His bride." 11

"No Christian denomination has ever taught such nonsense."

"What denominations are you talking about, Charles? You mean the churches that joined the mother of harlots? You don't want to see it. It was Satan's changeup."

"Before we leave I'd love to hear this new interpretation; wouldn't you Andrew."

Folding his arms the priest nodded.

"Looking at your smug faces says a lot. The heresies we taught are going to burn up at the judgment seat of Christ."

"Stop trying to read God's mind. He's our judge not you."

"Satan knew how to deceive. It was something we never expected."

"Which is?"

"Most pastors taught the saints would never war against the Beast. 12 When Kayin seized authority over the nations, most Christians didn't even believe in an Antichrist, much less recognize his mark."

"There is only one second coming!" blurted Charles. "The Word of God is going to catch up His elect before returning to earth at the battle of Armageddon. We are almost there."

Neither expected Louis' slow high-pitched whistle.

"That's another lie Satan has sown for two thousand years. The coming of the Lord actually has a beginning and an ending. Within His coming the Son will perform His Father's will. His coming began with the gathering of the elect by angels from the wrath to come. 13 When the fullness of the Gentiles ended, the Deliverer came to earth and fulfilled the Mystery of God, the salvation of Israel. 14 After Jesus marries His bride in heaven the Word of God will return at the supper of the great God, Armageddon, and cast the two beasts into the lake of fire." 15

"Is this when He sets up his so called earthy kingdom?" teased the priest.

"His second coming will end when the Lamb of God and His bride descend to a new earth inside a new heaven, the Holy Jerusalem." 16

"Please tell us you're done?"

"Only a seared conscience could miss this truth so late in the game."

"So you're saying you're more spiritual than us?"

"Absolutely not, your most Honorable, Excellency, Doctor, Reverend, Charles Everett Kyle. I'm certainly not as spiritual as you or Andy."

"I pity you, Cooper. Your faith is in your works. My salvation is not based by anything I do. I'm saved by grace alone. I am eternally secure. I'd hate to be in your shoes at the white throne judgment."

Striding toward the exit, the respected theologian wondered why he had ever come. In his mind, Louis Cooper was just another pastor who was never really saved.

"Hey, Charles, didn't J. W.'s wife read a letter he left behind?"

"What of it?"

"Heard J.W. regretted taking the mark of the beast, sure doesn't sound like someone who was eternally secure, now does it?"

From the bushes Reenie whispered, "Here they come."

"Any sign of Travis?"

"Not yet, Kurt."

"JJ, it won't be fun when Mercer hears about Death Angel. We should be underground by now."

A resigned Jake was going over their options when they heard the shrill of loud sirens.

"They've found Cassandra!" gasped Emma.

Accelerating through the back entrance of the park he wondered if he was too late. After hitting the brakes, the passenger's window went down.

"Where is everybody? Ree, it's cool."

"We're over here Travis! Excellent choice, bro. Who owns the nice wheels?"

From the driver's window she heard, "That would be me!"

"Gregggg, you've come back!"

"God changed my plans. I picked up Travis on Cherry; it was a divine appointment."

"I had the preacher pegged wrong. You could say he was moving in the zone when we met."

Jumping out, the former pastor playfully grabbed Kurt and Jake.

"Okay, dudes, what've you been up to? Seriously, the NWC has issued warrants for your arrest. That means we are way too hot an item for the Vineyard."

"Tell him, Reenie," encouraged Emma.

"I know how to get to the Santino's cave. It's got food and water. And we'll be protected from the bowl judgments too."

"It's worth the risk, Miracle Girl."

"Glory to God!" praised Kurt. "I just love camping."

Reenie hesitated as everyone piled into the van.

"C'mon, Travis, let's go."

"I don't belong."

"What do you mean? You rescued me from the Security Station. You saved me from Cassandra. You found Greg. We all love you; I love you."

"I know that now. Before Jesus came in the clouds, we didn't even know what love was. Jezebel made sure of that."

Tenderly she offered, "You can still come with us."

"And what happens when sores break out all over my face? Nah, I'll pass. Don't do this, Ree. I had my chances to follow Jesus; I just wasn't interested."

She wept as she hugged her brother for the final time.

"I wish it could have been different, I really do."

"Me, too, I'll always love you, Ree. Now get going, you don't have much time."

Jumping inside the van; the slamming of the door pierced her heart. She couldn't bring herself to look back. He didn't look either. He started walking. It didn't matter where; he just wanted to walk.

AN EVERLASTING KINGDOM

'Then the kingdom and dominion, And the greatness of the kingdoms under the whole heaven, Shall be given to the people, the saints of the Most High. His kingdom is an everlasting kingdom, and all dominions shall serve and obey Him.'
Daniel 7:27

Two lonely figures stood by the magnificent picture window. They were admiring the breathtaking view of Rome. 1 In the eyes of the world, this was the city of cities. For someone looking through spiritual eyes they would discern something completely different. This was not a city of truth but one of spiritual wickedness. Since Babylon, Satan had deceptively fed this religious counterfeit to the nations.

Reluctantly he confessed, "Our Master warned us the Christ would attempt to return to Zion."

"Did you say attempt?" seethed Kayin.

"So what has actually been accomplished?" pressed his false prophet.

"The seventh trumpet has sounded. 2 God has begun to reign." 3

"Does this mean we're giving up?"

"Not a chance."

"So how can we stop what has been decreed?"

"By feeding off the anger from the nations, destroying Israel at Armageddon is our best hope of regaining control."

"The Bible says the Ancient of Days is going to give the Son of Man an everlasting kingdom of peoples, nations, and languages! 4 The saints will obey the Most High."

Stepping away Kayin closed his eyes. Satan was summoning him into a dream like trance.

"I am the Abomination of Desolation who defiled the holy place of the Most High. 5 I am the Son of Perdition who was exalted above everything that is worshipped. 6 I am the Beast who overcame many saints during the Great Tribulation. 7 I am the Man of Sin who blasphemed God, His tabernacle, and His people in heaven." 8

The frail priest despondently stumbled out the door. Even from the foyer he could hear his ranting.

"Was it not I who made the earth tremble, who destroyed cities?"9

Waiting for the elevator, he thought about the most powerful leader the world had ever known. For a moment, he reminisced how mankind worshipped Joshua Kayin. The popularity of the WFM, their takeover of Jerusalem, the worldwide recognition of the NWC; their dream of what could have been was over. Deep down he knew they couldn't stop the wrath of God. He could only listen.

"Was it not I who spoke pompous words against the Most High? Was it not I who persecuted the saints? 10 Was it not I..."

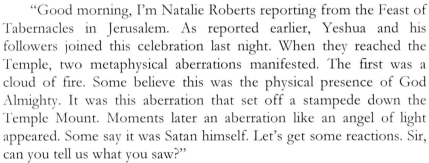

"Good morning, I'm Natalie Roberts reporting from the Feast of Tabernacles in Jerusalem. As reported earlier, Yeshua and his followers joined this celebration last night. When they reached the Temple, two metaphysical aberrations manifested. The first was a cloud of fire. Some believe this was the physical presence of God Almighty. It was this aberration that set off a stampede down the Temple Mount. Moments later an aberration like an angel of light appeared. Some say it was Satan himself. Let's get some reactions. Sir, can you tell us what you saw?"

"What an absolute mockery! Why the NWC allowed this imposter to interfere, I'll never know. His followers are fanatics."

"Some believe the devil appeared?"

"Utter nonsense!"

"What about the two Witnesses coming back to life?"

"Nobody believes they were ever dead."

Turning left, Natalie barely sidestepped a young lady kneeling on the ground. Her hands were covering her mouth.

"Hello, may I have your thoughts on the past week?"

"Zechariah predicted the Messiah would return to Jerusalem. 11 It was the glory of the Father resting upon His Son."

"Every religious authority present rejects such a literal

interpretation. Why do you believe this?"

"God Almighty promised to protect a remnant. Soon, the Lamb of God will split the Mount of Olives. He's going to lead those who believe in Him to safety."

"Why would He do that?"

"For protection from God's final wrath."

"If this is true then why aren't you following this Messiah to the Mount of Olives?"

After raising her right hand, she bent over and wept.

"There you have it everybody. You make the call. Tragically this charlatan has deceived many during this Sukkot celebration. Honestly, folks, we shouldn't be focusing on the antics of another spurious prophet. Our future as one people depends on..."

Fall was in the air. It was a special time for those who understood the importance of the final two Feasts. Amidst the charred hillside a few trees were changing color. No one was talking; not even Kurt. For the past two years, Satan relentlessly sent attack after attack against the Q Squad. The Holy Spirit countered with hundreds of miracles. Angels had intervened in response to their prayers.

"I don't see the road to the cave, Reenie? Where's our next turn?"

"See that small field on your left? It should be on the other side of it. Bret said a small pond is in the front of the cave; maybe a few trees."

Maneuvering between burnt bushes Greg spotted the dirt road. After passing three caves, the van stopped in front of several evergreens. Behind the trees was an infected pond littered with dead birds.

"Way to go, Reenie," cheered Emma. "A voice for the Lord."

She didn't reply. This is what she always wanted; to be used by God.

They could hardly believe it when they walked inside.

"Are you kidding me!" echoed Kurt. "This has to be a five star cave!"

In the middle of the cavern was a deep pit surrounded by narrow wooden benches. Sleeping bags and blankets were neatly tucked under the benches. Supplies were stored under a large ledge overlooking the ground floor.

"God bless Anthony Santino!" hollered a grateful Jake. "Over here, everybody! Look at these plastic containers of water! We're talking coffee, packaged food, apple juice, flour, canned fruit, gee, we've even got battery operated walkie-talkies."

Reenie softly shared, "Thanks for caring, Bret."

While everyone inspected the supplies, a curious Emma decided to climb the ledge to get a better view. Reaching the top, she froze. The letter was taped between two wooden sticks stuck in the ground.

"Hey, JJ, what's Greg up to?" asked a guarded Reenie.

"He's hiding the van. In case we need a quick escape. Here he is."

From tunnel two Greg threw Miracle Girl a brown paper bag.

"Wheeeee! Chocolate, marshmallows, and graham crackers, I say we celebrate our Savior's return with some hot chocolate s'mores."

A giddy Kurt announced, "It's party time for the Q."

The slender brunette remembered the evergreens outside the cave.

"Stick holders coming right up."

Sipping apple juice around the fire, Jake asked, "Hey, Greg, you never told us why you came back? Wasn't there trouble at the Vineyard?"

"Rueben Rodriguez is a Watchman that trained most of the staff at the camp. After praying with me, he offered to oversee the Vineyard while I was away. He's a great leader."

"You mean you'll be with us till the Millennium?"

"Lord willing. It took me a while to get what God was saying."

"Must be a lot of kids depending on you?"

"My doubts had nothing to do with the Vineyard. The divine warning I received was for Reenie. The Lord wants to use the Miracle Girl to save lives. Her mission will take place during the bowl judgments. The choice to obey is hers. We can't interfere. If Reenie agrees, she'll need our protection. What about it, Emma?"

"Count me in."

Jake simply nodded.

"Whoa," whispered Kurt, "I can hear the mission impossible theme."

Skipping back into the cave, Reenie joyfully asked, "Who wants honors?"

As Kurt attached marshmallows to sticks, she placed the chocolate on the graham cracker squares.

Looking at her eyes Jake knew something wasn't right. Then he saw the white envelope.

Playfully he asked, "You got something for me, Em?"

"Turns out this is the cave you saw in your vision. I found this letter on top of the ledge. Jessie must have hid here before leaving Alabama. Here you go, JJ, I pray you will finally get some answers."

Clutching her letter a thrilled Jake took off for the ledge.

The smoke from the roaring fire smelled great.

"Say, Greg, did you see the broadcast of Jesus entering Jerusalem?"

"Sure did, Kurt. He looked so different than I ever imagined."

"How insane was the resurrection of the two Witnesses? Nate Roberts turned pale after they went up."

God's end time puzzle was falling into place. His Word, which had suffered such ridicule, was shining for all to see.

While licking chocolate off her fingers, a relaxed Reenie shared, "I must say these s'mores could be the best ever. These won't last long, where's Jake?"

Everyone looked up toward the ledge.

"Miracle Girl, you could say he's visiting with an old friend."

"Will he be long?"

"Oh yeah," giggled Emma, "it'll be a while."

His abrupt release by his enemies was miraculous. Still, it was not easy for the freedom fighter to throw away his disguise. Matthias carefully avoided three Jordanian terrorists stationed near the base of the Temple Mount. Squeezing between a throng of people a young boy stumbled into him.

"Hold up, son. Why are these people so afraid?"

"Yeshua defeated Satan. The devil appeared as a beautiful white angel. Then it lost its light. That's when everybody freaked out. But I'm not afraid."

"Why are you in such a hurry?"

"Before the Lord fights the nations who fight against Israel, He has to split the Mount of Olives."

"How could that help His cause?"

"Yeshua's going to protect His remnant."

"What is your name? And where is your family?"

"I'm Jeremiah. I lost my parents last year. Sir, do you have a family?"

"Why do you ask?"

"I want to be part of Yeshua's family. I promised myself if I ever saw the Messiah I would give Him my heart. That's why I want to go to the Mount of Olives."

Grasping his arm, the Commander pleaded, "How do you know what you saw is true?"

"Only the Son of God can do what Yeshua did."

Aaron Glazer had never dealt with his pain. Nothing he tried could ever make it go away. He had come to believe the lie he would die with the horrors of war burned within his spirit. Yet, this young Israeli had just spoken the words that could unlock his bitterness.

"Jeremiah, can you make it to the Mount of Olives by yourself?"

"Sure I can."

"I wish you well."

Waving goodbye, the weary soldier began his journey up the Temple Mount.

"God bless you, my friend," yelled the boy. "I pray you'll find what you're looking for."

WHOM THE LORD CALLS

'...That whoever calls on the name of the Lord shall be saved. For in Mount Zion and in Jerusalem there shall be deliverance, as the Lord has said, among the remnant whom the Lord calls.'
Joel 2:32

Reenie loved spending time with her new friends. She was hoping for a spiritual time out when Jake returned from reading Jessie's letter. Greg had just finished praying for believers traveling to the Vineyard. While Emma served hot coffee, Kurt decided to hand out blankets.

"Thanks, Greg, what awesome chocolate s'mores."

"You're all worth it."

"C'mon, if you hadn't obeyed God none of us would be sitting around this fire."

"Emma, I'm with you tonight because the Lord used the testimony of my wife and two children. Somehow they convinced me not to register. Funny, I always thought I was being obedient to the Holy Spirit. Unfortunately, I had one slight problem. I wasn't saved!"

"You mean you were just going through the motions?"

"I looked the part, talked it, all while living a lie. My pride prevented me from yielding to God's conviction. I was listening to the wrong voices."

"Wow, Greg, I sure would like to hear some of the things the Lord has taught you; maybe some spiritual truths that changed your life."

"Okay, Reenie. God taught me this truth through the ministry of a friend named John Ryals."

"You knew him?" she groaned. "He used to be my pastor."

"John saved me from agents and helped me in rescue."

"Then why did he take the mark of the beast?"

"Many pastors believed the gifts of the Holy Spirit passed away with the apostles. They weren't listening to His voice when they registered. During the beginning of sorrows their focus was keeping their jobs. By the time they entered the Great Tribulation it was too late."

"Where is Pastor Ryals now?"

"The anguish was too much. One day he just walked away. John taught his congregation a real Christian could never be deceived and depart from their faith in the Lord."

"How could anyone believe that?" 1

"Kurt, the traditions of men deceived more Christians than we ever imagined."

"But how could you preach every Sunday without the Holy Spirit?"

"I was a proud legalist. My ministry was just a job. I thought I could obtain God's approval by conforming to a specific set of rules. Hearing and obeying the Holy Spirit doesn't mean much to a legalist."

"Not you, Greg?" questioned a surprised Emma.

"It's easy for someone who has never surrendered to God. I was self-disciplined, worked long hours, made sure my congregation followed our denomination's traditions. To the city I looked spiritual. Some pastors even looked up to me."

"But God knew."

"Yes, the Holy Spirit knew my motives were wrong even if the religious community had no clue."

"But didn't anybody see through your religious, uh..."

"You mean my mask, Kurt?"

"Yeah, how could you swallow something so phony?"

"I thought my works would get me into heaven. Some close friends rebuked me but I just brushed aside their warnings. Bowing his head, the former pastor prayed, "Father, salvation is a gift of Your love. We praise You for sending Your Son. We worship the Lamb of God who took away our sins by dying on the cross. We pray for the salvation of anyone who hasn't worshiped Kayin or received his mark.""

Thousands were still lingering beside the Temple. Some were waiting for the glory of God to reappear. Others were debating whether the manifestation of Satan was real. There was one more event left to accomplish before the Lord returns to heaven for His marriage.

Within the frightened crowd, a bewildered Matthias sat down on the ground. This freedom fighter had always fought for the defenseless. This was different. They weren't asking for his protection. He knew nothing about their pleas for salvation.

Clenching his fists he cried out, "The sheep are calling for their shepherd but He is gone."

He had always overcome by exerting his own strength. But now there was nothing more to give. He could feel his tears touching his hands. Aaron Glazer had always promised his soldiers he would never surrender. Ironically, at this moment, that's all he could think about.

Arm in arm, the mother and daughter cautiously made their way down the scattered hillside. Several times they had to fight off self-pity. Stepping around a soldier dressed in green army fatigues, her face turned serious, almost stoic. Bending over, Miriam placed her hand on his shoulder. Glancing up at her daughter she waited.

"Daddy, you made it!"

Spontaneously Miriam and Johanna fell to their knees. All three embraced in their first hug in twenty years. They could feel the tenderness of Yeshua in his grip.

"Daddy, have you become a believer?"

"Just moments ago."

"This is why this passage just popped into my mind. 'And it shall come to pass that whoever calls on the name of the Lord shall be saved. For in Mount Zion and in Jerusalem there shall be deliverance, as the Lord has said, among the remnant whom the Lord calls.' 2 Daddy, the Lord has saved you!"

"By believing you have received salvation atop Mount Zion," gushed Miriam. "Makes you feel clean all over, doesn't it?"

"All I remember is closing my eyes and seeing Yeshua's hand reaching out for me. I told Him I believe He died on the cross for my sins and rose again. Then after praying for forgiveness, I asked Yeshua to be my Lord."

The anger in his eyes was gone. His giddiness was something Miriam hadn't seen since their wedding day.

"I want to thank you both for risking your lives for me. The moment I saw your face in my office, Miriam, I knew the Lord was with you. The peace you had could not be faked. I always wanted it; I just never thought it was possible."

"Only by the blood of the Lamb! Daddy, did you see Satan bow to Yeshua?"

"No but I heard from a friend it was a miracle. Did you see it?"

"We sure did. Habakkuk prophesied, 'Look among the nations and watch-Be utterly astounded. For I will work a work in your days which you would not believe, though it were told you.'" 3

"I believe."

Reaching over, Miriam gave Aaron a warm embrace.

Wrapping her arms around her mother and father, Johanna Glazer led out in a prayer of protection for her dear friend, Ruth Lentz and her parents. Amidst the Feast of Tabernacles, all three worshiped the Lord atop Mount Zion.

This SWAT Force led by Doyle Mercer was made up of three teams; each having three soldiers. Outfitted with night goggles, they would track in complete darkness.

"Commander, their tire tracks reach a plateau of caves just up ahead. Then they disappear."

"This is a piece of cake. These kids are harmless."

"What about the Special Forces agent they murdered?"

"Who knows, maybe Tucker blew her away. She must have had enough of Cassandra."

"Sir, some of these caves have tunnels. If they're hiding; this could take longer than we anticipated."

"Santino knew what he was doing when he chose this area. He was once a Navy Seal."

"Where is he now?"

"Death Angel terminated him. You would've thought he might have fared a little better."

"Sir, if they see us before we see them it's possible they could escape through an inner tunnel, request permission to send two of my men to block the exit road."

"Denied! They can't be far. I repeat; no one shall attempt to apprehend any resister until I am present. Being busted by the NWC is the last thing on their minds. Now get going."

"I guess I'll go next. It sure seems like a lot more than two years since Emma and I got saved."

Looking into the fire, his hands clasped, his elbows resting on his knees; the redhead felt the unction of the Holy Spirit to testify.

"It happened when I was ten; something about me not doing my homework right. So my teacher wouldn't let me go on a field trip. My mom was so ticked off. On the way home she really let me have it."

"Kurt, what is wrong with you? You were told three times on how to do this assignment. Why won't you listen?"

"Looking back, it's easy to see. By listening, I would have to share what I thought. So to hide my fears; I became the class clown."

"And where did that lead you?" asked a curious Greg.

"The Holy Spirit showed me I was using my jokes like a fence to keep kids from hurting me. But the more they laughed, the lonelier I became. When you and Jessie arrived at the Dooley farm I was struggling big time. I had issues that needed to be talked out. So God brought someone who knew nothing about me; like a clean start. He used Jessie. I know what you're thinking. At first she laughed at my stories, even my one-liners. But I soon found out she wanted to go deeper. Jessie wanted to get to know the real me. She was saying, "I love you Kurt, I respect you, and I want to understand you.""

"Outstanding," whispered the former pastor.

"It was weird at first. It didn't matter how many times I interrupted her. Jessie never gave up on me. Her listening was so unselfish. When she would listen to me, I could feel God's love."

"She has a way of making you feel special," beamed Emma.

Kurt Abbott had just jumped the biggest hurdle of his life. His tears were more from joy than regret.

"God was saying if you listen, the fears tormenting me will go away."

"The Lord is leading you, bro."

"Thanks, Miracle Girl. God always cared but I resisted. So the Holy Spirit arranged circumstances which helped me listen. Jessie showed me a good listener allows others to share their problems, their sins, their hurts, even their dreams. Her dream was to find her aunt. Ever since she left, I've prayed God's perfect will for her and her family."

Holding her letter Jake silently thanked the Lord.

"Could you share how the Holy Spirit spoke to you, Kurt?"

"Sure Greg. While praying I saw an ostrich hiding his head in the sand. It was a picture of believers in the last days who wouldn't listen to the warnings by the Holy Spirit. And you know why? It was because they didn't want to be held responsible."

"Man is responsible even if he chooses to be willingly ignorant," the former pastor sadly confessed.

"How silly is that," posed Reenie. "Sounds like Wicca witches who don't believe in Satan."

"I realized I wanted to follow God no matter what it cost me. But I had so many questions. Will believers survive the seven bowl judgments? When will the Lamb of God return with His bride? Why does God allow Satan to deceive the nations after a thousand years? And when will the Son give His millennial kingdom back to His Father?"

"Wow, that's quite a list," kidded Reenie. "So what did you do?"

"I listened. That day I learned I didn't have to talk it up to hear from God. There is no magical formula. The key to hearing from God is to show reverence by listening."

"This is deep. Did you receive any verses while praying?"

"Sure did JJ. This is my call to the ministry. Jesus promised, '... For all things that I heard from My Father I have made known to you.'" 4

"So Jesus will reveal to us everything He has heard from His Father?"

"What a promise, huh, Reenie? The only way to become an obedient disciple is to be willing to listen to the Holy Spirit before we act."

The crackling fire seemed louder than usual. Everyone had their eyes closed; no one was talking.

ENTER BY THE NARROW GATE

'Enter by the narrow gate; for wide is the gate and broad is the way that leads to destruction, and there are many who go in by it. Because narrow is the gate and difficult is the way which leads to life, and there are few who find it.'
Matthew 7:13

Watching her brother share with such transparency was a joy for Emma. The past two years had been a real roller coaster ride. One moment they were completing a successful rescue; the next they were on the run. Her most painful memory was losing her parents. It happened the day they went underground with their new friend, Carlos Delgado. The Abbots had just finished a Sunday afternoon dinner. Their father was watching breaking news on the Middle East while their mother was stacking dirty dishes in the dishwasher. There was nothing left to do but walk out the backdoor. Grabbing their backpacks from the garage Kurt and Emma headed for the driveway. They could hear their mother humming a Beatle's tune from the open kitchen window.

"Hey guys, can you make a quick trip to the store for me? I'll leave the list on the kitchen counter. On second thought, I'll do it. You just finish what you've planned."

Emma could still remember her mother's haunting last words. Overcoming the guilt for not answering back took awhile. It was different now. She and her brother had been born from above. Jesus had become their pearl of great price. 1

"I want to thank God for choosing me to be a disciple. To see so many reject this honor was heartbreaking. Their refusal to be led by the Holy Spirit was an insult to the Spirit of Grace. 2 Being able to look back, I'm so grateful."

"It wasn't hard to feel His mercy, was it, sis?"

"Yeah, when you're battling the devil, God's shield of protection is mighty comforting."

"A real crash course in Spiritual Warfare 101," grinned Greg. "So, Emma, when did the Holy Spirit teach you to fight back spiritually?"

"It was when we got separated from you and Carlos. After I called a code green demons started throwing one lie after another. The house we were hiding in was like a war zone. Remember Kurt?"

Shaking his head the redhead raised his cup of coffee.

"Felt like a cloud of fear. It was so thick you could almost reach out and touch it. The apostle Paul exhorts us to fight the good fight of faith. That day, Kurt and I needed to discern what was coming at us. Talk about an Ephesians 6:11 encounter."

"Why do you think so many believers refused to fight?"

"Jake, I've asked the Holy Spirit that many times. Paul warned us to be aware of Satan's attacks. Without the shield of faith, the helmet of salvation, the sword of the Spirit, the girdle of truth, and the breastplate of righteousness, we aren't going to defeat any demon." 3

"The Word of God places part of the blame on the shepherds," Greg sadly reflected. "Many of us refused to teach on the consequences of His second coming; much less spiritual warfare. The lack of real discipleship was horrific. This is why so many saints were deceived for eternity." 4

A frustrated Jake asked, "Why pray if you don't believe it will help? So many assumed God would have His way no matter how they responded to Satan's attacks. How many times did Christians hide behind the excuse, there is nothing we can do, God is in control. Give me a break; what about our responsibility to resist the devil?"

An animated Kurt added, "What blew my mind, were the ones who surrendered. Instead of fighting back, they just rolled over and played dead. Imagine the enemy allowing a believer to sit on the sidelines during the days of the Great Tribulation. There ain't no way you can yield to Satan and serve a Holy God at the same time."

"So, Emma, how critical was intersession in defeating the devil?"

"At the top of my list, Greg, when I faced demons trying to destroy my trust in God, I knew I had to pray for discernment. After I got saved, I found out how fast my carnal nature can oppose what the Holy Spirit wants. Paul wrote, 'For to be carnally minded is death but to be spiritually minded is life and peace.' 5 Prayer is our lifeline in denying our flesh, defeating the Devil's lies, and living for God."

"'For as many as are led by the Spirit of God, these are the sons of God,'" shared Jake. 6 "I remember rescuing a teenager on the beach after the second trumpet sounded. His entire family had the mark. His running days were almost up. The boy got saved big time. Unfortunately, the honeymoon didn't last long. Satan really gave him the once over. Fear, sickness, confusion, he took a big hit."

"What ever happened to him?"

"Reenie, the high price of the calling of God can come sooner than you think. Jesus warned, 'Enter by the narrow gate; for wide is the gate and broad is the way that leads to destruction, and there are many who go in by it. Because narrow is the gate and difficult is the way which leads to life, and there are few who find it.'" 7

"Is Jesus saying most are going to hell? In my church, I never heard anything about spiritual warfare. No one even brought it up."

"Reenie, do you remember how Satan afflicted Job? Well, after a couple of attacks, this boy wasn't too excited about God. He was more focused on what it was costing him rather than loving God and hating evil. Serving the Lord was too much of a hassle. After visiting some of his friends who registered, he decided it just wasn't worth it."

Emma read, 'For though we walk in the flesh, we do not war according to the flesh. For our weapons of our warfare are not carnal but mighty in God for pulling down strongholds, casting down arguments and every high thing that exalts itself against the knowledge of God, bringing every thought into captivity to the obedience of Christ.'" 8 Doesn't this sound like we are commanded to fight?"

"Right on! What about James, Jesus' brother? He exhorts us to submit our will to God, resist the devil, and he will flee. 9 As believers we always have a choice. C'mon, sis, let's hear the passage that helped you defeat Satan's lies."

"That the God of our Lord Jesus Christ, the Father of glory, may give to you the spirit of wisdom and revelation in the knowledge of Him, the eyes of your understanding being enlightened; that you may know what is the hope of His calling...'" 10

The bobbing of heads and wide smiles was a popular affirmation among the Q Squad.

"After several attacks from Satan, I learned that it is better to be on the offensive than the defensive. Of course, when we fight spiritually we are extending the kingdom of God. This is why the devil tries to deliver the decisive blow, at the decisive point, at the decisive time."

"What was Satan's strategy against you?"

"Greg, the decisive time of his attack was when we were separated from everybody. Satan's decisive point of attack was overwhelming guilt right after I called code green. His decisive blow was to have us doubt God's protection."

"A big miscalculation!" grinned Jake.

"You know being on the offensive is just as much an attitude as it is an action. The moment we were attacked, I knew victory was just a prayer away. Jesus said, 'For where two or three are gathered together in My Name, I am there in the midst of them.'" 11

With the fire blazing, no one was noticing the tears running down the red cheeks of Reenie Ann Tucker.

A sea of faces blanketed the land. Although less than a mile away, their journey took several hours. From the bottom of the Mount of Olives, they could hear the worship of Yeshua in different languages. Most were giving praise reports. But none seemed greater than the salvation of Johanna's father.

"Is Yeshua really going to split the Mount of Olives?"

"Anytime now, Daddy."

"So when is Armageddon going to take place?"

"There are twenty-five days left till the great day of God Almighty erupts. 12 This is when Word of God will cast the Beast and his false prophet into the lake of fire."

"So when does the Millennium begin?"

"Forty-five days after the supper of the great God, Armageddon." 13

"What about us?"

"We will live on earth during the Millennium."

"I thought the earth burns up during the day of the Lord?"

"God's wrath will end after the seventh bowl. This world will be totally trashed. The Lord will restore the earth like the Garden of Eden by the first day of His thousand year reign over the nations." 14

Standing on the Mount of Olives, the Lord looked over Jerusalem.

"Are you ready, Johanna?"

"Yes, Mama, I want to be part of Yeshua's remnant."

"And you, Aaron?"

He was studying faces in the crowd. Their struggles, their dreams, it was all going to end.

"What about those who don't have the opportunity to follow Yeshua to Azal? There must be many unregistered Jews who still can be saved."

"Daddy, don't you want to be with Yeshua?"

"With all my heart, honey, my whole life I've made decisions based on revenge and hate. Now that I have a chance to escape it all, you would think my choice would be easy. I met a young boy just moments before I believed in Yeshua. He was all alone. There must be others just like him."

Miriam proudly asked, "Sounds like you want to be a Watchman?"

"The soldiers under my command have not worshiped Kayin or taken his mark. If God will make a way, I'd like to share the gospel with them."

Glancing back at her daughter, Miriam could sense the urgency of the moment.

"The Lord has changed your heart, Aaron. Your love for the lost is a gift from God. You have been granted a calling. The Holy Spirit is going to use you to win souls."

Gently he whispered back, "Incredible, some had a lifetime to share. I've got twenty-five days."

Reaching over she gave her daughter a big hug.

"Are you staying, Johanna?"

Breaking away, the tall brunette burst into tears.

"No way, I wouldn't have made it this far without you."

"What is the Holy Spirit telling you?"

"I don't know. Is God leading you to stay?"

"Physically, I'm totally spent. My destiny is in Azal. My focus will be intersession. Just after your father got saved, the Holy Spirit showed me He was going to use Aaron. Let's not forget, it ain't over til the Word of God appears in heaven with His angels." 15

"What about me?"

"Your father and I couldn't be prouder. When you were born, Aaron told your grandparents you would be a shining light for God. We praise the Lord for who you've become. Whatever decision you make, Johanna, it will never change our love for you."

Hugging her mother, she cried, "But I owe you so much."

"Now what would Jake say if he saw you like this?"

"He would say keep praying until I get an answer."

"Tell you what, honey; you seek the Holy Spirit for His perfect will. Then come and tell us your decision."

Holding hands, her father and mother slipped behind some teenagers praising their Messiah for the first time. Kneeling in the dirt, Johanna Esther Glazer began to pour out her heart in prayer. Miraculously, the Spirit of God had led her from a sleepy farm town in southeastern Alabama all the way to the feet of the Lamb of God.

"Sorry, Wes, Natalie hasn't returned our calls since her last interview... She was reviewing some pictures, next thing we know she's gone... Hold on, I'm not her babysitter... That's right, she checked out of her hotel... Joel Friedman is filling in... How should I know, Jerusalem is a madhouse... Trust me, somebody better come up with some answers, this city is about to explode!"

The uneasy producer had no choice but to call this early morning staff meeting.

"You heard me! Somehow, someway, we must explain it."

"Wes, how can we change anyone's mind?"

"Not change; just influence. How many of you have read the new NWC Consensus? It's simple; people are demanding an explanation of this week's bizarre events."

"Most Americans could care less, Wes. The average Joe on the streets knows the dying stopped the day the two Witnesses were executed. No one cares if they supposedly came back to life; that doesn't change anything. The dying has stopped!"

Another reporter asked, "What's your gut feeling, Wes?"

"Our lead story is the massing of troops around the world."

"What is Kayin's response?"

"He is with Michael in Rome. They have no comment."

"They can't run and hide. The silent treatment doesn't solve anything."

"Who knows what they're thinking? We can only speculate. Any suggestions?"

"How about a digital formatted presentation. We can fill it up with sound bites. It begins with the Witnesses' execution on Sunday and ends with yesterday's weird manifestation during the Feast of Tabernacles. Natalie saw it all. What's her take?"

Grudgingly Wes slowly replied, "I don't know."

"So let's get her on a conference call."

"She left Jerusalem a couple hours ago. She took a redeye flight home."

Several reporters stiffened.

"Yeah, yeah, it doesn't look good when the most popular News Anchor in America goes AWOL. Aren't you guys paid to tell me something I don't know?"

Their fire was almost out. There were no words to express their appreciation. Each had been given a gift in which no one could boast.

"I wanna thank God for the Q Squad," Jake gratefully shared. "Your support really helped me overcome the Devil's lies. Think of how many Christians who needed someone to care. I'm talking about risking your life for someone you've never met."

"Placing it inside Lance's tattered black leather Bible, Jake thought about how much to share.

"A lot of things make sense after reading Jessie's letter. She wrote how much of a blessing you all were. Let's face it; her chances of pursuing her aunt were slim without the encouragement from the Q. When you all met, Jessie's greatest spiritual need was to see a believer walking in God's authority."

"Authority?" laughed Kurt. "Is that word in my portfolio?"

"There is a vast difference between the world's power and the authority of Christ."

"But authority is power, isn't it, Greg?"

"Let's compare them, Emma. Who in the eyes of this world is powerful?"

"The Beast. Satan once gave him his authority over all the nations."

"This is true. Now what about the authority of Christ? Does Jesus force us to do His will?"

"We voluntarily do His will. The authority of Christ allows us the freedom to follow Him. Saints aren't really free unless we have the freedom to fail. Paul wrote, "Let this mind be in you which was also in Christ Jesus, who, being in the form of God, did not consider it robbery to be equal with God, but made himself of no reputation, taking the form of a bondservant, and coming in the likeness of men.

And being found in the appearance as a man, He humbled Himself and became obedient to the point of death, even the death of the cross.'" 16

Wiping away her tears, the Miracle Girl shared, "Setting aside His power as God; Jesus expressed His love by dying on a cross."

"Hallelujah!" praised Greg. "Jesus' authority flows from His love for us. Those who worshipped the Beast never got this. God's love is greater than mere power. Jesus' own family pleaded with Him to show His power. Immanuel chose a different path to communicate His Father's will. He withheld His power by laying down His life."

"What about now?" asked Emma.

"The Lord is still extending His love. It doesn't matter how well known you are in the eyes of the world, how rich you are, how much you've accomplished, or even who you know. The way of the cross demonstrated His love."

Standing to his feet, Kurt shouted, "You can't share the gospel without showing sacrificial love. You ain't got any authority if you don't have any love."

"Now there's a preaching machine!" teased Jake.

"Kurt's right," confirmed Greg. "In these last days, many Christians had a form of godliness but denied the power of the Holy Spirit. We can't communicate the gospel to the unsaved without allowing the Lord to crucify our flesh. Look at the pastors who purposely taught a watered down gospel to supposedly build up the body of Christ."

Raising his hand Jake's eyes got real big.

"Remember the famous Christians they paraded on TV? Think about it, when did Jesus ever use the rich and beautiful to prove how great His Word is?"

"Jesus is the stone the builders rejected!" preached Kurt. "The fishermen the Son of Man chose were no superstars."

Gradually their joyful sharing died down. His cracking voice spoke volumes.

"Jessie had so many questions. Man, she must have been like a sponge when she met ya'll. She really loves you guys."

"Jake, did you ever ask the Holy Spirit why you never met Jessie in Gulf Shores?"

"Lots of times, Greg, I never got an answer. Oh, Satan would whisper stuff like, God isn't hearing you because of your rebellion. He doesn't care about your circumstances anymore. If God really loved

Paul Bortolazzo

you, He would answer you."

"Anyone hear this broken record before?" giggled Emma.

Nothing could stop their fun around the fire.

"Remember when Jesus visited the home of Mary and Martha?" posed Jake. "You know, it's the old line, why can't I get an answer from God today? When the Holy Spirit led me to Gulf Shores I realized I could either choose an attitude like Mary or one like Martha."

Reenie sat back. She was beginning to feel like an outsider looking in.

"Hey, Jake, ease up on Martha. Somebody had to clean up."

"You think so, Emma? Was that really Martha's reason for not listening? Or was she avoiding the responsibility of obeying. When I pastored, I was good at doing that."

"Greg, are you saying you kept yourself busy because you didn't want to hear from God?"

"It can be a real smoke screen. Thank God His grace blew it away. I'm curious, Jake, why the Mary and Martha story?"

"I did a lot of praying. God wanted to use me but the mind games from the enemy were so overwhelming. I mean how can one become a mature Christian overnight?"

"Tell me about it," added Kurt.

"The answer is to grow in Christ. Of course the Devil would remind me of my past sins. The times I missed God's will was his favorite lie. For me Satan's condemnation over specific sins I committed was my biggest stumbling block."

"What about hurting people that never recover?"

"One of Satan's favorites Kurt, it was the Holy Spirit who convinced me I couldn't grow in Christ if I allowed Satan to bind me with his lies. So He gave me this verse. 'For He made Him who knew no sin to be sin for us, that we might become the righteousness of God in Him.'" 17

"Amen, bro, we are becoming the righteousness of God in Him."

"Once we are free to grow in Christ, it's an honor to hear and obey the Holy Spirit. I mean why did so many believers choose to receive the mark of the beast?"

After a long pause Emma shared, "They refused to admit Kayin was the Beast. Those who registered believed it had nothing to do with the Book of Revelation."

"To avoid persecution," offered Kurt. "They loved the things of the world more than God."

"Having a form of godliness but denying its power," reflected Greg. "Most were never taught how to renew their minds."

"Yep, these are examples of how believers stopped growing in Christ. My problem was that I couldn't make God answer my prayers the way I wanted. I was consumed with Jessie's safety. I thought of ways I could help her. I told the Lord I was willing to give my life for hers. Of course, He knew what was best for Jessie. I finally had to trust Him with her life. The answer was out of my hands."

"So when we are hurting and answers aren't coming, it's not because God doesn't care. It's just His timing is different than ours."

"It took awhile, Em, but that's what I learned. Remember when Jesus raised Lazarus' from the dead. 18 I wanted to know when the Lord would roll away the stone and deliver Jessie. So whenever I demanded an answer about her, I would lose the very peace I so much desired. As it turns out, He was answering my prayer, in His timing not mine."

"That'll preach bro," affirmed Kurt.

<hr />

In the pitch darkness of the early morning the taxi driver slowly exited her circular brick driveway. A light sprinkle of snow dusted the massive pine trees surrounding her multi-million-dollar lakefront home. Her car keys lay on the polished marble stairs. Her clothes were scattered across the bathroom floor. The smell of decay from the lake was coming through her bedroom window. A spilled bottle of pink sleeping pills lay on her nightstand. Sprawled across the white satin sheets of her king size bed Natalie René Roberts closed her eyes.

SIXTH DAY: THE MOUNT OF OLIVES

'And in that day His feet will stand on the Mount of Olives...'
Zechariah 14:4

All eyes were on the Watchman they affectionately nicknamed, Miracle Girl. Deep down Reenie Tucker wanted to testify, yet she didn't feel it was the right time.

"Praise God, ya'll are a bunch of walking testimonies. For me, it's kinda hard to be so transparent. I was just wondering what Jessie would say if she were here, how about it, Jake?"

Nodding, he carefully unfolded her letter.

"Dear Jake, there is so much I want to share with you. So I guess I'll start at the beginning. Do you remember when we first met? You were trying to find Mrs. Blum's English class and you stumbled into mine. I remember the goofy look on your face when I told you my class was Spanish. It didn't take long for me to realize how much I loved spending time with you. Looking back, I can see how God brought us together. Before the coming of the Lord, Satan was really harassing our friends who were witnessing to us. Luke, Hope, the twins, the Ryan's, each paid a price for preaching the days of the Great Tribulation would be cut short by the Son of Man. Of course, the attacks from the enemy were meant to keep us from finding the truth. One can feel pretty empty when you find out what you've been trusting in is a lie. I'll always cherish the moment we received Jesus as our Savior. Remember how much we wanted to rejoice with Elmer but his heart wasn't in it. Later, when the NWC executed him, I cried for a long time. The night we escaped from his church, I knew God had a purpose for our lives. The question haunting me was whether we would be able to serve the Lord together. I wanted this so badly.

When I got arrested at the Ryan's I realized how selfish I was. God wanted me to pray for you. He was calling us to different paths. It must have been hard for you to see me arrested. In a few hours my aunt and I will be leaving Alabama. There is someone special who needs our help. It may sound crazy but I'm praying this message of love will somehow find you, wherever the Lord takes you."

His tears gently fell upon some scattered ashes from the fire.

"Let's not forget our pact. We are going to meet in Jerusalem during the Millennium, remember? You won't believe this but the pastor you met at the Ryan's helped me escape from the NWC. Greg Hudson was such a blessing. He taught me a lot about Bible prophecy. I also developed a special bond with some other believers. Emma and Kurt Abbott and Carlos Delgado all helped me with God's will for my life. Their testimonies were so encouraging. It was so easy to fall in love with them. I pray for their safety every day. You would have really enjoyed them, Jake. Their worship for Jesus was so infectious. Let's search them out during the Millennium. Okay?"

"Praise God for Carlos," Greg tenderly whispered out loud.

An anxious Jake stood up.

"There are so many things I want to share with you. I never thought our lives would turn out the way they have. Jake, I love Jesus with all my heart. Paul wrote, 'The Spirit Himself bears witness with our Spirit that we are children of God, and if children, then heirs-heirs of God and joint heirs with Christ, if indeed we suffer with Him, that we may also be glorified together. For I consider that the sufferings of this present time are not worthy to be compared with the glory which shall be revealed in us.'" 1 I guess that says it all. Think of it, we are going to be able to worship Jesus as He rules over earth from within the New Jerusalem. I can still remember Greg's excitement when he taught the Q Squad this truth. That's what we called ourselves."

Kurt leaned over and pointed at Greg.

"I covet your prayers. Very soon I'll be facing some of the biggest fears of my life. Sure, I still struggle at times. I now know I'll never make it unless the Holy Spirit opens the doors. Honestly, I like it better this way. 'Likewise the Spirit also helps in our weaknesses. For we do not know what we should pray for as we ought, but the Spirit Himself makes intersession for the saints according to the will of God. And we know that all things work together for good to those who love God, to those who are called according to His purpose.'" 2

Sitting back down the Watchman didn't want the letter to end.

"Whatever is ahead, God will lead us. Here is a verse that reminds me of you. 'Who shall separate us from the love of Christ? Shall tribulation, or distress, or persecution, or famine, or nakedness, or peril, or sword? As it is written: For Your sake we are killed all day long; we are accounted as sheep for the slaughter. Yet in all these things we are more than conquerors through Him who loved us.' 3 Jake, to me you'll always be a conqueror for Christ. See you at His Throne. Love Ya, Jess."

After a dozen rings, the woozy celebrity picked up the phone.

"Natalie, it's Wes."

"What do you want?"

"What's going on? No calls, no notes. You left Joel hanging in Jerusalem."

"He can handle it."

"Are you up for this morning's interview with the Secretary of State?"

"Has Yeshua spilt the Mount of Olives yet?"

"Nate, we can't afford such foolish speculation."

"What do you suggest?" her words slurring together.

"I prefer a more ideological stance. Our objective is to foster hope."

"Listen to yourself! This is just a big game, isn't it? It doesn't matter what we saw. Let me guess this morning's headline."

"A possible World War III is our top priority."

"You can't just dismiss..."

"Sorry, this so called Messiah and His mob are old news."

"What do you want from me? Kayin has deceived the nations with his clever lies. God's wrath is just cleaning house."

Her close friend paused. Wes could feel her pain.

"You and I have been through a lot since the Peace Accord was signed. We were both in Jerusalem when Kayin's armies invaded. We also witnessed the assault in the Valley of Jehoshaphat. Who would've dreamed so many Jews could have survived."

"The remnant on the Mount of Olives will survive Armageddon."

"That's just it, Nate, several world leaders have agreed to stop this insanity. There doesn't have to be an Armageddon!"

In her mind she could see a mighty warrior. His eyes were like fire; his robe was dipped in blood. Angels dressed in white were following on white horses. Then she saw birds eating the flesh of dead soldiers. Slipping from her hand the phone bounced off the floor.

The sun on this Friday morning would be up soon. Their anticipation was growing. While sharing, Greg received a word of knowledge confirming their future. Before their first break, Emma understood her role. A short time later, while worshipping, Jake was given a vision of a struggle they would encounter. And of course, an excited Kurt could hardly maintain after getting a green light for the next twenty-five days. Their mission was coming together. Everyone had heard from God except one. A heavy anointing filled the cave as Jake read Jessie's letter. The Holy Spirit had been speaking all night. A divine exhortation was near. After several hugs, they resettled around a roaring fire.

A curious Kurt asked, "Say, Greg, what event are you looking forward to on the first day of Christ's thousand year reign over the nations?"

"Seeing Jesus rule from the House of God of Jacob would be amazing. 4 What about you?"

"Seeing an angel bind Satan in the bottomless pit would be sweet." 5

"I'd love to see how Jesus restores the earth after Armageddon," reflected an excited Jake. "Let's hear it, Em?"

"My dream is to see the bride descending inside the New Jerusalem. I've always held on to this hope. Wow, we're almost there."

Her red cheeks were a given; her soft sobs a beginning.

Moving over, Emma gently asked, "Are you okay, Reenie?"

"It's such a blessing being here with ya'll. Hearing your testimonies is like receiving a soothing salve in areas of my life that hurt the most. Being part of a remnant living during the Millennium is difficult to describe. It's all so wonderful. I feel like shouting it from the housetops!"

"Miracle Girl, what's your heart's desire? Besides the ones mentioned, what event are you really looking forward to seeing?"

Lovingly taking Emma's hand, Reenie gazed into the fire.

"Oh, I have one. It just sounds so unimportant. I remember it like it was yesterday. Smoke was filling up the cave I was hiding in. I thought I was going to die. I knew I couldn't do it on my own. Kneeling down to breathe, I begged God for help. Then I heard his voice. I wouldn't be alive today if the Lord hadn't sent Bret. Later, he refused to let me give up. In the end, he gave his life for mine."

Easing forward Greg shared, "Reenie, you'll see Bret again. John wrote, 'And I saw thrones, and they sat on them, and judgment was committed to them. Then I saw the souls of those who had been beheaded for their witness to Jesus and for the Word of God, who had not worshipped the beast or his image, and had not received his mark on their foreheads or on their hands. And they lived and reigned with Christ for a thousand years.'" [6]

"Bret is going to receive his glorified body on the first day of the Millennium!" yelped Kurt. [7]

Emma hugged her friend while Kurt gave Jake a high-five.

"When we first arrived here I was hoping we could just hang out. No agents, no mind games from Jezebel, I just wanted to enjoy a safe refuge with those who love God. This morning, I actually caught a glimpse of what Jesus meant when He said, 'If you were of the world, the world would love its own. Yet because you are not of the world, but I chose you out of the world, therefore the world hates you.'" [8]

"No joke, Miracle Girl, you've been through more warfare than any of us."

"Yeah, Jake, it's a real eye opener hearing you all share. Almost like a veil being removed from my eyes. Ever since I can remember, my spirit guide wanted to destroy me. I felt like a POW trapped inside my body. I was so terrified my friends would find out about Jezebel. To make sure it didn't happen; I play acted."

"Didn't your parents see the manipulation?"

"Greg, Jezebel used my parents to help shape my prison. Nothing I did was ever good enough. My folks would always say it could have been better. My fear of making mistakes would trigger confusion, disgust, most of all jealousy of others. It got so bad I couldn't trust anyone. I could hardly make it I was jumping through so many hoops."

"I can relate," added Jake. "My dad was a perfectionist. He could always find something wrong."

"I never felt good about myself; just a haze of disapproval coming and going. Travis would always take the blame for me. He knew something was wrong but was afraid to ask me."

"So you learned how to earn acceptance from your parents?"

"For sure, Greg, everything was based on performance."

"So how were you set free?"

"The Lord showed me what real love is by the sacrifice of other believers. It pierced my heart and all my bitterness just poured out."

"Walls come a tumbling down!" gushed a wide-eyed Kurt.

"When I felt His grace Jezebel left my body. And guess what? I had a vision of a spotless Lamb being sacrificed for my sins."

"Talk about getting a once over!"

Rolling her eyes at her brother Emma asked, "Reenie, how does it feel being free from Satan's grasp?"

"Like a totally different person. I can now see how God's grace has the power to turn evil into good. Remember Paul's thorn in the flesh sent by Satan? 9 Every city the apostle visited he suffered persecution from the hands of his own people. Well, Jezebel was the thorn in my flesh that needed to be removed. But I couldn't figure how to do it until God showed me. The key was to forgive Cassandra. After that, it was easy to receive forgiveness from the Lord."

"Cleansed by His blood!" praised Jake. "How do you feel now?"

"Better than I ever imagined. Jesus has wiped away my sins!"

"We are so happy for you, Reenie."

"Thanks, Greg. I wanna thank you all for the part you've played in my life. This is all so rewarding yet I can't help but feel there is something more. Like an unfinished task someone needs to volunteer for. Am I making any sense?"

"What type of task?"

"When I pray I see myself on some sort of mission, maybe it's for all of us; I don't know. I can hear children crying out for help. There's a shadow covering them so I can't see their faces. Does this mean God isn't done with us?"

"Reenie, I've been waiting to share this with you. This mission concerns your future. You are experiencing a specific anointing to accomplish something for God."

"Greg, how are we going..."

"Miracle Girl, this is your assignment."

"Why just me?"

"We aren't leaving," pledged Emma. "The Q is backing you up."

"How far into my future are we talking about?"

A confident Kurt replied, "For the next twenty-five days. Your mission will end at the supper of the great God, Armageddon."

"Reenie, for the past few hours the Holy Spirit has been speaking through our testimonies, our worship, and His word. Earlier this morning, I received a vision of you standing over Cassandra. She was whispering something. Did she say anything to you before she died?"

"It happened so fast, Jake, I don't remember."

A cautious Emma offered, "Cassandra said Satan would send others."

"Sound right, Reenie?"

"Something like that."

"In my vision I saw soldiers hiding in darkness. They're after Reenie."

"But why me when we are so close?"

Their young eyes instinctively turned toward their pastor.

"We have experienced too much to turn away from His perfect will now. The Lord has picked Reenie for this mission. He is calling the Q to protect her."

A playful Kurt kidded, "C'mon, Miracle, you can't get rid of us that fast. Besides, I'm not ready for retirement, are you?"

Raising her arms she prayed, "Father, not my will but Your will be done."

The first bowl of God's final wrath was near. Forming a circle around Reenie Ann Tucker, each overcomer fell to their knees in the damp dirt. Their new mission would begin and end in passionate intersession. 10

Huddled behind a rock formation, SWAT teams #2 and #3 were waiting on their Commander. The surveillance bug they planted near the mouth of the cave was working perfectly. While the Q Squad rejoiced in their Savior's love, one of the soldiers cursed.

"What's Mercer's angle in this operation anyway? He's sure taking his sweet time."

In darkness, Doyle led SWAT #1 down the crest of an adjacent hill.

"Whadda ya got?"

"Commander, it appears they're planning some sort of mission."

"I don't care what they're planning. In fact, we don't need any witnesses."

"I don't understand?" asked the confused leader from #2.

"There has been a change in your directive. Deploy your men west of the cave; #3 to the east. When I give the order, #1 will move in. All I want is Tucker. After taking her to our command post," execute the other resisters where no one can find them."

Sitting side by side, they were reminiscing.

"You know, Miriam, just after the elect were gathered during the Feast of Trumpets, I did some real soul searching."

"Me too."

"But you believed and I waited till now."

"Aaron, it's God who draws us. I was ready; you weren't."

"How bad will Armageddon be?"

"Armies from the world are coming to destroy Israel."

"Makes sense, armies from Jordan, Egypt and Syria are assembling their troops on Israel's borders."

"Matthias, your fighting days are over! You're now in the salvation business."

Staring at the remnant, he gratefully replied, "You're right, Matthias is dead. I'm not of this world anymore, am I?"

"Aaron, you've been fighting all your life. For years you've faced the harsh reality of physical casualties. Now you're entering a different kind of warfare; a spiritual battle having eternal consequences. Even though Satan's authority was stripped away at the seventh trumpet, God is still allowing demons to gather together the largest army ever assembled." 11

"What can I say? Fighting spiritual forces is new territory for me."

"This is why God has given me a scripture to encourage you."

"Would He really do this for me?"

"The Holy Spirit speaks His word into our real life situations in order to strengthen us. Your passage is I Corinthians 9:24-27. Paul is explaining his relationship with the Lord in the form of a race. As believers we are running a race; not for a perishable crown but an imperishable crown."

"So my race is for the salvation of others?"

"Yes, you're racing for souls. What you need to understand is you lack experience. The only way to be successful in this type of warfare is to use spiritual weapons. This can only be achieved by obeying the Holy Spirit in every trial you face. Don't be afraid to trust God, He is faithful."

"But I feel so weak spiritually."

Leaning over she whispered, "'My grace is sufficient for you, for My strength is made perfect in weakness.'" 12

"I don't understand."

"The Lord will soon show you."

They both smiled as their daughter greeted them.

"How are you, Johanna?"

"God is faithful, Daddy."

"You're staying aren't you?"

"How did you know, Mama?"

"You've always had a burden to be a rescuer for God. You will be a tremendous blessing to your father."

"Daddy, the Holy Spirit gave me I Corinthians 9:24-27. I saw a picture of a race. You and I were running alongside each other. Ahead of us were faces pleading to hear the truth. They were itching to run with us. Daddy, we're going to race for their souls."

"Did you see the finish line?"

"Yes, Mama, I saw a foursquare city descending from heaven." 13

"But how do we know if..."

She gently placed her fingers over his lips.

"My dear, Aaron Phinehas, some things we will never know. That's when our trust in God takes over. I'm going to leave you now."

Fighting back the tears, she backed away.

"This isn't a goodbye; we'll see each other during the Millennium."

"We love you, Miriam."

"I love you both with all my heart. Remember, no matter what, listen to the Holy Spirit."

Facing his daughter, Aaron meekly asked, "Are you ready, Johanna?"

Slipping her hand in his, she kissed him on the forehead.

"C'mon, Daddy, let's do this for the glory of God."

Squeezing through an opening in the crowd they began their jog down the Mount of Olives.

Pausing for a final look, Johanna spun around.

"I don't see her, Daddy."

"She's alright, honey, your Mother's gone to be with Yeshua."

THE END

Scripture References

Chapter 1
1. Mt. 24:30, 16:27, I Thess. 4:17
2. Rev. 1:7; 14:14-16
3. Rev. 1:13-14
4. Titus 2:13
5. 1 Thess. 4:14
6. 1 Thess. 4:16, I Cor. 15:52, Jn. 5:28-29
7. 1 Thess. 4:17, Rev. 7:9-14
8. Jn. 6:44, 1 Thess. 4:16-17
9. Rev. 12:6, Isa. 63:1-4
10. Lk. 21:20, Mat. 24:15
11. Mat. 24:29-31, Mk. 13:26-27
12. Rev. 7:1-4
13. Joel 2:1
14. Rev. 8:7, 2 Pet. 3:10-12
15. Rev. 8:1
16. Rev. 8:2
17. Rev. 8:3
18. Rev. 8:4-5

Chapter 2
1. Mat. 24:15, 29-31
2. Mat. 24:29-31, Mk. 13:26-27, Lk. 21:27-28
3. Mat. 16:26
4. Joel 1:15
5. Rev. 11:3
6. Jer. 4:14
7. Isa. 2:10-11
8. Dan. 9:24-27, Rom. 11:25-27, Rev. 14:1
9. Zep. 2:1-3
10. Rev. 8:1
11. Rev. 8:2
12. Rev. 8:3-4
13. Exo. 9:22-24
14. Zep. 1:3, Rev. 6:14-16
15. Exo. 18:19
16. Mat. 24:40
17. Isa. 35:1
18. Joel 3:12-14
19. Rev. 13:16-18; 14:9-10

Chapter 3
1. Rev. 21:18
2. Rev. 21:12

3. Rev. 21:14
4. Mk. 8:34-37
5. II Cor. 5:10-11, Rom. 14:10, Mat. 7:21-23
6. Mk. 8:38
7. Mat. 7:21
8. Mat. 7:22
9. Lk. 6:46
10. Mat. 7:13-14
11. Mat. 24:51, Rev. 20:13-14
12. Mat. 7:21-23; 24:45-51; 25:1-46
13. Rev. 12:7-8
14. Mat. 24:21-22, 30-31
15. II Thess. 2:3, Mat. 24:10
16. Rom. 11:25-27, Rev. 10:1-7
17. Rev. 10:7; 11:15
18. Mat. 24:29-31, Mk. 13:27
19. Rev. 8:1
20. Lk. 17:26-30
21. II Pet. 3:10
22. Zep. 1:2-3
23. Mat. 24:30-31, Mk. 13:26-27

Chapter 4
1. Rev. 13:15-18
2. Dan. 9:27a

Chapter 5
1. Rev. 7:9
2. Rev. 1:3; 22:19
3. Rev. 21:2, 9-10
4. Rev. 21:16
5. Heb. 11:16
6. Rev. 21:12
7. Rev. 21:14
8. II Pet. 3:10, I Thess. 5:4-6
9. Rev. 3:3
10. Rev. 3:22
11. Mk. 13:24-27
12. Mk. 13:24-25, Rev. 6:12
13. Mat. 24:13
14. Mat. 24:21-22
15. Rev. 3:10
16. Rev. 12:12
17. Mat. 4:1
18. I Cor. 7:5, I Thess. 3:5
19. Mat. 24:9

20. Lk. 17:26-30
21. Rev. 13:16-18
22. Rom. 13:1-2
23. Heb. 6:4-6
24. Mat. 26:24
25. Jn. 14:30

Chapter 6
1. Rom. 11:5, Rev. 7:1-8; 14:1-4
2. Lev. 23:24
3. Rev. 7:2-3; 9:4; 14:1
4. Dan. 9:24
5. Lk. 21:24, Rom. 11:25-27
6. Jn. 5:28-29
7. Jn. 6:40
8. Mat. 24:14
9. Rev. 13:18
10. Mat. 28:20
11. Heb. 13:1
12. Rom. 5:8
13. Act. 2:38
14. I Jn. 3:10
15. Rev. 14:6

Chapter 7
1. Mat. 24:33
2. Rev. 13:7
3. II Thess. 2:8
4. Rev. 19:20
5. Isa. 2:17, Rev. 12:12, II Pet. 3:10-12
6. Dan. 12:1
7. Dan. 9:27, Rev. 12:7-12
8. Rev. 13:5-7; 17:16
9. Rev. 20:4
10. Rev. 7:9-14, Mat. 24:21-22
11. Lk. 17:26-30
12. Eph. 4:11

Chapter 8
1. II Pet. 3:10
2. Joel 2:30-31
3. Isa. 13:9-10
4. Mat. 24:29
5. Isa. 65:17-20
6. Isa. 66:22
7. Isa. 59:20-21, Rom. 11:25-27
8. Dan. 9:24, Zech. 13:8-9, Rev. 10:7

9. Hos. 6:1-2
10. Gen. 12:1-3, 15:5
11. Rev. 14:1
12. Rev. 11:15
13. Zech. 14:3-5
14. Rev. 15:1
15. Zep. 1:2
16. Rev. 20:4-7
17. Zech. 14:16, Rev. 21:27

Chapter 9
1. II Thess. 3:3
2. Amos 5:17-19
3. Joel 2:31
4. Joel 2:32
5. 1 Thess. 4:17, Rev. 7:9-14
6. Lk. 21:13-15
7. Heb. 11:16, Rev. 21:9-10
8. I Pet. 4:19

Chapter 10
1. Rev. 14:9-10
2. Jn. 3:16, 18
3. Heb. 10:10, Col. 1:14
4. II Pet. 2:1
5. Neh. 2:1-8, Dan. 9:25-26
6. Dan. 9:24-27
7. Mat. 24:15, II Thess. 2:4
8. Rev. 13:2-5
9. Rom. 11:5
10. Rom. 11:25-27
11. Rev. 11:3-7
12. Jn. 5:28-29
13. Jn. 6:40

Chapter 11
1. Jn. 14:30
2. Gen. 15:18-21
3. Jer. 31:31-33
4. Lev. 23:1-44
5. 1 Cor. 15:51-52
6. Jn. 6:40
7. Rev. 14:9-11
8. Rom. 10:10
9. Mal. 3:18
10. Rev. 8:8-9

Chapter 12

1. II Cor. 5:17
2. Jn. 1:1-5, 9-14
3. Zech. 13:8-9
4. Rev. 9:11-21
5. Jn. 8:32

Chapter 13
1. Jer. 29:11-13
2. Jer. 7:16
3. Mat. 24:34
4. Rev. 22:12
5. Rev. 1:1
6. Rev. 22:10
7. Mat. 16:27-28
8. II Thess. 2:3, Mat. 24:10
9. Jn. 1:10-11
10. I Thess. 2:16
11. Jn. 17:8

Chapter 14
1. Rev. 8:8
2. Zep. 2:10
3. Zep. 1:6
4. Rom. 8:14
5. I Tim. 4:1
6. Rom. 3:23
7. I Cor. 15:3-4
8. Rom. 10:9
9. Mat. 24:40-41

Chapter 15
1. Heb. 9:28
2. Zech. 13:9
3. Rom. 11:25-27
4. Rev. 12:6
5. Rev. 14:4
6. Isa. 59:20
7. Rom. 11:26-27
8. Rev. 10:1
9. Rev. 1:16
10. Dan. 10:5-6
11. Dan. 12:11-12
12. Isa. 63:1, Rev 10:1-6
13. Rev. 7:1-4; 9-14
14. Hos. 6:1-2, Rev 10:7
15. Jn. 4:22
16. Rev. 11:8-9
17. Rev. 14:1
18. Rev. 11:15

19. Rev. 11:12
20. Isa. 6:8
21. II Pet. 3:10-13
22. Rev. 21:1-3
23. Isa. 65:25
24. Rev. 20:14
25. Mat. 16:27, 24:36
26. Joel 3:12-15, 1:15
27. Rev 1:7, Mat 24:29-31

Chapter 16
1. Rev. 7:9-14; 10:1-7; 19:11-21; 21:9-10
2. Gal. 6:16
3. I Chron. 16:22
4. Rev. 20:7-9
5. Rev. 20:10
6. Mat. 26:64
7. Rev. 22:12
8. Mat. 10:23
9. Mat. 24:4
10. Joel 2:30

Chapter 17
1. Rev. 20:10
2. Heb. 13:1
3. Obad. 17-21

Chapter 18
1. Mat. 28:19
2. Jn. 14:2-3
3. I Thess. 1:8-9
4. Zech. 14:16-17

Chapter 19
1. Isa. 26:19-21
2. II Thess. 2:8b
3. Isa. 2:12, 17
4. Zech. 13:8
5. Dan. 12:1-2
6. Dan. 10:14
7. Rom. 11:26-27, Dan. 9:24
8. Act. 1:6
9. Zech. 14:3, 12-14
10. Dan. 9:24
11. Jer. 31:31-33
12. Isa. 59:20
13. Zech. 14:3-5
14. Zep. 1:2

15. Isa. 36:35
16. Isa. 65:17; 66:22
17. Act. 5:39-40
18. Lev. 23:2
19. Rom. 11:11
20. Jn. 1:11-12
21. Lev. 23:5
22. Exo. 12:1-14
23. Lk. 22:7-19
24. Lev. 23:6
25. Psa. 16:10
26. I Cor. 5:7-8
27. I Cor. 15:20-21
28. I Cor. 15:22-23
29. Act. 1:4
30. Jn. 20:20-22
31. Act. 1:3-4
32. I Cor. 14:4
33. Amos 5:18-20, Joel 1:15, Isa 13:9-10
34. I Thess. 5:2; 4:16

Chapter 20
1. Rom. 8:1
2. Rom. 7:14-20
3. Exo. 15:22
4. Rev. 8:10
5. Zech. 7:9-12
6. Obad. 15-16

Chapter 21
1. Dan. 7:7-8; 24
2. Dan. 9:27
3. Titus 2:13-14
4. Mat. 24:29-31, Rev 6:12-17
5. Lk. 21:8
6. II Thess. 2:3
7. Mat. 24:9-12
8. Mat. 11:34-36
9. Rev. 13:3-18, 14:9-10
10. Exo. 20:13
11. Lk. 10:21

Chapter 22
1. Rev. 8:11
2. Mk. 13:11

Chapter 23

1. Rev. 8:11
2. Rev. 3:5
3. Rev. 19:20-21
4. Rev. 14:1
5. Jn. 3:19-21
6. Dan. 11:36
7. Dan. 11:45, 12:11, Rev 19:20
8. Lk. 21:12-17
9. Phil. 1:29
10. Jer. 6:17-19
11. Jn. 8:44
12. Rev. 3:5; 22:18-19
13. II Jn. 1:9
14. Rev. 12:11
15. II Thess. 2:3
16. Dan. 8:9-26
17. Jn. 10:22-23; 8:12, Rev. 21:9-10
18. Zech. 6:12-13, Ezek. 43:2, 4, 7
19. Rev. 17:9-10
20. Rev. 17:11
21. Isa. 59:20, Rev. 14:1-4
22. II Pet. 2:20-22

Chapter 24
1. Isa. 2:10-11
2. Rev. 20:8, Zech. 14:16-17
3. Mal. 4:5
4. Isa. 13:9, 13
5. Rev. 8:12
6. I Cor. 10:12-13

Chapter 25
1. Rev. 8:11
2. Rev. 8:12

Chapter 26
1. Rev. 9:5-11
2. I Cor. 3:16, Rom. 10:9-13
3. I Tim. 4:1
4. Mat. 24:3-31, Rev. 6:1-17, 2 Thess. 2:1-4
5. Mat. 24:4-5, II Pet. 2:1
6. Dan. 9:24-27, Rom. 11:25-27, Rev. 10:1-7

Chapter 27
1. Rev. 9:1-3
2. Rev. 8:13

3. Rev. 9:5, 10

Chapter 28
1. Heb. 13:1
2. Dan. 7:14
3. Jer. 44:15-30, 7:18
4. Jer. 7:23
5. Rev. 10:7
6. Isa. 62:11-12
7. Lk. 13:34-35
8. Rom. 11:25-27, Rev. 10:7, Dan. 9:24

Chapter 29
1. Rev. 9:16
2. Rev. 9:12-13
3. Rev. 9:15
4. Rev. 9:13-21
5. Deut. 31:29
6. Rev. 9:14
7. Rev. 9:15
8. Rev. 10:7
9. Rev. 10:1
10. Hos. 11:10
11. Hos. 6:1-2
12. Exo. 19:11
13. Rev. 9:13-14
14. Rev. 9:19
15. Rev. 9:18
16. Jn. 5:18
17. Jn. 1:29
18. Rev. 20:15
19. Act. 4:12
20. Lk. 17:30
21. Mat. 24:4-5, 33
22. Mat. 24:24
23. Rev. 3:5
24. I Tim. 4:1, Heb. 6:4-6
25. 2 Pet. 2:1, 20-22, Heb. 10:29
26. Rev. 22:18-19
27. Rev. 20:11-15

Chapter 30
1. Rev. 19:21
2. Mk. 16:16-20
3. Rev. 15:6
4. Mk. 10:27
5. Mk. 10:29-31

Chapter 31
1. Mat. 24:28
2. Mic. 2:12-13
3. Hos. 5:15
4. Rev. 10:7, Rom. 11:25-27, Dan. 9:24
5. Rev. 11:11
6. Zech. 14:4
7. Zech. 13:9; 14:5

Chapter 32
1. Act. 2:17
2. Rom. 10:2
3. Titus 2:13
4. Heb. 9:28
5. Zech. 14:4-5
6. Rev. 14:1-4

Chapter 33
1. Heb. 3:14
2. Mat. 24:15, Lk. 21:20
3. Zech. 13:8-9
4. Rev. 19:20
5. Jn. 3:16, 18
6. Mat. 25:41
7. Mat. 10:34-35

Chapter 34
1. Hab. 3:13
2. Rev. 16:19
3. Rev. 16:21
4. Lev. 16:30
5. Isa. 59:20, Rev. 14:1
6. Rev. 7:3-4
7. Rev. 13:1, 11; 6:8
8. Lev. 16:15
9. Rev. 11:19
10. Rev. 9:5
11. Dan. 9:24, Rev. 10:7, Rom. 11:25-27
12. Rev. 11:8
13. Rev. 11:10
14. Rev. 17:17

Chapter 35
1. Rev. 10:1
2. Act. 1:11
3. Isa. 10:20-23
4. Rev. 10:2

5. Rev. 12:11
6. Amos 4:11-12
7. Isa. 61:10-11
8. Isa. 62:1-5
9. Rev. 12:6; 7:1-8; 14:1-4
10. Mic. 2:12-13

Chapter 36
1. Isa. 63:1-2
2. Psa. 51:1-4
3. Zech. 12:7
4. Rev. 6:8; 13:11-13
5. Lk. 21:20
6. Joel 3:12
7. Hos. 6:1-2
8. Rev. 11:11-12
9. Heb. 9:28
10. Hos. 6:1-2
11. Isa. 62:11-12
12. Rom. 11:25-27
13. Act. 4:12, Jn. 3:16-18

Chapter 37
1. Mk. 10:33-34, Lk. 18:31-33
2. Jn. 1:14
3. Phil. 2:5-8
4. Mat. 16:15-16
5. Mat. 16:17
6. I Pet. 4:19
7. Col. 3:12-13
8. Isa. 27:13
9. Isa. 35:8-10
10. Hos. 6:1-2
11. Dan. 7:13-14
12. Jn. 17:5, Isa. 42:8

Chapter 38
1. Isa. 10:22
2. Rev. 11:11-12
3. Rev. 11:13
4. Exo. 23:16; 34:22, Hos. 6:11
5. Rev. 11:13

Chapter 39
1. Isa. 63:1-3
2. Psa. 118:25-28
3. Jn. 8:12
4. Mal. 4:1-2

5. Zech. 14:16
6. Rev. 10:7
7. Rev. 14:2, 15:2-4
8. Rev. 17:17
9. Isa. 59:19
10. Zech. 14:16

Chapter 40
1. Rev. 10:7
2. Rev. 11:15
3. Rev. 11:16-18
4. Rev. 11:19
5. Zech. 12:10
6. Rev. 1:12-16
7. Rev. 11:15
8. Rev. 11:17
9. Mat. 24:4-5
10. Zech. 14:4-5
11. Rev. 19:7-9
12. Rev. 13:7, II Thess. 2:3-4
13. I Thess. 1:10, Mat 24:29-31
14. Dan. 9:24, Act. 1:6-11, Rom. 11:25-27, Rev. 10:1-7
15. Rev. 16:14-16; 19:11-21
16. Rev. 21:2-11

Chapter 41
1. Rev. 17:9
2. Rev. 10:7
3. Rev. 11:15
4. Dan. 7:27
5. Mat. 24:15, Dan 9:27
6. II Thess. 2:3
7. Rev. 13:7
8. Rev. 13:6
9. Isa. 14:16-17
10. Dan. 7:25
11. Zech. 8:3; 14:3-5

Chapter 42
1. II Jn. 1:9, II Pet. 2:20, Heb. 10:29
2. Joel 2:32
3. Hab. 1:5
4. Jn. 15:12-15

Chapter 43
1. Mat. 13:45-46
2. Heb. 10:29

3. Eph. 6:11-18
4. Ezek. 34:1-24
5. Rom. 8:6
6. Rom. 8:14
7. Mat. 7:13-14
8. II Cor. 10:3-5
9. Jam. 4:7
10. Eph. 1:17-20
11. Mat. 18:20
12. Dan. 12:11, Rev. 19:20
13. Dan. 12:12
14. Isa. 51:3
15. Jud. 1:14-15, Rev. 19:11-21
16. Phil. 2:5-8
17. II Cor. 5:21
18. Jn. 11:41-43

Chapter 44
1. Rom. 8:16-18
2. Rom. 8:26-28
3. Rom. 8:35-37
4. Mat. 19:28, Lk. 22:29-30
5. Rev. 20:1-2
6. Rev. 20:4
7. Rev. 20:4
8. Jn. 15:19
9. II Cor. 12:7-9
10. Jam. 5:16
11. Rev. 16:13-16
12. II Cor. 12:9-10
13. Rev. 21:9-10

AUTHOR PROFILE

Paul Bortolazzo is devoted to teaching God's truth concerning the coming of the Lord Jesus Christ. This ministry offers a variety of outreaches including 'Til Eternity Conferences, End Time Seminars, College and Youth Presentations, and Bible Prophecy classes. If you would like more information about this prophetic ministry, please contact us. It would be a privilege to work with you by helping bring an end-times presentation to your church or area.

Paul Bortolazzo Ministries
PO Box 241915
Montgomery, Alabama 36124-1915

email:bortjenny@juno.com

www.paulbortolazzo.com

Please check out my website. This site was created to help empower the saints to overcome in these last days. It contains my books, teachings, radio shows, and YouTube's on the coming of the Lord.

.

'TIL ETERNITY

FACING THE CONSEQUENCES OF THE SECOND COMING

By Paul Bortolazzo

A non-fiction, student-friendly, chronological listing of the 70 Events coming before, during, and after the Coming of the Lord.

In this late hour, the love for the world is at an all time high. False teachers are turning many Christians away from the truth. Church leaders are refusing to judge between the righteous and the wicked; between those serving God and those who aren't. Such compromise will usher in the greatest persecution believers will ever experience. The only way to overcome will be through obedience to the Holy Spirit (Rev. 3:21-22).

'Til Eternity highlights the events coming before, during, and after the Second Coming of Christ. We will begin with the next event on God's end time calendar. After studying the last seventy events in order you will discover:
- *What events will warn His Coming is near?*
- *Who are the teachers deceiving so many?*
- *Where will His Coming end?*
- *When will the Great Tribulation be shortened?*
- *Why will the Beast overcome so many saints?*

Purchase online at Amazon, Barnes & Noble, and the author's website, in paperback, Kindle and eBook. Visit www.paulbortolazzo.com for links, prices, and more details.

CPSIA information can be obtained at www.ICGtesting.com
Printed in the USA
LVOW012133061111

253775LV00008B/32/P